Martina Reilly, formerly ~~writing a~~
number of bestselling novels, ~~...~~
Borrowed. She is also the auth~~...~~
books. Martina has worked as a ~~...~~
and does freelance columns for the ~~...~~
she acts, teaches drama and writes pla~~...~~

For more information, please visit www.martinareilly.info

Praise for Martina Reilly

'Like Marian Keyes, Reilly takes a cracking story and adds sharp dialog~~ue~~ and buckets of originality' *Scottish Daily Record*

~~...~~ the elements of an excellent read: mystery, drama and romance'

~~...~~ holiday read' *Closer*

~~...~~ ~~na~~ has the wonderful knack of combining sensitivity for a serious su~~bject~~ with a big dose of humour' *Irish Independent*

~~...na~~ Reilly's characters are so well observed . . . a substantial read'

~~...~~ ~~t~~o put down, laugh-out-loud funny . . . perfect holiday reading'
~~...~~ *Way*

~~...~~ s a star of the future' *Belfast Telegraph*

~~...~~ have the most hard-hearted reader wiping tears – and not just
~~of l~~aughter – from their eyes' *Irish Evening Herald*

'Good, solid entertainment' *Irish Examiner*

'Reilly has a wonderful comic touch, both in the way she draws her characters and in her dialogue . . . a brilliant read' *U Magazine*

'Brilliant' *Liffey Champion*

A MOMENT LIKE FOREVER

Martina Reilly
Formerly writing as Tina Reilly

SPHERE

First published in Great Britain in 2010 by Sphere
This paperback edition published in 2011 by Sphere
Reprinted 2011

A CIP catalogue record for this book
is available from the British Library.

ISBN 978-0-7515-4271-4

Typeset in Baskerville MT by Palimpsest Book Production Ltd,
Falkirk, Stirlingshire
Printed and bound in Great Britain by
Clays Ltd, St Ives plc

Sphere
An imprint of
Little, Brown Book Group
100 Victoria Embankment
London EC4Y 0DY

An Hachette UK Company
www.hachette.co.uk

www.littlebrown.co.uk

To all my nieces and nephews especially my two lovely godchildren – Jenna and Tom.

1

'MY FLAT JUST burned down,' Kate, my younger sister, announces quite chirpily from her end of the phone.

'*What?!*' My half-swallowed coffee comes back up again, only it comes out my nose. It's painful. I start to cough in between yelling out some more *whats?*

'It's OK, Andy,' Kate says soothingly. 'Well, obviously, my flat isn't. It's gutted. You should see it.' Behind her I hear sirens and noise and shouting.

'Are you OK?' I start to mop my nose with my sleeve. Hearing my alarmed voice, Baz, my big black cat, miaows from his basket in the corner of the room.

'Well, put it like this,' Kate says, 'I won't be needing the services your magazine provides just at the minute.' Then she laughs.

I work for a small magazine called *It's Your Funeral*. It's aimed at undertakers.

'Ha, ha.' Hearing her laugh relaxes me. 'Is anyone hurt?'

'No, we're fine. I don't know what happened. I think Luke was cooking and left the pan on.'

'Kate, that's awful. What will you do?' I'm sitting upright in my chair now, slippered feet planted on the ground, running my fingers through my unbrushed hair. One of the bonuses

1

of working from home is that no one sees what you look like. Which is just as well, as I'm in a dingy grey tracksuit and yellow t-shirt.

'Well,' Kate says, 'I was hoping to move in with you for a bit. Just until I get somewhere else.'

I don't even ask why she wouldn't move back to Mum and Dad's house. I can completely understand her not wanting to. 'Of course you can,' I answer without hesitation, acknowledging the fact that, though I love Kate, we've sort of grown a little apart in the last while. I hope we'll get on. 'No worries.'

'And Luke?'

Luke is her boyfriend. She lives with him in the flat that just burned down. Luke is a little odd, I think. He wears his hair long and braided. His clothes are baggy and he has a Johnny Depp *Pirates of the Caribbean* vibe about him. He works in a health shop, knows all about vitamins and organic rice and, on the side, teaches yoga to people. I've never really talked to Luke properly, just sort of observed him from the fringes, said hello, asked him how he is and had inane conversations with him about the weather. To have him suddenly living in my house, lounging about on my sofas while I try to think up things to say to him would all be a bit stressful. But then again, he is Kate's boyfriend, and she loves him, so . . .

'Sure.' I try to sound as if the prospect excites me. 'No problem. It'll be great to have some company.'

'Ah, thanks Andy, you're brilliant. We'll be around in a couple of hours.'

'See you then.'

She hangs up, and I abandon my job at the computer to go and make up the spare room.

2

LEXI WALKS. Sometimes she walks for hours on end in a sort of therapeutic way. She walks mainly through big open spaces, deserts or the outback, her feet encased in sandals or boots depending on the location. Now, though, she's ready for a change. Small towns appeal, small towns on the edge of civilisation. And she'd like to meet others too, maybe some sassy people who give as good as they get. In the last while, since she's been walking, she's met a variety of oddballs, some she's travelled along the road with, others she's ditched as soon as she can. Right now, she's wandering through what she guesses must be a canyon of some sort. She's walking along the basin, while on either side, steep walls of red dusty mountain rise upwards reminding her of an inferno. To the left and right of the narrow path, there are a variety of plants. She doesn't recognise any of them, their exotic, vibrant colours contrasting well with the red on either side. The sky is a vivid blue, the air perfect. The canyon is deserted.

Up until now, Lexi has just put one hiking boot in front of the other, taking the paths that presented themselves. She has wandered but never wondered where she's going. There are faster ways of travelling, but walking was invented for contemplation. In the last month or so, though, she's become a little restless. A bit bored with her own company, bored with whatever she's been trying to find. She thinks she might like to find a small town, maybe pick up some work, make some money, talk to a few people and then, when she's ready, move on again. That's the beauty of the life she's in – there are no real commitments. She can make friends and then move on when she likes. Life should be like this, she thinks.

A long time later, as the walls of the canyon recede behind her and the foliage on either side increases into scrubland, Lexi spots what she supposes must be grey kangaroos hopping about in the distance. She's so busy gazing at them that she almost trips over a signpost at a crossroads. It's like something from the Wild West, an old sign with the letters etched deep into it, on top of a pole. It's in the shape of an arrow, and declares that the town of Salue lies straight ahead. There are no indicators as to how far ahead the town is, but she is happy to have her destination decided for her.

Lexi grins a little, perfect white teeth contrasting beautifully against her lightly browned face. A little normal would be nice. She begins her walk to Salue.

3

THE SCREECH OF brakes and the roar of an engine announce Kate and Luke's arrival later that evening. I had expected them earlier, then panicked slightly when they didn't show, then panicked when I'd rung Kate to see where she was and there was no answer. I had visions of her running into a burning flat to rescue some ridiculous ornament she valued. Kate is a bit of a hoarder like that. Anyway, eventually I conceded defeat and was forced to ring my mother to ask her if she'd heard from Kate, and remarkably my mother was the voice of calm and reason.

'Kate. Oh yes,' she says airily, 'isn't she doing her radio show right now? I'm listening to her. She's talking about how sometimes the right man is not the right man for sex. It's all a little embarrassing.'

In the background my father snorts.

'Don't you be snorting,' my mother snaps.

'I have asthma.'

'I'll give you asthma,' my mother says back.

'And what exactly does that mean?' Dad asks in a weary voice. Then he hollers into the phone. 'Hello Andy, how are you?'

'Great, Dad.'

'Been anywhere nice recently?'

'Eh, no.'

'Don't go asking her that,' my mother whispers furiously. Then she turns back to me, attempting a laugh. 'Don't mind him, Andy.' Her voice lowers. 'He's gone out now, he's driving me mad.' She pauses. 'So is that all you rang for, to find out where Kate is?'

'Yes. She, eh, had a problem this morning with her flat. She's coming to stay here for a bit.' I decide I'll break the news to her and save Kate the job. Telling my mother bad news is a delicate business, sort of like holding out your hand to a dog you're not sure of. Then when the reaction is a favourable wag of the tail, only then do you venture closer.

'Oh yes, the big fire,' my mother says, not sounding that bothered. 'She told me. The flat was gutted, apparently. Nothing survived. She'll be out of it for months.'

I blink at my mother's cavalier attitude. 'OK,' I say slowly, 'once you know.'

'Yes, I know. Will you stop hovering!' This latter part to my father, who has obviously come back into the room.

'Hovering suggests an ability to levitate,' my dad says back. 'So technically—'

'Bye Mum,' I say hastily. 'Talk at the weekend.'

She barely hears me, what with Dad driving her mad.

I remember this as I buzz Kate and Luke up. Kate arrives in first, dragging an enormous plastic bag of belongings behind her. She's finding it quite difficult to manoeuvre it as tight miniskirts and sky-high heels are not ideal for this sort of situation. Luke follows with two equally enormous bags, one in each hand.

'I thought you lost everything in the fire,' I say in disbelief as they and their baggage fill the limited space in my hallway.

There is a tiny beat of silence.

'Well, not everything . . .' Kate says. Then, giving me a flash of white knickers and tanned leg, she bends over and drags a state-of-the-art espresso machine from her bag.

'Obviously.' There is no way that amount of stuff can fit in my place.

'Would you have preferred it if we'd lost everything?' Kate asks teasingly.

'Don't be ridiculous.' I roll my eyes. 'It's just, well, it looks to me as if you lost *nothing*.'

Luke sets his bag down with the grace of a panther. He shakes his dreadlocked head and bestows a grin on me. 'You know Katie,' he says languidly to me as one of his long fingers brushes a remaining dreadlock from his face, 'she has tons of crap.'

'Hey!' Kate objects.

'Our place was too small for it,' Luke continues, unperturbed, 'so my mother stored it for us in her spare bedroom, which was lucky as it would all have been burned in the fire.'

'You must have rescued the espresso machine, though.' I nod to where Kate has placed it on top of the bags. 'I remember you had that in your flat.'

Kate scoffs a little. 'No offence, Andy, but when were you last in our flat?'

I shrug, blushing a little. 'Dunno.'

'Yeah, exactly,' she says. 'Luke's mother lent us this. I told her you always use rotten instant coffee, and she was appalled.'

A faint smile lifts my lips. 'Am I supposed to be eager for you to stay at this point?'

They both grin at me.

'Sorry.' Kate nods an apology. 'So, can I plug it in? I'm gasping.'

'Sure, go on.'

I follow her into the kitchen while Luke goes on downstairs to drag up the remaining bags. I dread to think how much stuff they must have. I think one little bedroom will not be enough for them. Some of it will have to go back to Luke's mother, though I don't say it just then as it might seem a little tactless.

Kate plugs in the machine and pulls a bag of coffee from her coat. She is a caffeine addict, she often admits proudly. She blames her job; says a lot of the time they just sit around brainstorming and drinking coffee. She's a DJ on Dublin Live, and she got the job when she called up one of the programmes to complain about the lack of women DJs on their station, so they offered her a trial. She has the same husky voice as I have, but that's where the similarities between us end. Kate is alive, if you know what I mean. Her whole body zings with energy, and she has a real 'hey look at me, I'm here' vibe. I used to be a little like that – people did look at me when I entered a room. I suppose I could have been called beautiful. Now, though, with the scar running from my left ear, across my cheek and halfway down my neck, people look at me for a whole different reason. When it happened, the medical staff delicately stitched me up, assured me that it would fade in time and sent me home. Now, over a year later, it's still as noticeable as ever. The violent red has faded to a sort of pink, but it's not something the average person would miss when they looked at me. I try not to look at me too often.

8

I smile a little as I watch Kate, in her tiny little skirt and tight top, prance about my small kitchen humming a tune as she goes about fixing up the espresso machine. I say a little prayer that nothing bad ever happens to her.

'One or two shots?' she asks me cheerily.

'Two,' I say. I'll need it. I plan to stay up late.

'Luke,' she calls out, as her boyfriend slams my front door closed, 'one or two shots?'

Luke enters, filling the small kitchen with his presence. His long limbs sprawl in all directions when he sits down on the chair opposite mine, making the space seem even more cramped. Even though it's a wet night he's wearing sandals, I note in amusement. Sandals and a faded pair of brown flared cords. The only concession he's made to the rain is a big green parka jacket with a furry hood. I'd never have put him and Kate together in a million years. 'None,' he says. 'I'll just grab a glass of a water in a sec.'

He looks at me for permission.

'Don't be doing that,' I smile. 'My place is your place for the next while. Treat it the way you treated your own place.' Then I wince. 'Well, just don't set it on fire.'

Kate laughs as she places a coffee in front of me.

Luke nods lazily and gives me a small salute. 'Message received.'

Then Kate pours him some water and places it in front of him. He pulls her onto his lap and she squeals. He nuzzles her and laughs.

I smile at their obvious happiness. Then, memories of me and Chas on a park bench, me on his lap as he tickles me surface so suddenly that my poor old heart seems to squeeze up with pain and ridiculous tears pop into my eyes. We'd had

9

four perfect months before life came along and ruined it for us. Four months of fun. Even though it was almost two years ago now, it seems like only yesterday.

I turn away suddenly so that Luke and Kate don't see.

4

A BLUE AND WHITE banner mounted on what appears to be
a steel pole welcomes Lexi to the town of Salue. She
stops walking just outside the town limit and absorbs her first
glimpse of what she hopes, for a short time at least, will be
somewhere she can stay. As far as she can make out, the only
road, from this direction into the town, is the road she is
currently on. A narrow strip of path to the left leads from it,
and a sign says 'Beach'. Up ahead, a little beyond the banner,
Lexi can see three shops, two on one side of the wide road,
one on the other and all fronted by red cobble paving. The
shops are small and the dusty road appears deserted. Lexi
starts walking again, taking in everything she passes. The first
shop, which has a green exterior, is called Hats Off, and
peering in, Lexi sees a variety of hats in different colours, all
for sale. Most of them are wide-brimmed and trimmed with
flowers or ribbons. Lexi's own quirky green baker-boy hat
suddenly looks a little cheap by comparison. Still, she wouldn't
swap it for anything. The next shop appears to sell music.
Black on the outside and inside, she notes, the shelves and
walls are also black. It's called Doug's Original Music. She
wonders what kind of music this Doug person sells. Not classical, by the looks of the place.

The only shop that seems to have an occupier is the weirdest one of the three. Lordi's Angel Shop is the sign over the door. The writing swirls and loops and appears as eccentric as the door, which is white. A big picture of an ordinary-looking angel with fluffy white wings is stuck to it. Or painted onto it, she can't tell which. Lexi grins. This shop she has to see.

She enters and is slightly overawed by the amount of things on the shelves and floor and dangling from the ceiling. In fact, the stuff on the ceiling appears to be levitating. There are big angels, small angels, angels in every colour of the rainbow, angels made from every conceivable material, advertisements for angel cards, for angel drops – whatever they are – for guardian angel mascots, for angels to pray to. A large poster with a prayer on it is on the wall behind the desk. A man is sitting there, and he looks up as Lexi approaches.

'Wow,' Lexi exclaims.

The guy behind the counter stands up. He's dressed from head to toe in white: tight white jeans, white cowboy boots and a white shirt. A white cloak, tied at the neck, billows from his shoulders. He's a lot taller than Lexi.

'Wow,' she says again.

The man acknowledges the 'wow' with a small inclination of his head before holding out his hand. 'Lordi,' he says.

'Lexi.'

Lordi comes out from behind his counter and smiles. She can't quite work out if he's handsome or not. Maybe it's just hard to think that way about a guy in a cloak. His hair is dark, his skin pale. The piercing blue of his eyes lends his face a mesmerising quality that it wouldn't otherwise have had.

'Would you like to buy something, petal?' Lordi asks, sweeping his arm in an arc.

'Oh yeah,' Lexi says, 'but the money situation is tight. I pray to the angel of money all the time, but she ignores me.'

'The angel of money?'

'Eh, sorry, that was just a joke.'

'Oh.' He doesn't seem to find it at all humorous. He just sounds baffled. 'Right. Well, as you can see, we have a vast array of angels to choose from here. I normally study customers and tell them what angel suits them. Are you staying around for a while?'

'I hope to, but I better warn you, I don't believe in angels.'

'No matter.' Lordi folds his arms. 'I do, so I'll still let you know. Your angel will whisper to me.'

The man is a complete nut case. She wonders if she should leave, but something about him fascinates her. Odd people have always captivated her. 'What got you into doing this?' she asks.

'Why does everyone ask me that?' Lordi exclaims.

She can think of a reason or two but she doesn't say so. 'It's OK if it's private,' Lexi says. She doesn't want someone to know all about her, and she's not comfortable with lying.

'It's not private.' Lordi smiles for the first time. He sits down on a big angel chair that has wings sprouting from the back. As he sits, the wings flap for a second or two. 'I've just got weary of explaining it.' He crosses his long skinny legs. 'It was my own experience. I was in an accident twenty years ago. My car collided with a lorry. It ended up under the lorry, and I was taken to hospital barely breathing. They say I died for a minute or two on the table as they were working to repair some internal bleeding. I remember very vividly seeing

13

an angel. It wasn't like the representations I have here.' Again his arm sweeps the confines of the shop. 'It was beautiful, but not in the way we think of beautiful. It had more substance than that definition of beauty. Anyway, like the old cliché, she told me that it wasn't my time, and I remember a large thump as if I'd been pulled back to my body with a magnet.'

The term nut job is too mild, she thinks.

'So I've made it my mission in life to spread the angel message. The first shop I started, my proper one, is just off Piccadilly Circus in London, and obviously I sell directly on the internet.'

She wonders if he makes much money from it.

'I make enough money to pay my expenses and to live on, and the rest I give to charity,' he says, as if reading her mind.

'Right,' Lexi says. A charitable nut job. Not a bad combination.

'People think I'm mad, but that's their business.' Lordi stands up. 'Feel free to browse, and call in any time. I'll try to work out your angel.'

'Thanks.' Lexi smiles, then says, 'I'm looking to make a few quid, actually.' She indicates her clothes, her hair, all of which need some improving. 'Are there any jobs in this place?'

'Jobs are hard to get.' Lordi tells her something she knows already. 'You could try walking further into town. It's a fairly small place. One main street, you're on it. Keep going. You'll see a gallery and a coffee shop, the town hall and some other venues. When you come to a t-junction, the left way leads to the beach. A lot of artists live down that way. You might have seen the footpath to the beach from the direction you came. It circles right around the left side of the town. The other road leads out of town to the surrounding towns.'

14

'Well, thanks for that verbal tour, Lordi.' Lexi nods a goodbye.

'Be seeing you, petal,' Lordi says.

'Count on it.'

Back outside, Lexi decides to keep moving.

'I'll pray for a job for you,' Lordi says from his doorway.

'I'd appreciate that.'

It was nice to talk to someone new about everyday stuff, she thinks.

It has been so long.

5

IT'S AFTER THREE in the morning when I turn off my computer. My eyes feel as if someone has poured sand into them but to be honest, I'd had such fun talking to Kate and Luke that I'd been reluctant to leave their company and come up here. So instead, I'd chatted to them until they'd gone to bed and then come up. As my computer screen goes black, my eye falls on a picture of Lexi. It's one I have on a shelf, just at eye level, and I must look at it about a hundred times a day. I don't think I've ever seen it at this hour of the night, when the full moon outside has bleached my office into monochrome. In this light, Lexi looks all alone on her shelf, surrounded as she is by knick-knacks. Her face is a pure white in the moonlight, and her red-lipped grin looks eerie as the shadow of one of the largest teddies I have, positioned beside her, falls across her face.

Lexi was my best friend ever. We met when we were in primary school, and after I forged her mother's signature on her half-done homework we were inseparable. Alexandra was the name the teachers and her parents called her, but to me and the rest of the world she was Lexi. And she looked like a Lexi, way more than she'd ever looked like an Alexandra. Alexandra was a prim name; Lexi was the name of someone

16

with an untameable spirit. She had a wanderlust that did not include turning up for school every day. Instead, she'd hoist her bag on her shoulder and find adventure. I thought she was impossibly glamorous. She hung out with exotic people, or at least they'd seemed exotic to me at the time. Really they were just older teenagers who smoked hash and bunked school too. But the fact that they'd even talk to Lexi, never mind let her hang out with them, showed what an amazing personality she had. Lexi's formidable light washed across me too, so I became quite cool by association. I never did see what she saw in me.

As we got older, we blagged our way into the celebrity areas of nightclubs. Lexi used to pretend that I was a top model, despite my five-foot-two frame, and that she was my agent. She spoke in such a cheeky way to the bouncers manning the door that all they could do was laugh and let us by. Then she'd give them a seductive wink and we'd fall about the place giggling madly. When Lexi was around, you were guaranteed fun and terror in equal measure.

And she always managed effortlessly to acquire really quirky boyfriends. I mean, they were never the most attractive men in the room, but somehow, because they were with her, they were the most desirable. I always liked her boyfriends better than I did my own. Well, except once, when I'd dated Lexi's older brother, Chas. God, he'd been fun too. But that turned out to be a mistake, and thinking about him hurts so I don't do it too often.

I pick up the picture of my friend and study it hard. I remember the day it was taken, the first day of our big adventure out in the real wide world. We were twenty-seven, a little old, maybe, to be backpackers, but we had both promised

17

ourselves that when we had enough money to do it right, we'd go. We weren't planning on working a hell of a lot. When the time finally arrived, I was reluctant to go as I had been seeing Chas for four months. I kept hoping he'd ask me to stay, or that he'd invite himself along with me and Lexi, but he hadn't. I suppose, like me, he thought that four months with someone didn't give them the right to disrupt plans the other person had been making since before they came along. But he did say he'd wait for me, and that come Christmas he'd fly out for a month to Australia to meet us. I was on a countdown from that moment. In the picture, Lexi is wearing her green combats and a white t-shirt. Her black Doc boots are laced up and a green baker-boy hat holds her hair back from her face. She shaved it all off a month into our travels, saying that it cooled her down. Beside her is the most enormous rucksack, stuffed with her tent and sleeping bag. Lexi is grinning so much, it makes me smile.

I wish I knew where she was. Is she on a new journey somewhere? Is she dead, as most people seem to think? Wherever she is, she has left me behind for the first time in our lives, and I am so lonely without her. I can still hear her voice and her laugh. If I close my eyes really hard, I can sometimes hear her teasing me about my lack of boyfriend or lack of a life. But without her, I feel like a flower that is wilting from the absence of light, and if that sounds a bit melodramatic, then maybe it's the artist in me. I always did tend to make a big deal of things, as my mother is so fond of telling me. 'Oh,' she says, 'that's the curse of being creative. You've the imagination for it, anyway.'

I smile at the thought of my mother with her practical no-nonsense attitude. Then I put Lexis's picture carefully back on the shelf, the shadows leaping to cover her face.

Closing the door of the little office bedroom as quietly as I can so as not to wake Kate and Luke, I tiptoe into my own room and fall into bed fully clothed.

A yowl of rage makes me jump upright and Baz emerges from my bed, hissing and spitting. You do not mess with Baz when he behaves like that. I allow him some time to cool down by hopping back out and waiting patiently as he examines the terrain of the bed for a spot to settle down on. He walks in tight circles for ages before curling up right in the centre with a look in his eyes that seems to say, Do not mess with me again. Now I glare at him, but knowing it's unwise to move him, I squash myself into a corner of the bed and try to get some shut-eye.

At least, after beavering away on the computer half the night, I'm tired enough to fall asleep.

6

PETER'S GALLERY IS an ultra-modern building taking up quite a chunk of space on the street of downtown Salue. It looks inviting, and what's even more interesting is that there is a 'Help Wanted' notice stuck on the enormous front window. Maybe the angel of money wasn't so far-fetched an idea after all, she thinks jokingly. She wonders what the job will entail. She has some knowledge of art, though maybe the job is just being on reception in the gallery, or displaying paintings to their best advantage on the walls. She could do that easily enough. Nothing ventured, nothing gained, she thinks as she ascends the grey steps to the blond-wood front door.

Entering the building, her first impression is that the foyer is stark, with bright-white walls and pale floors. Large windows slant golden light onto the reception desk, behind which sits a dark-haired, dark-eyed man. He looks vaguely oriental, and she wonders if he speaks English. If he doesn't, she's in trouble. Languages have always been her Achilles heel. She sees that his name is Peter Smith, so that seems a positive indicator that he might speak English. Peter straightens up as Lexi approaches. She senses a sort of desperation in the action. Then Peter's eyes seem to take in her dishevelled appearance and his shoulders slump a little again. She winces inwardly. She probably should have put on something a bit more conventional, though suits are not really her thing and even if she had one, which she doesn't, she knows it'd look ridiculous.

'G'day,' Peter says in what is unmistakably an Australian accent.

She's relieved. She leans across the counter and takes some comfort in the knowledge that Peter is wearing a tracksuit and trainers. 'I see you have a job advertised.'

Peter raises his eyebrows in surprise. She has a feeling that he was hoping for a more glamorous applicant. 'Have you experience workin' in a gallery?'

She shrugs. 'Uh-huh.'

'As in?'

'Well, what will my duties be?'

Peter gestures towards a door. 'Take a squizz in there and guess.'

'A squizz?'

'Look in there,' Peter repeats, sounding impatient.

Lexi does as she is told. The door opens onto a beautiful square room, the walls, like the foyer, painted a brilliant white. She glances back over her shoulder at Peter.

'Do you notice anything strange about that room?'

'No, it's a nice room.'

'It's a room to show pictures.' Peter sounds stressed. 'But there *are* no pictures, are there?'

'Um, nope,' Lexi shrugs. 'Are they all sold?'

A pause.

'This place is full of artists,' Peter explains after a bit. 'An' I thought that by buying this land and building this gallery, I'd be flat out with artists wanting to exhibit. But no one wants

21

to come here.' He shakes his head. 'They make enough moolah selling their pictures directly.'

'You never investigated this when you built the place?'

It's the wrong thing to say. Peter folds his arms defensively.

Before he can answer, Lexi goes on quickly, 'So, you want someone to talk artists into coming here?'

'Yes.' Peter seems glad to ignore her earlier question. 'I need an ambassador for the place. I'm good at business, but not too hot in the conversation stakes. For some reason I thought it would change when I opened this place, or by being here, but it hasn't.'

Lexi has met a few people like that along the way. They somehow thought that by getting away from their everyday, they could become something better than they used to be. But they found that, like their home lives, there were always going to be problems once they'd committed themselves to staying in a certain place, forging links with people. It was probably the reason she travelled a lot here, though to be fair, she'd been born talking.

'I'll do a deal with you,' Lexi says suddenly. 'For every artist I get, you double my hourly wage for a day.'

Peter takes a few moments to consider her offer. 'OK,' he eventually answers, 'though if you fail to get at least one artist by the end of two weeks, you're out of here.'

'You're on.' Lexi shoves her hand out to shake his. Peter stands up. He's taller than her and has an athletic build. She guesses from the expensive-looking tracksuit and trainers that he is pretty well off. For here, anyway. 'Prepare to be dazzled.' She grins.

'It's the artists you want to dazzle,' Peter says back. 'Not me.'

Sense of humour bypass alert, she wants to snigger, but wisely, she doesn't.

She spends the night sitting on the beach. Of all the places she's been, beaches are her favourite. The waves, the moon, the stars. Further along she can make out the flickering flames of a beach fire. It's somehow very peaceful.

She has a funny feeling about all this. A prickling up her spine. But in a good way.

7

I NEVER NORMALLY WAKE before eleven and even then, I usually lie still for a while listening to the unique clicks and ticks of my apartment. It relaxes me. Then eventually I tear myself from the bed and grab some breakfast before beginning work at around midday. I find it's easier to sell ads to people after lunch, when they've mellowed out a little. And when I've woken up a little, too. I normally spend the afternoon designing the pages for the ads I've sold and then, if I've time, I mess about on my computer, keeping in touch with my Facebook friends and gaming. This morning, however, the sound of the radio blaring loudly from the kitchen jerks me out of an uneasy sleep. Baz purrs like a Porsche in my ear, and I discover that during the night he has crept closer to me than is normally wise and now has his nose pressed up against my cheek. I freeze and wonder how to move without annoying him. Downstairs, Luke laughs at something Kate has said and I remember that they are living with me now, for a bit.

'Hey, Baz,' I say in the wheedling, cajoling voice he seems to like and which I have perfected, 'would you like some food?'

Baz stares at me unblinkingly, green eyes boring into my

brown ones. Then to my relief, he languidly sits up and stretches, arching his back and pushing his head right back. I get the chance to turn over and look at the clock. It's eight. I've only had five hours' sleep. I groan, before hauling myself out of bed, pulling on a dressing gown and shambling down to say 'hi'. Baz follows me like a prison guard escorting his prisoner.

'Hey,' I smile sleepily at my two house guests. They look as if they've been up for hours. Luke is in his usual hippyish garb, brown cords and a t-shirt bearing a slogan about saving the earth. Kate, her long brown hair in a gleaming French plait, is the picture of health in a glittery top and tight jeans. She looks as if she's heading for a night on the town and not into work.

I yawn widely, reach into the press and take a tin of food out for my cat. He miaows constantly until the entire contents of the tin are deposited into his bowl.

'I have never seen such an enormous animal,' Luke observes in admiration.

Everyone who sees Baz says that. The cat is the size of a small dog. He has the build of a panther and is probably twice as intimidating. *You do not mess with the Baz*. That's Kate's catchphrase after he scratched her once for trying to lift him up.

'I think he's still growing,' I say. It's not a boast, more a cry of despair.

'Here, puss.' Luke holds out his hand and makes the whispery noise cats apparently love.

Baz looks up, marginally interested, then turns away in disdain.

Luke grins.

The radio starts to play a theme tune. I'm glad I remembered to tune it into Kate's station before she arrived yesterday. Kate, however, scoffs at the tune. 'It's the new morning show,' she says, indicating the radio with a wave of her hand. 'That DJ is crap, I think.'

Luke rolls his eyes. I get the feeling it's not the first time Kate has slagged off the DJ.

'Is he?' I plonk down onto a chair, my voice croaky with tiredness.

Luke solicitously pours me a coffee.

'Ah, thanks.' I reach out and take a slice of toast from the table and spread it with copious amounts of butter, enjoying the way it all melts in. Yum.

'He's the new hotshot guy they poached from RTE,' Kate says as she holds her mug out for Luke to fill. 'I dunno, I think the management in our place are rubbish. I should have got that job.'

'Well,' says Luke, and having poured coffee for both of us, sits down and butters himself a slice of bread. 'Maybe, you know, you are too cutting-edge for a morning show. Like, I don't think it would be right for schoolkids to be listening to you yabbering on about female orgasms first thing in the morning.'

'Eh, I can talk about other things, you know,' Kate snaps uncharacteristically, sounding hurt. 'I'm not totally one-dimensional.'

'Ah, damn,' Luke teases, but Kate doesn't smile. Instead she throws him an exasperated look as she picks up her bag.

He laughs.

She doesn't return the smile. 'I'm going,' she says instead.

'OK, well, have a good day now,' Luke nods, unperturbed

26

by her display of pique. 'Give that DJ a big thumbs-up from me!'

'Ugggh!' Kate glares at him. Then she pointedly says goodbye to me before stalking out of the room. A second later, the front door slams hard.

I wince, hating the idea of being caught in the middle of a domestic.

'She's fecking mad,' Luke says fondly as he grins at me across the table.

'Well she is now,' I say back, and we both laugh a little.

This is followed quite rapidly by a silence. Now that it's just me and Luke, I don't know what to say. I really don't know him all that well, and it's been so long since I've had a stranger in the flat, I really don't know how to make small talk any more. Luke doesn't seem to sense my unease. He lies back in the chair, his legs crossed at the ankles, and calmly finishes his bread. As the silence grows, I get edgier while he seems to find the lack of conversation quite relaxing. Just as I'm about to make some excuse to leave, he asks, 'Any plans for today?'

I seize the topic with as much enthusiasm as an unemployed man suddenly being offered a job. 'No.' I shake my head and pour some more coffee. 'My aim today is to sell one more ad for the magazine, then I'm finished for the week. It's mad. What with the way things are, you'd think our advertising would have slowed down, but it's as good as ever.'

'That's 'cause you've the gift of the gab, like your sister.' He smiles as he thinks of Kate and I feel a little pang. A sort of envy for her. She's so lucky.

'I guess,' I agree, though I don't add that Kate is better at face-to-face chat than I am.

Luke seems to eat a lot for such a skinny man. Like Baz, he doesn't seem to put on weight. He butters more bread, settles back in the chair and then asks, 'And after you sell your one more ad, any plans?'

I shrug. 'Not really. I'll probably spend some time laying out the ad. I'm the designer for the magazine too.'

'Oh yeah. Cool.'

'Then I'll email it to Alistair, that's my boss, and after that, I dunno . . .' My voice trails off.

There is a silence. I get the feeling Luke thinks I'm a bit of a loser.

'But that's just weekdays.' I grin. 'I mean, on Saturdays, I go sky-diving and do a little rally-car driving in the afternoon. Then I see who I can rope into heading out at night.'

Luke smiles at my feeble attempt at humour. 'Kate and I will volunteer, if you like.'

'I didn't say where I was going.'

'Doesn't matter.'

'To see the folks?'

'Rewind. No way.'

I laugh. My parents think Luke is a bit of a freak. I suppose he is, in some ways. There is the way he dresses for a start, then there is his whole mind-body-spirit take on life. Though, to be fair, anyone who is a little left of centre is seen by my parents as an exotic being. Their lives are lived firmly in black and white, and any shades of grey are viewed with incredible suspicion. Any slightly odd person that comes into their sphere is talked about for weeks. There was the time Linda Ryan, a neighbour from up the road, took to jogging. My mother was appalled that a woman with big breasts should go about jogging in tight t-shirts and bright green tracksuit bottoms. She commented on it every time Linda jogged past our house. My father seemed to indicate by his silence that he was not adverse to the spectacle, and that caused more trouble.

To me, their way of life is slightly claustrophobic. I don't know if that's why I chose Lexi as my friend, or had a whole host of ridiculous-looking boyfriends in my time. Most of them could have had their own spots in the Addams Family films. It probably explains why Kate became a shock jock, though her ability to shock my folks wore off a long time ago, I think. My mother, after a long time avoiding it, is an avid listener to her show now. Kate jokes that my mother's patronage has sent shares in her street cred nose-diving. Though I believe she is privately chuffed that Mam supports her. Which is more than can be said about her encouragement of me. Selling ads in a trade magazine for funeral directors is not something my mother is comfort-able with me doing. I think it reminds her of her own mortality. The fact that I gave up offers of top jobs in graphic design to take it convinced her that I was having some sort of a mental breakdown. But I reckon this job has saved my sanity.

'So are you really going to spend a Saturday night in with the folks?' Luke asks, breaking into my thoughts.

'They look forward to it,' I answer, knowing that the words 'Andy' and 'loser' are going to be for ever entwined in his brain now. 'I bring up a box of sweets and we share it while watching the telly.'

'That conjures up gentle images of an ad for a nursing home,' Luke says with dreamy sarcasm.

'Ha, ha.' I smile despite my mortification. He's right, though. 'I know it sounds crap but,' I pause, and admit with a little difficulty, 'I don't like going out much anyway.'

Luke's eyes soften a little. 'Because of your scar?'

'Well, no.' I'm flustered now, and my face flames red, I know it does. My hand rises defensively to my left cheek. 'I'm just not—'

'Your scar isn't so bad,' he interrupts me.

That halts my bumbling fibs. I gulp slightly and say, a little more bitterly than I mean, 'Thanks for the lie.' I can't meet his eyes.

'No lie.' He shakes his head. 'You'd hardly notice.'

Now that *is* a lie. 'Ta.'

'I mean it,' he says and boy, he can lie convincingly. 'Like when I met Kate, she told me not to stare at you too much, that you didn't like it on account of your scar. I was expecting you to look like something out of *Alien*.'

Before I can react to that, he goes on. 'But you don't. You look grand.' He nods. 'Totally grand.'

I feel tears start underneath my eyes and I blink. I wish I did look grand. I wish so much to look grand. I mean, it's not that I was ever vain or anything, but I took it for granted that people used to look at me and think that I was good-looking. My skin was my best asset. A no-blemish, peaches-and-cream complexion. And while I was never great at being the centre of attention, I did enjoy the compliments. But with the scar, there were no more positive comments. Instead, people either avoided looking at me or they looked at me for a whole different reason. I felt that no matter where I was I was being whispered about, speculated on, felt sorry for, and my natural shyness increased.

In fact, it increased so much that going outside has become impossible for me, and meeting strangers is now a regular feature of my nightmares.

My eyes must look teary because Luke's eyes crinch up in concern. He pokes his dreadlocked head across the table at me. 'Have I upset you?' he asks apprehensively.

I wave him away. 'No. I just wish I could believe you, that's all.'

'Well, I'm only telling you what I think,' he says. He stands up and takes his cup to the sink. 'The rest is up to you.'

I watch as he pulls on his old parka jacket. Bending down, he laces up a pair of trainers. 'Well, I'll be off,' he says. 'I've a bit of a stressful morning ahead.' He doesn't sound that bothered. 'The place I teach the OAP yoga in? Well, they're closing it down.'

'Oh, that's awful!' I know from Kate that he loves teaching yoga.

'Yeah. I mean, I don't make any money from it, but the old folks that come along will miss it. I'm going to phone around a few places today in work and see if there's anywhere available on the cheap.'

'Oh. Well, fingers crossed.'

Luke gives a lopsided grin. 'Something will come up. See ya.'

'Good luck hunting.'

'Ta.' He nods to me and places a big corduroy cap on his head. 'See you later.'

When he's gone, my little apartment is plunged back into silence. Funnily enough, I feel a little glad that I'll see him and Kate later on.

* * *

31

Hey Alistair, I type shortly afterwards, *you owe me a one-hundred-euro bonus. Ten thousand euro-worth of ads sold.* I press send, and almost immediately Alistair's response comes back.

You beauty!!!!

I laugh, he always makes me laugh, and type back, *No need to exaggerate.*

He mails back, *No exaggeration. Fancy some celebratory wine tonight? Discovered a nice dry white at a funeral recently, and while I know you don't appreciate the finer things in life, you will enjoy this. (Actually you could do some research on wine at funerals. Maybe sell some ads?) You on for tonight?*

Why not? I type back. *I could do with a good chat to you – helps me sleep.*

Hilarious. See you later.

I reply back that I'll be here and, grinning, close off the email.

Alistair is quite simply the best boss I've ever had. He has taken, in the last five months or so, to bringing over a bottle of wine every time we sell out our ad pages. In the beginning, he'd send me the wine through the post from one of those online wine companies but then, last May or so, he'd arrived at my door, uninvited, clutching a bottle of wine in his hand. The company had gone bust, he didn't want me to be without my wine, he hoped I didn't mind. I had minded, but Alistair is one of those people who have no social nous, and I found that oddly appealing. Whereas anyone else might be mortified at my embarrassment, he had smiled and told me how much the wine cost and that he couldn't trust it to the post. What would have happened if it had got smashed? And somehow, I'd found myself laughing at his appalled face as he'd contemplated the

32

smashing of his gift, and I'd invited him in. Since then, he has taken to calling over at least once a month, and I really look forward to seeing him now.

I suppose he makes me feel like a normal person.

8

L IGHT CREEPS UNDERNEATH the canvas of Lexi's tent. She lies still for a few seconds, savouring the silence. There doesn't seem to be another soul around. The fact that most of the places she has travelled through are pretty deserted doesn't bother her. It's nice to hear only the click-click-clicking of her feet as she wanders, exploring valleys, red mountain trails, scrubby outback and sometimes huge stretches of land with houses dotted about the place.

After about half an hour, she is ready to go. Her job, as has again been outlined by Peter, is to talk to any artists she can find and get them to sell their stuff through the gallery. She can't wait for the challenge. After all, she doesn't exactly have anything to lose except her time, though a few bob would be nice. She isn't a fool: she knows it's going to be hard to locate all the artists, and even harder finding out when they are around to chat. Still, if there is one thing she is good for, it's talking.

She sets off, her black boots slung across her shoulder. To her surprise there are other tents on the beach. She's never seen that before. There's one massive one, like a mini canvas castle, and she wonders who on earth could be bothered to own such a ridiculous monstrosity. On and on she walks. Up ahead, a guy in jeans with a bright yellow t-shirt is standing, his hands sunk into his pockets, his face impassive as he stares out to sea. He turns as Lexi approaches. He's not bad-looking, she thinks, his hair a dirty tousled blond, his teeth impossibly white in a tanned face.

'Hey,' she says.

'Hey.' He nods back. Then, having given her the once-over, he turns back to stare at the sea.

'Waiting for your ship to come in?' Lexi asks, grinning.

'You never know.'

Lexi gives a bit of a laugh and turns to leave, before pausing. 'Eh, I was wondering if you could help me,' she asks, smiling.

'Were you?'

Oh, a smart arse, she thinks with a roll of her eyes. She feels a little irritated that he doesn't seem to react to her looks. Most guys fall over themselves in their eagerness to help her. Still, he hasn't actually refused to help. 'Yeah, it's not a biggie or anything. I'm just wondering where all the artists hang out? I mean, this is a place for artists, right?'

'It is.' There is a slight pause before he tears his eyes away from the horizon and looks at her. 'Are you looking to buy some art?'

'Mmm, I suppose that's one way of putting it.'

'One way of putting it?' he repeats.

'You tell me where these guys are, I'll tell you the other way.'

He laughs. 'They don't all hang out in the same place, you know.'

That's condescending. 'Right. Thanks for that. That's been very helpful.' She turns to leave and hears him laugh again.

'I do some stuff,' he says. 'I'll show it to you.'

35

'Now?'

'God, you're keen.'

'Well surely you're keen to sell?'

'I'll sell it anyway.'

A smart arse and cocky, she thinks.

'Not for as much as I'll sell it for you.' Lexi folds her arms in a cocky gesture of her own.

'You're an agent?'

An agent? Would that impress him? 'I might be.' She hoped that was sufficiently enigmatic.

'For real?'

Oh, for God's sake. She wasn't one for giving false hope. 'I work for Peter's Gallery,' she admits. 'The gallery in town? It's my job to coax artists in to display their work. There is no fee for that, you only pay when you sell. And you will sell. That place looks amazing.'

'Er, no, thanks all the same. I'm mainly here to get inspiration, anyway. Strange place this.'

'What have you got to lose?' she presses, reluctant to let him change the subject. 'You could actually make more money than you are now.'

'I'm doing fine.'

Lexi takes a look at his jeans and t-shirt. 'Not that fine.'

'I happen to like these clothes.'

'So you like being in the minority, do you?'

'You'll do well with an attitude like that.'

'I hope to.' Feck it, he wasn't going to be persuaded. She starts to trudge away.

'You'll find most of them about ten minutes walk from town,' he calls out. 'Just take the road and keep going.'

She raises her hand in a gesture of thanks.

'Good luck, you'll need it,' he calls with a laugh.

She ignores that.

She'd have to do better than she had with him. That hadn't been very successful at all. When she reaches the top of the sand dune Lexi puts on her socks and boots. Hopping lightly down towards the road, Lexi takes her time as she begins the walk to town. She needs the time to come up with a strategy. No point going in feet first. The best thing to do is to put herself in the position of an artist. Well, that should come easily enough. She concentrates. If she were an artist, what would entice her to commit to a gallery when she could make a perfectly good living without anyone interfering? Why would she display her work behind doors when she could sit on a street and display it to the world? She thinks about this as the sun rises higher in the sky and ahead of her the road seems to shimmer in the heat. What could she say to someone?

And then, just as Lexi reaches the hat shop on the outskirts of the town, it hits her. It's so obvious she laughs. Artists, despite their laid-back attitude, are fiercely competitive. Well, she thinks, the best ones are. She remembers Chas quite suddenly and how, when he'd started out, he'd been desperate to display his pictures and paintings in a gallery in Dublin city centre. He'd known it would launch him. And the more the gallery refused, the more desperate Chas became. He'd even ditched his air of carefully cultivated coolness by camping outside the gallery one night, his pictures displayed in frames so that he could catch the curator before opening time. His tenacity had succeeded, and he'd got an exhibition of his own that had launched his career. He'd been hungry and competitive. Lexi stops walking, her head to one side. So, she thinks, how best to bring out the bloodthirsty edge in these artists? A competition would seem the obvious answer, but her competition would have to have an angle, something to make it different from other ones.

And when the idea comes, it's so obvious she wonders why Peter never thought of it.

Genius!

9

I'T'S EIGHT O'CLOCK. Kate and Luke have gone off to the cinema with some of their friends. They did ask me to go with them but, as Alistair was coming over, I refused. I wouldn't have gone anyway. I'm dividing my time, while waiting for Alistair, between watching reality TV and messing about on the computer. I bless whoever invented the internet every day of my life. It's brilliant for keeping someone like me, who doesn't like going out at all, in touch with people. Right now I've logged onto my Facebook page. Julie, my very first ever Facebook friend, has just announced that her period is three weeks late. She hopes she's pregnant. Amber, another friend from the US is moving house but will stay in touch with us all. And Laura posts a joke about a strawberry and a plum that makes me laugh out loud. I mail them all back, and then spend a few minutes before Alistair comes playing about with some designs for this month's magazine cover. What I like about working for *It's Your Funeral* is that the creation of each page is a challenge. I used to work for a glossy, and it's all happy, cheerful you-go-girl design. That's what I call it, anyway. And while there's nothing wrong with that, it bored me.

That's why I agreed to go travelling with Lexi in the first

place, to escape the tedium of greens and classic blues. But a funeral magazine, now there was an offer I couldn't refuse. The pay isn't great, but the idea of how to make a page work appealed to me. It has to look sombre yet offer hope – I mean, how do you do that? With massive difficulty, as it happens. Another big plus was that I could work from home.

I'm about to try out a particular shade of grey as the background colour of the lead page when I hear Alistair's car pulling into a parking space outside. Even though I'm not looking out the window, I know it's his car as it has a very distinct sound, like an eighty-year-old man with acute bronchitis. When I tease Alistair about it, he rolls his coal-black eyes and tells me in a superior tone that his car is vintage. And a classic. I just tell him that it belongs in a classic car boot sale. Peeking out the window, I see his long frame climbing out of the bucket seat. He's carrying a bag, presumably full of nice wine and, as he slams the door, he glances up at my apartment. I save my work and lightly hop downstairs to buzz him up.

Alistair and I met at the funeral of my grandmother nearly a year ago. He had been her next-door neighbour at the time, and he had promised her before she died that he would organise her funeral. Obviously it wasn't a random offer on Alistair's part – he and his family are the local undertakers. Anyway, they did a great job, if you can call a funeral that. My grandmother was buried with all the pomp and ceremony she'd loved in life, and the family and mourners went to a local pub for lunch afterwards. I hadn't been as reclusive then as I am now, but I was still sitting at a table deep in the snug of the pub, hidden from view, waiting for Kate to come back down with a pint, when Alistair slid into the seat beside me. I'd flinched, wishing he'd sat on the other side of me, the scar-free side. I braced myself for a 'what happened you' or, even worse, for it to be embarrassingly ignored, but Alistair genuinely seemed to pay no attention to the red welt running down my face. Instead, without any preamble, which is typical of him, he asked me if I was the granddaughter who was the graphic artist. He was the first person in about a year to ignore my scar and ignore it honestly. It wasn't that he avoided looking at it, it was as if he didn't see it. Or as if it didn't matter to him. I was stunned for a second at the unusualness of it before I nodded and told him yeah, I was a graphic designer. And he asked if I was working and I said no, I was on disability leave. He didn't ask why, though looking back, he probably knew as my granny would have filled him in.

Alistair is a man that old women like to chat to. He's the guy that mothers wish their daughters would settle down with. I guess if he'd been born in another century he'd have fitted in better than he does in this one.

'Great,' he'd said, then bumbled, flushing, to a halt. 'Eh, not great that you're on disability, but great that you're un-employed. Well, eh, not great for you, obviously, but great for me.' He'd stopped. Heaving an exasperated sigh, in which I fully expected him to kick himself, he asked me straight out if I'd work for him. He was starting a magazine for the trade, he said, a magazine for the bereaved and the dying and would I like a job designing it. I told him he'd referred to under-takers, bereaved and death in one sentence, and was there any way he could make it more enticing? He had flushed some more before laughing, and I had smiled. The first real

41

smile in a while. Even now, thinking of it, my eyes water a little. I'd been so sad. Then Alistair said the magic words, 'You can work from home.'

And so our partnership had been born. Initially Alistair was to write up features and sell ads, and while he was great at the writing, he couldn't sell condoms in a brothel. So I waded in and offered to have a go. He was sceptical at first, as he'd really only known me after my accident, when I'd morphed into the solitary, antisocial weirdo I am now, but make me faceless and give me a phone and I become even more social than the person I used to be. It's like I'm braver when no one can see me. So now I sell ads and design the pages. It's a lot, but I love it. I work from home and my boss is a pushover – how much better can it get?

Alistair comes in and hands me the bag containing two bottles of wine before divesting himself of his coat. As befits a guy that does the odd funeral nixer, he's dressed head to toe in black. Black jacket, black jeans, black polo neck and black Doc boots. I am not a fan of polo necks on guys, but on Alistair it has a certain appeal. Alistair's clothes lend him a look of a man not to be messed with, and I mean 'lend' because it's sadly deceiving. Alistair, despite the serious clothes, is actually a very quiet guy. His voice is soft and gentle and has a beautiful tonal quality to it. His every action is hesitant and slightly apologetic.

He nods to me and hands me a bag. 'A lovely Pinot in there,' he says.

'I beg your pardon?'

'Your juvenile sense of humour is absurd.' He rolls his eyes, smiling a little. 'Uncork it, it's beautiful. I discovered it at a funeral last week. It's bottle-fermented, much like Champagne. Gorgeous stuff.'

Now it's my turn to roll my eyes. I would drink anything, as he well knows. A bottle costing three euro would go down as easily as a bottle costing fifty. Alistair, however, is a big wine snob. He swirls it about and sniffs it and sips it and says things like, 'Oh, you can taste the oak.'

Why would anyone want to taste oak, I joke.

I uncork the wine and pour it into two glasses. Alistair follows me into the sitting room, holding the bottle in one hand and his glass in another. Baz is sprawled across the sofa. I sit down gingerly, trying not to disturb him. Alistair sits down at the far end. It's like a big chasm of cat separates us.

'Here's to you,' Alistair says smiling as he lifts his glass in a toast, 'my best worker.'

His only worker. 'Yeah, here's to me,' I agree.

Baz opens one lazy eye.

Alistair moves a little further away. So do I. Then we look at each other.

'Maybe I'll see if he'd eat something,' I say, 'then I can lock him in the kitchen.'

'Might be a good idea,' Alistair agrees. My cat makes him nervous. Well, Baz makes everyone nervous. He's quite vicious; he hisses a lot and tends to bite people who are foolish enough to want to pet him. He's a maverick, only seeking comfort when it suits him and, being honest, I'm afraid to refuse when he presses himself against my legs and purrs.

'Hey, Baz,' I cajole. 'Come on, come on.'

Baz eyes me sceptically.

I hop into the kitchen and find his bag of treats, which I then shake under his nose. He looks from me to Alistair as if he suspects some sort of a trick before jumping lightly down from the sofa and following me back out to the kitchen. I fill his bowl to the brim, then close the door on him.

'Mission accomplished.' I grin as I sit back down.

'That cat is evil,' Alistair announces. 'Are you not afraid of being alone with him?'

I giggle a little, and take a sip of wine. 'He reminds me of a lot of guys I could mention. The guy that gave him to me, for one.' Unfortunately the last sentence comes out sounding a little more bitter than I'd intended.

Alistair manages a smile, though, and wisely doesn't comment.

The silence that envelops us then doesn't bother me. Being with Alistair is not a strain because, even though we only see each other once or twice a month, we are comfortable with each other. Probably because we're both living life on the fringe of things. Tonight, though, even in the silence, Alistair is a bit edgy. He seems to be working himself up to say something. I know this because he keeps running the tip of his tongue over his lips and swallowing hard. I hop up and pull some tortilla chips from a press and tear them open.

'Spill,' I order, as I shove the packet towards him.

He looks momentarily startled. 'Pardon?'

He says pardon a lot. His manners are those of a gentleman in the old-fashioned sense. It's quite charming, actually. 'You,' I nod, still urging him to take a crisp, 'you're working up to say something, aren't you?'

He reaches into the packet and takes a handful. Placing them on his lap, he smiles a little ruefully. 'You know me well.'

There's not much to know, I don't think. Alistair lives a

predictable life; he reacts in predictable ways. Our conversations mainly consist of him telling me about weird funerals he's attended with odd mourners, which makes me laugh.

'Go on.' I'm smiling. This version of Alistair is not one I'm familiar with. This person who seems ever so slightly shifty. A sort of embarrassment creeps into his dark eyes. He angles his body a little away, and seems to scrutinise his wineglass. 'You won't find the answer sitting at the bottom of a wineglass,' I joke.

'Funn-ee.'

More silence.

I watch as he takes a deep, shaky kind of breath. 'OK,' he plunges like a dog into a river, 'I, eh, met a girl.'

'Pardon?' Now it's me with the weird manners. I'm slightly startled at the admission, to be honest. 'What?'

'I met a girl,' he snaps. It's the mortification, I think. 'I really like her.'

'Well, that's great. Good for you.' Alistair is not a guy that would dive impulsively into anything, I don't think. He's probably been mulling over this girl for months.

He shifts about uncomfortably. 'Yes, yes it is.' He pauses. 'I suppose.'

'You suppose?'

'Well,' he swirls his wine about, 'I don't really know her.'

'You've met a girl, you think she's nice and you don't know her?'

'You're laughing.' He sounds almost hurt.

'I'm laughing.'

His gaze flicks up to meet mine. A trace of a grin appears. 'I met her when I did a phone interview with her for the magazine. Flower arranging for funerals on a budget?'

'Oh yeah, last month's issue. That was a good piece.'

He nods modestly.

'So you interviewed her, but you didn't see her?'

He flushes. 'I did the second time,' he says defensively. 'She dropped some pictures into me for the pages. Her email broke down.'

'Maybe that was her excuse to meet you.'

'Really? You think?'

'Could be. And?'

'And nothing. But last week, I rang her up to arrange to give her pictures back, and then I asked her for a meal. I hadn't planned to, it just sort of came out.'

'Good for you!' I punch him lightly on the arm.

Instead of smiling, he looks slightly anguished. 'Yeah, well, you'd think so, wouldn't you?'

I stare blankly at him.

'I really like this girl, Andy, I know I don't know her but I really want it to go well.'

'Obviously.'

'And you know me,' he goes on slowly, as if each word is a careful step across thin ice, 'I'm not great with women.'

It's true that Alistair's manner takes some getting used to. He's shy and tactless at the same time. His body language is awkward and self-conscious. But when you get to know him, like I have, he's incredibly sweet and funny in a sort of bumbling Hugh Grant kind of way. There is a charm to his utterances that one only recognises after a while. 'Yes, you are.'

He raises an eyebrow.

'OK, you're no Don Juan, but that's a good thing.'

46

He ignores this. 'I thought you might know what to do. What I should say to impress her.'

'Me?' I half laugh. 'What makes you think I'd know?'

'You're a girl,' he says, as if stating something I didn't know already. 'I thought, you know, you could give me some insight into the female mind.'

'Every woman is different, Alistair.' I set down my wine-glass and start munching on a large handful of crisps. 'Just get to know her. Be interested in her.'

'I am interested in her.'

'Not in that way, you fool.' I make a face and he offers me a smile. Alistair's smiles are another cute thing. The word 'offer' is so appropriate. He smiles as if he's not quite sure you'll accept it, and when you do, his smile broadens and he actually looks quite handsome. 'Right, you know she's inter-ested in flowers, so show an interest in that.'

'OK.' He nods. 'I would have done that anyway. What else?'

'I don't know.' My love life at the moment is as barren as a sixty-year-old woman. 'Just be yourself, I suppose.'

'Eh, no, I'd rather not.'

I laugh. 'So, who are you planning to be? She already knows you're an undertaker and she's still agreed to go out with you.'

'I'm not a full-time undertaker,' Alistair says. 'I edit a maga-zine too.'

'True, she might find that interesting. Ask her about herself. Her family. What she likes to do.'

He nods. 'And what if she asks me about myself?'

'Tell her.'

He shifts about uncomfortably. 'I'd rather not. I did that to the last girl I went out with and she never returned my calls.'

'More fool her.' I scoff. 'What's so bad about you, anyhow? If I liked a guy, nothing he could say would put me off.'

Alistair looks unconvinced.

'OK, let's pretend we're on a date.' I put my wineglass down and straighten up. 'Now, I'll pretend to be her and you be you, OK?'

He hesitates before nodding, 'OK.' He doesn't sound too sure. Though he too puts his glass down. Then he coughs before assuming what he must think is a casual pose. 'Hey Mandy,' he stops. 'That's her name,' he tells me before continuing. 'Hey Mandy, eh, how's things? I, eh, booked a restaurant, I hope you'll like it.'

I nod encouragingly. 'Right, so we get into your car,' I say. Then add, 'Chances are she'll ask about your car.'

His face lights up. 'Oh, good. Well, it's a 1978 Corvette Stingray with a five-litre petrol engine and an automatic gearbox, featuring—'

'No!' I interrupt, trying not to laugh. 'No. Just tell her it's a vintage car and that you like vintage cars, and then you ask her something about herself. Maybe ask her if she was always into flowers, or something.'

'Oh.' He flushes. 'OK. So I divert the conversation from myself and onto her.'

'Sometimes. Not all the time, as she'll want to know about you too. Just make sure you tell her things she'll enjoy hearing about.'

'OK. Like what?'

48

I suddenly realise how little I know about Alistair. 'I dunno, talk about what you like. Your taste in wine, for instance. Maybe she's like you about wine.'

'Hmm.' He pauses, then raises his gaze to mine. 'Can I ask you a personal question?'

'No.'

'Would you like to be kissed on a first date?'

'Was that the personal question?'

'Yep.' He grins a little at me.

'Rule number one,' I hold up a finger, 'girls like it when guys actually listen to them. A no is a no. But, seeing as it's not too personal a question, the answer is, it depends on how much I like the guy. If I like him, I'm very happy to kiss him.'

'So how will I know if she likes me?'

'You just will.'

'I don't think I will.' He shakes his head before picking up the bottle of wine. 'Like some more?'

I push my glass towards him. 'Look, just be yourself. You're a nice fella.'

He looks a little surprised at that remark. 'Ta.'

'It's true.' And I really mean it. Alistair will never sweep a woman off her feet. His attraction is much more slow-burning, I suspect.

To my surprise, he leans across and lightly kisses me on the cheek. 'Thanks, Andy.'

I push him off playfully. 'That is a boss taking liberties with the staff.'

He laughs loudly.

It's only afterwards that I realise he has kissed my scar.

I wonder how he could have. I feel strange that he did.

Happy that he did, I guess.

Maybe Luke is right, and my scar isn't as bad as I think it is. Maybe it's all in my head. Or on my face, I think in a rare moment of wry humour. But Alistair kissed it, and that must mean *something*.

10

LEXI FINDS PETER doing push-ups on the steps of the gallery. He looks a little ridiculous, and she laughs to herself. When he spots her, he straightens up and manages a smile. He's wearing the same tracksuit he had on when they first met. His trainers are different, though, and his hair has changed too. It's spikier, more tousled and modern. It suits his oriental features.

Lexi doesn't wait for him to greet her. Instead she plunges in with, 'I think we need to run a competition.'

'What?' He's bewildered.

'A competition,' Lexi repeats, walking up the steps to the gallery and entering the foyer. Behind her, Peter almost trips up in his eagerness to follow her. 'We run a competition, and the best pictures from the best artist get displayed.'

When there is no response, Lexi turns to face him. 'Well?'

He barks out a sort of laugh. 'A competition?' He folds his arms. 'Running competitions takes time. I don't have any bloody time. This gallery will cark it.' At her puzzled look, he adds, 'Die. This gallery will die.'

'You have all the time in the world.' Lexi waves his concern off and perches herself on the edge of the desk.

'It's costing me,' Peter says. 'Every day this building is

costing me.' He studies Lexi with her Docs and her three-quarter-length green jeans and her white and green t-shirt. 'You might have all the time in the world, hon. I mean, you're just travelling about. I'm not. I want to make a go of it here.'

Her first impulse is to think how sad he is. But she pushes it away. Even though she isn't staying put, she too wants to make a go of it, whatever 'it' is. 'I'm telling you how to succeed,' Lexi says, and if she could have sounded any more passionate, she would have. 'Look, Peter, asking artists to come in here is ridiculous. I already met a guy this morning who laughed at the suggestion. You need to bring out their vanity, their ego, their competitive streak, make them feel that it's a prestigious thing to be in here.' She pauses, reluctant to reveal anything about herself, but finally she says, 'I know someone who used to be a full-time artist.'

'Yeah?' Now she has his attention.

'Yeah.' And she tells him about Chas, and of how he'd queued up to get the gallery to display his photos and pictures.

'Chas Ryan?'

Lexi is surprised that Peter has heard of him. Maybe the man had some knowledge about art.

'Uh-huh.'

'You know him?'

Lexi dips her head. 'Yep. Anyway, he—'

'D'ya think he'd judge the competition?'

Oh, shit. Lexi should have known that was coming. Contacting Chas was not something she was prepared to do at all. 'I dunno.'

'If he judged the competition, it might get a lot of attention. His paintings are awesome.' Peter seems excited now. He pokes

52

his head towards Lexi's. 'How well do you know him?' he demands.

'I used to know him quite well,' Lexi says hesitantly. 'Now, not so much. Anyway, he doesn't paint any more, he gave it up. He only does photography now.'

'Yeah,' Peter was still grinning, 'which is why his pictures are so damn exy. Just think, if you could get him to judge, we could go really big with this competition.'

It was no use, she had to nip this in the bud. 'He won't judge it,' she says. 'I was just using him to demonstrate the power of,' she sought for the words, 'the power of ego.'

'You won't know until you ask.'

'I do know, and I'm not asking.' Lexi folds her arms.

'Well, then, we'll just have to go back to plan A.'

'That won't work.' Was this man stupid, she wondered? 'I've already explained that no one will exhibit here. It's not worth their while.'

'And you've been in this town how long? Two days?'

Lexi says nothing. The trick now, she thinks, is to present the angle to Peter in an offhand manner, make him think he thought of it himself. 'OK,' she shrugs, 'well, there's no point in me sticking around. You go and run your gallery into the ground if you like.'

'Hey, hang on.' Peter follows her to the door. 'Are you shooting through on me?'

'Wow, a hundred points for observation.' She smiles to herself. Not exactly the greatest put-down in the world. She's going soft in her old age.

'Oh, don't go.' Peter stands in front of Lexi, looking as desperate as his gallery. 'Why don't you just go talk to the artists? You've only chatted to one, that's no indicator.'

'OK.' Lexi nods and immediately he relaxes. 'So, what would you like me to say: "Desperate gallery owner, fears going broke and wants you to exhibit with him?" Something like that? Or maybe, "Peter's Gallery is running a worldwide online art- gallery competition to find an artist worthy enough to exhibit with them?"' Lexi cocks her head. 'Which sounds better, d'you think?'

He says nothing.

'Well?' she pushes.

'Worldwide?' He rolls his eyes.

'Yeah, aim high and you'll get somewhere, I reckon. Might not be worldwide, but still . . .'

'Online.' It's a statement, and he's smiling.

'Yeah, makes perfect sense. Also, it widens the scope of entries. All the artists have to do is submit a scan. It's a risk, but still . . .' She lets the sentence hang.

Peter's smile fades. 'But who'll judge?'

'Will you forget about that for a while!' Lexi snaps.

'Well, they'll want to know that.'

It's a reasonable point, she has to agree.

'I mean, for posters and promotion and stuff,' Peter goes on, sensing a weakening in her position. 'We need someone.'

She thinks hard. Does she know anyone else who would do it? Well, there is . . . but no. That would blow her whole world right open, and she doesn't need that.

'No,' she lies.

'Chas Ryan would be bonzer. And if you know him, it'd make a ripper competition.'

'There are many other artists out there,' Lexi says.

'In the meantime,' Peter goes on as if she hasn't spoken,

'go down town and start spreading a few rumours of a big competition, see what feedback you get.'

'So you're going with the idea of a competition, then?' Lexi can't help the cocky body language.

'I guess.' He nods. 'It makes sense.'

'Do I get money for the idea?'

'Fifty?'

It's more than she expected. 'Yeah, I can live with that.'

He has a nice-sounding laugh.

11

I TURN TO THE design of the front page. All the copy is now in, and the magazine is due out in a week's time. Something is still not quite right about it, though. Alistair has done a massive feature on hearses and their costs this month, and he'd asked for a black car to adorn the cover. Black is hard to work with. Well, I find it is. I've tried grey, no go. Red is too gaudy. Maybe white? Or cream? I begin to try out various combinations when my mobile rings. Flipping it open, I don't recognise the number.

'Hello?'

'Andy, Luke here.' In the background, I can hear a lot of noise. People talking. 'Shusssh,' Luke says, and immediately there are mumbled apologies followed by silence.

'Impressive,' I joke.

'That's me,' he says back. Then adds, 'Look, Andy, I've a favour to ask. A biggie.'

I grin a little. He and my sister are in my house, they are eating my food and their stuff takes up nearly all the free space in the place. How much more massive a favour can he want? 'Shoot.'

'You can say "no",' he says hastily. 'I'll completely under-stand. The yoga place was shut down this morning. We all

56

arrived here and couldn't get in. I thought I'd another week to run, and I haven't managed to get anywhere yet.' He takes a deep breath. 'What I'm asking is if I can hold my classes in your place until I find somewhere else. Your front room would fit us all comfortably. There's only four people in this class.'

'My place?'

'I know it's a biggie.'

My heart starts to flutter and I feel a little breathless. I haven't had strangers in my house since the accident. That's well over a year and a half ago. The thought of it makes me feel sick. They'll see me and stare at my face or, even worse, they'll pretend that the scar is not there. I don't know if I'd be strong enough to handle the humiliation.

'Oh, Luke, I – I dunno.'

'No worries,' he hastens to reassure me, though it's hard to miss the deflation in his voice. 'It's no big deal. It's your place, I just thought I'd ask. No worries.'

His immediate understanding makes me feel guilty. And I know he actually means what he says. I take a deep breath. 'It's not that—'

'Hey,' Luke interrupts, 'I know if you could, you would. I shouldn't have asked. It was stupid of me. It's just that I'm a bit desperate.'

'Are we going somewhere else, pet?' a voice in the background asks Luke. It sounds like an old woman.

'Not yet, Mabel, just gimme a few more minutes.'

'OK, pet. Now I hope we're doing the back-strengthening exercises today. That's what you promised last week and—'

'I know, Mabel. Just gimme a minute, I'm on the phone here.'

'Oh, of course. Of course.'

'She's as blind as a bat,' Luke lowers his voice. 'Sorry about that.'

'Blind but not deaf,' Mabel shouts as Luke chuckles.

'Are they all old?' I ask.

'Yep,' Luke says. 'The classes I do here are the OAP ones. It's sorta my good deed. I don't get paid for them.'

Ouch. That makes me feel worse. And maybe old people in my house wouldn't be too bad. I'll have nothing in common with them. They'd be far too mature to judge me on my appearance or maybe, I think, they'll be all as blind as Mabel. Then I feel mean for thinking that. But if I stay out of the way, then . . . 'OK,' I say to Luke. At the word, sweat pops up so fast on my hands that I lose my grip on the phone for a second. 'Come over, but stay in the room downstairs. I'll be upstairs, don't . . . you know . . . let them bother me. I need silence when I work.'

The last sentence is a lie. He knows it, as I normally have classical music on when I create. But still, human voices would definitely not help me concentrate.

'You sure?' Luke sounds as if he's trying to suppress his delight.

'Totally. Just, you know . . .' I don't finish. I think he knows what I'm trying to say.

'There's only four of them. They'll be grand. Thanks Andy.'

'No worries.'

Twenty minutes later, I hurry from my front room back up the stairs. I've tried to make it more spacious for Luke and his yoga people. I've pushed the sofa to the wall and taken the coffee table out to the kitchen, where it now sits in the centre of the floor. Baz is safely ensconced in my bedroom. I've just reached the top of the stairs when Luke unlocks my front door and enters the hallway. He stands back to usher a number of people in. I disappear from sight and listen as he tells them all that his friend has lent him the use of the front room and to be as quiet as possible. There is a lot of good-natured shushing and exaggerated tiptoeing. Then the door to the front room clicks shut and there is a sudden quiet.

I return to my work, my fingers tapping across the keyboard. From below, every now and again I catch Luke's gentle voice followed by the faint murmurings of others. After about forty-five minutes, the strains of a relaxing CD drift up to me.

I've just got the shade of cream matched up well with the ebony black when the class ends. Luke bids them all goodbye, and they thank him.

'Say thanks to your friend,' someone says. 'He's a lifesaver.'

'She,' Luke corrects, 'and I will.'

Then the door closes and I hear Luke as he hops lightly up the stairs. The man should have been a dancer, he's so graceful. Probably as a result of all the yoga. He knocks gently on my office door and pops his head around.

'Hey Lifesaver,' he says, 'lunch is my treat. What would you like?'

'Ah, there's no need.'

'There is. You just saved me a lot of cash.' He comes into the room and peers out the window. 'There they are.' He grins, pointing out his students as they emerge from the building down below. 'They're a gas bunch, and they're so enthusiastic.'

I follow his gaze and see three women and one man, all

in the mid- to late-seventies age bracket, chatting avidly to each other as they cross to the car park.

'See the woman in front? The one with the blue track bottoms.'

'Uh-huh.'

'That's Mabel. She rang up Dublin Live this morning when we were standing outside the building waiting to get in. They initially refused to put her on air, so when Kate heard about it she said she could go on her show. The other three have promised to ring up to support her.'

I gawk at Luke. Kate's programme? Kate takes phone calls on sex-related queries and reads out lurid stories from the day's newspapers. What possible place could yoga and an OAP have on Kate's programme?

Luke grins as if reading my mind. 'Yeah, I know,' he says. Then his eyes cloud over slightly. 'But they haven't a hope. The place is gone now, and there is nothing they can do about it.'

'Maybe someone listening in will offer somewhere.'

'A massage parlour? A brothel?'

We both grin. Then he shrugs. 'So, lunch?'

'Go on then. I'll have a roll. Lots of salad stuff, some cheese and no onion.'

He bows. 'No problem. I'll be back in ten.' He jingles his car keys and leaves.

Luke has left for his real job in the health food shop by the time Mabel makes her radio debut. He didn't ask me to listen, but I wanted to, more out of curiosity than anything else, just to get to know the four people who had tromped into my house earlier that morning. And who probably would

60

be tromping into it every week until they found somewhere else.

The DJ, if you can call Kate that, as she doesn't play any music, introduces Mabel. 'And now we have Mabel, an old-age pensioner. So, Mabel, your yoga centre was closed down this morning, was it?'

'It sure was,' Mabel says smartly, and immediately I like her. 'It was in a community centre, run by the local authority, and the classes were free, run by a lovely young man who wants to give something back to society. Now with the centre closed, we've nowhere to hold our yoga classes. I wish to ask if there is anyone out there who would help us find somewhere.'

'Well, go on then,' Kate encourages.

So Mabel succinctly explains about the yoga, and how important it had become in her life and in the lives of her friends. She'd been in a car crash, she says, and doing the exercises had helped ease the pain in her back. It was also a way of meeting other people of her own age and making friends. 'I was quite lonely,' Mabel says, 'but now I feel I have support.'

'I have a listener on with a suggestion,' Kate says. 'OK, go on Declan.'

'Find another yoga class,' Declan snorts.

'It's not that simple,' Mabel snaps. 'Were you not listening? The classes were free! I couldn't afford to pay, and neither could my friends.'

'Welcome to the real world, honey,' Declan drawls. He sounds like a brothel owner to me. 'Everyone pays for everything.'

'I get the feeling,' Mabel says icily, 'that you are not inter-ested in this item. That you feel it is not of sufficient interest.

You'd rather have some blonde bimbo on talking about underage sex, or something.'

Declan snorts back a laugh. 'I really don't think—'

'No, you don't think,' Mabel interrupts. 'I am an OAP, and this class means a lot to me. The instructor is a fine young man who is excellent at the various exercises, especially when it comes to people of my age group. He didn't abandon us the way the people at the centre abandoned us, the way you seem determined to, no, he held the class in his friend's flat this morning. Thank God for people like him. I bet that if I had a bit more glamour, I'd get a lot more sympathy out of you, wouldn't I?'

'That's ridiculous,' Declan says patronisingly.

'It is not,' Mabel snaps. 'Appearances count for a lot in this world, don't they? Well, I can tell you with absolute certainty, one day you will be old and looking for help, and maybe you might remember this conversation and wish you'd treated me differently.'

'Caller on line five,' Kate interrupts hastily.

'I'm Fred,' a man says, his voice trembling nervously. 'And I agree with Mabel. It's an ageist society we live in. Growing old can be lonely, especially if you have no family nearby, and classes like this are a godsend.' He pauses, and sort of spoils the moment by admitting, 'And I'm in Mabel's yoga class too.'

'Hi Fred,' Mabel says. 'Did you get home all right today?'

'I did. I managed the walk without a bother.'

'That is fantastic. You probably only had indigestion then.'

'Yes, those Rennies you gave me worked a treat.'

I find myself grinning at the exchange.

Then another caller comes on to support them. Soon all

four are on air, and they are joined by at least another fifty people, all wanting their say on how lonely it can get when you grow old.

Mabel finishes up the slot with, 'Please help us find a place to hold the sessions. If we were a group of twentysomethings, I bet we'd have got somewhere by now.'

'Mabel, can I ask you if the yoga helps with that enormous chip on your shoulder?' an unsupportive caller chortles.

'How dare—'

Kate cuts whatever else Mabel has to say by wrapping up the slot. 'And next,' she says, 'we're talking sex!'

Well, there's a surprise, I think wryly.

12

THE GUY WITH the yellow t-shirt is on the beach again, the ninth morning in a row. Only now he is sans t-shirt, obviously having removed it at some stage. He is sitting on the sand, his elbows resting on top of his knees, watching the sea. He doesn't speak as Lexi approaches. He only ever talks if she talks to him.

'We don't want your pictures for our gallery now,' she calls out as she passes him.

'I didn't want your gallery for my pictures. Ever,' he calls back.

Ouch. She'd asked for that. 'Well good.'

'Good.'

Lexi has to grin. She can't see his face, but maybe he's grinning too. 'Oh, and by the way,' she calls out when she's at a safe distance from him, 'I've seen better six packs on a turkey.'

'I've seen nicer faces on a horse.'

She laughs, unoffended, and starts the walk to town. She does this stroll a lot and by now, she recognises the stones on the road and the flowers in the verges. Each day, though, there is something new to spot. Today a weird-looking bird hops up and down in a nearby bush. It's a sort of cockatoo, she thinks. It's the most gorgeous-looking bird she has ever seen.

The town seems particularly deserted this morning. She's met all the owners of the shops now. Normally, passing the hat shop, Cissy, the owner, would call out a cheery greeting, but for some reason she's not in. Cissy is a tall, leggy, dark-haired woman who dresses in the shortest skirts and the tiniest tops even on the rainiest days. Not that there are many of those. When Cissy is around, as far as Lexi can see, she spends her days stalking up and down the town's streets, enjoying the effect her undulating walk and flirty little skirts have on the other residents. Lexi is convinced that Peter has a crush on her, as he makes a point of jogging by her shop every day.

'Hey Lex,' Doug, the tall rangy guy who owns the music store lifts a hand to her. He is in his usual black t-shirt and tight jeans. The t-shirt has an AC/DC logo emblazoned across it. Today he has a ridiculous-looking hat perched sideways on his head. 'Hoar you t'day?'

'Hi Drug,' Lexi calls back, making him laugh. The man was incomprehensible a lot of the time. 'Sell anything lately?'

'I'm geeting so desperate I t'ink I'll sell my body.'

'Prepare for bankruptcy, so.'

'Yor so smart you'll cut yersel'.'

'I'm so *sharp* I'll cut myself,' Lexi corrects him.

'Go.' Doug makes whooshing motions with his hands. 'Have a bad day, go on. Make my dreams come true.'

'A Lexi day is a good day.' Lexi bows, and he makes a sound like a snort and laughs.

Lordi's shop is deserted, a forlorn angel guarding the front door. A sign slung around his neck informs the reader that it is in fact none other than St Peter.

As Lexi continues on, she thinks suddenly that of all the places she's travelled to, this town is turning out to be quite the nicest. And it isn't because of the white sandy beach or the dramatic red mountainscape that can be seen from a distance, it's the others she's met. They make her laugh, she makes them laugh. Not that she knows them on any intimate level or anything, but she doesn't need to. She came here to escape, to reinvent, to re-imagine a normal kind of life, and she reckons that a lot of the people here are doing the same. If escape is what is needed, well, she reckons that this quiet, dusty settlement is definitely the place to come. She passes the gallery and heads in the direction of the town hall, a big, barn-like building situated on the right-hand turn of the t-junction. It's the first building most travellers go to when arriving in Salue, as it helps them get to know what's going on in the place. Outside, in the grounds, Peter is waiting for her. He's ditched his tracksuit and is dressed for the occasion in a fancy blue suit and bright white shirt. It makes him appear quite suave. His shoes – a designer pair, no doubt – are black and highly polished. Lexi winces. Still, according to Peter himself he is loaded, and as she isn't, the best she could manage is a pair of unripped denims and a brand new funky hat courtesy of Cissy's shop. Her top is a faded yellow that suits her colouring.

'Hi Pete.' Lexi raises her hand in greeting.

'G'day. Are you ready?'

'Yep.'

Together they walk past the gaudy-looking town fountain, which consists of an enormous and very ferocious-looking fish spouting water from its mouth.

'Whoever designed that should never have any work displayed in a gallery,' Peter jokes.

'Agreed.' Lexi nods.

They enter the large, high-ceilinged, multi-windowed building and make their way to the reception desk. There is no one there. Peter sits on a purple sofa just inside the doorway. 'Jay said he'd be a bit late.'

Jay is the guy who knows what's going on. As far as Lexi can make out, there is one of these men in every town here, though Jay seems to be particularly prominent. She finds him pompous and self-important. Though, to be fair, he's not a spoofer. He really does have his finger in every pie.

Lexi remains standing. It's the first time she's been inside this building, and she's impressed by the number of notices that line the walls detailing the events happening in the town and in other towns in the vicinity. That's what they need, she thinks, only their notice has to stand out.

A stunning piece of artwork dominates the wall above the reception desk. It's blue, green and red and seems to depict the emergence of building and development, at least that's what she thinks it shows. Lexi crosses towards it and peers at it more closely. 'Wow, who did this?'

'A bloke by the name of Styles,' Peter tells her. 'When I saw it, I asked him to exhibit but he knocked me back.'

'Is he still living here?' Lexi continues to study the picture, the whirl of colour, the shapes of buildings and trees, looking almost as if they were being created by a force other than man.

'Dunno. What if he is?'

'Mm, I suppose it doesn't matter.' Lexi finally turns around. 'But he's good. I like that picture.'

'Yes, I paid him a heap for it.' Jay suddenly appears from behind them. His Australian accent is more pronounced than Peter's. He comes towards the two of them, hand extended, dressed in a flashy silver-grey suit and pinstripe shirt. His blond hair and tanned face lend the impression that he is an oily, slick operator. He's a businessman, but has the smoothness of a consummate politican. 'Peter, g'day. Long time no see. And?' He looks questioningly at Lexi. 'It's Lexi, yeah?'

'Uh-huh. I work with Peter in the gallery.'

Jay nods. 'An offsider, huh? Business better now, Peter?'

'Eh, not exactly, no.'

'Right, well, now that I've put my huge foot in it, what can I do you for?' Jay sounds embarrassed.

'We're organising a competition,' Lexi answers, knowing that Peter will be flustered. He gets very sensitive about the car crash that is his gallery business. 'And the winner will get the chance to exhibit in Peter's gallery. He's offering prize money too, aren't you, Peter?'

Peter nods. 'We think that it will help boost the profile of the gallery, especially the way we're structuring the competition.'

Jay nods. 'Go on.'

So Peter explains to him what they have in mind and finishes with, 'And we need your help. We want this to be a ripper competition, not just local. Lexi and I feel that we could make it a global event, with the right publicity.'

'Global?' Jay sounds sceptical.

'Yes.' Lexi nods. 'Peter's gallery is gorgeous; it's capable of displaying anything to advantage. I think this could be a unique competition. First thing we need is to advertise it locally, and then in the towns nearby. We were hoping you could help us with that.'

Jay nods, then crosses to his desk. 'Yes, I can help you. I have a condition, though.'

'What?' Peter asks.

'I want the town's name to be used at all times. I want this town to get publicity, as well as your gallery. Agreed?'

'No worries,' Peter says. 'In fact, we'll have a link on the competition site with directions on how to get here, and maybe some pictures of the place.'

'That should increase visitors.' Jay nods.

Lexi says nothing. An increase in visitors is not what she wants. Who knows who might spot her then? Still, if more visitors come, she'll move on.

'Right.' Jay looks up. 'I'll prepare a list of names you can contact in all the towns nearby. Or at least, ones that I know of. Some of them might have changed. Do you have an email?'

Lexi hesitates, but Peter rattles off a website address. 'It will redirect email to me,' he says.

'And you both have a list of artists you're going to contact,' Jay asks. It's not a question, more a statement of fact.

'Uh-huh,' Lexi answers anyway.

Jay looks up. 'Well, that's it then.'

'Eh, no,' Lexi says. 'We were wondering if you'd do us the honour of putting this up in the town hall.' She holds out the poster. 'It's the poster for the competition. We were also wondering if you could do it for free.' She makes that up on the spur of the moment. 'I mean, if our competition is going to be giving you publicity and all.'

'Yes, and I'm giving you a list of contacts,' Jay says back.

'Paying is not a problem,' Peter interrupts. 'I'll pay whatever it costs.'

If Peter could have killed Lexi with a look, he would have.

If Lexi could have kicked Peter, she would have. 'It was worth a try.'

'It'll be a standard fee,' Jay says. 'And as your poster is rather large, it is a discount of sorts.'

'We don't need a discount,' Peter says.

'Yeah, but we'll take one.' Lexi laughs.

'Whatever you decide.' Jay points to a spot on the wall. 'Now just there is a prime position. People will see it when they come in as it's right opposite the door. Normally we charge more for that, but we won't.'

'I don't need discounts.' Peter is miffed.

'He does.' Lexi ignores him. 'Thanks for that, Jay.'

Jay grins. 'I'll be talking to you both again.'

'Sure,' Peter says, before turning on his heel and stomping out of the building.

'Oops, think I've upset him now,' Lexi says.

'I'll have the poster up by tomorrow,' Jay, still grinning, informs Lexi. 'You can come and have a squizz at it then.'

'Ta.' She nods her thanks and runs out in search of Peter.

He must be in a right huff, she concedes, because he has gone without waiting for her or saying goodbye.

13

LUKE IS SITTING on the sofa, Kate on the floor at his feet. With one hand he's running his fingers through her auburn highlighted hair and with the other, he's flicking through the pages of a local telephone directory, which is balanced quite precariously on his knee. They look so comfortable together, so right.

My favourite soap, *Coronation Street*, has just started on the telly.

Kate shifts slightly so that her arm rests on Luke's knee. 'Want some help?'

'Nope.' He lightly kisses the top of her head. 'I'm just having a look to see if there are places that might be available to hold my senior-citizen yoga class. I don't want to abandon it. I mean, they've come on so much that it'd be a shame.' He flips over another page and scans it.

'They might find another free one,' Kate says. 'I know you think you're one of a kind, Luke, but you're not.'

'And I thought she loved me,' Luke says, tugging on Kate's hair and grinning across at me.

'I do. Didn't I put your old lady on my radio show, and get the face eaten off me by my producer?'

'Why? I thought the producer was the one who has the final say on who gets air time.'

'She does. I told her I had a raunchy friend called Mabel who was going to talk about how yoga positions help in senior sex.'

'No!' Luke splutters out a laugh.

'Yep.'

'You told your producer that?' Luke chortles. Then, as Kate nods again, he laughs some more. 'Jesus, Mabel would wither up and die!'

'So what happened? Did your producer go mad?' I ask, smiling too and admiring her nerve.

'She did, but I just blamed Mabel. I told her the silly old bat chickened out.'

Luke hugs her tight and kisses the top of her head. 'I love you, d'you know that, Katie Fitzsimons?'

'Mmmm,' she responds, flapping him with her arm. 'Well don't ask me to get publicity for your classes again so.'

'You're welcome to use here as long as you like,' I surprise myself by saying.

'Ah, no,' Luke waves me away. 'You've been good enough already.'

'I mean it,' I say. 'It was no bother today, you didn't even disturb me.' I pause and admit, 'To be honest, having people around was kinda nice.'

Kate's eyes light up and she beams over at me. 'Really?'

I wince inwardly at her big smile. Hastily, I add, 'Anyway, until you get somewhere else, the offer is there.'

Luke nods in his slow way. 'Ta. I appreciate that, Andy.'

I turn back to *Coronation Street*, trying to ignore the look that passes between Luke and my sister. It's a communication of

72

sorts, and I know it's to do with me. I try not to think about what it might be. I fix hard on the dilemmas going on in the fictitious TV street. What I love about soaps is that no matter what disasters befall the inhabitants, things somehow sort themselves out. People survive to go on fighting, or make an exit to a better life, or die. Nothing like that happened to me. When my disaster struck, I survived but ended up moving sort of sideways, which in hindsight was not a particularly good thing. I don't mean to sound ungrateful, I'm glad I'm alive, and to be honest, I don't know in what other way things could have panned out. But the way they did, or the way I handled them, was all wrong. I have no idea how it all went so pear-shaped, how I ended up so stuck. 'Cause I am stuck, I think. Stuck in this apartment, for a start.

'Andy, d'you fancy coming with me to call on the folks,' Kate asks, moving out from under Luke's arm. 'I haven't seen them in weeks, and Mam keeps texting me to come over.'

I glance involuntarily to the window. It's seven forty-five and mid-October, so it's dark enough outside to hide me if we happen to bump into anyone. And I know from experience that there won't be many people in the corridor of my building at this time of night. The man who lives beside me only seems to go out at weekends, so we hardly ever bump into one another and when we do, I have perfected the art of keeping my head down and to the side, so that my scar is not immediately visible. I don't think he's ever noticed it. These thoughts flick through my head in rapid succession, like a general planning a military blitz. I come to the conclusion that the walk to Kate's car will be trauma-free. Pressing 'record' to make sure I get the rest of *Coronation*

Street, I tell Kate that yep, I will go with her to visit our parents.

Half an hour later, Kate pulls up in front of our parents' house. It's the best-kept house on the road. My mother sets a lot of store by outward appearance: her garden grass must never grow more than an inch, her flowers must be in straight rows. Her house must gleam and smell of polish. Her windows have to shine. And my mother must always look well groomed.

Kate must have rung to say we'd be calling, as no sooner have we parked behind Dad's car than they both come to the door to greet us.

My mother, as usual, stands slightly in front of my father. 'Hello girls!' she says loudly.

Dad nods a silent greeting.

'Hey!' Kate says cheerily. 'How are the best parents in the world?'

'Oh, she's looking for something,' Mam laughs, flapping her hand as Dad smiles and rolls his eyes.

'No. It's all true.' Kate nods, slamming her car door. 'Look at you both, out to the front door to say hello. How many other parents would do that now?'

'I don't know,' Dad quips wryly, 'maybe you should discuss it on your show, might make a change from all the sex.'

'Easy now, you don't work in radio.' Kate walks by him, grinning. 'Borrrrr-ing!'

My mother has the sofa covered in a throw, to keep it clean, though how it would get dirty when they have very few visitors is a mystery. Kate and I sit down. The telly is switched to *Fair City*, the RTE soap. Again, a place where awful things happen and people get by.

'It's coming up to an interesting bit,' Dad says, thumbing to the television. 'The girl who's leading a fake double life is about to be unmasked. She was spotted with her pimp by her husband.'

'Sounds completely bizarre.' Kate grins.

'About as bizarre as your show,' my mother clicks her tongue. Even though she listens to Kate's show, she still feels she has to disapprove of it. 'Tea or coffee?'

'My show is not bizarre,' Kate smirks.

'Your mother has a point.' Dad nods, surprising us by agreeing with her. They normally disagree on everything. 'It makes for very uncomfortable listening, especially for me and Lil.'

'Well, maybe you both should invest in some softer chairs.'

My father laughs despite himself as my mother clicks her tongue again before repeating loudly, 'Tea or coffee?'

We all opt for coffee, and Mam exits to make it.

'So, how are you?' Dad turns to me.

'I'm good.' I nod, trying to ease the look of concern in his eyes. They worry a lot about me. 'I'm enjoying the magazine more all the time. It's fun.'

Dad doesn't look at all convinced. 'But it's for funerals.'

'Yeah, I know.' I grin.

'Hmm. And that funeral fella you work for, how's he?'

My dad is hopeless at names. 'Alistair is good. He's got a new girlfriend.'

My mother comes back in with a tray. 'Move over, Donald,' she orders, and my father obliges by shifting up on the sofa to allow my mother to squeeze in and put down a tray of biscuits and cake. 'Who's got a new girlfriend?' she asks.

So I tell her, and then I end up talking about how he came

over for a drink to celebrate me selling loads of ads. My mother looks meaningfully at Dad.

'He's got a girlfriend,' I repeat, knowing that in their desperation to see me out and about, they'll read all sorts of things into the visit. 'Alistair is just a friend, he is my boss. I am not interested in him in that way.'

'Oh, that doesn't mean anything,' Mam says brightly, as she lays plates, cups and saucers in front of us. She's very formal like that. 'I wasn't interested in your father in that way either.'

'Ha!' Dad snorts and rolls his eyes. 'You couldn't keep your hands off me.'

'Yes,' Mam nods, straightening up, the tray under her arm, 'I wanted to strangle you.'

'Ooh, kinky sex,' Kate smirks. 'What a brilliant topic for my show. Want to come and talk about it, Mam?'

'Kate!' both my parents say together as I dissolve in laughter.

'Sorry,' Kate says, not sounding sorry at all.

She really does try to shock them. It's as if her whole life is built around getting a reaction.

'As I was saying,' my mother goes on, 'sometimes you realise you love someone who initially doesn't even register on your radar.'

Dad doesn't look too pleased by the remark. 'Thanks,' he mutters drily.

'In fact, I used to think your father was a bit of a drip,' Mam continues, oblivious to Dad's mounting dismay.

Dad glares at her. 'Thanks,' he says again.

'So what changed?' I ask, hoping she'll say something nice.

Mam looks at Dad, her head to one side, pondering the

76

question. Her forehead creases up. 'I can't remember,' she finally states, sounding baffled.

'Thanks,' Dad says for the third time in a distinctly pissed-off voice. He turns up the volume on the TV. The *Fair City* theme tune blares out.

'Donald, that's rude,' Mam snaps.

'I'd rather hear the telly than listen to you,' he snaps back.

I stiffen. All my life they've had rows like this, out of the blue, from seemingly innocuous conversations.

'*Fair City* is good, isn't it?' I say brightly.

My diversion doesn't work. 'What do you mean?' Mam demands. 'What's wrong with listening to me?'

'Oh I don't know,' Dad says airily, 'everything.'

Kate and I glance at each other.

'You can get your own coffee for that.' Mam picks up his cup and saucer. 'I'm not serving you.'

'Oh, the disappointment is eating me up.'

'I wish someone would come along and eat you up, give us all a bit of peace.'

'That's a ridiculous remark, Lil.'

Mam can't think of something to say to that, so she turns on her heel and marches from the room.

Again, Kate and I look at each other as Dad jabs the remote crossly, flicking it from station to station. Eventually he settles on a programme entitled *The Fifty Stone Man*. The three of us gawk as an enormous man fills the TV screen and talks about how he can't get out of bed. 'Hey, Lil,' Dad calls, 'maybe you did have a point, look at this guy. He'd eat anything, I reckon.'

'Dad, that's awful,' I say. 'The poor man.'

'He doesn't have to listen to your mother. He's lucky, I reckon.'

His remark is followed by my mother slamming down the tray and ignoring him for the rest of the evening.

'Do you think they love each other?' I ask as we drive back to my flat. I am shattered, as usual, by the visit. Being with my parents is like struggling to breathe in a stormy ocean. Right now, I feel as if I've been thrown up on the beach, gasping for air.

'Well, they're still together,' Kate says cheerily, unfazed. Then she adds, 'When I was a kid, I was terrified they'd get divorced.'

'Really?' I'm surprised. Kate had been wild as a teenager. She'd spent her days fighting with both of them, not caring that her outbursts made things worse. She'd smoked, come home drunk at thirteen and had to repeat her Junior Cert as she failed most of her subjects. Meantime, I'd strived to keep the peace at all costs. 'I thought I was the only one who worried about that. I remember trying to organise a truce between them once, and both of them told me to butt out. To be honest, I sometimes think they enjoy it.'

'Hmm,' Kate eyes me mischievously, 'maybe the make-up sex is to die for.'

I flick on the car radio, really high, as she laughs, before joining in with her.

14

'YOU SAID YOU knew Chas Ryan.'

Lexi folds her arms in exasperation. Peter is annoying her big time. He has Chas Ryan on the brain. 'I knew him. Not any more. Anyway,' Lexi says, trying to put Peter off, 'if you get him to judge, you'd have to pay him big money.'

'You are obsessed with money.'

'Oh yeah, that's why I sleep in a bloody tent. I'm obsessed with stopping you from splashing money about on the wrong thing.'

'I have heaps of it.'

'So you say.'

Peter walks towards the gallery door.

'Where is it, then? What else do you do?' she calls after him.

'Mind your own bizzo.' He turns back to her. 'I really am not happy to tell you that. All you need to know is that yep, your idea is ripper. Now let me make it work.'

She can understand his reluctance to tell her about his other businesses, she's not happy revealing parts of herself, either. 'Fair enough, but I'm not contacting Chas Ryan.'

There is a pause where he doesn't respond. 'OK.' He finally nods. 'I'll sort out the judge. I can call in a few favours, but it would have been so much better for me if you'd handled it. I don't have time on my hands to be going around looking for a judge.'

She doesn't either. She resents him saying that. 'There must be other people I could try and ask.'

'No. Leave it.'

'Are you trying to make me feel guilty?'

'Would it work if I was?'

'No,' she lies.

He laughs a little. 'You can go call into the various towns and get those posters hung. Meet with any artists you can find, talk to any of them that you can.' A pause. 'You'll be good at that.'

'Thanks. I think.'

'And email a press release to the papers. Someone might pick up the story.'

'Will do.' Jesus, she thinks, this'll take *ages*.

He smiles. 'And don't look for money off advertising space,' he warns her as she turns to go. 'It makes us look cheap.'

'Hey, I am cheap. I only charged fifty for my genius idea. I reckon I deserve more.'

'Lesson in business: never undersell yourself.'

'Lesson in business: don't mess with the Lex.'

'I'm scared, that's my teeth chattering you can hear.' Then he cracks a smile. 'I'll pay all the expenses you have plus double, how's that?'

She blinks, amused. 'It's OK. For now,' she adds.

He laughs.

She watches as he jogs out of the foyer and into the sunlit street.

Doug, long dark hair falling across his face, is lounging in the doorway of his shop. He never seems to have any customers, probably because he only stocks heavy metal music and, as far as Lexi knows, the whole heavy metal scene is a bit of a niche market. That fact doesn't seem to bother or to have registered with Doug at all.

'Hey Lex,' he calls as she approaches, 'I'm thinking of going somewhere today, you fancy it? I could do with company.'

'That was well put.' Lexi nods. 'I understood every word.'

Doug laughs good-naturedly. 'Well?'

Lexi shrugs. 'Why not. I've a pile of stuff to deliver for Peter, but it can wait a while. I haven't gone AWOL in ages. Where are you thinking?'

'There's an amusement park I can recommend, that's if you like that sort of thing.'

She laughs delightedly. 'Bring it on.'

Cissy and Lordi are persuaded to tag along as well. Cissy wears a tight white skirt and a top that reveals more than it covers. Her hair, long and gleaming like polished ebony, swings down her back, almost to her waist. Her high red shoes, with impossibly thin heels, match her new livid red highlights.

Lordi looks downright weird, with his long hair and flowing white robes. A massive crucifix, that could be classed as a dangerous weapon, hangs around his neck. And Doug, with his drainpipe jeans covering his skinny legs, reminds one of a walking pair of chopsticks. Lexi, even with her Doc boots, green three-quarter-length jeans and fishnets, looks the most normal of the four of them.

The amusement park is quite large, and Lexi whoops in delight at the enormous wooden rollercoaster that dominates it. Sprawling out in every direction, as far as the eye can see, are more rides than she can possibly count. Ferris wheels, roundabouts, smaller coasters, boat journeys, ghost trains. A world of imagination and excitement. The place is half deserted, which is great.

'Cool,' Lexi exclaims. 'OK, which thing first?'

Cissy points to a carousel and admits shyly, 'I love those. Let's go on that.'

Lordi eyes Cissy sceptically. 'You'll be done for exposure if you try to sit astride anything,' he comments, sounding a little embarrassed.

'Oh bring it on, my man, bring it on,' Doug snorts.

Lordi laughs.

'That's some reaction from a guy selling angels,' Cissy says crossly.

'He sells angels. Doesn't mean he is one.' Doug grins. Then adds, as he eyes her up, 'And neither are you, from what I can see.'

'If you say any more, I'll hang you both by Lordi's crucifix.' Cissy pushes by them and climbs with little difficulty up onto the carousel. 'I'll just sit sideways, won't I?' she says.

'All riders must straddle the horse.' Lordi points to a sign. 'You'll be thrown off, petal.'

'I'll take my chances,' Cissy says, her long legs crossed, her shoes gleaming under the lights of the ride.

'No side-saddle allowed!' booms an announcement.

There is no arguing with that, so Cissy grumpily climbs down and stomps off. Lexi, feeling a little sorry for her, joins her on the ground.

'You didn't have to.' Cissy smiles.

'I thought it'd be a better laugh from this perspective.' Lexi grins back. 'Look at the state of Lordi going round on a horse.'

Cissy laughs. 'He looks like something from the apocalypse!'

They crack up.

Later, after they've spent about three hours hopping on and off rides, they find a spot in a local park and sit down.

'Well, that was a great idea.' Lexi nods to Doug. 'I enjoyed that. Thanks.'

'Yeah.' Cissy nods too. 'I think we should go somewhere like this once a week.'

'Only if you wear that white skirt, though,' Doug jokes. 'And Lex, you're going to have to get out of the jeans. I bet there's a great pair of legs underneath those.'

'You ditch the drainpipe jeans, I'll ditch my ones.'

'I'm not that desperate to see you.'

'Ha, ha.'

'So?' Cissy looks at them all. 'Any takers for a once-a-week outing? It'd be nice to get to know you all properly.' She pauses. 'I was too shy before this to approach you, Lordi and you, Doug.'

'You didn't mind teasing us by walking up and down the street, did you, though?' Doug smiles.

'That was different,' Cissy says primly. 'Anyway, Lexi here has sort of brought us together, and I've had a great time.' Another pause. She looks around again. 'So, anyone on for meeting up regularly?'

Lexi says nothing. She's not sure if she really wants that much intimacy. Talking and having a laugh is one thing, really connecting is another. Still, if the worst comes to the worst, she can always pretend, though it would make her feel a bit bad. The three of them seem so nice. They'd think she was weird if they knew her, of that she is certain.

'I'm on,' Doug says. He lies back in the grass and stares up at the sky, which is rapidly turning from blue to gold. 'Jesus, I wish I was able to stay here for ever.'

The other three say nothing. They don't have to. Easy companionship, no ties, just out having fun. Who wouldn't want that for ever?

'Preferably somewhere free,' Lexi says. 'Or somewhere not too expensive.'

Doug laughs. 'I'm with you there. It's nice to relax when you don't have to worry about cash.'

'Liberty angel,' Lordi says suddenly, and they all look at him.

'That's the girl for you,' he nods to Doug. 'You need to be free of stress about where money is coming from. Buy her. She'll do the business.'

'You are so full of shit,' Doug snorts.

'Don't knock it until you try it.' Lordi is not offended. 'If she doesn't work, then feel free to insult me.'

'Nah, I'd rather just insult you, thanks.'

Lordi shrugs.

'What angel would work for me?' Cissy asks, sounding shy.

84

'My dear,' Lordi stands up and bows elaborately, 'you are an angel.'

'Doug is right,' Cissy giggles, 'you are full of shit!'

They laugh, and even Lexi is happy to agree to a once-a-week outing.

15

INDICATING RIGHT, I turn into a large, sweeping driveway. It's the entrance to Lexi's parents' house. I visit them every three weeks or so. It started about two months after I'd been discharged from hospital and now, almost a year later, I'm still hopping into my car Sunday nights to say 'hi' to them. It was a bit awkward at first, as their son had just dumped me to take up a job in India, but by not mentioning the elephant in the room, we managed to evict it. Sort of. My eyes still stray to photos of him on their mantelpiece, and on the odd occasion when one of his parents mentions him, I have to physically restrain myself from wincing. But it's worth it because I mainly come here so that Lucy and Bob, Lexi's parents, know that I've never forgotten Lexi, and that I still care. I imagine it'd be heartbreaking for them to think that I've just got merrily on with my life while their daughter remains missing.

Lexi's folks live in a huge, five-bedroomed house at the foot of the Dublin Mountains. Pulling in to the right of the door, I park my little Ka. It looks so teeny beside Lexi's dad's Merc. To my dismay, I see another vehicle in front of the door, a massive jeep, one of those fuel-guzzlers that always set my teeth on edge. Tonight, though, I focus less on the carbon footprint of its owner than on the fact that Lexi's folks have a visitor. I sit in my car, unable to move, my heart slowly picking up pace as all sorts of scenarios tumble about inside my head. Will their visitors look at me? Make me feel like a freak? My hands are clammy on the steering wheel, and I start an internal argument as to whether I should go in or not. Maybe I'll go home; I might be intruding. Just as I shove my key into the ignition, the front door opens and Lexi's dad, Bob, waves at me from the doorway.

'Andy, hello! I thought it was you.' Bob looks a lot like Lexi: he's dark and always has a smile on his face. In the last year, understandably, it's tempered with a barely hidden pain behind his eyes. But for me, he always manages to be cheerful. 'Andy,' he calls again, striding towards me.

I pull the key back out of the ignition and, taking a deep breath, I hop out of the car, doing my best to smile.

'Hey.' I walk towards him. My voice only shakes a tiny bit. 'How's things?'

'Good, good,' he says. 'Come on in, Lucy has the kettle on.'

It's nice to know they expect me. I glance towards the jeep, keeping my tone casual, not wanting to betray the anxiety that is threatening to overwhelm me.

He hesitates before saying, 'Charles is here. He's moved back for a bit.' A pause. 'Are you OK with that?'

Chas. I should have known that that horrendous jeep was his. The thought of seeing him when I haven't met him in over a year makes a big lump of horror wedge itself in my mouth. But at the same time, he's not a stranger; he's seen me when my face was a mushed wreck. He's seen me when the scar was full of ugly stitches and swollen and taking up half my cheek. He's seen me on the hospital bed,

87

with bandages and tubes and big purple bruising covering almost my entire body. Chas has seen me when I have been at my very worst. So now, hearing that he is inside the house, I feel two completely opposite things: relief and dread. In equal measure. And of course, I wish I'd dressed up in something more glamorous than a pair of combat trousers and a hoodie. It's not the sort of thing I'd ever have let him see me in when we used to date. It's not the sort of thing I'd ever have worn before, to be honest.

'Andy,' Bob peers at me, 'are you OK with that?'

I realise that I've been staring at Chas's car, my mouth half open. 'Uh-huh,' is all I can manage. 'Sure. It was ages ago, we're all over that now.'

Bob looks relieved. 'That's what he said too; that's good to know.'

I walk alongside Bob into the house. Well, that's *very* nice of Chas, I think. It's easy for Chas to say he's over it, he bloody dumped me. I cried for weeks over him. When he left, it was as if a big hole had been blown right through my universe. I hadn't realised until then how much I'd invested in us. When he left, I missed everything about him. Everything. I especially mourned the fact that with him, as with Lexi, life had been a laugh. I'd also been myself. Most times when I fancied a guy, I was a hopeless babbler but with Chas, I had just slipped into an easy intimacy. Maybe because he'd already known me from his sister. And then, four months into our relationship, Lexi and I had gone travelling, and barely eight weeks later, we'd had our accident and I'd ended up in hospital for two months, and later, just as Chas and I were rebuilding our shattered lives, he had got a cool job and—

'Andy's here,' Bob calls out to the empty hallway, interrupting my thoughts.

'I've just got the kettle boiled, Andy love,' Lucy answers from the kitchen, 'go on into the front room.'

It's where we usually sit, watching whatever happens to be on on Sunday-night TV. Because I've been coming for so long now, none of us feels the need to talk all the time, or entertain each other; we sit and eat sandwiches and cake and tell each other our news. If we have any. Most times I have to invent news, as I don't want them to know that I spend all my time indoors.

Bob ushers me into the room, and I have to actually concentrate on not gasping as Chas glances up at me from the sofa. His time away seems to have changed him, physically at least. He's more tanned and a bit thinner than when he left. The tan makes his black hair appear even darker and shinier. His eyes are the same smouldering brown I remember, but his whole rugged, lived-in appearance is in contrast to the cool, effortlessly groomed guy he used to be. Instead of the designer shirts and high-fashion denims he used to wear, he's dressed in a brown t-shirt with a faded orange shirt over it, the buttons undone. A pair of old, though clean, jeans encase his long legs, and one of his red socks has a hole in it, through which his big toe pokes out. A pair of old trainers lies discarded on the floor beside him. Chas *never* wore old trainers.

I take all this in in a matter of nanoseconds. It's like a flash of sudden illumination in dark gloom. I realise horribly that a smattering of whatever power he had over me a year ago still remains. I know this because when he smiles uncertainly at me and says 'Hi' in a suitably chastened voice, my knees get all shaky. Chas has a smile that promises wickedness and fun and though, right now, it's a little watered down, its effect on me is still devastating. I experience a huge sense of loss.

'Hi,' I say back. I'm proud that I don't sound as mixed-up as I feel.

Bob looks from one to the other of us. 'I'll just help Lucy with the supper things,' he says, almost backing out of the room. 'Leave you two to catch up.'

I sit in the chair furthest away from Chas, making a big deal of looking all around as I do so. My scar is hidden from this angle – not that it matters with him – but it is a force of habit. I wish again that I'd worn something a little more flattering, though none of my stuff is that great. It's hard to get clothes right when you buy all of them online.

Chas is studying me, I can feel it.

'How have you been?' he asks.

'Great,' I say back, trying for nonchalance.

'I was sorry to hear about your gran.'

I jerk at his words, turning without meaning to towards him. He has shifted position as well. From his previous casual slouch on the sofa he is now crouched forward and staring at me intently, his hands clasped between his knees.

'Were you?' I say, by way of response.

He flinches a little. 'Yeah. 'Course I was. She was great.'

'She was,' I agree. 'Thanks.'

He nods.

Then, haltingly, not wanting to but knowing that in order to appear as well adjusted as I'm trying to make out I am, I say, 'How's your job going?'

My enquiry surprises him, I think. 'Good.' He swallows a little and continues, 'I'm doing a project now in Ireland, which is great. My agent, Audrey,' he smiles a little at the name, which makes me wonder if she is more than just his agent, 'got it for me. It means I can stay here and reconnect with the folks.' He grins. 'Not quite as edgy as India, but nice to be home.' Chas is a freelance photographer; he goes where the work is. 'I'm preparing for an exhibition, too. You?' he asks. 'Mam tells me you're working in graphic design again?'

He must have asked after me, I think. 'Uh-huh. Small magazine, though. We're going a little less than a year. It's for funerals.'

The word funeral makes him recoil.

'I sell ads too,' I continue quickly. 'I'm quite good at it.'

'Great. Well done.' He nods in approval, before adding solemnly, 'It's good to see you, and thanks for calling in here, too. I know Mam and Dad appreciate it.'

I pull my gaze away from him. It's like I'm drinking him up, and I so don't want to. Chas has charm in bucketloads. He knows how to say the right thing, knows how to make you feel good, and then he seems to forget. 'I like seeing them,' I answer, my eyes following the swirl of design on the carpet, concentrating hard on where it starts and how it ends. It's hard to figure out, I have to screw up my eyes to see it.

Neither of us says anything at all then. My heart has slowed. This first awkward meeting has gone a little better than I thought it would. I must be stronger than I give myself credit for.

'Well,' Chas says, standing up and stretching, his brown t-shirt riding up and giving me a flash of toned, tanned midriff, 'I'll head to bed. I only stayed up to say hello. 'Night, now.'

'Eh, night,' I barely manage to whisper. There he goes, I think, admitting that he only stayed up to say hello to me.

And what does that do? Makes me feel OK about him. I damp it down. He knows the right things to say, that's why he said it, my rational brain thinks. He probably stayed up to fight the jetlag so he could be all right in the morning.

When he leaves, it's as if he takes so much more out of the room than just himself. I suddenly find I can breathe again, and my shoulders, which I must have had hunched, relax back. I spot the remote for the telly on the arm of the sofa and use it to flick on the Sunday-night movie.

In the kitchen, I hear Chas bidding his parents a good night and declining offers of food. 'I'm knackered,' he says. Next I hear him as he climbs the stairs to his room.

When Bob and Lucy join me, I'm almost completely relaxed. Lucy pours me a cup of tea and Bob offers me a salmon sandwich. And except for Lucy asking me if everything is all right, and my reply that everything is fine, followed by their looks of relief, it is just a normal Sunday night.

16

<u>Artists – do you need</u>:

Worldwide exposure for your work?
Free gallery display?
A substantial cash investment in your career?
Of course you do . . . Soooooo – take a look at this!

Peter's Gallery in Salue is holding an online-only
art competition to find the next big thing in the art
world – if it's **you**, this will change your life.

For entry forms, links and details, email
Petersgallery@yahoo.com

Closing date: 1 December next
Entry fee: $10 or equivalent

THE FINAL POSTER is up. Lexi grins as she puts it on the wall of another anonymous town. She is glad that she isn't responsible for funding the prize money or finding the judge. Her job is mostly done. All she has to do now is to email newspapers and radio, and hope that some journalist somewhere will pick up on it and run with a story. Peter has agreed to talk to the media if they decide to contact the gallery. Which they probably will do. The whole concept is a bit of a first, she thinks.

17

LUKE AND KATE are squabbling about something. Again. I love having them stay, but honestly, it's weird being outnumbered in your own home. Especially when it's a couple. I hover outside the door of the kitchen, unsure if I should enter or not, but Kate spots me and waves me in.

'Maybe you can settle this for us,' she says as Luke rolls his eyes behind her back.

'I know you're rolling your eyes, Luke,' Kate says smartly.

'I think I might just steer clear,' I say, in what I hope is an upbeat manner. 'I just came in for a juice.'

'Do you or do you not think he is crap?' Kate ignores me as she highers the volume on the radio.

'You're not still going on about him, are you?' Now it's my turn to roll my eyes.

'She is.' Luke nods. 'She's like a rabid dog with a kid in its mouth.'

'I am not like a rabid dog,' Kate snaps. 'That's a horrible thing to say.'

'Well, then let it go,' Luke says mildly. He shoves his arms into his parka jacket and his hands into big woolly gloves. Then, as he wraps an equally woolly, bright yellow scarf about his neck, he adds, 'He got the job, you didn't, happens every day, darl.' He attempts to kiss her but she scowls at him, so he shrugs. 'See you, Andy,' he says instead.

'Yep, bye.'

Kate sticks her tongue out at him as he leaves.

Then he's gone in a slam of the front door.

'Honestly, he never, ever backs me up,' Kate says, glowering at me as she begins the hunt for her tiny fake-fur jacket. 'I used to think he was cool, but he's just a guy who's afraid to stand up for himself, so he won't stand up for anyone else either.'

Finding her coat, she slips her arms into it, then pulls her long hair out from under its collar so that it lies in sexy disarray all across her shoulders.

'I very much doubt that.' I find a carton of orange in the fridge and pour myself a glass. I watch as she rummages about, looking for her big furry bag. 'Under the chair,' I say.

'Thanks.' She bends down and pulls it towards her. The blue and red skirt she is wearing is the shortest I've ever seen on anyone. At least she's teamed it with a pair of bright red tights so it has an air of being half decent. 'And you're another one,' Kate continues as she checks the contents of her bag. 'I've never heard you arguing with anyone ever before, either.'

I shrug. 'My opportunity for doing that is a bit limited, don't you think?' I gaze around the room.

Kate doesn't smile. She really is in a foul mood. 'I mean, you even let your grumpy cat have his way all the time.'

I laugh a little. 'You try shifting him when he doesn't want it.' I grin. 'He'll scratch your eyes out.'

'Yeah, and most people would have him put down for that.'

She doesn't mean it; she's just in a really bad humour for

96

some reason. Kate adores animals. 'Good idea.' I tip the glass at her. 'I'll definitely consider that.'

Her eyes widen in disbelief, then she sighs and plonks down on a chair. 'Sorry,' she mumbles, staring at her fingernails. 'You know I—'

'I know.' I smile. When she doesn't look up, I place my glass on the table and sit down too. 'What on earth is the matter with you?' I ask. 'Poor old Luke, you have made his mornings a misery. Maybe you're better off not listening to Dublin Live at all.'

'Have you ever tried not to look at a car accident?' Without waiting for an answer, Kate says, 'Totally impossible.'

'Luke is right, though,' I venture. 'You didn't get the job, you should let it go. Your show is still great.'

She doesn't reply, and I have the eerie feeling that I've just said the wrong thing, though I don't know why.

'And I'm sure there'll be other chances,' I say, not sure at all. 'On other radio stations.'

'Yeah, maybe,' Kate says, standing up again. For some reason she looks sort of sad. 'Anyway, I'd better go. See you this evening. I'll bring dinner in.'

'OK, thanks.'

I spend the rest of the morning catching up on washing and housework. This month's magazine has now been put to bed, and I always take a day off in semi-celebration. Though ironing and polishing would hardly be called a celebration by most normal people. But I'm a bit of a saddo, in that I get satisfaction in seeing my ginormous pile of washing cut in half. Maybe it's what my life has been reduced to. Before the accident, I performed these tasks as a necessary evil, only doing them when I wasn't living it up with Lexi and Chas and other friends that I used to see. Now, for lack of anything else to do, I've turned into a clean freak. I suppose tidying my little apartment is the only control I have over anything. The only place I don't clean is wherever Baz has decided to lay his huge bulk. I'm just about to throw a load of jeans into the tumble dryer when my intercom buzzes.

The unexpected caller in the middle of the day is something I dread. Still, the good thing about living in an apartment is that I don't have to physically answer the door – I can just tell them to go away via the intercom.

'Hello?'

'Andy, it's me.'

Alistair. I wonder what he wants. I'm suddenly glad I've got a visitor. 'Come on up.'

Alistair has never called before during the day. In fact, as I put the kettle on, I wonder just what Alistair does on his day off. I suppose a funeral or two with his dad. I can't see him shopping or hanging out in a pub with a load of mates. I wonder if he has any mates. Do undertakers hang about together when they finish a job? Go for a coffee? They probably do.

He arrives in just as I'm spooning some coffee into a couple of mugs. He looks good, too. A nice pair of black jeans and a cool-looking, v-necked chunky black jumper with a bright white t-shirt underneath. 'Good, a strong coffee, just what I need,' he says as he slides into a chair. He runs a hand across his face and proffers a tiny grin. 'Had a mess of a weekend.'

'Yeah?'

'I brought Mandy out?' he reminds me.

'Oh yes.' I nod delightedly, then at his look of unease I temper it with a 'Did it not go well?'

'Not going well would be an understatement,' he says with a hint of a glum grin. 'I would bet my life that for her, it was the most pointless and boring date of *her* life.'

'Oh, I'm sure it wasn't that bad.'

He doesn't answer, and I wait until I've made us both a mug of coffee before I say, 'OK, spill. What happened?'

'This place looks nice,' he says by way of reply. 'You've been cleaning?'

'Yep. Once a month, big clean-up.'

'Right.' He takes a sip of coffee and winces. 'Oh, that's strong stuff.'

'Kate's influence.'

There is more silence.

'So,' I press, 'what happened with Mandy?'

Alistair sighs deeply and puts his mug down. 'Nothing,' he says. 'Nothing happened at all. That's the problem.'

'She stood you up?' For some reason that makes me really mad. How could someone—

'No,' he says in a resigned sort of tone, 'she looked *stunning*. Black dress, silver shoes, silver bag. Cool silver coat. Stunning.'

'So what was the problem?' His pissed-off look puzzles me. 'That sounds great.'

'Not if you've booked a bloody pizza parlour for a meal, it isn't great,' Alistair says back.

I smother a smile, wanting to laugh and yet feeling so sorry for him.

'I took one look at her,' Alistair continues, 'and thought to myself, this girl doesn't think she's going out for a pizza. Like, I wanted to keep it casual. No pressure or anything.'

'Yeah, that was a good idea.'

'Well, it didn't seem that way, looking at how she was dressed. So I crossed my fingers, prayed for a miracle and brought her to The Ivory.'

The Ivory is the most expensive place in town. 'Wow.'

'Only I hadn't booked it, had I? And the place was jammed. They cut their prices, apparently. So I lied and told the guy on reception that I had a table booked, but they insisted that I hadn't, and I insisted that I had.' He swallows a bit and continues. 'And they said, "No, you haven't" and I said, "Yes, I have". Well, you get the idea. After about half an hour I was asked to leave.'

'You had a row in a restaurant on a first date?'

'I know,' he winces. 'It was for her benefit, so she'd believe I had booked it. Like if I'd backed down, she wouldn't have believed me, would she?' He takes a gulp of coffee. 'So then I ask her if she'd be happy with a pizza. That I know a great little place. So she says "yes", and I'm delirious until we turn up at my original restaurant and they tell me I'm too late for my table, that I'll have to wait. And I say, 'cause I'm afraid she'll find out that I lied in The Ivory, "Too late for what, I never booked", so they tell me that they can't seat me at all then. So I tell them I have booked. And they say that I just said that I haven't. And I tell them to please check if they have a table, and they say they haven't. And it sort of goes on and on until I'm told to leave.'

'Oh, Alistair.'

'Yes,' he groans. 'So I offer to bring us somewhere else and she tells me to forget it. And I offer her McDonald's, and she gives me this look.'

'I can imagine.'

100

'Yeah.' He glances up at me. 'I think she thought I was an asshole.'

'You should ring her and explain,' I say. 'Tell her you panicked when you saw how well she looked.'

'I tried. She didn't even let me explain. She just said, really nice, that she didn't think going out with me was a good idea.' He shakes his head and smiles glumly as he fiddles with a teaspoon. 'Ah well, another one bites the dust.'

'If you like her, you should keep trying,' I say. 'Show her you're serious.'

'She'll really think I'm a loon then.'

'No, she won't,' I sit down. 'Send her some flowers with a big "I'm sorry for our disastrous date" card.'

'I don't know if it's worth it.'

'Only you can decide that,' I say. 'But if you really like her, you've nothing to lose.'

'Would you do it?' he asks.

'Yeah, if the guy was special enough.'

'Hmm.' He stares once again at the tar-like substance in his mug. 'I'll think about it.'

'Good man,' I grin.

'Don't patronise me,' he smirks. 'It's not my fault I'm a hopeless socialiser. If you'd been helping out at funerals since you were twelve years old, your interactions with the living would be pretty limited too.'

'Twelve?' I'm a little bit shocked. From the corner of my eye, I notice Baz slink into the kitchen and pad towards his feeding bowl, which is empty.

'Yep. I had nightmares the first time I saw a dead body. My dad joked that I took the fun out of funeral.'

'You poor thing.'

He shrugs. 'Oh, I got used to it. The nightmares stopped about two weeks ago,' he jokes feebly. He runs a finger around the rim of the coffee cup as a hunk of hair falls across his forehead. He brushes it away as his gaze meets mine. 'But you know, after that, I never felt I had much in common with other kids.'

'You must have done some sports, or had hobbies in common?'

'Nah. No football for me on a Saturday.' He sounds a little bitter. 'I spent my time writing ghost stories in between learning the art of embalming.'

'Christ.'

'Yeah, he plays a pretty big part in the whole funeral thing too.'

I giggle. 'Stop!'

Alistair grins. 'Oh, I'm half joking, it wasn't so bad. It makes for a good story. Anyway, thanks for the coffee. And the advice.' He grins again. 'D'you think we could have an agony aunt in our magazine? You'd do well.'

'I'll pass.'

Baz miaows. We both ignore him. 'D'you want to stay for dinner? Kate is getting takeaway.'

'Nah, thanks all the same. I'll head off.'

I walk him to the front door and he turns to me. 'I'll post on a copy of the magazine when I get them back from the printers. Should be tomorrow.' He tips my nose with his finger. 'You did good this month, soldier.' Baz startles us both with a menacing hiss. Turning abruptly, I see my cat crouch down, his back hunched, about to spring. He always does that when I ignore him.

'Jaysus!' Alistair exclaims.

'You are a bastard,' I say to Baz. I tell Alistair to let himself out, and as the door closes, I stomp towards the opened tin of cat food which is on the kitchen counter and scrape the remainder into his bowl. Baz sits patiently while I excavate the tin before sniffing at the food and, as if he is doing me a favour, he begins a delicate nibbling on his chicken pieces in gravy.

'I could get you declawed,' I say, as I dump the tin in the bin.

Baz looks impassively at me before beginning to eat again.

I think suddenly of how wonderful it is to be so sure of yourself as to not give a shit. That's the way Baz is. The way Kate is. Me and Alistair, well, we could learn a lot from both of them.

'I could,' I say again. I take the risk of petting Baz behind his ear. He purrs briefly. 'But I won't.'

18

A T FIRST, I don't quite know what the commotion is. I'm
up in my office, making out a list of potential advertisers
for this month's magazine and mailing my Facebook friends,
who I seem to have neglected in the last couple of weeks, when
I hear Luke's voice. That's not surprising, as he's teaching his
yoga class in my front room again. What is surprising, however,
is that instead of Luke's soothing murmur, his voice has risen
and I, who have become quite a good reader of voices, can
detect a faint note of panic in it. Next, there is the tiniest of
shrieks and some pounding about. My heart quickens a little;
it all sounds quite frightening. I hear a door banging downstairs and someone going into my kitchen. I remain, fingers
poised over my keyboard, afraid to move.

Someone seems to be crying, too. The person in my kitchen
is clattering around a lot. What the hell is happening? Baz,
who has been lying quietly on the floor, suddenly stands up,
his ears pricked, his mouth curled, ready to hiss.

Now I recognise Luke's step on the stairs. 'Andy,' he sounds
a little freaked, 'Andy?'

'What?' I don't know why I'm suddenly scared. 'What?' I
open the door and peer out at him, afraid someone else will
be with him.

Luke's face is bleached of colour, and I think he's shaking. His appearance shocks me so much that I forget about not wanting to be seen by anyone. 'What is it?'

'Fred is in a bad way downstairs, we think he's having a heart attack.'

Fred, as far as I can remember, is the guy who walks to the classes. He has a limp. 'Oh God,' my breath catches, 'did you ring for an ambulance?'

'Uh-huh. It's on its way. Have you any aspirin? They said to give him some in case it is a heart attack.'

'Sure, yeah.' I step out of the boxroom office, then jerk to a halt, remembering suddenly about others being in the house, but Luke has charged ahead of me down the stairs and after hesitating a second or so, I follow him. Sweat is beading my forehead and I'm sorry to have to admit, it is more out of fear of meeting people than it is for poor Fred. But I'm still doing it. I'm meeting four people I have never met before and I'm hoping they'll be too freaked to stare at me. Three of them, all women, peer anxiously at me as I pass the dining room on my way to the kitchen. Luke has rifled the presses in a futile attempt to locate aspirin. I haul a chair across the floor, then, standing on it, I pull my medicine box from the highest press. Fingers shaking, I locate the box of painkillers, heaving a sigh of relief that I have them.

'He has to chew them,' Luke says as I pop out two tablets and hand them to him. He swings around quickly and heads to the front room. After another panic-stricken second, I decide to follow. Fred, an elderly man, is sitting on my sofa, which is tight up against the wall. He looks a little weird in his grey tracksuit bottoms and t-shirt, which says *Surfers Do It Standing Up*. He is ashen-faced, and is clutching his left arm,

105

wincing in pain. Three women stand anxiously by, all in various pastel-coloured tracksuits with sweat bands holding their hair back from their faces.

'Here mate,' Luke hands Fred the aspirin.

The five of us watch him as he chews.

Luke looks at his watch. 'They said five minutes. I'll go outside and see if I can flag them down.'

He disappears out the door, and I'm left with Fred and the women. We all look awkwardly at each other.

'Sorry about this,' Fred rasps out.

'Don't be,' I try to sound sympathetic. God, it's been a long time since I talked face to face with a stranger.

'Don't be,' one of the women scoffs. 'He's wrecked our yoga class with his carry-on.'

There's a titter of laughter, and Fred smiles a little shakily.

'My husband thought he was having a heart attack once,' a pink-tracksuited woman says, sitting in beside Fred, 'but it was just indigestion.' She pats his arm. 'A big fart, and he was as right as rain.'

'I hate the word fart,' one of the other women says.

'Heart attacks can kill,' another one of them volunteers. 'The biggest killer in Ireland, so I heard.'

'Yes, well, Fred doesn't want to hear that, do you Fred?' the woman in the pink tracksuit, sitting beside Fred, snaps, glaring at the woman who has spoken.

'Heart attacks run in families,' the same woman goes on. 'My second cousin's family, now there was a breeding ground if ever there was one. Chips for dinner, sausages for tea, a few pints in the evening, fried eggs for lunch, deep-fried onion—'

'Aghh!' Fred suddenly moans, startling us all. He clenches

106

his arm hard and squeezes shut his eyes. Then, to my horror, he falls back against the sofa and goes limp.

'Oh Jesus!' I cry. 'Oh shit!'

The woman who's been harping on about her second cousin's eating habits screams, while the woman on the sofa starts some kind of DIY CPR on him.

'Where the hell is my phone?' I say. 'I'm ringing the ambulance again.'

Just then, the sound of wailing sirens can be heard. I cross to the window and see an ambulance tearing up the street as Luke waves desperately, trying to get their attention.

Pink Tracksuit has now abandoned CPR and is instead taking Fred's pulse. The other two flutter about like squawking hens, being completely useless. The ambulance pulls up outside and I buzz them up.

A silence descends as we watch the men do their job. Luke stares horrified at Fred's motionless body. 'When did that happen?' he asks.

'A few seconds ago.' I wrap my arm about him, wishing Kate was here to comfort him. He barely notices.

'There is a pulse,' Pink Tracksuit says, standing aside as the ambulance men take over. 'It's quite faint, though.'

'OK.' The paramedics nod. 'What can anyone tell me about him?'

'Well, his name is Fred,' the same woman says. 'He's got no family that we know of, and he's a member of our senior citizens' club.'

'Fred,' the ambulance man starts calling him. 'Fred!'

'We gave him an aspirin,' I speak up. 'He swallowed it.'

All eyes swivel in my direction, and I want to dissolve into the carpet.

'Good work.' The ambulance guy grins at me reassuringly.

Ten minutes later, Fred is carried from my apartment, bits of tape wiring him up to machines. Luke offers to go with him to the hospital, and the ambulance man tells him he can travel with them.

'You go, Luke, we'll be fine,' one of the women says. 'We'll meet you there.'

Without replying, Luke leaves.

The silence is instant once he's gone. The hustle and bustle is replaced with a shocked stillness. All of a sudden, I'm conscious of being me again. Of being a scarred face among perfect older ones. The panic begins to seep through my feet and up to my legs. Sweat coats my palms and I want to hide. Then, quite suddenly, Pink Tracksuit starts to sob.

'Oh, honey,' the woman with the disastrously eating second cousin embraces her. 'Hey, it's OK. He'll be fine.'

'He said he wasn't well and we laughed at him,' Pink Tracksuit sniffs.

'I know, I know.'

'We've had a bit of a shock,' the woman who hates the word 'fart' says.

'Of course you have,' I answer back, empathy for them all washing away the panic. 'Look, come out into the kitchen. We could all do with some strong tea. You sit down and I'll make it. Then I'll ring Luke and see how Fred is doing.'

'Oh yes, yes, that's a good idea,' Disastrous Second Cousin says, leading Pink Tracksuit out. They're followed by the Fart Hater.

As they sit down, I turn away and focus on the tea-making. I also pull some biscuits from a press and ask if anyone would like a sandwich. To my surprise, they all declare that they're starving, so I butter a pile of bread and make some ham sandwiches and they tuck in. Once the tea is poured, I feel that I have no choice but to sit among them.

'Well,' Pink Tracksuit, who seems to have recovered slightly, says, 'thank you for this.'

'No problem,' I answer, suddenly shy.

'Andy, isn't it?'

'Yes.' I'm glad I've worn my hair down so that it falls across my face.

'That's an unusual name for a girl.'

'It's Andrea really,' I explain, and they all chorus that Andrea is so much nicer than Andy and that they'll call me Andrea in future.

'Well, I'm Eileen,' Pink Tracksuit says.

'Hi,' I say back.

'Evelyn,' Disastrous Second Cousin says.

'Hi Evelyn.' She is the biggest member of the group, huge and buxom with lots of cleavage on show. I'd say Luke got an eyeful every time she bent over.

'I'm Mabel,' says the Fart Hater.

'Oh, you were the woman on the radio!' I say. 'You were very good.'

Mabel preens. She tosses her iron-grey hair back from her face. 'I thought so,' she says without a hint of modesty, 'but they cut me off. They kept putting me on hold and asking what sexual positions I was going to talk about.'

I turn away so she won't see me laugh.

'I think they were trying to shock me because I'm old.'

'We're not exactly old,' Eileen says a little indignantly. 'I'm only seventy-three.' This last part she says to me.

'And you don't look a day older,' Evelyn says back, smirking.

Eileen glares at her.

'By the way, thank you for the loan of your apartment, Andrea,' Mabel, who I guess to be the peacemaker of the group says, changing the subject.

'No problem.'

The conversation then turns to speculation on how Fred might be, so I pick up my phone and dial Luke's mobile. It goes to answer machine. We all look at each other a little anxiously.

'I have a car.' Eileen dangles her car keys. 'Would anyone like to go into the hospital?'

Mabel and Evelyn agree that that might be a good idea.

'I'll just ring my daughter and tell her not to expect me this afternoon,' Eileen says, taking a state-of-the-art mobile phone from her handbag. Holding it at arm's length, she presses in a number.

'You need glasses,' Evelyn mutters, as Eileen shoots her an irate look.

When her call is answered, Eileen proceeds to yell all the news into the receiver.

'And a hearing aid,' Mabel giggles.

I smother a little smile and begin to clear away the tea things. One by one the women pull on their coats and pick up their bags and fluff up their hair. It's as if they're off to a carnival.

'Tell Luke to ring me with any news,' I say as they turn to leave.

'Oh,' Mabel seems a little surprised. 'Would you not like to come with us?'

Into a hospital? Where I'd spent two months recuperating after the accident? 'Eh, no, no I have a lot of work to do,' I say. 'Thanks anyway.'

110

'Ohh.'

'Oh, what a pity.'

'Oh, dear, work, how awful. However will you concentrate?'

'I'll manage,' I say.

'Well, thank you for the tea.'

'And the sandwiches.'

'Yes, thank you for the tea and the sandwiches.'

'Give my best wishes to Fred,' I call after them.

They all promise to do so before tromping out and plunging me back into being on my own. Well, except for Baz, who now creeps down the stairs, looking suspiciously from left to right.

'Fat lot of use you were.' I crouch down as Baz comes to me, purring. In an unusual move, he winds his body in and out affectionately under my hands. 'Oh, maybe there's hope for you, Baz, eh?' I scratch behind his ear and the purring abruptly stops. What I have done to offend him, I don't know, but, tail twitching madly, he stalks off.

'You're just like the guy who bought you,' I call after him. 'No matter how much I love you, you still walk away!'

His answer is to curl up in his basket and ignore me.

Cheeky fecker!

19

LEXI SITS CROSS-LEGGED on the sand, Lordi beside her. They are at the water's edge, and the smallest of waves wash up just a few inches shy of their feet. She likes Lordi a lot; there's a sort of calm about him that makes her feel good. Safe, even. The beach, with its bright white sand and sheltered cove, is not the most exciting one for surfers or water enthusiasts. Further out, the sea is flat and as shiny as the underside of a silver saucepan. The sky is its usual vibrant blue, which mingles nicely with the horizon and the sea, so that you can't tell one from the other after a while. Lexi is running a palm across the sand, staring at her slender fingers and comparing them with Lordi's enormous ones.

'My,' she jokes, 'what big hands you have.'

Lordi looks. 'All the better for—' he stops and thinks. 'Well, I don't know, really.'

Lexi giggles.

Lordi holds his hands up and studies them. 'They are big, aren't they? I never really copped that before.'

'Too busy selling angels?'

'Yes, I suppose so.'

They are quiet for a bit.

'What made you say that to Doug?' Lexi asks.

'Say what? I've said a lot of things to him.'

'Liberty angel,' Lexi says. 'You said he needed a Liberty angel.'

'He does.'

'How do you know?'

Lordi shrugs. 'I just do. If I spend enough time with anyone, I can tell what they need.' He looks directly at Lexi. 'With Doug, it doesn't take a genius. His shop does no business. He's constantly on about how much things cost. He told me last week that some things he'd purchased were repossessed as he couldn't meet the repayments. He needs to get out of that cycle, it's toxic.'

'Poor Doug.'

'Yes. I told him I'd give him a Liberty angel but he won't take charity. And he thinks I spout a load of rubbish.'

Lexi smiles.

'As do you.'

'No, I don't.'

Lordi quirks an eyebrow.

'Not really,' Lexi amends.

'Promise me one thing,' Lordi says.

'What?'

'Promise that when I tell you what angel you need, you'll buy it.'

She guesses she has nothing to lose. 'OK. Deal.'

He nods. 'Good, because you are a puzzle. I have to think carefully about you. You don't talk much about yourself.' He stops. 'In a place like this, where most of the people are just passing through, they tell me things about themselves because they think they'll move on and never meet me again. But you . . .' He doesn't finish the sentence.

113

'What do you want to know?' She is intrigued. Curious. But he is right, she doesn't like talking about herself, afraid of how people will see her.

'What happened to you? Something terrible definitely happened to you.'

She squirms. 'Something happens to everyone.'

He laughs. 'See. That's what I mean.'

'I was in a crash.' She pauses, stunned that she's even told him. 'Just like you.'

He nods. 'Was it bad?'

Now it's her turn to nod. She can't reveal any more about it, it would be too painful.

'OK.' Lordi touches her briefly. 'Thanks. I will let you know.'

Lordi is either some wonderful, undiscovered mystic or completely barking, she isn't sure which. 'Do you wear clothes like that in your shop in London?' Lexi asks.

'I'm not totally insane,' Lordi says, making her smile. 'Do you think I'd survive two minutes in London wearing a robe and a cape? No.' He shakes his head. 'When I am working there, I wear the normal garb. Shirt, jacket, trousers.'

'Good to know,' Lexi says. 'Do people take you seriously there?'

'Only if they want to.' He doesn't seem bothered by it. 'I have my regulars. I have tourists, which I don't really like because they think the angels are souvenirs. I have to make sure they bring the right ones back for their friends. Though it's easier to read people in London, obviously.'

'Obviously.' Barking mad, she decides.

'Hey,' Yellow T-Shirt arrives up and stands in front of them, blocking the view of the sea. 'This looks cosy.'

114

'Oh, it speaks without being spoken to,' Lexi drawls.

Yellow T-Shirt laughs and flops down beside them.

'Eh, hello? Private conversation here.'

'I see you're running a competition in the gallery,' Yellow T-Shirt states, not in the least bothered by her comment.

'She is,' Lordi says, answering for Lexi. 'And it was all her idea and apparently there are quite a lot of entries coming in. At least, the paper I read yesterday told me so.'

'It did?' Lexi asks. 'Which one?'

'London *Times*. Just a tiny paragraph.'

'Oh, cool, I didn't know that. I must see if I can get hold of a copy.'

'So,' Yellow T-Shirt says, 'it's a successful competition, eh?'

'So far, so good, thousands of entries,' Lexi lies. 'It's going to be very successful. Only the best need apply.'

Yellow T-Shirt laughs, throwing back his head and giving her a glimpse of his tanned throat. It's oddly erotic. 'Cool. Well, in that case I'd better get my paintbrush out.'

'I said the best,' Lexi quips, 'not the most desperate.'

Yellow T-Shirt laughs again, and Lordi joins in.

'So how you been?' Yellow T-Shirt angles himself towards Lexi. 'I've missed you on the beach in the mornings.'

'Busy,' she replies.

'Yeah, hanging posters, I heard all about it.'

'Really? I thought all you did was stand about all day and stare at the sea.'

'I do that too.' He is unoffended. 'Then I paint, then I go for walks, then I meet people.'

'That sounds just too exciting for me.'

'Yeah, well, when you're boring, these things do seem a big deal.'

115

Lordi laughs before standing up. 'Well, I'll go and leave you two to slug it out. I'll be seeing you, Lexi. Oh,' he stops and turns around, 'Cissy says she has just the place for us to go next Wednesday. Are you interested?'

'Yeah, I should be free. Let me know the time.'

'I certainly will.' Lordi turns around and walks off down the beach, his cloak billowing around him.

Lexi doesn't know what to say to Yellow T-shirt now that they're alone. She's not normally shy, and while it had been easy and a bit of fun to shout out greetings to him as she passed, now that they seem to be on conversational terms, it's different.

'So, like I said, I missed you.' Yellow T-Shirt grins.

'Well, I'm back now, so you can get your fix of insults any time you like.'

'Good.' To her dismay he stands up. 'Be seeing you around.'

And then he too walks off.

Damn! Why hadn't she done it first?

About ten minutes later, she stands outside the gallery looking for Peter. There is quite a crowd about. Lexi enters the building and sees at least twenty more in the foyer. Wow. Peter is behind the reception desk, directing them to the exhibition room. When he spots her, he crosses towards her. 'How's my wonderful offsider?' he beams.

'I liked you better when you were cross,' Lexi answers.

'It's amazing. *You're* amazing.' Peter ignores her comment. 'We have managed, in the space of three weeks, to put ourselves on the map. There have even been articles in the press.'

'Yeah, Lordi told me there was a piece in the London *Times*.'

'Lordi, the drongo with the cape?'

'I presume a drongo means a nice guy?'

Peter ignores that too. 'Just this arvo, I've opened me mailbox and there's emails from everywhere looking for application forms and information on how to come here. We should be paid commission on the visitors.'

She suddenly thinks of Doug. 'Maybe you should put a notice up in the gallery and on the website about local businesses,' she says. 'There are cool shops just a walk away from here. One guy even sells his own music. You can download it and everything. And I know they could all do with some help.'

Peter nods enthusiastically. 'Yes, why not,' he says. 'Onya. Share our great fortune.'

'Well, it's not a great fortune yet,' Lexi reminds him before he gets carried away. 'You have to find a judge, for one thing.'

'Shussh!' Peter glares at her. 'Stop. People will hear. It's OK. I've approached people. They've to get back to me.'

'Just don't leave it too late,' Lexi warns.

'I won't.' Peter strikes a confident pose. 'With the amount of attention this competition is getting, any artist would be proud to be involved.'

She guesses he's right. She bloody hopes he is. They'd look like fools if they had no judge.

'I've spent the week emailing a select group of artists to see if they'd be interested in submitting work.'

'Yeah? How'd you select them?'

'I trawled the websites of the best galleries to see if I could get info on anyone who'd had work displayed in the last five years. Took yonks.'

'Oh, aren't you a busy beaver,' she teases.

117

'I am,' Peter seems to preen himself.

'So, tell me, how many people have been in today?'

'I dunno. Heaps.' He almost does a dance, he's so high on excitement.

Not for the first time is she suspicious of Peter's business credentials. What hard-nosed businessman would get so excited about this stuff? 'Well, do you need me to help? Do you want me to take over here?'

'No worries. I'm loving it. This is the coolest thing to happen to this gallery. You knock off, hang out with your drongo friends. Enjoy!' He makes whooshing motions with his hand before turning with a wide beaming smile to a woman who has crept up behind them to ask him something.

'My friends are not drongos,' Lexi calls out, 'or they're no more weird than you, business boy.' She is gratified to hear the woman laugh as Peter glares in her direction.

Blowing him a kiss, she exits into the perfect blue-skied day.

20

M Y INBOX PINGS and I click on the icon. It's Alistair.

This arrived for you today in the magazine inbox. Unusual, huh?

The attachment is entitled: *Peter's Gallery. Go online to find out about our art competition.*

My heart flutters a little. My stomach rolls. I scroll down the message.

Dear Artist

I am sending this invite out to any artists who have exhibited with prestigious galleries in the past. I wish to invite you to enter a unique art competition. At Peter's Gallery, we are looking for the next big thing in the art world. This competition could be for YOU!

Underneath is the poster telling me all the things I can win if I enter. It makes me smile. It's been a long time since I've been classed as an artist, and it feels good, though I know there is no way I can enter this. No way. Aside from everything else, I haven't painted since before I went travelling, which is almost two years now. I painted a lot when I was with Chas, in fact, I only ever seemed to create when I was content. Happiness brought out the best in my art. After the accident, I couldn't do it any more. I was a different person. And even though the accident happened well over a year ago now, I couldn't pick up a brush. My confidence would be on the floor. What am I thinking? My confidence *is* on the floor. And it's not just with the art. My whole life is a lack of confidence. An eight-inch scar has gouged out more than just my face.

Then my phone, which I always keep alongside me, bleeps. It's Alistair.

I never knew you painted!!

I send a message back: *I never knew you cared.*

He replies: *'Course I do. Gives you a whole other image (ha ha). You going to enter?*

I text back: *I've about as much chance of winning as you have of making me laugh.*

He texts back: *I still tried it though, eh? What have you got to lose?*

I text: *Nothing. But gave it all up a while ago.*

He texts back: *So start again.*

I grin and don't reply. Alistair hasn't got the hang of texting at all. He doesn't seem to realise that in certain cases, it might actually be cheaper for him to ring me. If I reply now, he'll text again. One time we were swapping texts for about an hour before I picked up the phone and told him to stop. I turn back to my screen. My phone bleeps.

Well, why don't you think about it?

Sighing a little, I'm forced to text back: *I might if you stop bloody texting me!!*

Bleep-bleep. *Deal.*

I smile. Put my phone down.

It bleeps again. *Do we have a deal??*

He's doing it on purpose now. I text: *Feck off.*

He texts: *Haaaaa!*

I grin, and let him have the last word. I better get down to doing some work. The whole monthly magazine cycle has come around again, and I've my list of phone calls to make and pages to design. The rhythm of getting a magazine out has always appealed to me. It's predictable, provided everything slots into place. Interviews, articles, copy. It's hard to concentrate because even though I know in my heart there is no way I should enter the competition, I can't help but feel that maybe it might be good for me. The idea of painting was something I'd really wanted at one stage, just to make my living from selling pieces of art, whether it was on the street or in a gallery. Of course, I knew I had to be realistic. The chances of actually living off it were slim, but at least two years ago I was prepared to give it a try. It was another reason I'd agreed to go travelling with Lexi – to live, spread my wings, explore other places. We were going to go everywhere we could, walk, take boat rides, rough it on long, heat-soaked train journeys.

Lexi was dying to visit Australia. She wanted to do as much of it on foot as she could. I don't think she ever got it into her head how enormous the country is. We knew neither of us would care if we reeked of sweat or grew filthy. The experience was the main thing. The plan, of course, was that when I came back I'd be able to paint what I'd seen through traveller's eyes. Chas had given me lessons in photography so that I could snap all the sights we'd see along our way. I hadn't decided whether to concentrate on landscape or portraits, though landscape was my passion at the time.

And then, about eight weeks into our travels, the bus we'd been on careered down a mountain. I still dream about it, flashes of memory bubbling up despite spending my waking hours trying to forget the whole thing. The images are horrible. I was found the next morning out cold on the mountainside. Apparently I'd signalled the helicopter and they'd seen the flash of bright blue of my tattered rain jacket among the other shades of the mountain, but I can't remember doing that. How would I have been able to signal when my arm was so smashed up? But the rescuers insisted that I had. When they eventually got to me, I was unconscious. The hospital and the flight home to Ireland to be treated there is a blur. Lexi's body, despite an intensive search, was never recovered. Now, though, I think wryly, this would-be landscape artist is landlocked between four walls. Even I can smile at the irony. I haven't been out socialising with friends my own age in . . . I do the maths . . . in well over a year.

Just then my computer pings. There's another message in the inbox.

You should definitely go for it! Alistair.

I have to laugh. I don't reply, though, not wanting to encourage a day-long email conversation. Anyway, I'm still not sure if entering would be the right thing to do, though the idea of picking up a brush again and mixing colours and seeing the way they change appeals to me. Suddenly I think, what on earth is stopping me painting for myself? Even if I don't enter, there is no reason why I can't just

122

mess about with a canvas and a few brushes and see what happens. My heart picks up pace. I could drag my stuff out of hibernation and set it up in my bedroom. The little thrill of excitement I feel makes me realise quite suddenly how much I must have missed it.

In the months following the accident, I couldn't paint, it was mentally too hard. There was nothing in my head, only a blank where emotion should have been. Some artists use pain to do their finest work, though I think they must have had a bit of distance before they did so. Maybe that's what I had now, a little bit of distance. And while I'm not exactly completely content, I am happy in my own weird way. I could try to paint, I suppose. Try and see what comes out. As Alistair says, I have nothing to lose.

I stand up, curiously invigorated. I haven't felt this way in ages. I'll haul my gear out of storage, set it all up and see if it's still usable.

Just then, the front door opens.

'Just us,' Kate says.

Kate and Luke are drenched to the skin, even though they've only crossed from their car to the apartment. They shake themselves down in my hallway. Kate peels off her fake-fur jacket. Luke removes a sopping parka. Jesus, I'd somehow missed the fact that it was raining waterfalls outside.

I decide to abort my search for the moment to find out how Fred is. 'How's Fred?'

'Stable,' Kate answers. She takes off her impractical red shoes, and scarlet-painted toenails glitter under my hall light. 'It's been a long day, though.'

'Give me your jackets, I'll hang them in the loo.'

When I've placed both jackets on the heated towel rack in

my bathroom, I join them in the kitchen. Kate is bustling about, filling up the kettle and offering Luke biscuits from the press.

'He's hardly eaten all day,' she says, as if she's his mother or something.

When she'd heard what had happened, she'd gone straight from her show to the hospital to be with him. And because he insisted on staying, so did she. She looks a lot worse for wear than he does, as hospitals and Kate don't mix too well.

'I've some ready meals in the fridge,' I offer, 'you can shove them in the microwave. Be a lot better for you both than a heap of biscuits.'

'Great.' Kate pulls the frozen cartons from the freezer and examines them. 'He's hooked up to all these machines,' she explains, making a face, 'and the smell in the place. Ugh.'

'It is a hospital.' Luke speaks for the first time. Then, heaving himself to his feet, he says as he runs a hand through his dreadlocked hair, 'Look, I think I'll head to bed, I'm wrecked.' Without waiting for us to answer, he leaves the kitchen.

Kate slides into a chair beside me and whispers, 'It's really shaken him. He's acting all weird. He hardly spoke to me all day. There were three women in the hospital too who were really old, and they never stopped talking. And because Luke wasn't talking, they felt they had to include me.'

'They were probably the women from Luke's yoga class.'

'They were. And when they found out I was your sister, they went on and on about how you were so nice and how you'd made them sandwiches. You scored a big hit there, Andy.'

'Really?' I am ridiculously delighted by the comment.

'Yep.' Kate heads to the microwave and puts in her ready meal. 'And when they found out I was the DJ on Radio Dublin

124

Live, they started asking me when they could go on again. I told them that the breakfast show might be interested, so they're ringing it.' She giggles like a naughty schoolgirl. 'I told them that even if they were told "no" to keep plugging away, that they were fond of persistence in the radio world.'

'Oh, Kate.'

'I'll make a few enquiries for them with some other people, don't worry.' The microwave pings and pulling out her pasta, she pokes a fork into it and gives it a quick stir before putting it back in again. 'So, what did happen with this Fred fella? Between those women talking about your sandwiches and Luke being all upset, no one has really told me at all.' She removes the pasta from the microwave and begins to fork it into her mouth.

I pour her a glass of water and tell her as she eats.

'How awful.' Kate stops swallowing long enough to gawk at me. 'Well, he looked in a bad way, even though they said he was stable. And he's got no family, the poor man. The doctors said that it'd be nice for him to have visitors every day, so Luke volunteered and so did the women.'

'He must have other friends?'

Kate shrugs. 'Dunno. No one really knows. The cops called to his house and there was no one else around, and the neighbours didn't seem to know him that well. In fact, one of the women was saying that it was just as well he had his heart attack at yoga and not at home, as he could have lain there for days without anyone knowing.' Kate seems to relish the drama of it as she adds on an emphatic nod, jabbing her fork in my direction, 'Can. You. Imagine?'

I'd never thought of that. Imagine if the man had no one watching out for him, he could lie for days without anyone knowing. How sad. I get a shiver up my spine as, without warning, I project into the future and see me, an old maid, ancient and bent over, locked inside my house, having a heart attack and, because I've cut myself off, there is no one to help me. No one to notice if I don't appear for a few days, because I've never appeared. No one to ring Kate and tell her her sister has been injured because they know nothing about me. No one to feed my pet, who is so hungry he might start to feed on me . . .

'Are you OK?' Kate asks, looking at me in concern.

'What? Yeah.' I smile and reach for a biscuit to give myself a bit of a sugar hit. 'Just having weird thoughts. Don't mind me.'

'About what?'

I shrug, 'Oh, nothing.'

'Go on. I love weird thoughts. You should hear the people that ring in to my radio show.'

I flush a little. 'It wasn't like the people who ring your radio show.'

'Oh, damn.' She feigns disappointment. Then she quirks an eyebrow. 'Well, go on, I still want to know.'

I shrug. 'It was nothing. Just wondering, you know, if one day I'll be a Fred.'

Kate frowns, drawing her eyebrows towards each other. There is the longest of pauses, and I wish I'd said nothing. It's humiliating, having her study me like this.

'You want to be a man?'

Oh, God. I splutter on a laugh. 'No, you fool!' Then I stop laughing, realising abruptly that I have to explain it, and not really sure I want to. 'Forget it.'

'Jesus! How can I forget that?'

'She means will she be alone,' Luke says from the doorway, and now I really want to curl up and die. It's bad enough admitting my total-loser status to my sister, without her boyfriend hearing it. 'Sorry,' he smiles a little ruefully at me, 'I came down to kiss this lady good night. I forgot.' Then he adds, 'You won't be a Fred. Believe me.' He crosses to Kate, stoops down and kisses her so tenderly on the lips that it makes my heart bleed. Well, obviously that's a figure of speech. And not a very good one, considering the day's events. Kate reaches up and caresses his stubble-covered jaw before he pulls away and nods a good night to me.

'Well,' I stand up now, 'I'm going to go to bed too.'

'Hey, not so fast.' Kate pulls me back down. 'Luke is right, you know. You will not be a Fred. You'll always have me. I mean, you're older than me, right, so you'll die first.'

'Gee, thanks, that's a consolation.'

'And,' she pauses before continuing, 'you will not be stuck in this house for ever. You will get out and make friends again, so you will. You made three new friends in those old women already. You just say the word and you can hook up with them.'

'Right. Ta. Yoga and bingo do not appeal.' I'm trying to keep it light.

Kate laughs. 'Seriously, though, it's not as if you're claustro-phobic, or whatever the word is.'

'Agoraphobic,' I correct automatically.

'Yeah, you're just a little self-conscious about that bloody scar. I mean, those women today, they never even mentioned it to me.'

'They had just seen someone have a major heart attack. They probably had more important things on their minds.'

'Oh they did, yeah,' Kate nods, 'like their appointments with their hair dressers and their piles of washing, though how they could have piles of washing is a mystery, and the fact that Eileen's husband is eighty this week and she has no present for him, and how she'll have to buy him something and had anyone any ideas. But that she can't bring him for a meal out as he gets severe indigestion from eating late at night.'

I grin.

'So,' Kate says, winking, 'you are not a hot topic of conversation, Andy, which must come as a shock to you. People don't consider your scar as being worthy of talking about.' She pats my hand. 'So, off you go to bed.'

I totally believe that she's telling the truth, but I think that maybe the women had already talked about me in the car on the way to the hospital, or that maybe they just hadn't wanted to mention it in front of Kate. So I just grin back at her, pretending that I'm happy to hear it.

''Night,' I say.

''Night,' she says back before jabbing the pasta. 'This stuff is putrid.'

'Yeah, I know. I normally get it for Baz.'

It's a mean joke, but her shriek is so worth it.

21

J UST OVER A year ago, Dad, at my insistence, had put all
my art stuff away. I remember telling him to throw everything out, to bring it to the dump or give it to a charity shop.
He'd stood calmly in the face of my fury and slowly taken a
big fan paintbrush from the pile I'd thrown on the table. He'd
felt it, touched its softness between his fingers and, his eyes
downcast, had declared brokenly, 'It's such a shame.' And I
don't know why, maybe it was the way he said it, or the in-
offensive way the brush looked held between his big hands,
but suddenly I'd backed down and agreed that he could store
my stuff for me in case I ever needed it again. Of course, I
never thought I would. All my creativity had frozen in the
wake of the accident, but now, somehow, I suddenly felt like
having a brush between my fingers and loading it with paint
and making something real. Not a picture on a computer
graphic, but something I could touch and feel and smell.

I discover now that Dad had stored all the bits and pieces
of my former hobby right at the back of the highest press in
my bedroom, and that getting it down is no joke. I'm standing
on a chair, and the press is still a foot above my head. Baz
gazes at me impassively from the bed, ready to spring away
if anything threatens his comfort. So far, I've managed to pull

down a large unused canvas and, with major effort, an easel. I fell off the chair during that procedure, and now have quite a swollen elbow. I flex it a little, just to make sure it isn't broken, before standing back up on the chair and attempting to grab a little white plastic bag that is tantalisingly out of my reach. The smaller items are impossible to get to. My fingers tip the edge of the white bag and I inch it forward slightly. Dust rises and catches in my throat and makes me cough so much that I have to get down, leaving the unopened bag where it is. It occurs to me that I'll have to ask someone to help me, I'm way too small to get things down and I don't possess a step ladder, as there is nowhere in my apartment to store it. It's a bit of a bummer, as I'd wanted to keep my painting a secret just in case I was totally crap. Still, Kate and Luke were bound to notice, especially if I used oils, as the smell of the paint would be really strong.

I decide to give up – temporarily. Maybe I'll ask Luke when he comes back from visiting Fred. Since Fred collapsed in my flat Luke has barely left the hospital. He took a week off all his work commitments to do so. He really is a very kind man. I think too he feels a little responsible, though the doctor has assured him that it's not his fault. Kate, despite the fact that it makes her skin crawl, drops into the hospital for an hour around eight at night before bringing Luke home. And the three women from the yoga class are taking it in turns to spend a couple of hours each day with him too.

Fred is still in intensive care, and the doctors will be making a decision on his treatment in the next couple of days.

Luke has brought him in, from me, a Get Well card and a pile of magazines that I got Kate to buy. Ones about yoga and things that I think might interest him. Luke has said that

Fred used to teach history, so I got him a magazine about that. I'd like to go in myself, but I just can't. First, going outside into the street would terrify me: all those people who would see me, all the looks, the pitying glances, the false, bright, 'determined to ignore my face' smiles. And second, even if I did by some miracle manage that, I don't think I could venture into a hospital at all. I spent two months lying flat on my back after my own accident, two months of pain and tears with the smell of disinfectant all around me. Its odour is imprinted on my brain. And even though everyone was so kind and nice, and even though I was lucky, I can't go back there. Not yet.

Eventually, I stop coughing and turn to survey the two things I have managed to haul from the press. Both are lying across the bed, and I assemble the easel and place the canvas on it. Of course, it's way too big a canvas for me at the moment. I'd rather paint on something smaller; just take a few baby steps until I see what I can still do. I wonder where my pictures are? I'd quite a collection of unsold pieces before I went away with Lexi. They don't seem to be here, at least not that I can see. Maybe my dad got rid of them, or stored them somewhere else. For the first time I'd like to revisit them. It'd be a bit like seeing a place I used to love many years ago. I wonder suddenly if any of them are on the internet. I used to be one of those saddos that googled myself, relishing the mention of my name whenever I came across it. Sometimes a picture I'd done would be displayed – well, once a picture I'd done was displayed – and I remember the small thrill I'd got when I'd seen it. The whole world could view my painting if they wanted, was my thought. In fact, I realise it was probably how Peter's Gallery had found my name. So, not stopping to think, I sit down and Google 'Andrea Fitzsimons'. There are about seventy-five hits. Seventy of them are not me. I find reference to myself somewhere in the middle of the group.

Andrea Fitzsimons displays her latest painting Rua *in a showcasing of new talent in Dobson's Gallery in Dublin. She says the in . . .*

I click on the link, and the piece which appeared in *The Irish Times* pops up. Of course, even though I should have anticipated it, I'm not prepared to see myself scar-free, but there I am. My face is perfect, though I'm sure at the time I'd been moaning about a spot or something. Like a traveller parched for water, I peer intently at the screen. My finger trembles slightly as I press on the picture to get a full-size image up. Wow, was I once so confident? I'd always felt a little shy, but in this picture I'm facing the camera fearlessly, my brown eyes wide and cheeky-looking. My hair was short then, framing my pixie-like features and high cheekbones. I'm wearing a daring red top, tight and plunging. Bright fire-engine red lipstick contrasts with my pale make-up. I'd worn black leggings that night, I remember now, as the top was akin to a short dress. My lips are puckered in a crimson pout. I smile a little. I'd forgotten I used to think that pouting accentuated my cheekbones.

There is a lot about the old me that I've forgotten, or that I have chosen not to remember. I think I did it to help keep me sane. To my left, hanging on a stark white wall, is my painting *Rua*. 'Rua' means red in the Irish language, and refers to a dog or red hair, not the colour red on its own. My painting was of various shades of red: strawberry blonde, crimson, vermilion, coral red and lots more. It could have been a sunset, or the gleam of a red setter's coat or glossy hair. The picture is vibrant with shade layered upon shade, and it looks like it could move under the touch of a finger. It was meant to portray the fact that nothing was what it seemed. Though the picture was called Red, it was actually not a true red. And the fact that it could be interpreted as a painting of hair, or the streaks of a sunset, meant that what you thought was just an illusion.

It hits me now that I'd deliberately chosen my violent red top to clash with the picture. God, I grin to myself, I really was kind of pretentious back then. In fact, I was very pretentious. The picture did sell, though: a man with a weird red coat and lecherous eyes had bought it. I remember not having a lot more to say on the topic of appearances, and had moved on. I'm about to see what else is written about me when I see the photographer's name listed at the end. Charles Ryan. Chas had taken it? I find I can't remember that. He used to send pictures into the papers when he was starting off all right, I remember that, but the fact that this was one of his pictures is a blank, which I find strange as everything Chas and I did seems to be burned onto my memory with a branding iron. I can remember our first meeting – I was ten, he was twelve. Our first kiss, which took place in a darkened cinema after he'd rung me to say that Lexi was ill and couldn't go out with me that night, and would he do instead? I can recall our first official date, which took place in a darkened cinema, seeing as the last cinema outing had been so successful. I remember telling Lexi about us, and she'd been sceptical until she realised that we were mad about each other. Yes, I realise, I'd been truly content in those days, even if I did work for a women's magazine designing pastel pages – a job I hated.

I log out of that site and scan the other four entries. The

first three are not that interesting, just my name among a heap of other names as someone to watch, and the final entry is one in which I'd been nominated as Designer of the Year in the Magazine Awards for my work on *Trend*, which was the women's magazine I used to work for. I was responsible for the overall look of the magazine and I did a good job, I suppose, though I never really enjoyed it, I don't know why. Anyway, I didn't win. A music magazine took the accolade that year and they deserved it, the work of the designer they had was visually stunning. There isn't a picture of me on the site, just a mention that I was a contender. I log out. Five Google entries is not that bad. For someone who lives like a hermit, at least there's a record of my existence beyond my own sphere.

Which is pretty cool, I think.

Alistair arrives a couple of hours later, just as Baz and I are settling down for some rubbish daytime TV. It's my lunch hour, and I relish the dramas that unfold on badly written soaps.

'What are you doing here?' I ask as Alistair, grinning a little manically, bounces into the hall. 'Three visits in one month. Do you fancy me, or something?'

He quirks an eyebrow. 'I was beginning to think you fancied me,' he counters.

'OK, too surreal for me.' I put up my hands in a gesture of surrender. 'You can explain all over a coffee.' I gesture to the coffee pot. 'Pour yourself one. I'll be in the front room. Alexis is about to seduce Jeremy, and she doesn't know he's her stepson.'

'Wow,' Alistair calls after me, 'that's going to be some reunion. Where are the mugs?'

'Dishwasher!' I wish he'd stop talking as, just as I plonk down on the sofa, Alexis announces her intention to bed Jeremy.

'OK.'

A few minutes later, he's joined me in the front room and brought a packet of biscuits with him. 'It's like this—' he begins.

'Shush!' I know it's rude. But I've been following the plot for weeks, and am dying to see how it unfolds. Alexis is swaying seductively in the light of a red lamp as Jeremy watches her, completely mesmerised.

'It's important,' Alistair interjects.

I ignore him.

Alistair heaves a big sigh. 'You need to hear this.'

'You need to shut up,' I warn jokingly.

He sighs in an exaggerated way and shakes his head.

'Shut. Up.'

'Fine.' He is amused for some reason. But he shuts up, and we both watch the badly acted but compelling scene in which Jeremy's eyes almost pop out of his head as this woman, fifteen years his senior, does a ridiculous dance in front of him. Then the credits roll.

'Ohh,' I groan, 'what a cop-out. It's not on again until next week.'

'I'll set my DVD for certain,' Alistair says wryly.

'You would if you followed it.' I'm still miffed. 'Now,' I take a biscuit from the packet and ask, 'what do you want? I hope you haven't changed the publication date for the magazine, as I've only just started ringing around for ads.'

He shakes his head. 'Two things. The first is a really good thing but,' he shrugs, 'with the reaction I got from you, I don't think you'll care.'

135

'What is it?'

'Are you really sure you want to hear my really good news? Like,' he shrugs nonchalantly, 'there isn't a ridiculous programme you want to see where, oh, I dunno, women have sex with aliens and they find out that—'

'What is it?' I punch him lightly. 'It was hardly more important than Alexis and Jeremy.'

Alistair sits up straighter; he seems to be relishing this. 'It's the reason I came over, actually,' he says. 'I wanted to see your face.'

I groan. 'So you do fancy me!'

'Hilarious.' He acknowledges the joke with a nod of his head and then pauses before he says, 'In fact it's fabulous news. For you,' he nods to me, points to himself, '*and* for me. Though mainly for you.'

'So it's something to do with the magazine?'

'Uh-huh. You, my fabulous, wonderful employee, I am reliably informed, have more than a shouting chance for the Designer of the Year for the Magazine Awards.' He grins broadly. 'What do you think of that?'

His words floor me. The fact that, only hours earlier, I'd been reading about being nominated the last time is weird. Plus I didn't know I'd been entered.

'Well?' Alistair presses, eyebrows raised.

Me? Designer of the Year? Our magazine is less than a year old. 'Really?' My voice is small, a little disbelieving.

'Really.' He grins wickedly. 'Really,' he confirms again. 'I entered you, I wrote a piece pretending to be you and hey, isn't it great? I was talking to a guy who's well in there, and he said your stuff was as brilliant as ever.'

'Oh God.' I'm overwhelmed. To be in with a shout for an

award for designing a magazine that promotes good funerals, well, I would have said that was practically impossible. I wonder if it's a sympathy vote. I'd been well known in my field, I'd been offered jobs when I came back and had declined them all until Alistair came along offering more than sympathy.

Alistair studies me, his head cocked to one side, still smiling, totally delighted for me. 'Ah, come here,' he suddenly says, holding out his arms and scooping me into them. 'Well done, you!' He hugs me hard, patting me on the back. 'You're a flipping genius, do you know that?'

Tears are pooling in my eyes now, and I have to blink them back. 'It's – it's great,' I gulp out. 'Are you sure?'

'I wouldn't be here if I wasn't. Apparently it's between you and the designer of some business magazine. I just had to drive over and tell you. Isn't it great?'

And then it hits me. The awards are given out at a big dinner held in December. Everyone dresses up and gets their hair done and it's like the Oscars of the Irish magazine world. I pull away from Alistair, and he must notice something because he asks, 'Are you OK?'

'I can't go, though,' I say to him. 'You know that. Besides, December might be a busy month with Christmas holidays and all, less time to do the same amount of work.'

He looks as if he's been expecting that. 'Just enjoy the fact that they love your stuff,' he says. 'Forget about being there.'

His words make sense. I don't have to go. It might look bad if I don't, though. I remember the first time I was nominated, God, I'd so looked forward to the evening, spent a fortune on my dress and half a day in the hairdresser's. But things change, people change, jobs change.

Alistair looks at me encouragingly. 'Your artwork is brilliant.'

Again, tears spark. 'Thanks. And you're the best editor a girl could have.'

He smiles and wraps a companionable arm about my shoulder. 'Thanks.' But then he spoils the moment by saying, 'Oh yeah, and the second thing I want to tell you is never advise me what to do in a romantic crisis ever again.'

'Huh?'

'The whole' – he makes quote signs with his fingers as he says it – 'buy her flowers thing? Tell her the truth?'

'Oh yeah. Did it not work?'

There is a faint grin on his face, though he winces slightly. 'It might have, only we forgot one tiny little detail.'

'What?'

'She owns a flower shop. Apparently I bought flowers from her rival.'

'Oh crap!' I clasp a hand to my mouth and begin to laugh. 'Shit!'

'Hmm.' Alistair rolls his eyes. 'I know. It was a disaster. I walked into her shop with this ridiculously expensive bunch of yellow and white flowers, I dunno what they were but they made me sneeze. And a customer in her shops says, "Oh, they're lovely, where did you get them?" and I said, "The flower shop on the corner," and off she trots, out of Mandy's shop.'

'No!'

'Yes!' he copies my tone. 'Oh – fucking – yes!'

'Sorry,' I say meekly.

'She told me to get out. Like she didn't shout or anything, she's a really quiet girl and she has a really girlish voice, but she was really cross. So I said I hadn't thought, and I offered her the flowers and she asked how would I like it if

138

she took out an ad in a rival funeral magazine, and I told her that there were none, and she said but if there were, how would I feel? And I told her that she was so nice I would forgive her. And she said if the rival funeral magazine was taking away our advertisers, how would I feel? And I said I would still forgive her because she has to be mindful of her business, and obviously she wants her ad to reach as many people as possible, and that if my magazine wasn't up to it, well then, it was my tough luck, and she didn't seem to know what to say to that. So I just left then.'

'Oh.'

He makes a face. 'So, I just thought that in order to make it up to her, we'd give her a free ad, front page.'

He's bonkers. 'That's prime space.'

'She's a prime girl.'

'And you are a prime idiot.'

He grins. 'Nothing ventured, nothing gained. And I would like you to ring her and tell her that we're doing it. I don't mind making a grand gesture, but what's the point if she doesn't know? You will get commission on the ad, so don't worry about that.'

It hadn't occurred to me. 'And what do you hope to achieve?'

He shrugs and blushes a bit. 'I like her, Andy. I want her to like me. I think she might, if I didn't keep messing up.'

'Jesus.' I'm impressed at his devotion. Alistair never runs after girls and it's not because they fall over themselves to get to him, it's more because he has no confidence in himself. This Mandy must be special. 'This girl I have to meet,' I joke.

Alistair winks. 'You will,' he promises me.

I wish I could believe that. Unless its via webcam, it's probably never going to happen.

'You *will*,' he says more emphatically, as if sensing my mood. He wraps an arm about me. 'You switch on some more TV crap and I'll fetch a bottle from my car. I meant to bring it in. Grade A Champagne, to celebrate!'

'You're my kind of boss.' And I totally mean it.

22

ALISTAIR AND I are pretty smashed when Kate arrives back with Luke later on. We've had a bottle of Champagne and are onto our second bottle of wine. It's cheap plonk, but at this stage we don't really care. Baz has had enough of the two of us laughing over nothing, and has taken himself out of the picture and found refuge somewhere else in the apartment.

'Well, isn't this great,' Kate throws an amused look back at Luke. 'I like your management style, Alistair. Can I come and work for you?'

Alistair, emboldened by drink, nods emphatically. 'You so can. You'd be a big draw in my magazine. Only thing is,' he slurs, 'you'd never be as good as your sis-is-ter. She is in the running for a Ma-ma-ma-magazine Award.'

'A Ma-ma-ma-magazine Award,' Kate giggles, imitating him. 'Well, that sounds wonderful, what is it?'

'Deeee-signer of the Year!' Alistair says with aplomb, waving his wineglass about and sloshing me with droplets of booze. 'We're celebrating.'

'Celebrating,' I agree, ignoring the fact that I've been baptised in red wine. 'Join us.'

'I'll get the glasses.' Luke smiles. 'We're celebrating too.

Fred should be OK, according to the doctors. He's having angioplasty.'

'Angio what?' I ask.

'It's where they blow up—'

'Ew.' Kate holds up her hand. 'Let's not go into details. Let's just celebrate.'

Luke heads off into the kitchen and comes back with a couple of glasses.

Alistair shakily pours them a drink before emptying the last of the drops into my wineglass. 'All gone,' he says.

'I'll go out and get another bottle.' Luke stands up. 'Shame for the party to end too early.'

'My kind of boyfriend.' Kate laughs as he ruffles her hair.

All's back to normal in paradise, I see to my relief, as Luke bends down to kiss her.

It's ten o'clock. We've sent out for pizzas and garlic bread to soak up the alcohol, though I reckon we'd need the EU food mountain to do the job. At this stage, I know if I stand up the room will unexpectedly tip sideways. Despite this, I'm more relaxed than I've been in a long time. I'm sitting sloppily back on the sofa, my stockinged feet pulled up and curled under me, listening to the others chatting away without any real idea of what they are talking about. They probably have no idea what they are saying, either. The conversation rolls in waves about the room, and I enjoy the rhythm of it and the way it's punctuated by laughter. Alistair has discarded his shyness and awkwardness and is entertaining Luke and Kate with a story about the time he'd crashed on the way to a funeral. I've heard the story before.

'I was driving this family to the church,' he slurs, 'my

142

very first driving stint, as I normally sat with my dad, in the hearse.'

Luke and Kate find this very funny, for some reason.

'Anyway,' Alistair continues over their laughter, 'there's this sort of partition thing in the family cars that divides the driver's seat from the back seats and it's soundproofed, and this family had it pulled over so it was really quiet, you get me?'

'We get you,' Kate says.

'So, I'm driving along,' Alistair mimes a steering wheel, 'all nice and calm, when the next thing, I feel a tip on my shoulder and a voice from the back says, "Here's the church now".' He does a fair impression of a bog accent. 'Well, I jumped like a fecking hare on speed and swerved, crashing the car into the pillar of the church. I was so used to being with my dad in the hearse that I thought it was a voice from the grave.'

Luke throws back his head and laughs loudly. I catch Kate looking fondly at him. I think she's relieved he's actually laughing after the week he's had.

Alistair smiles in that bewildered way he has when he has told a funny story. 'They sued me for mental distress. It was nothing to what I suffered in that moment.'

More laughter.

The pizzas arrive and Luke, who seems to be the most sober, goes down to collect them. Soon, we're all munching happily. 'So what made you decide to set up the magazine?' Kate asks him.

Alistair shrugs. 'Have you ever been to loads of funerals in a week?'

'Eh, no.'

Luke chuckles.

'Well, I hated it.' Alistair has suddenly become serious. He is silent for a second, placing his wineglass on the floor before meeting Kate's gaze. 'I absolutely hated it. All that sadness, that grief.' He shakes his head. 'Nah, not for me. So, I decided to do the magazine. I could write, I knew about funerals, it seemed logical.'

No one says anything for a bit, catching the glumness of Alistair's mood. 'And you're glad you did it?' Luke asks, breaking the silence.

'Gladder than if I didn't,' Alistair says. And that seems to be the end of it.

'I gave up being a solicitor to teach yoga and work in a shop,' Luke cheerfully admits. He indicates his grey sweatshirt and tracksuit bottoms. 'I hated being a solicitor, and I also hated the way I had to dress. In the end my mother told me to give it up. So I did.'

'Good for you.' Alistair nods.

'Good for your mother,' I add.

'And good for me.' Kate snuggles up to Luke, the pizza slice in her hand drooping and dropping pineapple over him, which he plucks up and pops into her mouth. 'He came on my show to talk about the benefits of yoga.'

'I did.' Luke looks down at her.

'And,' Kate trails a free hand across his chest, 'he got me all hot and bothered explaining about the doggie position. And the snake.'

'Cobra,' Luke corrects her, spluttering on his wine. 'And the Dog.'

'Anyway,' Kate tosses her hair back, 'it was yummy. He was yummy.'

144

'And you were yummy.' Luke kisses the top of her head.

Alistair looks faintly embarrassed at this display.

'See what I have to put up with,' I say, slurring badly. The food has done nothing for my spinning head. 'The carry-on of them. They've no respect for old maids like me.'

'Old maid,' Kate snorts. 'That's your own fault. If you went out you'd get a man.'

A shocked silence, followed quickly by an air of unease as the two lads look at me. I'm suddenly feeling incredibly sober. I'm hyper-aware that I am holding a glass of wine, and that two seconds before I had a smile on my face which is now rapidly dying. Embarrassment sweeps right through me like a hot flush because while everyone knows that I don't go out, I constantly hedge the subject with euphemisms about not liking the social scene and being uncomfortable with people. But Kate saying that it was all my own fault, well, that's a bit of a shocker. And it's even worse because we all know it's true. I'm glad the lights are muted as I'm sure my face is burning. I can't look at anyone. I stare at my half-eaten pizza slice and I'm suddenly not hungry. 'I don't want to get a man,' I mutter, trying to keep my voice from shaking.

There is more awkward silence, as if some delicate boundary has been breached, which it has.

'Sorry,' Kate says, immediately making me feel worse.

'Sorry for what?' I say, trying for a casual tone. 'It's no big deal, I don't want a man.'

'That's not what I meant,' Kate says. 'I meant sorry for—'

'More wine?' I interrupt, holding out the bottle.

The silence is worse this time. The bottle wavers in my outstretched arm.

'I think it's time for bed.' Luke yawns widely. It looks fake

145

to me. 'I'll never get up in the morning. Come on you,' he stands up and holds out his hand to Kate, dragging her up with him. ''Night all.'

''Night,' Alistair answers for both of us.

Kate says nothing as Luke leads her from the room.

'More wine?' I ask Alistair. I can't meet his eyes. Instead I focus on the bottle. When he doesn't answer, I say, 'No? OK, all the more for me, so.' I drain my wineglass and fill it halfway up again.

'She didn't mean it,' Alistair says awkwardly.

'Sorry? What?' I feign confusion.

'Your sister,' he says, and his voice is embarrassingly gentle. 'She didn't mean it in a bad way.'

'So she meant if I did go out I wouldn't get a man?' It's a feeble attempt at a joke.

'No. She didn't mean to hurt you,' he says.

'She didn't hurt me.'

'Look . . .' Alistair angles his body towards mine. He suddenly seems completely sober. 'You don't go out, we all know that. Stop trying to make it normal 'cause it's not, Andy.'

'I know it's not, but I can live like that. I don't have a problem with it.' I feel too hot all of a sudden.

'Well, I guess we do,' Alistair says calmly. 'It's a shame. You are a beautiful girl, you've a great personality and you need to get out.'

My eyes fill up. I want to crawl into a space somewhere and hide.

'Here.' He pulls a hankie from his pocket. 'Don't cry.'

'I'm not going to cry,' I say tearfully. I look at his white cotton hankie. 'And what sort of a man goes about with a hankie in his pocket?'

146

'A trained undertaker,' he says with a smile.

I take it and twist it between my hands. This, no contest, is the most excruciatingly embarrassing moment of my life.

'Kate just meant that you are wasted staying in, Andy,' Alistair goes on. 'I think so too.'

'I don't want to talk about this. I'll go out when I'm ready.' My voice wobbles. I take a shaky slug of wine.

At that moment, Baz appears in the doorway, miaowing. He positions himself at my feet. I reach down and pet his black back and he arches it appreciatively. It's a good excuse not to look at my boss.

'I hope you will, Andy.' I'm aware that Alistair has stood up. He must be leaving, which is good. He attempts to peer into my face, but I can't look at him. 'And when you do,' he continues, 'if you haven't got a man, I'd be happy to be seen with you.'

Baz hisses and Alistair steps back.

'Thanks,' I say, a little bit touched but even more morti-fied now. A charity date, I don't think so. They all think I have a major problem, I realise suddenly. Even though I've never admitted it, even though they've never admitted it, even though my refusals to go anywhere have been passed over with an 'oh, well, maybe next time', they'd all known the extent of my phobia. 'But I am fine,' I rally suddenly. 'I know I used to go out a lot before, but, well, the . . .' I struggle over the word, 'the accident made me realise that it's nice to stay close to people you know.'

'And it is,' Alistair agrees. 'But you're on your own here.'

'Anyway . . .' I stand up. 'I'll get to bed now, too. Thanks for coming over.'

'No problem. And congratulations again.' He doesn't

attempt to hug me, and I'm glad. It would feel too much like sympathy.

I walk him to the door, watch as he leaves and then, closing the door after him, I press my back to it, inhaling sharply, holding in my horror at what has just been said, I damp down the embarrassment and blink back my tears. I realise I'm still holding Alistair's handkerchief.

When I finally feel as if I've regained some control, I flick on the alarm and head upstairs.

23

I CAN'T SLEEP. I've barely closed my eyes in two days. Kate's words keep circling about in my head. And though she apologised for them, it doesn't take away from their truth. I don't go out. It's a fact that I've been ignoring for way too long. Or maybe 'ignoring' is the wrong word. I didn't go out, but somewhere in my head, I'd kept promising myself that one day I would. Which somehow made everything all right. Meantime, however, everyone is noticing that I'm becoming . . . reclusive, and they're probably all talking about me behind my back, which is why I've become reclusive in the first place. I've found that it's hard to trust the surface of people. What they say is not what they really think. During the two sleepless nights, I recall vividly the incident that slid underneath the shaky foundations of my confidence after the accident. I have tried to block it out, but have never succeeded. I've never told anyone either, it hurt too much. And besides, I'm ashamed that it has had such a profound effect on me; I think somehow that it makes me as superficial as the people I try to avoid.

I was two months out of hospital at the time, and my face still looked a mess, at least it did in my eyes. My scar was red and raw-looking, snaking its way down my face. Make-up only made it worse. I was like two people, perfect on one side, damaged beyond repair on the other. And like my face, my whole personality was in transition too. But I was making the best of it. Or at least, I was trying. I never complained, I always tried to be in a good mood. I even made jokes about it. And as the doctors kept telling me, two months was no time. I had to give the scar a chance to heal. Anyway, I think I was behaving a little like I am now, I was fooling myself that one day I actually would be OK about it. Then, one evening, Chas asked me out to meet some friends of his. I remember that I hadn't wanted to go, and I don't think he really did either, but both of us were trying hard to put our devastated lives back together. It was his first night out since the accident too. Not knowing what had happened to his sister was slowly killing the Chas I knew, and I wanted a chance to do something for him. He'd been so good to me since the crash.

I remember now, with a yearning that surprises me, how he'd taken my hands in his and gently kissed both my palms while keeping his wicked brown eyes pinned on mine. 'You are gorgeous,' he'd said, his gaze intense, his voice quiet. 'I am bloody mad about you. I love everything about you. My friends love you too, you know that.' He paused before adding, 'And I really don't think I could go on my own.' That swung it. I would have died for that guy, so I agreed. I would go for him. And a little for me. My counsellor had told me to try to go out.

I can still remember what I wore, probably because it was one of the last times I'd dressed up. A short, flirty little patterned skirt, plenty of fake tan, high red shoes – I had a thing about red – and a cute ruffled white blouse. My hair, which had grown since I'd started travelling, I left loose and it hung about my face like a curtain. I hadn't been secure enough to tie it back. Chas had lifted up a strand, pushed it behind my ear and gently leaned over and kissed my scar. The gesture made my eyes water, and it does now, too, as I remember it. Then without saying any more, he'd loped his arm about my shoulder and led me to his car.

Chas, in those days at least, was a poseur. A very nice poseur, but a poseur none the less. I loved that about him. I loved his vanity, I loved the fact that we looked great together. I loved that I could tease him and he'd never take offence. His hair had been shoulder-length, glossy and dark, a touch of the Georgie Best about it. There was nothing casual in its casualness, though. It fell perfectly around his perfectly chiselled face. A sparkling white shirt contrasted with his Italian looks. The shirt hung casually over a pair of distressed denims. Expensive dubes adorned his feet. Chas's whole appearance exuded a carefully cultivated air of shabby chic. He loved being the centre of attention, loved women looking at him. Chas had the magnetic personality of his sister, and he used it to devastating effect. But he was a good guy.

When we arrived at the pub Chas, maybe sensing my unease, or maybe looking for support himself, wrapped his arm protectively about my shoulder and led me in. His mates were sitting at a table right at the back, and I steeled myself to walk right through the whole pub. The place was heaving. It was noisy and loud, but when Chas and I made our entrance, people still noticed. They always noticed the two of us. We made a striking couple. And for about one blissful hour, I bathed in that fact. Denied to myself that my scar was that bad. No one seemed to notice it at all. Everyone told me how

151

well I looked. For one hour, my life was back on track. I knew I could do this.

And then I went outside for a smoke.

Another thing I did in those days.

One of Chas's friends was outside taking a call on her mobile. I lit up, stood back to allow her some privacy and overheard: '—really awful-looking. Honestly, I feel so sorry for her. She's making the best of it but she'll never hang onto him now . . . Oh, it's *huge* . . . all down her face. Honestly, you'd feel so sorry for her. I'd prefer to be dead than look like that.'

And on it went.

I'd like to think that I could have gone up to her and said, 'You already do look like that', or something equally caustic, but I didn't. I hadn't the confidence. It was my looks that had given me confidence in the past, I realised in that instant. My looks were the root of my identity, and now that they were gone, I felt as if I had been robbed of my very self. So, instead of making a witty rejoinder and putting her in her place, I'd quietly stamped out my cigarette and hidden in the shadows until she left. I didn't have the courage to walk back inside. I couldn't face them all now that I knew what they were really thinking. I had no cash to hail a taxi as my bag was under the table in the pub, and besides, I did not need a third degree from a taxi driver. So I'd stood, hidden in shadow, growing colder and colder, unable to even cry. I was numb, the way I'd been for a while after the accident. Humiliation tried to crawl in but I shoved it aside, preferring not to think about it.

Eventually Chas had come looking for me. He'd asked me on a laugh what I was doing. I told him I wanted to go home.

I know I sounded angry, and I was. I was angry at him for giving me the hope that I did look OK. I was angrier at him than I was at the girl. Chas looked into my face and asked me what had happened, but it was too humiliating. I just told him I didn't feel well. So he'd gone back inside, fetched my bag and coat and driven me back to the flat. Maybe I should have told him. But he'd told me I was beautiful, and I knew now that my perception had been right all along. He had lied. I couldn't trust him. His friends had lied.

I never said anything in the weeks that followed. Instead, I'd pushed him away, too angry and ashamed to talk about it. Some weeks later, he'd got the job in India and had asked me to go with him. I refused. He asked me if I would wait for him. I said that if he loved me he'd stay. The truth was, I couldn't go halfway around the world when I was terrified of walking down the street. And I think I'd wanted to punish him for that night, however unfair that might have been.

We'd parted barely talking to each other. The only thing I'd left of him was Baz.

That girl had been right. I hadn't been able to hang onto him.

The only good thing to come out of it was that I hadn't smoked a cigarette since.

But that's not good enough, I realise now. I feel incredibly sick as it hits me what exactly I have to do. No amount of internet chat, or texting, or making phone calls is going to replace what I've lost.

I have to get my life back.

Somehow.

24

O<small>N</small> W<small>EDNESDAY</small>, C<small>ISSY</small> brings Lexi, Doug and Lordi to a forest.

'Enchanted Forest.' Doug reads the garish sign that hangs, apparently in mid-air, over the entrance. 'Well, that's good.'

'Really?' Cissy smiles.

'Yeah, really. Can I enchant some cash my way?'

Cissy giggles, but Lexi doesn't feel that Doug has meant to be funny. In fact, it sounded quite bitter, the way he said it. Things must be pretty bad for him.

'Have you been here before?' Lexi asks Cissy.

'A couple of times, but it's such a big place it's always different. It's so cool, and there are really weird plants growing, and I take photos of them and design hats around them.'

'That doesn't sound very enchanted.' Doug folds his arms. He's wearing a black t-shirt with *I Dig Doug's Music* scrawled across the front of it.

'I think,' Lordi says calmly, 'that the word "enchanted" is a tad misleading. I think it means enchanted as in enchanting.'

'Oh, round of applause for the English scholar.'

There is a bit of a silence. None of them seem to know quite what to say, so they wisely say nothing. They walk past the entrance, Lexi bringing up the rear. She's behind Lordi's billowing white cloak, and she soon loses sight of it as there is fog all around her, which is incredibly disorientating as the world goes blank for about five seconds and all she can do is walk forward, hoping that she's heading onwards.

'It's meant to be a Harry Potter moment.' It's Cissy talking. 'You know, the bit where he takes the leap of faith and walks through the wall at Platform Nine to Platform Nine and Three-Quarters, and finds himself in a nicer world. Well, this is why they have this.'

'Nice idea,' Lordi says.

When the fog clears, Lexi sees that the other three are waiting for her.

Lordi pretends to look at a watch on his wrist. 'What took you so long, kiddo?' he asks.

'Time,' Lexi answers and they all laugh, even Doug.

'This is my favourite route,' Cissy says, indicating an ordinary pathway to her left. 'It's like something from Willie Wonka. Come on.' She prances ahead, her tiny feet encased in little white flat plimsolls.

The path has definitely been created by a master of imagination. Flowers that reach to Lexi's waist align both sides of the walkway. They look like miniature umbrellas, all of different hues. There isn't any order to the way in which the colours are arranged either, which is nice, she thinks. It's freer and more joyful that way. The flowers seem to sway in a light breeze. Behind the flowers, like gigantic sentries, are the trees. Tall, reaching so far into the sky that it's impossible to see how far up they go, they have branches that are perfectly aligned so that one tree flows into the next and into the next, a wall of unbreakable green. This wall prevents any light from penetrating, so that the only illumination is along the

155

path upon which they are walking, much as the light from a skylight. Lexi turns her face upwards, catching the light.

'Wow,' Lordi exclaims. 'Fabulous imaginative structure to this place.'

'I know,' Cissy says. 'I'd love to know who designed it, or came up with the concept. Come on, this way.' She beckons them towards a gap in the trees. 'Wait until you see through here.'

They watch as she disappears. Lexi climbs in after her and stands gaping. She is on a hill, light flooding in from every direction. Down below, Cissy is running towards fields and fields of yellow flowers, bigger than daffodils and a lot sturdier too, as they spring back up again after Cissy has run through them.

'Come on,' Cissy calls. 'Come on.'

Lexi runs to join her. The yellow flowers are deceptively large, even bigger than the umbrella-like ones. She is enchanted by the way they almost make it up to her shoulder. And enchanted is the right word; it's an aptly named place. Cissy is ahead of her, dancing along in her sparkling white t-shirt and tight little shorts. Lexi follows, and then stops abruptly as Cissy disappears from sight.

'Cissy?'

'Here.' Cissy's head pops up. 'Come on, lie down in them, it's an experience.'

Lexi joins her, lying on her back alongside her friend. The world suddenly turns yellow and gold. The flowers are like giant tulips, she sees now. 'Wow,' she says.

'Isn't it funny how, when you lie down, it all looks so different?'

'Yep. It looks even better, and I didn't think it was possible.'

Cissy sighs, obviously content.

Lordi flops down beside them and they are soon joined by Doug, who has walked at a slower pace.

'Lie down, Drug.' Lexi turns towards him.

'I'd rather sit,' he mutters.

'It looks better when you lie down.'

'Sometimes no matter how much you look at a thing, it never looks better.'

No one says anything for a bit.

'You didn't have to come,' Cissy eventually pipes up. 'You're spoiling it. This is my day out and I want to enjoy it.'

'I'm not stopping you enjoying yourselves among these ridiculous plants.'

'Hey,' Lordi says. 'That really isn't called for. You are casting a shadow over the day, you know.'

'Yeah well . . .' Doug stands up, pushing his long hair from his face and giving Lordi a mock salute. 'I'll leave so.'

'Oh, come on.' Lexi hastily scrambles to her feet and reaches towards him. 'Don't be like that. What's up with you?'

Doug shakes his head. 'Nothing. Nothing,' he repeats. 'But I'm not great company at the moment.'

'Did you buy the Liberty angel?' Lordi asks.

'Liberty fucking angel,' Doug scoffs. 'Jesus, if you sold me a Liberty fucking *archangel*, it wouldn't sort my problems out.'

'So there is something bothering you.' Cissy sits up now too, her dark hair falling over her shoulders, her massive brown eyes appraising him.

Doug doesn't reply, but neither does he leave. He remains standing, his hands in the pockets of his jeans, staring away from them.

'You should either buy an angel from me or order one on the internet,' Lordi says.

'Will you shut up about that angel,' Doug snaps. 'Jesus!'

'It's not Jesus, it's a Liberty angel and it will help.'

'I bought one, OK?' Doug says then. 'Not from you, though.'

'Thanks for the support,' Lordi says drily.

'I didn't want you to know,' Doug mutters. 'Anyway, it hasn't worked.'

'That's because you doubt it.'

'Give me a break.'

More silence.

Cissy pats the ground. 'Come on, Doug, sit down. Fighting with us won't sort anything out either.'

He seems torn but after a second or two, he plonks down beside them. Lexi sits down too.

They all look at each other.

'Maybe we can help,' Cissy breaks the silence. 'We can listen and give you advice, and let's be honest here, it's not going to go any further.'

'I'm crap at advice,' Lexi tries to joke. 'So whatever I say, ignore it.'

'I've already given mine.' Lordi lies back down, his hands behind his head.

'So, you've got me and Lexi.' Cissy beams.

'And what a lucky guy I am,' Doug jokes feebly.

Cissy laughs. 'Go on, what's the problem? This can be your day to tell us all about yourself.'

It takes a second for Doug to begin. When he does, his voice comes in fits and starts, like an old car attempting a jump-start. 'It was good in the beginning,' he says wryly. 'My life.'

That makes them laugh a little.

'Then I got into music, and that was good. I was doing well. I wrote my own stuff, recorded a couple of albums.'

'Really? Would we have heard of you?' Lexi asks.

'Dunno. I was in a band.' He pauses as if not wanting to tell them the name, and then decides to go for it. 'Mike and the Misfortunates.' Doug pauses. 'Which was apt, considering what happened.'

'What happened?'

'Our albums flopped and we were dropped by the record label.'

'Bad choice of name,' Lordi speaks from his position on the ground. 'You set the band up for failure.'

'Will you shut up with the mumbo-jumbo nonsense,' Doug says.

'Sorry.'

It doesn't sound as if Lordi means it.

'So what happened then?' Cissy has moved nearer to Doug, her long legs stretched out in front of her, the palms of her hands planted firmly in the grass behind her.

'Well, the contract we'd signed was a bit of a dud, as it happened. We agreed that any money lost on our albums had to be repaid to the record company, but of course, we'd blown the lot. I now have no house, no car, no furniture and my girlfriend informed me by text last night that I'm officially dumped. I mean, you'd think she'd tell me to my face.'

'Wagon,' Cissy says.

'Bitch,' Lexi offers support too. 'Were you with her long?'

Doug doesn't answer, obviously not wanting to go there. 'Anyhow, my attempt to promote my music through my shop has to stop. I can't afford to keep the shop any more.'

159

There is silence for a minute as they all look at him. Even Lordi hauls himself from the ground in surprise. 'You never said it was that bad,' he says.

'Yeah, well, I don't make it my business to tell my business.'

'Eh, you just have.'

'Are you trying to piss me off?' Doug glares at him.

'I am merely trying to inject some levity into what must be a tense situation.'

'Well, don't.' Doug stands up. He looks down at Cissy. 'Thanks for the outing, Cissy, but I'll be leaving soon.'

'Oh no.' Cissy stands up now. 'Don't, come on. Let's try to hang onto your shop here, at least.'

'I wish,' Doug says. 'I love it. Being here, being in the shop, I forget about the hassles in my life. It's another reason the girlfriend dumped me. She says I spend more time here than I should.'

'Do you?' Lordi asks. 'That would not be a good idea. You should be with your girlfriend.'

'Yeah, well, I happen to prefer it here. I like being with you lot.'

'Me too,' Cissy says loyally.

Lordi shakes his head and lies back down.

'I prefer here too,' Lexi says. 'It's like a holiday for me. And you three are odd but nice.'

It makes them laugh.

'I could sell your music through my shop,' Cissy says suddenly. 'The rent would stay the same.'

'No,' Doug shakes his head. 'I couldn't have that.'

'Why not?'

'It's charity.'

'You can pay me back when you can. I'm not spending

160

any more than I already am, and your music could entice people into my shop who might buy a hat. It's a win-win.'

'I couldn't get people into my own shop.'

'No offence, but your shop was all black and you look a bit weird. It probably put some customers off.'

'No offence?' Doug says, laughing. 'Thanks.'

'You should change your image.'

'Eh – no.'

'What do you think?' Cissy asks. 'Of my offer?'

'Oh, I dunno.'

'If you close the shop, you might not come back here,' Lexi voices what she imagines the others are thinking. 'We'd miss you.'

'I would come back.'

In the distance, there are voices. Others are emerging from the gap in the trees and exclaiming over the flowers.

'Think about it,' Cissy says.

'I don't do charity.'

'It's not charity, it's friendship.' Cissy looks around at them all. 'Isn't that what this is?' she asks. 'Friendship?'

Lexi nods. She is suddenly happier than she's been in a long time. These three are her first friends since . . . well, since she dropped out of her life. They might not be the type of friends she'd ever imagined making, but there was a time when she'd begun to imagine that she might never make any again. 'I'd take the offer,' she says to Doug. 'And what's more, I'll see if Peter will play some music in the gallery to promote you – that's if you have any gentle tracks.'

'I could write one.' Doug seems overwhelmed.

'And I'll give you a massive Liberty angel for your shop,' Lordi says to Cissy. 'And a Friendship angel.'

161

'And can you give us a big sheet to hide them under, too?' Doug asks, but it's a joke. He takes a second to look at the three of them. 'Thanks, you lot. I didn't come here to find friends, I just wanted to promote my music after the band failed.'

'So now can we lie down and look at the flowers?' Cissy asks. 'And not talk, just be?'

'Sounds incredibly boring, but let's give it a go.' Lexi lies down, and immediately the view is a blend of yellow flowers and blue sky.

Beautiful.

25

'COFFEE?' KATE ASKS as I enter the kitchen on the third day after her drunken comment. Without waiting for an answer, she hops up from Luke's lap and pours me a drink. Luke looks at her in amusement, then winks at me.

'Toast?' Kate asks brightly. Again, I don't have to answer as she slides two pieces of toast onto a plate and presents them to me.

This has been the pattern for the last two mornings, and I stifle a smile.

As I pick up my cup, Kate hovers about, and then bestows on me this big, quite creepy, sisterly smile.

'Oh Jesus.' I hold up my hand. 'Enough, Kate! You don't have to do this. I told you, it's fine. You think I'm a weirdo recluse—'

'Oh no, I never said that!' Her eyes widen in shock. 'I never did.'

'No,' Luke joins in to defend her, 'I didn't hear her say that.'

I know I'm trying to be all flippant, but calling myself a weirdo recluse does hurt a bit. 'All right,' I concede, 'you didn't exactly say that. But you did say that I never go out.'

Kate winces, then hops about from foot to foot, looking nervous, which is odd as she's never been nervous of me in her life. 'Mmm, yes, I did say that. But I was wrong. You go to our folks and Lexi's folks and—'

'Only under cover of darkness,' I say quietly, halting her. 'You are right.' I meet her gaze. 'I don't go out. I've spent the last two days doing a lot of thinking, and it's me that should be apologising, you only told the truth. I—'

'Oh no—'

'You were right, Kate.' I say it firmly, so she knows I mean it.

She seems taken aback at the admission. 'I wasn't trying to hurt you, you know that, right?'

'Uh-huh.' I take a bite of toast and suddenly remember that I haven't buttered it. It tastes rotten. All dry.

'I mean, if you want to stay in, that's your business.'

I don't reply. Instead, I pick up my knife and scrape some butter across the toast. I've always been amazed at the effect butter has on things. It transforms them. I'll probably be massively fat by the time I hit forty, with the amount of butter I eat. My mother always complains about it but as my dad says, what's the point of eating dry stuff if you hate it?

'I need to get my life back,' I blurt out.

I'm as shocked as they are by what I've just announced. Like I just told Kate, I'd been thinking about what she'd said. I'd also been thinking about Alistair and his new girlfriend, and how I might never get to meet her, how she could be all wrong for him and I wouldn't be able to warn him. Or the fact that I'd been nominated for a Magazine Award and I'd miss out on the event. The fact that Chas is back and I can never tell him what I'm doing now, while he gallivants about the country taking pictures. Life, despite the fact that I'm stuck, is going on without me in it. I need to do something proactive to help myself, but I hadn't planned on announcing it straight out like that. In the silence that follows, I stare at my delicious buttery toast and slowly raise my eyes to look at Kate and Luke. 'I need to get out into the world again and have some fun.'

Kate's mouth opens and closes and opens again. Then she gushes, 'You so completely do!'

I manage a smile. 'Thanks for your support.'

'You can come out with me and Luke at the weekend,' she slides into a seat beside me. 'We're heading to the pub with a load of mates and—'

'Oh, I dunno.' I find I can't even eat my toast now. I feel a little sick with the admission. 'That might be too much. Maybe I could start slowly.'

'Come out with just me and Luke?' She arches her eyebrows.

'Eh, no, I was thinking more like . . .' I search my mind for something I feel I might be able to do. Somewhere in there, the advice of the counsellor I'd had after the operation for the scar comes back to me. 'Somewhere easy and quick. Maybe, I dunno, the local shops to buy bread.'

'Oh,' Kate sounds unimpressed. 'Well, that's not much fun.'

'I think that's great.' Luke shoots Kate a warning look. 'You can build from there, eh?'

'Oh yeah.' Kate nods now too, sounding completely insincere. 'Brilliant.' Then she brightens. 'There's a gorgeous guy who works there. You'll like him.'

'Thanks,' Luke says drily.

'Well, not as gorgeous as you, obviously,' Kate says, it as if it's not obvious at all.

'Obviously.' Luke smirks at her.

165

'Obviously.' Kate crosses to him and rubs her nose against his. 'Obviously, obviously, obviously.'

'Can you both be honest with me?' I interrupt them suddenly, another thought bubbling to the surface.

'Honest?' Kate stops teasing her boyfriend long enough to look at me. 'What d'ya mean?'

I gently, though with shaking fingers, pull my veil of long brown hair away from the corner of my face. Pushing it behind my ear, I turn my scarred cheek towards them. 'I need to know what you really think of this.'

Their smiles vanish. Kate blinks a little rapidly. 'Oh, Andy . . .' is all she says.

'I need to know,' I say firmly. 'I can't go out unprepared. I did once, and . . .' I pause, not wanting to go there. Instead I settle for, 'Well, I'm not doing it again. So?'

Luke is the first to answer. 'I told you when I came here,' he says, sounding chilled. 'It's not that bad. I mean, you can see it, it's like a thin line down your face, but it's not horrific or off-putting. Not to me, anyway.'

'You told her that?' Kate gawks at him. 'I told you not to mention her scar to her.'

'And when have I ever listened to you?' He rolls his eyes as if the very idea is preposterous.

'Asshole.' Kate elbows him. Then she turns to me. 'He's right though, Andy. It's much better than it used to be. I mean,' she snorts as she says it, 'it used to be awful. Awwwful. But it's fine now. Really. I think you make a big deal of it.'

'You never said it was awful before!' Ridiculously, I feel a little indignant.

'You never told me to be honest before.'

166

She has a point.

'So it's not noticeable?'

Their hesitation gives me the answer.

'It's noticeable,' Kate picks her words as carefully as she picks her shoes, 'but not,' she makes a face, '*that* noticeable.'

'Great,' I deadpan.

Luke splutters out a laugh. 'Not *that* noticeable.' He mimics Kate perfectly, making us both laugh a little. He turns to me and grins broadly. 'Your scar is barely noticeable, Andy. It's there, but it's overlookable.'

'Overlookable,' Kate snorts. 'Rewrite the English language, why don't you?'

'Thanks, guys.' I think they barely hear me as Luke wonders if there is a word 'classtastic' to describe Kate – classy and fantastic.

It makes me smile to see that though I have just made one of the most momentous decisions of my life, they're more interested in coining ridiculous words.

'Smoochable,' Kate says as I leave. 'That describes the guy in the corner shop.'

'Ouch!' I hear Luke mock-groan.

'Screwable, that's you.'

And they laugh.

The jungle drums must have got going, as my mother arrives over at lunchtime. Dad trots along behind, carrying a plastic bag containing a dry Madeira cake and some oranges. 'Kate told me the news,' my mother announces before she steps into my apartment. 'You're going to go out again. Andy, I'm delighted.' She enfolds me in a hug, and over her shoulder I can see the tenant from the apartment opposite glancing curiously at us. I've never seen him in daylight before, a small, overweight little man who is obviously inspired by the seventies for his dress sense. I smile at him from over my mother's shoulder.

He winks back at me.

My mother lets me go and steps inside. My dad follows her and, not being one for displays of affection, he just nods to me as he hands me the plastic bag. 'The usual,' he says.

My parents love dry Madeira cake. It's cheap and tasty. It's the one thing they both agree on.

I lead them into the kitchen where Luke is sitting at my table, poring over a health food book.

'Oh,' my mother says, taken aback at seeing him there. 'Eh, hello, Luke.' She gingerly sits opposite him and takes in his dreadlocked hair and hippy clothes. He's outdone himself that morning – he's wearing a colourful stripy top that looks as if it was hand-sewn by a blind person. His cords are green and faded and he's barefoot.

'Hi.' Luke nods, flushing a little. 'How are things with the two of you?'

'Fantastic,' Mam answers.

'All right,' Dad says at the same time, sitting down beside my mother.

There is a pause.

My mother turns to my father. 'All right? What do you mean by that?'

'I mean that things are all right,' Dad says.

'I said they were fantastic.' My mother folds her arms.

'Well, you've got me, haven't you? And, well . . .' Dad shrugs. 'I've got you.'

Luke guffaws. Then realises that he probably shouldn't have, as he goes red and turns hastily back to his book.

'Thank you,' my mother says to my father. 'That's very nice. Thanks.'

There is a silence.

'It was a joke,' my dad says mildly.

'Well, I only said things were fantastic as Andy is finally getting her life back together. I didn't say it because I have you.'

'I know that,' Dad says. 'And Andy getting her life back is fantastic.'

'I believe you and Kate are going to walk Andy to the corner shop,' Mam says loudly to Luke, as if the man is deaf and not just reading.

He glances up.

'I won't need a convoy,' I interrupt.

'Two people isn't a convoy,' Mam says, still eyeballing poor Luke, who looks as if he'd rather leave.

'We're there to do whatever Andy wants us to do,' Luke stutters a little.

'Very good,' Dad says as he reaches out to take some Madeira cake that I've just sliced. 'That's the best way.'

'Well, we're delighted,' Mam says, and she sounds emotional. 'You've no idea how worried we've been, Andy. I mean, there you were, in all day, your only company that morose cat you have, spending your time designing covers for a funeral magazine. Who knows what was going through your head. I was going out of my mind. I was so relieved when you let Kate move in with you.'

'Well, in fairness her flat burned down.' I pour scalding water into the teapot and swirl it about.

'Oh yes, yes, that.' Mam nods, and there is something in her voice which is odd. A high note or a quiver or a—

'How is the refurbishment coming along?' Dad asks Luke. 'I believe it was pretty badly gutted.'

There's a perceptible pause before Luke closes his book, which is entitled *Herbs for Health*. 'Uh-huh,' he says. 'We were only grateful no one was killed.'

'Absolutely.' Dad takes another slice of Madeira. 'That would have been a tragedy.'

'Can you not wait until Andy pours the tea before you gobble up all the food,' Mam snaps.

'Obviously not,' Dad says calmly as he bites into his second slice.

I hastily fill the cups so as to avoid any more arguments. Luke takes this as his cue to leave. 'Be seeing yous.' He pulls on his heavy green parka jacket and slips his feet into an old pair of flipflops. 'I'm just heading to work in the health food shop.'

'Bye Luke,' I call out after him as the front door closes.

'I wonder, do they have any shampoo in that shop he works in?' my mother says.

'I quite like his hair,' my dad says. 'Maintenance-free.'

Mam clicks her tongue but makes no comment.

I pour myself a cup of tea and sit down with them, mentally preparing to put up with the onslaught of their bickering and answer all the questions my mother is bound to have. Instead, there is silence as I reach for the milk. Stirring it into my tea with a finger, I glance at the two of them.

They are both looking at me. I squirm under their scrutiny. 'What?' I ask on a half-laugh.

My dad clears his throat. 'We're thrilled,' he says swallowing hard. 'We want you to know we'll help all we can.'

'Oh.' My eyes rake over the two of them. I'm suddenly ridiculously touched as I swallow back unexpected tears. 'Well, thanks.'

Mam's hand finds mine across the table and surprisingly she says nothing, she just squeezes it. Hard.

I ask Dad a little later to get my art stuff down from the press for me.

'Oh,' he says, 'are you going to paint again, too?'

I shrug, 'I was thinking about it. I'll probably be crap.'

'You couldn't be any worse than some of the people in my art class,' my mother says. 'Honestly, they can't even draw a circle.'

'You go to an art class?'

'Most people can't draw circles,' Dad says before she can answer me, 'only a real artist can.' He starts to ascend the stairs to my room.

'And you'd know how?' my mother calls after him. 'Do these facts just come to you as you lie on the sofa all day?'

'Yes,' he answers with conviction, 'they do.'

'Up here, Dad.' I hasten him into my room and point to the press where the rest of my stuff is, heading this potential squabble off at the pass. Dad pulls across my bedroom chair and, because he's taller than me, he can easily pull the bags down. There are two of them. One, I see, holds a few tiny canvases. The other has my brushes.

'There we are now.' Dad swipes the dust from his trousers and smiles at me. 'I hope to see some lovely pictures the next time I'm here.'

'You might see pictures,' I grin, 'but lovely they might not be.'

171

'I like a few flowers,' my mother says, 'or a hen. They're my favourite type of pictures. All that swirly stuff you did, Andy, never really appealed to me at all. Do a nice rose, or a tulip.'

I suppress a smile. I'm not a rose or tulip kind of girl. 'Yeah,' I say, 'maybe.'

'Righto,' Dad says, 'we'll be off, leave you to it.'

There is a pause. We stand in a sort of awkward triangle. Then my mother looks at my father, and through some unspoken consensus they both enfold me in a hug.

26

I RUN MY FINGER down my list of potential customers and stop at a photo shop. They specialise in enhancing pictures. I guess I can sell an ad to them. I dial their phone number and wait. Two seconds later a bright male voice says, 'Hello, Photoshop Pics.'

Downstairs I hear Luke letting his yoga students in.

'Hi,' I say back, just as brightly, yet I lower my voice to get that gravelly, husky tone into it that men seem to like. 'My name is Andrea—'

'Nice name,' the man at the other end of the phone interrupts. He sounds like he's grinning.

'Yeah, my parents certainly thought so.'

'Do you look anything like the other Andrea?'

'The other Andrea?'

'Corr, Andrea Corr. Now there's a girl with an apt surname. One look at her, you'd just go *Corrrrr.*'

It makes me laugh. 'Can I tell you why I'm ringing now?'

'You haven't answered my question. Do you look like Andrea Corr?'

'The image of her.' I'm grinning.

'OK.' The man sounds interested now. 'You can certainly tell me why you're ringing, Andrea.' He drawls out my name, and his inflections make me sound a little like a porn star.

I take a deep breath and deliver my sales spiel. 'Well, I work for *It's Your Funeral* magazine and—'

The man erupts in laughter. 'A funeral magazine? You work for a funeral magazine? Is this a joke?'

'No, it's not a joke. I do. It's a magazine dedicated to the business of burial. It's, eh, very successful.'

'Oh, and here was me thinking that the business of burial was a dying trade.'

If I had a cent for every time I heard that one . . .

He laughs at his joke, but I don't. Instead, I doodle a picture of a star on a blank page in front of me as I wait for him to stop.

'Oh, sorry,' he apologises eventually, as my deafening silence works its way down the phone line and into his consciousness. 'I didn't mean to laugh at you, it's just the joke I was laughing at.'

'I know that,' I answer, grinning. 'I just happen to have heard that joke before.'

'In another life?' More laughter.

'I'm wondering if you'd be interested in taking an ad out with us.' I speak over the laughter this time. 'I see from your ad in the *Golden Pages* that you do photo enhancement. A lot of people who come through funeral homes and who wish to put a photo of their loved one on an acknowledgement card often wish they had photographs of better quality.'

'Well,' the man says, 'if it was up to me, I'd definitely take an ad out with you. You've a lovely voice.'

'Thanks.' I roll my eyes and grin again.

'But I only work here, I don't own the place.'

'Gosh, and you sound so important.'

In fairness to him, he laughs. 'Putting you through to the boss man now,' he says. 'And a tip – tell him you're delighted Man U won at the weekend. He'll buy an ad for definite.'

'Thanks.'

The phone clicks at the other end. Click. Click. Click. As I wait for it to connect, I sigh and hope I make the sale. If I do, I've only another ten or so to sell. It was easier this month, due to Alistair giving a whole page to the flower shop. I suddenly remember that I haven't rung Mandy to tell her, so I'll make that the next call. I'm just jotting this down when an impatient male voice breaks into my reverie.

'Hello? Yes?'

I get through my sales pitch without interruption, and then in a moment of genius send my coffee mug crashing to the floor. 'Sorry,' I apologise, 'my mug just fell. It was my favourite, too, my Man United one.' OK, not the smoothest transition from selling ads for a funeral magazine to Man United, but I'm still a little pleased at my quick thinking.

'I hate Manchester United,' the man says from the other end. Then, to my gobsmacked horror, he hangs up.

I stare at the phone for a second, and then it dawns on me that Photo Shop Boy set me up. He just lost me a sale. And I even laughed at his jokes. I feel a little hurt and betrayed and very annoyed all at the one time. Damn it, I think, redialling, I'll give him a piece of my mind. I'll ask him what he—

'Andy, come here a second, would you?'

My finger freezes over the phone pad. It's Luke. What does he want? His yoga class hasn't left, as far as I know. At least, I haven't heard them leave. I glance quickly at the clock on my laptop; it's ten minutes off the hour, so they should be just finishing up now. Yes, I can hear voices from downstairs. Oh shit, I suddenly wonder if someone else has been taken ill? No, that'd be too much. But that morning I'd seen a headline on my computer about two members of the same family dying in different locations when they were struck by lightning. Oh shit!

'Andy!' Luke calls again.

'Maybe she's not here.' I recognise Eileen's voice. So at least she's still alive.

'No, she's in,' Luke says. 'Andy!' he calls once more.

'What?' I call back, hopping up from my chair and bolting out the door to the top of the stairs. Luke and Eileen are at the bottom, in the hall, looking up at me. 'What?' My eyes dart from one to the other. 'What's happened now?'

'Oh dear,' Eileen says guiltily, 'have we traumatised you so much that you think every time we come here there'll be a fatality?' She doesn't wait for me to answer. Instead she continues, flapping her hand in the direction of the kitchen, 'It's just that we have a few nice cakes we'd like to share with you, you know, to say thanks for being so kind and taking care of us so well after Fred's unfortunate episode.'

My hand darts automatically to the back of my head as I realise that my hair is pinned up in a scraggy sort of bun. They'll get a full view of my face. I'm also wearing pyjamas.

'Unfortunate episode,' Evelyn scoffs, coming to join Luke and Eileen at the end of the stairs. 'It was a cardiac failure.' She says the last two words like a dog chewing a particularly meaty bone. 'No point in dressing it up, Eileen. Thirty cigarettes a day, was it any wonder? Would you like a cake, Andrea? I hope so, as we got them for you.'

'No pressure.' Luke laughs.

I smile a little, and think that I should. It is nice of them, after all. It'd be rude to refuse, and anyway they've seen my face already so it's no big deal to them, and it'll be good practice for tomorrow when Kate and Luke take me out shopping for bread. 'OK, thanks, that's very nice of you all. I'll, eh, just throw on some clothes.'

They smile happily at me and disappear back into the kitchen.

I unpin my bun, shake my hair out and pull on yesterday's jeans and a blue sweatshirt. My feet still encased in my fluffy slipper-socks, I join them downstairs. Baz follows on my heels.

'I told them you wouldn't mind if they put on the kettle,' Luke says. 'I hope that was OK?'

'Of course it is,' I answer. 'You're just down for the washing-up.'

Baz miaows from his position at my feet. He likes to be fed whenever I eat. It's foolishness to refuse him.

'Hey bud.' Luke, as usual, attempts to pet him but Baz hisses in annoyance and follows me towards the press where I keep his food. He shows a remarkable disinterest in the three women.

Mabel, however, seems to fall for his ebony charms. 'Oh,' she exclaims, 'you have a cat. What a monster! I have a cat too, they're such lovely animals, aren't they?'

'Eh, not this one,' Luke pipes up, but it's too late. Mabel scoops an unsuspecting Baz up in her arms and attempts to cuddle him. His body becomes rigid and, claws extended, he lets out a ferocious yowl. Even I jump.

Mabel drops him as if he's on fire, which in a way he is. Baz lands on all fours, his back arched. He's like something from *The Omen* as he hisses at her. He really is quite a magnificent animal when he's angry.

'Baz!' I snap, and he starts to hiss at me too, as if it's my fault someone picked him up without his permission.

Then he stalks off out of the kitchen.

'Oh, he doesn't like you, Mabel, does he,' Evelyn chortles.

'He doesn't really like anyone,' I stammer. 'He's not used to company.'

A bit like his owner, I know they're all probably thinking. And they'd be right.

'He was abandoned as a kitten, and I think he finds it hard to trust.'

'How sad,' Eileen says. 'The poor creature.'

'You should let him join your yoga class, Luke,' Evelyn laughs again, seeming to think the whole incident is highly amusing. 'It might chill him out.'

'The only thing that would do that is a deep freeze,' Luke banters back. He glances at Mabel. 'You OK?'

'Animals normally like me,' Mabel says faintly.

'Normal animals like you, you mean,' I comfort her. 'Baz is not your run-of-the-mill cat. He barely lets me pet him.'

'I can see where you got your scratch from,' Mabel nods. 'Did he do that?'

To my embarrassment, she points to my face. Automatically I put my hand up to shield it. I think I'm going red. So they had noticed . . .

'No,' Luke answers for me, 'she got that in a bus accident just over a year ago.'

The three gasp. 'Oh, no!'

'A bus accident?'

178

'How awful!'

'So, who wants to cut the cakes?' Luke calls.

Their attention is drawn away from me and back to the feast at hand. Evelyn begins calling out orders. Mabel has to set the table, Luke can make the coffee, she is going to cut the cake and, she looks at Eileen, 'There really isn't much you can do.' Eileen bristles and glares at her.

'As for you,' Evelyn says, turning to me and ignoring the dagger looks of her yoga companion, 'you're the guest of honour, so sit down and take it easy.'

'You join me, Eileen, you can keep me company.'

'Yes, yes I shall.' Eileen sits in beside me.

I prepare myself to answer questions on the car accident, but instead Eileen asks, 'Baz is an unusual name for a cat, isn't it?'

'Not for that one.' I roll my eyes. 'I originally called him Blackie, but Baz just suited him better. Short for Bastard.'

'Oh.' Eileen seems a little taken aback at the word, and I remember that she hates the 'fart' word. 'Well, OK,' she nods, tittering uneasily, 'that makes sense now.'

Ten minutes later, the five of us are drinking coffee around my kitchen table. Next week, they tell me, Fred will be back, and they didn't want to have a party then as cake wouldn't be good for all the clogged arteries in his heart, so that's why it had to be this week.

'We're going out to clean his house for him tomorrow, so it will be dust-free when he gets back. He's all alone in the world, which is very sad.'

'Well, he has us,' Eileen says.

They all agree that indeed Fred has them.

I pick out a huge slice of cream sponge. 'Thanks,' I say shyly,

179

as they all watch me bite into it. 'I really don't think I deserve it, though. I just made a few sambos.'

'And you give us your place for yoga,' Luke reminds me.

There are murmurings of agreement.

'Oh, by the way,' Eileen interrupts, 'before I forget—'

'Which should be five minutes after she remembers,' Evelyn snorts.

'Do you mind?' Eileen glares at her. 'I am sick of your digs.'

Evelyn shrugs but doesn't apologise.

'I have organised a timetable for looking after Fred, and I'll bring it next week so we can see if it suits everyone. I've also included times for going for walks with him and—'

'When my second cousin had his heart attack, he wasn't able to walk for about a year,' Evelyn interrupts.

'Are you sure he didn't lose his leg?' Eileen giggles, obviously a little braver since she told Evelyn to cut out the smart remarks.

'There is no need to be so sarcastic,' Evelyn snaps. 'His heart attack was so bad the doctors said they'd never seen anyone survive one like it.'

'Well then maybe he was dead, and that's why he couldn't walk for a year.'

I laugh, and Evelyn grudgingly smiles too.

'Well, if Fred can't walk, we'll push him in a wheelchair,' Luke says.

They all agree that yes, this is what they'll do.

I smile. Despite their bickering, these three women are so comfortable with each other. I envy them their friendship. I haven't had that in such a long time. After the accident people did call, but when I began refusing to go out, I suppose they

180

just got fed up and drifted away. I can't blame them. It's what I wanted at the time, to be left alone with no one pressuring me to go anywhere. Besides, they were never as close to me as Lexi was. Or Chas.

I long for friends, I realise suddenly. Ones I can talk to, confide in, bicker with. Real flesh-and-blood friendships. OK, I've got Alistair, I suppose, but he's my boss too, so it's not the same. Maybe when I get back on my feet I'll join some sort of yoga class and meet people too.

This, for instance, is the first time in almost two years that I've had coffee with people I don't really know. It feels like putting on an old, loved jumper. Not extraordinary, not even thrilling, just as if it's normal and comfortable. I'd never have said before that coffee with post-menopausal women would be my natural element, but I'm finding it surprisingly easy to enjoy. Across the table, Luke is digging into a cream slice. Icing sugar falls like dust onto his clothes and Eileen reaches over, laughing, and brushes it off him. He catches me looking and winks over. And I know that I want more of this easy, no-strings normality.

I will go to that shop and buy bread, I tell myself. If it's the last bloody thing I do, I'm going to get out there.

27

S HE CAN'T HELP it. She has to google him. So, when she
should be working, she trawls the internet for information on Mike and the Misfortunes.

And . . . bingo.

*Mike and The Misfortunes were a very promising heavy metal
band based in London who had one hit single, 'Daydreams'. It
reached number one and two in the British and Irish charts respec-
tively. The band released two albums,* Death by Fire *and*
Economy, *neither of which charted. The band subsequently
broke up.*

Below the article was a picture of the five band members.
Their faces were in slight shadow and to be honest, it was
impossible to know which one was Doug, but the five lads
looked like stereotypical musicians. Long hair, faded jeans
encasing lean legs, white t-shirts, arms folded and semi-
bored looks on their faces as they lounged languidly against
a heavily graffitied wall. She found it sad to think they'd
once been so promising, and were now in dire financial
straits.

Their music can be downloaded here.

A red button flashed. It said 'download' in big black writing.

One press and some details, and the album was installed on the hard drive.

Next thing was to approach Peter with it.

28

B ROAD DAYLIGHT. I'VE never understood that expression before, but now I think I do a little. With Luke on one side and Kate on the other, I'm stepping outside my apartment for the first time in nearly a year. In daylight. The brightness makes everything look so much bigger, broader. Night-time hides nooks and crannies, stops you seeing too far ahead. Daylight washes over everything, making it gleam and shine and dazzle. Things you might never notice at night leap up to capture your gaze, rivet your eyes so that you can't look away.

The door to my apartment is off-white. It has a big scratch going down it. The carpet in the foyer is bleached where the sun catches it. The lift to the foyer looks a little grubby on the outside. The foyer appears vast and bright, the postboxes polished, their stainless steel glinting in the hard light. The doors to the outside look huge and heavy. I freeze. Kate and Luke don't know, but I've been dry-retching all morning.

They look at me questioningly.

'It's so big,' I say, and I know I don't make any sense to them. 'All this.' I gesture weakly around. 'In the daytime.'

Kate looks at Luke, who looks back at Kate.

Kate is the one to speak. 'Don't you want to do it?' I can hear the disappointment in her voice.

If I had a choice, then no, I don't want to do it. But do I have a choice?

'Maybe if you just, I dunno, stand outside the front door and then come back in, how about that?'

I consider it. My knees are trembling, which surprises me. I can feel my heart beat in my throat, like a bird has got trapped in there. And I suppose it's true. I've been trapped inside for so long.

'Well?' Luke asks. 'It's your call.'

I think of him with his yoga class yesterday. Strangers who became friends. The laugher. The banter between the women. The only contact I have with the world is when I tap away on my computer or chat on the phone. I suddenly feel awfully sorry for people like me who live like that, confined between four walls, afraid of what might happen, so they ensure that nothing happens. It can't be me any more. I take a deep breath, ready to throw myself onto the pyre, and I look at Kate. She's dressed all cool and casual, in a pair of tight jeans and a lime-green sweatshirt. There is a pair of sunglasses perched on top of her head, holding back her glorious mane of hair.

'Can I take your sunglasses?' I ask in a moment of inspiration. They'll give me the impression of night-time and make me feel more closed in.

Kate looks a little startled, but she pulls them from her head and hands them to me. 'I'm only wearing them to keep my hair back, it's not exactly summertime out there.'

I don't care. I put them on and immediately relax. 'OK,' I nod, 'let's go.'

Luke strides ahead and pushes open the front door. Immediately the noise of the day rushes towards me. Night is so much quieter on my street. Today there are lorries and trucks and cars all crawling along, engines chugging, horns blasting, radios blaring from wound-down windows. Someone with a barking dog jogs by, a kid cries, there's the jangle of keys, the crash of something falling, a shout, a roar. The bleep of the traffic lights. The traffic moves, and is replaced by more traffic. It's as if a whole year's worth of sound assaults me. I gasp again.

'Andy?' Kate has gripped my arm. 'Are you OK? You've gone a bit pale.'

'I'm fine.' I try to sound fine, though behind the sunglasses my eyes are squeezed shut, as if that somehow will block out the noise. I steady myself against her. 'Sorry to be such a wuss.'

'Take your time. You're grand.' She points down the road to where a sign saying Roy's swings a little in the slight breeze. 'That's the shop. It's only twenty seconds away.'

'I'll walk in front if you like,' Luke offers. 'That way, all you have to do is look at me.'

'Do you want her to get sick?' Kate snorts, and Luke laughs, a deep rumbling sound.

'That would be great, Luke, thanks. Sorry to drag you into this. You must think Kate's family are totally for the birds.'

He just smiles and starts to walk. Kate holds onto my arm but as we get going, a young fella who has been standing around gawking at us, says loudly to his mate, 'Look at the two lezzers.'

'I am not a lesbian,' Kate turns around to him, thereby

186

letting me go, 'and if I was, it's not a big deal, you know. Why don't you grow up?' She attempts to catch me again but I shrug her off. It's my first time out in two years, I have a massive scar on my face which I'm afraid people will comment on, I really do not need puerile schoolboys giving me a lesbian tag on top of everything else.

I square my shoulders and follow Luke as he strides along. Due to Kate's exchange, he's moved further away than I thought. He disappears into Roy's, and I hurry to follow him.

I've never been in Roy's before as I do all my shopping online. It's bigger than I would have imagined, with everything laid out in an easy-to-find manner. Kate has already given me directions to the bread, as I really didn't want to wander about in a panic looking for it. But it's nice to be among real things again. I want to reach out and touch the shelves of biscuits and squeeze orange after orange. I'd like to lift up the shampoos and smell them, or spray a bit of deodorant and decide which one I'd like. But of course I don't. Other people are there, and I know one or two of them have glanced at my face as I make my way to the bread, my head down. I'm so tempted to walk about with my palm concealing the scar but I'd look even odder then, so I keep going, Kate and Luke following behind like anxious parents of a toddler that's just learned to walk.

I find the bread and give it a squeeze to see if it's fresh. It is, so I pick it up and turn to go back to the cash register.

'Hold your head up,' Kate whispers as I pass her. 'You look like a shoplifter.'

I realise that I've been staring at my shoes a lot, so I

gradually lift my gaze to focus straight ahead. Kate and Luke allow me to pass them, and again they fall in behind me. Nearer and nearer I draw to the till. There is only one open, and there is a little bit of a queue. I stand in line and wait my turn. A woman with a screaming toddler seems to be having difficulty finding her purse. From behind my glasses, I can see how flustered the woman is getting as the child screams and throws himself down on the floor in a temper because she has refused to buy him a treat.

'I'm sorry about this,' she calls timidly to the rest of us as she fumbles about in an enormous black bag, which seems to have more compartments in it than the Orient Express. Eventually she pulls out a black purse, shiny to match her bag, and her hands are shaking so much her money spills out everywhere.

'Sorry, sorry, sorry,' she calls again, flapping her hand and blushing. Her child meanwhile has grabbed a fistful of coins and is dancing around the place chortling that he won't give her the money back.

'Should give him a smack, love,' someone says loudly.

The woman blushes some more, and after paying scurries away, her child dancing boldly ahead.

'Well,' Kate says, 'no matter what happens to you, Andy, it's not going to be any more embarrassing than that.'

'Um, yeah, I guess.'

And then the kid sitting in the trolley in front of us starts to look at me. He does it quite subtly at first, his head cocked to one side, a puzzled sort of look on his face. I pull slightly back from his eye line and Kate looks questioningly at me. I say nothing, but the boy has now stood up in the shopping trolley and is peering over Kate's head at me. I angle my face away from him, sweat breaking out on my palms.

'Mammy.' The boy is tugging his mother's sleeve, all the while looking at me.

Oh God, I want to die. He'll announce it to the whole shop.

Again I turn away from him, only making it more obvious this time.

'Mammy.' The boy is now tugging and speaking with more urgency.

'What?' his mother is preoccupied, placing her items on the conveyor belt. 'What is it?'

'That girl . . .' There's no mistaking it now, as his chubby finger jabs in my direction.

My stomach heaves. Why did I decide to do this? I can't have everyone staring at me, I just can't. And yet if I run, they'll stare too.

Luke has his arm suddenly in my arm and Kate is glaring balefully at the boy, who doesn't seem to notice, he's too intent on staring at me.

'That girl, look Mammy.' The boy giggles loudly and one or two people look at me. 'She's wearing sunglasses and it's not even sunny.'

Oh God. Kate hiccups back a laugh, and beside me I can feel Luke shaking slightly. Meanwhile, all eyes are trained on the freak with the sunglasses.

I smile through my mortification. 'I've had an eye operation,' I lie. 'Have to wear sunglasses for a bit.'

'Oh.' The mother looks mortified. 'I'm sorry about that,' she indicates her son, 'he's always commenting on people.'

189

'Sure, that's kids for you,' Luke says cheerily. 'If it isn't one thing it's another.'

The mother smiles at us and then turns away.

'He has funny hair,' the boy pipes up, and is silenced by a lollipop shoved into his mouth.

29

PETER IS NOT that keen. He remains silent as Lexi tells him all about Doug and how he's now bankrupt, and that maybe by playing his music in the gallery his albums would get more notice.

'I've listened to the album, the first one,' she says, 'and it's very good.'

'Galleries don't need music,' Peter replies somewhat loftily. 'They're meant to be places of relaxation.'

'My arse.'

'I mean it.' Peter sounds as if he does. He stalks over to the reception desk and ensconces himself behind it. Adjusting his suit, he continues, 'I'm not a record shop, Lex, I'm here to run a gallery and thanks to you, things are looking up. We've over a thousand entries so far, with an average of fifty a day coming in. The online novelty has really taken off. But,' he pauses, 'I really can't have any music.'

Lexi follows him over to the desk and leans across, staring at him. 'If you don't play his music, I'll tell everyone that you've no judge for the competition.'

'As it happens, I do have a judge, or at least I should by the end of the week.' Peter turns his back on her, obviously disgusted. 'And I don't like being blackmailed.'

Lexi steps back in the face of his obvious disapproval. She supposes it was a cheap shot. And he's probably right – galleries are not normally places of music. But still. 'I'm sorry, Peter. It's just that Doug is a mate.'

'You hardly know him.' Peter is dismissive.

'I do know him. I spend more time with him, Lordi and Cissy than I do here.'

'Look, I'm sure he'll appreciate your efforts but Lex, you have to understand that if I want to be taken seriously, I can't go promoting music for people *you* know in *my* gallery.'

'Don't people take big hotshot businessmen seriously anyway?'

'Sure they do, but big hotshot businessmen, as you so disparagingly call them, have to take themselves seriously first.'

'I wasn't being disparaging. I was only—'

'Anything else?' He pretends to be working.

'Will you at least listen to it? He even said he'd write something special for the gallery if you like.'

Peter sighs. 'Fine. I'll listen to it. Send it to me, I'll listen on the computer.'

'I already did.'

He allows himself a laugh.

Lexi smiles back. After a second's pause, she asks if he needs any help.

'No, take off. I'm heading out now for a run. Go spend some time with those friends you seem to have made. If you get a chance, you should go view the competition entries online, Lex. Some really great stuff from some really good artists. I put the best ones on the first few pages.'

'Has Yellow T-Shirt done anything?' She tries to make it

a casual enquiry. There's something about him that interests her. Maybe it's his disinterest.

'Yellow T-Shirt?'

'The guy on the beach who always wears the yellow t-shirts and stares out to sea.'

'I'm never at the beach. Does he call himself that? Yellow T-Shirt?'

Lexi nods. 'To me, anyway.'

Peter shrugs. 'Maybe he's afraid you're a crazed stalker.'

She smiles.

'Well, I don't think we have any entries from a Yellow T-Shirt.'

Lexi nods and turns to leave. 'Don't forget to check that album out, d'you hear me?'

'Aye, aye, boss.'

'That's what I like to hear.' He is still laughing as she exits.

Yellow T-Shirt is, as usual, sitting on the beach facing the sea. He turns as Lexi approaches. 'Hey.'

'You busy pondering the questions of life and death?' she teases as she sits down beside him.

'I was, but now I'm pondering how to get rid of unwanted attention.'

'Madly funny.'

He smiles briefly. 'You?'

'Nothing better to do. There's no one around this morning except for you. How's the painting going?'

'Good.' He turns back to the sea again. 'Better than before, at least I think so.'

'Did you enter the competition? Aside from here, it's been mentioned in the national papers in Ireland and England.'

'You show-off!'

She smiles. 'So? Did you enter?'

'I did.'

She feels flattered, for some reason. 'Let me guess, you painted the sea?'

He laughs.

'So, what's your picture like, then?'

'Blue.'

'Jesus, you crack me up.'

He laughs again. 'Well, I painted the sea and the horizon.' He stresses the 'and'. Pointing out towards the sea, his hand traces the line of the horizon. 'From here, it's hard to tell them apart, eh?'

'Yep.'

'I think what I was trying to do was figure out where solid ground ends and the sky, fantasy, begins. You know, the line between one and the other. Real life and imagination. Being on holiday as opposed to being in real life.'

'Sounds good.'

'I don't know if I got it right, though. That's what I'm doing here.'

'That's like looking at an exam book after the test.'

'Yeah, I guess.' Yellow T-Shirt nods, and after a second or two, he heaves himself to his feet. Looking down on her, he asks, 'Did you enter?'

'That'd hardly be fair.' Lexi stands up too. 'Anyway, what makes you think I'm an artist?'

'I dunno.' Yellow T-Shirt shakes his head, seeming surprised suddenly. 'I just assumed . . .'

'What else did you assume?'

He laughs. 'Well, you mightn't want me to answer that.'

194

'Go on.'

'OK, like everyone here, I assume you're looking for some fun, or an escape, a diversion, a break before you go back to your real life.' He waves his arm around, encompassing the beach and the village and the sun and the sea. 'This isn't really a place to spend all your time, is it?'

Lexi can't answer for a moment. His words hit her hard. Recovering, she asks, 'So, I take it that's true for you too?'

Yellow T-Shirt shrugs. 'I'm just here to check it out.'

'Oh.' That's a disappointing answer.

'I wanted to know where the horizon lies. You know, the line you can't cross.'

'We all know that.'

'I don't think people do.' He nods to her before beginning to walk away. 'Don't get trapped being here.'

'Hey!' She runs to catch up with him, a thought striking her. 'You're leaving, aren't you?'

'My picture is called *Fine Line*.' He offers her a small smile. 'See ya, Lexi. If I win, you'll see me about, yeah?'

She's hardly got to know him. She thought she'd have ages to find out about him, but his air of mystery wasn't an act, he really didn't want to talk or interact. He just wanted to be here, to observe, so that he could paint his bloody pictures. 'Are you leaving?' she asks again.

'Yep.' He holds out his hand and touches her. 'Check out the picture.'

'I will.' She feels like crying, she doesn't know why. She guesses that she just hates when things leave her life un-expectedly, and she'd got used to seeing him in his position by the beach. To being slagged by him and slagging back.

It's ridiculous, almost as if he has become part of her life. 'What's your name?'

'It's on the picture.'

Of course. 'Come back someday. Just for a visit.'

He doesn't reply.

Lexi thinks he will never return.

The picture is on the website, and it's magnificent. It's blue, very blue, but there is still that distinct horizon there. If you want to see it, you can, and if you don't it just makes the picture look like a blue canvas. It gives her the shivers just looking at it.

She searches for a signature, and there it is – Yale Thomas Styles. Yellow T-Shirt. She traces the picture on the computer screen and remembers another one of his pictures hanging in the Welcome Centre of Salue. She googles his name.

Nothing.

'Good luck, Yale Thomas Styles,' she whispers.

30

'H EY,' I say into the receiver, 'how you doing? It's the girl that looks like Andrea Corr here.'

There is the slightest of pauses. A wariness in the way the man at the other end drawls out a 'Yesss?'

'Is it you I was talking to the other day?'

Another pause. 'Eh, were you the girl selling the ads for the funeral thingy?'

'That would be me,' I reply chirpily. 'And it's not a "funeral thingy", it's a magazine. And I am ringing to say that I did not appreciate the way you set me up.'

'Did you not?' He sounds a tad defensive.

'Not only did you cost me an ad, but you probably cost your boss money, too. Think of how many sales you might have got from a little bit of advertisement.'

There is silence from the other end. It seems to go on for ages.

'Hello?' I say.

'I'm thinking,' the man says back.

Despite myself, I smile. 'Very funny.'

His voice has a smile in it too as he says, 'OK, look, I'm sorry about that. I did feel a bit guilty about it afterwards. It was just a prank. It's a thing we have going, me and Joe.

197

That's the boss. He's a City supporter, and I'm United. I couldn't resist it.'

'Yes, well, I have a job to do, and I'd appreciate not getting dragged into your . . .' I can't think how to phrase it. 'Games,' I finally say, omitting the 'childish', as it'd probably annoy him and I don't want to do that. At least, not unless I have to.

'Sorry about that. How about you let me buy you a drink to apologise?'

I'm slightly taken aback. 'Do you always offer to buy your callers a drink?'

'No. But then again, they don't all look like Andrea Corr.'

'Neither do I.'

'You mean you lied to me?' He attempts an anguished moan. 'And I trusted you!'

'Just like I did you.' I smirk.

'Touché.' He pauses, then asks jokingly. 'Do you look as sexy as you sound? Your voice is pure Harley-Davidson.'

I ignore his attempt to soft-soap me. My motto when selling is nothing ventured, nothing gained, and I'd been so close to selling an ad to his boss. 'I'm ringing to ask if there is any chance, seeing as I obliged you with a good laugh, of you spending a couple of weeks putting the idea of advertising into your boss's head. Then I ring him again, and *voilà*.'

He hesitates before saying, 'Uh – I dunno. He is my boss. I can't tell him stuff I don't know is true.'

'He'll still be making the decision whether to advertise or not,' I say patiently. I kind of like the idea that he has some scruples.

'Hmm.'

'I just thought it'd be worth a shot. I mean, you did lose me a sale. I was so close.'

198

'Yeah?'

'Yep.'

'If I refuse?'

'Nothing lost. I'll just think you're a bit of a loser.'

'Jesus, I can't have that. And if I agree?'

'All to gain, maybe.'

'And if I agree and you make the sale?'

'I will be grateful for ever.'

'Oooh, sounds promising.'

I roll my eyes.

'OK. You've got a deal. But if it works out, I'll take you up on the "grateful".'

Yet again, I ignore his comment. 'OK. Thanks. I'll be in touch in two weeks' time.'

'Looking forward to it.'

I laugh again and hang up. That's one sale I hope to get.

Next, I dial Alistair's mystery woman.

'Hello?' A nice voice, I think. Cheerful.

'Hi, this is Andrea from *It's Your Funeral* and I just—'

'*It's your Funeral*? The magazine?' The voice has changed from cheery to instantly suspicious. I curse Alistair for this.

'Yes,' I say. 'And I—'

'I don't want to take out an ad, I don't want a piece done, I want nothing more to do with that magazine and its creepy owner.'

'Oh right, well, that's pretty decisive.' I am at a complete loss. 'So, eh, you don't want a free one-page ad in prime position, then?'

A pause. 'Free?'

'Uh-huh.'

'Listen, honey,' now the voice has gone from suspicious to caustic, 'there is no such thing as a free ad. What does Alistair want me to do now? Tell everyone my business is crap? Fight with every restaurateur in the country? Sleep with him?'

'I think he'd like the last offer all right,' I joke feebly, and she slams down the phone.

Shit.

Two seconds later, the phone rings. It's Alistair.

'I have just had a terrible email from Mandy,' he moans. 'What did you do?'

'Nothing,' I lie.

'You told her I wanted to sleep with her!'

'It was a joke,' I say feebly. 'Your girlfriend has no sense of humour.'

'She is not my girlfriend, and hardly likely to be now.'

'I'll ring her back. Explain.'

'Do not!' He pauses. 'I'll think of something.'

'Will I run the ad?'

'Just let me think. I'll get back to you.' He hangs up.

He's going to a lot of effort for no return, I think as I dial Mandy back. Whatever Alistair says to her, I reckon I have a better shot. Of course he'll kill me if it goes wrong, but then again, he can't really fire me.

'Hello?' Again the bright cheery voice.

'Hi,' I match hers. Then, without explaining who I am, which will make her hang up, I'm sure, I say hastily, 'A full-page ad, no strings, only joking about having to sleep with him. He's mad about you, a complete idiot when it comes to dating, but a brilliant man, what do you say?'

As expected, she is stunned. Then she says, 'Pardon?'

'An ad, no strings,' I say.

'An ad, no strings?' she repeats.

'As an apology from a guy who is spectacularly bad at dating. Who saw you in your dress and felt he couldn't bring you to his pizza place.'

'Does he tell you everything?'

'Oh no,' I lie. 'Absolutely not, but he wanted me to ring you about the ad as he was sure you'd hang up on him. I'm his saleswoman. He's my boss.'

'You could refuse to do that sort of work for him. Does he threaten to fire you if you don't do what he says?'

'I hope not.' I manage a laugh. 'He told me not to ring you again.'

She laughs uneasily, no doubt aware that my fate might lie in her hands. 'He's a bit odd, isn't he?' she manages eventually.

'He's shy,' I say, feeling annoyed that she would think lovely Alistair odd. 'It makes him ridiculously awkward, but he's not a psycho or anything. He's used to dealing in grief and dead people. Not in girlfriends.'

'Oh.'

Shit, I think I've put her off.

'And he's kind and into vintage cars and reading, and he's into our magazine and, well, he's also into you, actually.'

There is a silence. 'Are you his mother, or something?' she sounds wary. 'You seem to like him a lot yourself.'

I make a scoffing sound. 'Well?' I ask.

'OK,' she agrees slowly, sounding a little shell-shocked. 'Right . . . well . . . I'll take the ad. But I can't guarantee that I'll take him.'

'That's good enough for now.' I heave a sigh of relief. 'Is there anything he can do to make himself more appealing to you?'

'Yeah, he can start by ditching the black.'

'I'll let him know.'

'Bye now.' She sounds as if she's smiling.

'See you.'

I type an email. *She'll take the ad. Not you, though, until you ditch the black. Maybe not even then unless you start acting the way I know you can act, which is NORMAL.*

He takes his time replying. I'm about to call him when my inbox pings.

I told you not to ring her.

I type back: *Did you? Sorry.*

He types: *Apology accepted. What colour would suit me?*

I type: *Something bright, as you're so dark. Blue or red.*

He types: *Ta. Good work.*

I log off. It's been a good day.

31

Two trips to Roy's, one without the glasses. One to my 'stuck in the seventies' next-door neighbour, Bert, to ask to borrow some milk. One trip to return the borrowed milk. That was scary, as he had a load of friends visiting and they all thought that I was his mystery girlfriend and they crowded around the door to see me, whooping and cheering. I wouldn't mind, but the man is definitely in his fifties and his friends were all grey and balding, but as Kate says, when men don't settle down they start acting younger again. I've also had tea with the yoga ladies and Fred. No one seemed to notice my scar, or if they did, they were great at hiding it. Drip by drip, like a bucket filling with rainwater, my confidence is slowly building. I'm sure the slightest tip will send a lot of it splashing out, but I'm determined to keep going. Today I've decided to go to Roy's without Kate and Luke. I haven't told them because for some reason Kate is a bit stressed out over a meeting she has to go to about her show.

I'm in the foyer trying to get myself psyched up to go out.

'Hello you!' It's my next-door neighbour, Bert, the one with the mystery girlfriend. Judging from his appearance – a royal-blue cardigan and red shirt, which is opened to reveal copious amounts of chest hair – she'll soon be an ex-girlfriend.

'Hi Bert.' I try out a smile, despite the anxiety crawling away at me. 'How's things?'

'Oh, you know,' Bert rocks on his heels, 'fabulous!' He slaps his hands together and smiles. His teeth are dazzling, he's obviously had them bleached. 'Well, can't chat. Places to go, you know.'

'Uh-huh. See you.'

He nods at me and I watch as he struts confidently out the door. It's only then I notice his red Doc boots. They make me smile.

Then it's my turn to exit. As I push the door open, I realise that the noise isn't as shocking as it was at first, but it still gives me a start. I take a deep breath, let the door swing shut behind me and then, like a high diver, throw myself into the throng.

I'm on my way back, high on the thrill of my achievement. I managed to stroll around Roy's at a steady pace, smelling the deodorants, pondering which bread to buy, the one with the nutty bits or not. I even chatted with the cashier about the weather as I handed over an exorbitant amount of money for a few groceries. But I'd gladly have paid double, I'm so giddy on the freedom of knowing that I can go outside and pick up whatever I like in the local shops whenever I feel like it. It's a heady feeling, as if I've just been given the world back to play in.

And then I see him. Standing outside my building, looking up at my window, his hand shading his eyes from the glare of the sun.

Chas.

And then he turns, and his gaze falls on me.

My heart lurches so violently that I think I might be sick. He pauses for a second before raising his hand in a silent greeting. Then he smiles that familiar smile, the one that I seem to have known all my life, and starts to move towards me. I realise suddenly that I've stopped dead in the middle of the street and that people are passing me by and looking curiously at me. I give myself a mental shake, swallow hard and start to walk towards him. He looks the same, but different. He seems to have abandoned his dress sense completely, and is wearing a tattered pair of jeans and an old leather motor-bike jacket over a grandfather shirt. Even his trainers have seen better days. His face, though, despite the short hair, gives me the same pang it always did, only this time it's tinged with sadness. As usual, he has a camera slung around his neck.

I wish I'd bothered washing my hair, so that at least I'd look half decent. My own old jeans and faded red sweatshirt are rivalling his for dinginess.

'Hey.' Chas smiles again, though it looks a bit forced. His eyes don't crinkle up in the way I remember. 'I was actually just about to call in on you.'

That's a bit of a shocker. 'Why? Is everything OK?'

'Uh-huh. I, eh . . .' He pauses and fiddles with the camera strap. Awkwardly, he mutters, 'I just wondered if you'd like to go for a coffee?'

'Why?' I am suddenly sweaty. How can I go for a coffee? I can't trust myself in an unfamiliar place just yet, especially with a guy I used to love so bloody much. His every gesture reminds me of how much we've lost.

'I dunno. Just to have a coffee.'

'I, eh, I'm sort of busy,' I answer lamely.

'Oh.' His smile dips. 'Tomorrow, maybe?'

205

He'll keep going until I agree, I realise. Then he'll know from all my refusals that I'm a total reclusive loser. He'll also uncover the fact that for the last year, I've been lying to his parents about my great life. The humiliation would kill me. 'I can manage a quick coffee now if you want to come up to my apartment?' Without waiting for him to answer, I push open the door to the foyer and he follows behind. I'm acutely aware of him standing at my shoulder as I press the button for the lift. When it arrives, he stands alongside me. I can smell his freshly laundered clothes and the aftershave he uses. I take in the tanned hands and the clean nails. The lift pings to a stop and I exit hastily, him bringing up the rear. I wonder what he wants? I ache to touch him, but it's the worst thing I could do. Already I'm crying inside.

'This place hasn't changed,' Chas remarks as he follows me to my door.

'It's only been over a year since you were here,' I say a little shortly.

'I know, but . . .' He doesn't finish his sentence.

Opening the door to my apartment, I'm suddenly assaulted by the mess. I hadn't noticed before, but I cringe as I see it through my visitor's eyes. It's as if a scud missile has landed in the middle of the hallway, making clothes explode every-where. About ten of Kate's jackets are either hanging at the end of the stairway or piled in a heap on the floor. She'd tried them all on before going to her meeting, asking me which ones made her look more professional. An abandoned haversack of Luke's lies underneath a plastic bag containing knick-knacks they've salvaged from their flat. A skirt hangs from a doorframe. Trying to ignore it, I step gingerly into the kitchen where a pile of laundry is heaped beside the washing machine ready to go in. I step over it to get to the kettle.

'Kate and her boyfriend Luke are staying with me for a while,' I explain, indicating the mess. 'Their flat burned down.'

'Jesus!'

I am conscious that he has slid into the chair he always sat in when he came here. Again my poor heart aches a little. My back to him, I fill the kettle, water splashing onto my hands and spotting my clothes. I'm actually nervous. Nervous and sick. I wonder what the hell he wants. Just as I'm about to ask, Baz slinks into the kitchen, miaowing plaintively, looking for food.

'Hey.' Chas swivels on the chair to look at him. 'Blackie, mate, how are you?'

'His name is Baz,' I say back. 'I changed it. It suits him better.'

'Hey Baz.' Chas rubs his fingers together and calls the cat.

Baz gazes at him, his head cocked to one side before trotting delicately towards him and purring delightedly as Chas rubs his back. Traitor.

'I think he remembers me.' Chas is also delighted. 'D'you remember me, eh?'

Baz purrs even louder.

'He's like that with everyone,' I lie childishly. 'He's a very friendly cat. Hey Baz,' I call and tap a fork against his tin of food, determined to get him away from this interloper.

Baz abandons Chas somewhat reluctantly. I pile some food into his dish and wish he was human so I could berate him for his disloyalty.

'You've taken good care of him.' Chas admires the enormous feline that the once cute kitten has become.

207

Chas had given me Baz when I was discharged from hospital after the accident. My mother had not been impressed. 'You can hardly look after yourself, and he thinks you can manage a cat.'

But apparently Chas had been under the impression that an animal was therapeutic. How wrong he'd been, though he hadn't stuck around long enough to find out.

'What do you want?' I ask, the words spilling out of my mouth without me even being aware I was going to ask.

Chas flinches, before tearing his eyes from Baz. He fixes me with a solemn gaze.

My stomach flips.

'You were never a girl for beating around the bush.' He half smiles.

I'm not going to fall for his easy charm. 'Well?'

Chas swallows a little, perhaps taken aback by my apparent coldness. 'I dunno. I just . . .' He stops abruptly; his eyes flit to his hands, then up to meet mine again. It seems to me as if he is thinking about what he should say. 'Well,' he begins again, 'ever since I saw you at the folks' house, I've had this urge to talk to you, I dunno why.' He sounds embarrassed. 'I guess, well, I sort of missed you, missed the fact that you knew Lexi, and I realised it when I saw you that Sunday.'

I'd missed him too. I'd never not realised it though. I'd just decided to live with it. Seeing him here sitting in his old place hurts me more than I'd ever imagined. 'Talk to me about what?'

'I dunno. Anything.'

'Nuclear war? The possibility of the government losing the next election? What?'

He seems a little stunned at my flippancy. But it was either that or burst into tears.

'I just thought, you know, we could be friends.'

'Friends? Why?' I can't be friends with him. How can I be friends with someone I thought I had a chance to be with for ever? With someone who didn't seem to understand that?

'Andy, don't be like this. We got on great. We were close once.'

'Until you left me for a job.' My voice wobbles. It still hurts.

'I didn't bloody leave you! I asked you to come with me.'

'And I said no and you still went.'

'I had to work!'

'I had just been in a bad accident, I had lost my best friend and you thought I'd uproot and go with you?'

'Well, being here was doing you no good. You wouldn't go out before I left; you wouldn't look for a job. I thought it would be good for you. I knew it would be good for me to get away. And,' he falters a little, swallows, 'don't you forget, Lexi was my sister.'

'I know that.' I'm instantly contrite. My voice softens. 'I know she was.'

'I just wanted you to come with me,' he says.

'Well, Chas, I wanted you to stay with me.'

He swallows hard and winces.

'I mean, if you cared about me you would have stayed. As far as I'm concerned, you looked after yourself. You upped and left.'

He looks at me and for an instant his eyes seem to fill up with tears, but I think I imagine it because he stands up and glares at me. 'Fine. If that's what you think.'

'What else can I think?'

209

'Forget it, Andy.' He sounds pissed off.

'You're the one that brought it up.'

'D'you know what?' He shakes his head, 'I think I'll go.'

'Well, get out of here then.' Even as I say it, I realise I'm hurting myself.

'Fine. I will.' He turns to leave, then pauses before turning back towards me. Now he is angry, because his voice rises and he jabs his finger at me. 'D'you know what? You're a great one for blaming stuff on me, but you seem to conveniently forget that you left *me* to go travelling with Lexi. Did I stop you? No. And why not? 'Cause you and Lexi had talked about it for so long, way before we ever got together. I knew you wanted to do it and I wasn't going to stand in your way, even though you'd have been gone for a bloody year.'

'Yeah, well, if it bothered you that much you could have come with us!'

'You never asked me.'

'Did we have to? All you had to do was say you wanted to come.'

'All you had to do was say you wanted me there.'

We glare at each other across the table, a year of mis-understandings lying between us. I finally snap out, 'You said you were going!'

But he's on a roll. 'When I wanted to go away, you dumped me. You wouldn't wait, would you? I was happy to wait for you.'

'Don't go twisting things—'

'It's not twisting things from where I'm standing!'

'Well, go and stand somewhere else then.'

Baz miaows frantically from the floor.

'And don't go upsetting my cat.'

210

'Jesus!' His eyes narrow. 'You always were a self-centred cow.'

'Oh, that makes me really want to meet up with you! Did you leave all your charm behind in India?'

'I wouldn't meet up with you now if you were Our Lord.'

'If I were Our Lord, I wouldn't have created you in the first place.'

His answer to that is to stomp out of my apartment, slamming the front door. I have a fleeting sense of pride in my final comment before bursting into tears.

Two hours later, all thoughts of Chas have been firmly buried under a mountain of work. My red eyes have cleared up, and I've told Baz how awful he was to go and be friendly to such a man. Still, what Chas had said about me leaving to travel with Lexi niggles a little. Maybe, part of me says meekly, maybe he does have a point. But he'd never said for me not to go, so how was I to know he wasn't that happy about it? And why hadn't he just been honest with me? Why hadn't he asked to come with us? Probably for the same reason I hadn't asked him to come. Because we'd only been together for four months, and I hadn't wanted to pressure him, hadn't wanted him to think that I was planning a huge future for us in case it would scare him off. If he had wanted to come, I imagine he'd have asked. And besides, his photography was taking off, and I didn't want to jeopardise it for him, but maybe, maybe I should have offered him the choice. But then again, he could be dead or missing now, too, so maybe our misconceptions had saved his life. It's the only positive thing to focus on.

And he'd still left me for India anyway.

I shake my head. Concentrate on work again by running down my to-do list, and see that I've a teeny bit of designing to do on one page, and am in the middle of calling up the programme on my computer when Kate arrives back. The furious way she slams the door reminds me of Chas earlier, and I catch my breath.

'Everything OK down there?' I call, not really expecting much of an answer.

'Everything is shite!' To my horror, she dissolves into tears.

Abandoning the computer, I rush down to see what's up. She's sitting at the kitchen table, the heels of her hands pressed against her eyes.

'Kate?' I am unsure what to do, scared of what she's about to tell me. I have a dread of bad news. 'Sorry,' she sniffs, lifting her face briefly to take in my concern, 'I didn't want to cry outside.'

'What's happened?' I move closer to the table, heart pounding, hands sweaty. 'Is it Mam? Dad? Luke?'

She shakes her head and relief washes over me. 'Well, it can't be too bad then,' I say. Ever since the accident, nothing bar death bothers me.

She splutters out a tearful laugh before beginning to sob again.

I do a Mammy on it. I squash in beside her and rub her back, muttering soothing things like 'shush' and 'hush' and 'it'll be all right'. Finally I wrap my arm about her shoulder and pull her to me. 'What's wrong? Tell me, go on.'

'They fired me,' she hiccups. 'They fired me.'

I think I'm hearing this wrong. 'Sorry? They what? Who did?'

'They-fired-me,' she annunciates, before more tears drip

from her eyes and she scrubs them away with her fist. It's a curiously childish gesture and I hug her again.

'Your job? The radio station?'

'Uh-huh.'

'Why? Can they just do that?'

'Clause something-or-other of my contract says they can, especially if I don't deliver the goods.'

'What goods?' I'm lost. I hadn't been expecting this at all.

'Sex talk, sex calls, crap, in other words.'

'But I thought that's what you did do.'

Kate manages to look indignant for a second before her bottom lip wobbles again. 'You're so right, that is what I did. Total crap.'

'I didn't mean—'

'And I wanted to change it and I have been changing it, have you not been tuning in?'

I never listen to her show. There is something quite unsettling hearing your younger sibling talking about sex on the radio. 'I work in the afternoons, so no.'

'Well, I slowly started introducing other topics. I had Luke's old lady on, what's her name, Mabel, you remember? Well, that caused massive trouble for me. And there have been others over the past few weeks, and my researchers got in trouble over it and they blamed me and they were right, it was me. Anyway, today the bosses told me that if I didn't toe the line, I'd have to go. So I resigned.'

'So you weren't fired?'

'Well, it's the same thing. I've no job.' And she's off again.

'But I thought you loved doing your show?'

'When I started off I did. But I want a new challenge. I was brilliant at the interview for the breakfast show, but I didn't get

213

it because they wanted a big name for it. And Andy, I know I would have been better. But I'm sort of stereotype-cast or whatever it is you call it, everyone thinks I'm nothing but a dirty talker.'

'They don't.'

'They do.' She looks crossly at me. 'Remember the paper last year? Kate Talks Dirty?'

'Hmm.' She'd been discussing the merits of recycling, and they'd used a photo of her in a swimsuit standing beside a clothes recycling bin.

'And I'm sick of hearing words like,' she scrunches up her pretty face, 'like dick and mickey and slammer, hammer, pump, boner, salami, cock, ding-ding, every bloody day. I mean, men are not that interesting.'

I struggle to suppress my grin. 'Stop!'

She smiles a little ruefully too. 'Don't tell Luke I said that, though.'

I laugh again. 'Come on.' I pat her on the shoulder. 'I'll make you a coffee and, Kate, if the show made you uncomfortable, you were right to leave.'

She's about to answer when the phone rings. I hesitate, not wanting her to think a phone call is more important than her crisis but she says, 'Go on, answer it.'

I pick up the receiver as Kate takes over making the coffee. 'Hello?'

'Is anything wrong with Kate?' It's my mother, who seems to be hyperventilating. 'I'm listening to her show now and there is a man doing it. He says Kate is gone. Gone where? That's what he didn't say! Is she in hospital? Is she sick?'

'It's Mam,' I mouth to my sister.

'Hello? Hello?' Mam calls. 'Andy, are you there?'

214

Kate takes the phone from me and without any preamble says, 'I've left my job.'

Mam's answer is a shriek that makes me wince. Then she says something.

'I wasn't being fulfilled,' Kate announces.

Mam shrieks some more. Then obviously hands the phone to Dad, as Kate's next words are, 'Hi Dad.' A pause. 'Yes, it's true . . . yes, I've left . . . yes, they can.'

Meanwhile, I've made some coffee and when she finally finishes her call, she sits beside me and grins ruefully. 'They're delighted. I've mortified them for long enough. They're glad they don't have to feign support any more.'

'Mam's words?'

'Yep. Dad's were,' she screws up her eyes and doing a high-pitched, passable imitation of Dad, she says, 'It's to be quite nice weather for the next while, so maybe you should just go out and enjoy it. Get fit. Get a hobby.'

I laugh.

Kate smiles briefly before going suddenly serious again. 'I have a few bob saved so I can keep paying you rent for a bit, but—'

I wave her away. 'Forget it. I don't need it.'

'I can't stay for free.'

'Luke pays his share,' I answer, suddenly realising that I don't want the two of them to go. I've been on my own for way too long. I was lonely, only I hadn't known it. 'And if it makes you feel better, pay me back when you get a job again.'

'Thanks,' Kate says gratefully.

'I like having you both here,' I admit, flushing.

Kate suddenly turns away from me. Her face goes really red, and just as I'm about to ask her if she's OK, she says,

215

'Oh shit,' in a determined sort of voice which makes me jump.

'Pardon?'

'Look, Andy.' She turns to face me, her gaze boring into mine. 'We haven't exactly been entirely honest with you. Me and Luke.'

This is a curveball. 'You haven't? Why?'

'It was Mam's idea. She was worried about you.'

'What was?'

She seems to be steeling herself. 'For me and Luke to come here, to keep an eye on you.'

At first, what she is saying confuses me, and then it all slots into place. Mam's reactions, her blasé attitude to Kate's narrow escape from a fire. The amount of stuff they managed to 'save' from a burning flat. I think a little of me knew all along. I don't know if I should smile or feel offended. In semi-disbelief, I say softly, 'So, there was no fire, then?'

'No,' Kate winces. Then hurries on, 'Though to be fair, Mam was desperately worried about you. She thought you were going to do . . .' her voice trails off and once again she flushes, 'well, something stupid, so she begged me to keep an eye on you.'

I had no idea I had worried my mother that much. 'Really?' My voice is a shaky whisper.

Kate nods.

Guilt washes through me so swiftly that I can't even look Kate in the face. Maybe Chas is right when he says I'm self-centred. I'd been so wrapped up in my phobias that I hadn't noticed the effect it was having on everyone. My poor parents thinking that I was going to . . . going to . . . I can barely bring myself to think the word *suicide*. They must have been

216

petrified. And all this time, I realise now, their incessant phone calls and bits of useless gossip were their way of keeping me in touch with the world. I'm ashamed of myself for putting them through that. Ashamed that I hadn't noticed their concern.

'. . . And so Mam thought that if we said our flat had burned down you'd take pity on us. I told her that there was no way you'd fall for that.'

I'm so glad I had. Maybe I'd even wanted to. Maybe I knew it was my only hope of crawling out of the hole I'd dug for myself.

'Anyway . . .'

'I'm glad you and Luke are here,' I interrupt her. 'Poor Luke, getting dragged into my dramas. But,' I feel honour-bound to say it, it's only fair, 'I can promise you that I'm not going to do myself in, so if you and Luke want to move out and get yourselves somewhere, it's cool. You can still come and take me out, though. Think of it as visiting your old granny in a nursing home.'

'Stop, that's awful,' I'm delighted to hear her giggle. 'You're not like that.' She gives me a bashful grin. 'And anyway, where can Luke and I go now? I've lost my job.'

She has a point. 'So you're here to stay, are you?'

'For the moment.'

'Well, that's good. I'm really glad.'

And I so am.

D AD LOOKS SURPRISED to see me calling over in the middle of the day. I haven't been at my parents' house before sunset for about eighteen months. As I pull into the driveway, Dad stands up to greet me. He pulls his gardening gloves off and stamps his feet hard on the ground. His legs always go numb from kneeling down, he complains. Mam says it's just an excuse for him to get out of work. 'This is a surprise!' he calls delightedly. I notice that he's got a ridiculous brown battered hat perched on the top of his head and a white plaster across his nose.

'Come on in and I'll make you a cuppa.' Dad begins to usher me in in front of him. 'Eh, we'll go around the back way, you know the way your mother hates dirt in the hall.'

I do indeed. I push open the side gate and call out a cheery 'hello' to my mother.

'Oh, she's not here,' Dad says, 'she's gone to her art classes.'

'Oh, right.'

'Every Tuesday from twelve to two. She's very good. Here . . .' He pushes open the back door and removes his wellies. 'You put on the kettle and I'll show you her watercolours.'

As I fill the kettle, it occurs to me how much of other peoples' lives I've missed out on. I wonder what else my parents do that I hadn't known about. Is Dad a karate expert? A computer hacker? A—

'What are you smiling at?' Dad arrives back, holding some watercolour papers.

'Just wondering what else the two of you do that I don't know about.'

'Not a lot,' he says good-humouredly, rolling his eyes. 'Now, here you are, what do you think of those?'

He lays five pictures down on the table. They are landscapes, all copied from bigger pictures, some of which I recognise. It's very competent art. It'd be interesting to see what she'd do from real subjects. 'Wow,' I pick one up, 'that's good. I like the way she did the water in that.'

'That's what her tutor said.' Dad is as proud as if he'd done them himself. 'He said it had movement. Your mother says that it's very important to have movement.'

'It is.' I suppress a smile. 'Fair play to her. I never knew she liked to paint.'

'Oh, she loves it. Sure it wasn't from the ground you licked it, you know.'

'It's such a relief to know where I got my talent from.' I grin. 'I always thought I was Mam's love child from another relationship.'

'Sure, who'd have her,' Dad snorts. 'He'd want to be a brave man with a strong stomach.'

'Dad!'

He laughs and pours the tea.

When Mam arrives back, rather than being happy to see me she's convinced something is wrong. In fact, she seems to think that I might be about to tell her that Kate has slid into depression after leaving her job.

'No,' I say. 'In fact, she's pretty upbeat. She has had a brainwave, apparently.'

'Oh.' Mam frowns. 'Do you like the sound of that, Donald?'

'Whatever makes her happy.' Dad nods to Mam's very professional-looking art folder, which she has laid on the table. 'Let's have a look at what you did this week.'

Mam is suddenly bashful. 'Oh no, it's not done yet, I have to finish it. And besides, I'm sure it's not up to what Andy can do.'

'It probably is,' I say. 'I haven't painted in ages.'

'Have you not started yet?' Dad says, pushing a plate of biscuits towards me. 'You were very good.'

'I was OK.' I don't tell them about the way I've hesitantly drawn a few sketches of my house and my rooms, I don't know why. Maybe I don't want to get their hopes up that things are going to revert to the way they used to be. I don't think they ever will be like that again. 'Go on, show us, Mam.'

My mother acts as if she doesn't want to, but I know from her demeanour that she does. In fact, if she hadn't wanted to, even Leonardo Da Vinci couldn't have persuaded her. Coyly, she produces her picture from her folder. 'We used a photograph of fruit,' she explains. 'I think I got it right.' She holds the photo out alongside her picture.

It's a monochrome picture of a bowl with oranges, apples and bananas in it. Black and white is incredibly difficult to achieve in watercolour, mainly because a lot of tutors won't let you use black, so you have to make it up.

'That's really good.' I mean it. She's even got the texture right on the skin of the orange. Even in the grey shading.

She looks proudly at me. 'My tutor said I should consider entering it in that competition, you know the one that's been in the paper?'

'The online one?'

Mam nods. 'Yes. You can scan it in for me, Andy. All you have to do is get an entry form, pay, scan it, post it to the address and that's it. It'll be seen all over the world when people go into the view.'

'View?'

'I think she means site,' Dad answers for her. 'And you don't post it, Lil, you email it.' He looks at me. 'I'm doing a computer course in the tech.'

'Whatever.' Mam dismisses his knowledge with a wave of her hand. 'Andy knows what I mean.'

'I do.' And I also know she hasn't a hope of winning. The entries are of such a high standard that even I haven't a hope of winning. 'Well, I'll enter it for you if you want me to.'

'I might as well. Sure I probably won't win, but I definitely won't if I don't try.'

'You've a great chance,' Dad says loyally. 'There is lots of movement in it.'

'Pardon?' Mam looks crossly at him. 'Are you trying to say it's blurred?'

'No,' Dad shakes his head. 'No. Not at all. It's very good.'

'You said it had movement. How can a still life have movement?'

'Right. Oh.' Dad nods sagely. 'I see your point.'

Mam's lips narrow and I'm sure she's about to say something caustic, so I butt in. 'The reason I've called in is to let you both know that Kate told me there was no fire in her flat.'

They are silenced for probably the first time in their lives. Mam looks guiltily at Dad. Dad smiles uneasily back. They remind me of two kids who know that they'll be punished.

'Was there not?' Mam says weakly.

'You know there wasn't, Mam.' I try not to smile at her attempt to extricate herself from the situation. 'I also want to tell you both,' I look from one to the other as I say softly, 'that I'm not planning on jumping from a bridge in the near future. I promise.'

'Oh, good,' Dad says, sounding uncomfortable. 'Fantastic.'

Mam can't speak. 'It's not that we didn't trust you—' Her voice falters and Dad takes her hand in his and squeezes it.

'I know,' I continue quietly. 'But I would never do something like that. I saw how devastated Lexi's family were to lose her; I'd never do that to you and Dad.'

'Oh Andy,' my mother sniffs, blinking hard.

'We did lose you, though,' Dad mutters. 'In a way.'

His words floor me. I hadn't looked at it like that.

'There is more than one way to lose someone,' he goes on. 'We just wanted to bring you back to us.'

'Yes, we did,' Mam gulps out. 'We wanted our Andy back.'

'And I'm trying.' I touch her sleeve gently. 'Here I am, in the daytime. Kate and Luke are responsible for that.'

Neither of them can speak now.

'I'm sorry if you were worried,' I go on. 'I didn't realise—'

'Come here.' Dad pulls me into an embrace. He's manky

with soil from the garden, but I don't care. 'Of course we were worried, but that's only because we love you.'

'We do,' Mam mouths before catching my hand.

The terror I'd had earlier of driving in daytime seems worth it for this moment.

33

L EXI WAVES AT Cissy and Doug who are sitting at a table outside the town's only coffee shop. Cissy is wearing one of her signature skintight, short, frilly dresses, with horizontal white and lime-green stripes. It would have made the average woman look ridiculous but Cissy isn't an average woman. With her giraffe-like legs and slender body, she carries it beautifully. Doug is in his usual tight black jeans and t-shirt. There is a graphic image of a skull emblazoned on it.

'Hey.' Lexi slides in beside them. 'How's things?'

'Lex!' They pounce on her as if they haven't seen her in ages. 'Where were you?'

Actually, they probably haven't seen her for a few days, she suddenly thinks, surprised. She'd been so busy that she hadn't noticed her neglect of them. 'Just busy,' she shrugs. 'How are things with the two of you?'

They exchange a laugh. 'Good.' Cissy smiles. She touches Doug's hand. 'This guy has moved to the best shop on the street.'

'I have.' Doug nods. 'It was quite traumatic, actually, closing my shop, but I think we're going to work very well together, eh, Cis?'

'Well, your music suits my hats.'

'Maybe we could include a built-in iPod in every hat?'

'Maybe we should.'

And they laugh.

Lexi looks from one to the other. 'Am I missing something?' Actually she doesn't think she is. They seem very cosy together, and she suddenly feels like an interloper.

'No,' they both say together.

''Cause I think it would be a mistake to get too close at the moment. You do have a lot of stuff to sort out, Doug.'

'Who are you – Dr Phil?' There is no mistaking the hostility in Cissy's remark.

'Wrong sex, for a start,' Lexi tries for lightness. OK, maybe she shouldn't have said what she did, but the way they are together makes her uneasy. She's always been under the impression that Cissy has a childlike naivety about things, as if she hasn't experienced much of real life at all. Even the designs of her hats reflect it: wide brims and flowers, pastel colours. Little-girl hats for grown-ups. She thinks Cissy could be hurt very easily. And Doug, well, he's been so miserable, he reminds her of an abandoned puppy. Not a good combination. Two needy people in what could only be an artificial relationship. Men on the rebound, bad idea.

'We're cool,' Doug says dismissively. 'Cissy is only helping me out.'

'Yes, that's all.'

She gets the feeling that Cissy is disappointed by the remark. 'OK. Sorry for presuming.' She tries to change the subject. 'I had a talk with Peter the other day about your music, Doug. He said he'd listen to it and let me know. I'll get onto him today, if I can find him, and see if he's interested.'

'Oh, I wrote a special track for the gallery, actually,' Doug says shyly.

'It's perfect,' Cissy gushes.

'It's the first thing I've written all year that I'm happy with,' Doug adds.

'And you should be happy with it.' Cissy nods vigorously. They're like a double act, she thinks. 'Brilliant. Well, get it to me and I'll give it to Peter. The competition is closing tomorrow, so a selection of the best artwork will be on display every day until the final. I'm sure he'll use it.'

'Thanks, Lex.'

'Greetings!' Lordi arrives. 'I've been looking for you everywhere.' The 'you' is directed at Cissy. 'I've got those two angels for you, you can pick them up whenever you like. The sooner the better, though.'

'Lordi, thanks. That's so nice.'

'So the bigger the angel, the better they work, is that it?' Doug asks, but he's joking.

'The bigger the belief, the better they work, actually,' Lordi pronounces, sitting alongside Lexi. 'Now, if you two would like to go say, now, and sort that out, I'd have no objection to that.'

Doug cups a hand to his ear. 'Is that clanging the sound of a hint dropping?'

'I think it is.' Cissy stands up. 'Come on, Doug, let's go.' Tossing her hair back from her face, she totters off, swaying sexily. Doug waves a lazy goodbye and lopes along after her.

'Is it my suspicious mind, or is there something going on there?' Lordi turns to Lexi.

'Well, you and I both,' Lexi says. 'I think it would be the worst idea ever.'

226

'Yes,' Lordi agrees. 'A collision between a rabbit and an artic is the image that comes to mind.'

Lexi smiles at his dryness. 'Yeah, but who is the rabbit?'

Lordi shrugs. 'Both of them, I think.' He pauses. 'And what about you?'

'What about me?'

'You haven't been around in a few days. Been busy?'

'Yep.'

'Or is it maybe the star attraction's gone, and you now have no interest in hanging around the town or the beach?'

She knows what he means but he's wrong. 'You and the other two nutters are the main attraction for me.'

He laughs. 'Not beach boy?'

'No, not beach boy.' He means Yellow T-Shirt. 'He only came here to paint, he told me. His real name is Yale.' Even talking about him gives her a pang. She does miss him. And she doesn't know why; it wasn't as if she knew him that well.

'What a perfectly awful name.'

'Isn't it?' she agrees with a grin.

'Well, we all have our cross to bear.'

She thinks that that is true. She wonders what his is; he seems so together for a guy who sells angels. 'What's your cross, then?' She's half joking, not really expecting him to answer.

'I wooden like to say.'

'Ha, ha.'

Lordi laughs. 'My cross?' he says. Then there is nothing until he adds, 'Well, I suppose the worst thing that ever happened to me was the crash, the one that my wife died in.'

'Oh, Lordi.' She's taken aback, not sure how to respond to his frankness. 'You never said you had a wife.'

227

'I know.' He pauses even longer this time.

Lexi remains silent. Why did she have to ask? She should have known better than to ask Lordi; should have known he'd tell her. And she hadn't really wanted to know.

'I used to wish I'd died alongside her but as you can see, that was not to be,' Lordi continues. 'Still, I believe she's somewhere out there, so that keeps me going.'

'That's good you believe that.'

Lordi nods.

'I wish I could.'

'Everyone is different.'

'No, I wish I could because,' she swallows, won't let herself cry, 'because, well, I couldn't deal with what happened after my crash and I – I ran away from it all. I've been running ever since. I just want to hide away. I wouldn't feel so bad if I had your faith.'

Now it's Lordi's turn to remain silent.

She swallows. It's so hard saying the words, it's the first time she's voiced this fear. 'And the worst thing was,' she stops, then starts again, hoping her voice sounds more in control, 'the awful thing was, I was with my friend on the bus and we were fighting with one another the day it happened, and we weren't speaking. And then . . .' She stops.

Lordi waits for a few seconds, then, as it becomes obvious that she's not going to say any more, he stands up and puts an arm about her. 'You have to let it go.'

Lexi shakes her head. 'I can't. I said some terrible things to her. We were fighting over the fact that we'd nearly missed the bus for the tour we were to go on. I was the one who hurried her onto the bloody bus, for God's sake. Why couldn't we have missed it?'

228

'If you had,' Lordi says softly, 'I bet you never would have come here, and you never would have met me. Now, wouldn't that be a real tragedy?'

She hiccups out something between a laugh and a sob. He's such a nice man.

'You never would have said horrible things to your friend if you knew there was going to be a crash, would you?'

'No.'

'I'm sure she knows that. And I'm also sure she said horrible things back.'

She'd called her a controlling cow, and said that she wished they'd not bothered going away. She'd called her a user and needy and pathetic. But she knew she hadn't meant it, not really.

'You come into my shop. You need a Healing angel, and I'll give you one and you can hang it up in your tent and touch it every night before you go to sleep.'

'I don't really believe in all that, you know.'

'Well, think about it.' He gives her a final hug before letting her go.

'I will.'

He attempts to bend down and peer into her face. 'You've not told anyone this before, have you?'

'No,' she says in a small voice.

'Maybe you should.'

How can she?

'Now, petal,' he says, 'I'm away for a few days. I'll be back here in my shop on Thursday if you want to call in. And remember, letting go takes time. I know.'

She watches him leave, hardly able to believe that she's just told her most shameful secret to a man that is still, in essence, a stranger. A nutty, but lovely stranger. She'd never been able to tell anyone about the row before. She had hoarded it to herself, letting it fester inside. The feeling of shame, that she'd never be able to change it, that helplessness of not being able to pull time back and just say something like 'you are the best friend I ever had, thanks', was killing her. It was so shocking to think that that might never be, that she'd have to live the rest of her life knowing and regretting her final words to her friend.

34

I HAVE A DREAM that night, the strangest dream I've ever had. I've dreamed it before, only not in this way. Not with this ending. It's me and Lexi in Tasmania. The sun is beginning to set, sending streaks of red and violet and gold across the sky. We're running like mad to catch the bus to bring us on a night-time tour of the region in the mountains. We're late, both angry with each other, though it would be fair to say that I am the crossest. Lexi is in a sulk, stomping along in her combats and flipflops. The bus is about to pull out when we arrive. Some of the other passengers clap as we board, and shout out good-natured insults at us for holding them up. Lexi doesn't smile; instead she marches right to the back of the bus and slides into a seat, sitting right in the middle so I can't get in beside her. I don't let it bother me; I sit with someone else, a dorky man who is on his first trip away. His first trip ever, I think, as he tells me about the email he's sent to his mammy and daddy at home. Lexi is peering deliberately out the window, not looking at me at all, and I so want to reach over and tell her I'm sorry. I so do. I mean, I said horrible things to her, but then I remember what she said to me and I resist trying to make amends.

The bus trundles along, the roads getting higher and higher

and steeper and steeper and narrow and narrower. The views, streaked with the setting sun, are breathtaking. Oohs and aahs issue from all sides of the bus. Cameras flash. I wish I was beside Lexi so we could talk about it.

And then the bus driver exclaims loudly, the bus swerves and in slow motion, I see us tumbling over and over and over, down, down, down. I see people being flung from ceiling to floor like rag dolls and windows smashing as bodies fly out, and wide, gaping mouths as people shriek and scream. Blood splatters the walls like paint being squirted from a canister. I see bits of broken camera shattering and splintering, but I hear no noise. It's like a silent horror, a slow-motion movie in my head. Then everything goes black. I normally wake up at this part of the dream, sweating and frightened. Instead, in the dream, I'm waking slowly up, cold and freezing on the mountainside. Dawn light is creeping across the rocks, there is no breeze, no noise, only the bright red light of a rising sun. I'm lying on my back, wondering what I'm doing here, wondering if I'm in a dream and why I feel so cold. Then, in the distance, from what seems like far away, I hear the sound of an engine. It grows louder little by little, and I realise that it's coming from above me. I move my head, there's something sticky on my face, I can feel it squelch as I lift up my cheek from the rock I seem to be lying on. A helicopter, I think. It's a helicopter. I blink and my eyes hurt. Bits and pieces of the night before flit into my head, images too horrible to remember. And up above, in the blood-red sky streaked with gold and blue, the helicopter hovers and some primal survival instinct kicks in. I know I have to signal to it. To save myself I have to signal to it. And I lift an impossibly heavy arm. Pain rips through me as I wave. The pain is so bad that I black out.

And in the blackness, I suddenly see Lexi.

And she's smiling. She's smiling like she's stayed with me all night on the mountain just so she can save my life.

And in my dream, I'm smiling back.

I wake up, and I'm crying.

But I'm happy too.

35

'OK, SEXY ANDREA, I'm putting you through. Remember, you owe me a drink if you get the sale.'

'How could I forget when you keep reminding me?' I feign a laugh. As he connects my call, I wonder how I'll get out of this bargain he seems determined I keep. In fact, how did I get into it? Even if I have made the decision to take a short walk to the local shop in broad daylight, I very much doubt that my new-found bravery will extend as far as going for a drink with a guy who's helped me get a sale. Alistair would be appalled, I think with a small grin. He'll be convinced that letting guys buy me drinks in exchange for ads is akin to prostitution. It would probably be better not to mention it to him.

'Hello?'

It's the impatient boss.

'Hello,' I say. 'I'm ringing on behalf of the—'

'Yes, I'll take a full-page ad.'

'Pardon?' It takes a lot to stun me: this response flattens me.

'A full-page ad, is that a problem?'

'Eh, no, that's great.'

'Right. Well, I'm a busy man, I'll trust you to come up with the text, just email it to me beforehand. I'll transfer you back to Graham.' A little awkwardly, he adds, 'I hope this'll help you keep the job.'

'Keep the—' But he has cut me off.

'Hi, that was quick, you really are good!' Graham says, in what is obviously a big fake admiration voice.

'What exactly did you tell him?'

'Just that you were my girlfriend and you were in a new job, and in order to keep it you had to sell a full-page ad every month. I also might have mentioned that you had a sick mother who needed a full-time nurse. He can relate to that, his mother is sick too.'

'That's horrible.' I almost mean it.

'It is – but hey, now you owe me a drink.'

'I have a sick mother. I can't go gallivanting about all over the place.'

He laughs, then adds, amused, 'It's OK. I was only joking about the drink.'

'Oh.' I feel a little relieved, though he sounds like a nice man.

'I'd be happy to settle for just full sex.'

'Funnee.'

'Aw, I'm not that creepy that I'd expect a drink from you,' he says. 'I am sorry about losing you the ad first time around.'

'I'd never have sold a full-page ad first time around.'

'With that voice? You'd have sold me two full-page ads.'

'You charmer.'

'I do like to think so. Anyway, if you're passing by any day, call in and say hi. I'd love to see the face that goes with that incredibly sexy voice.'

For some reason, a massive lump materialises in the back of my throat. Imagine, I think, if I was well, if I had no scar, the laugh I could have going to see this guy. The idea of just calling in on him as I pass his shop seems so outlandish right now.

'Hey, you still there?'

'Yeah.' I swallow and say in as upbeat a voice as I can manage, 'OK. If I'm passing I'll definitely call in. Meantime, I'll send you on a copy of the magazine when it comes out.'

'It'll have to do, I guess,' he says mournfully.

'For now,' I say.

'I like the sound of that.'

I hang up, smiling.

Downstairs, Kate's phone is ringing non-stop. Since the media got hold of the fact that she resigned from her job, there has been a deluge of calls to her mobile.

'Your mobile is vibrating again,' Luke keeps saying in a dirty voice to her.

She's been so much more relaxed in the last couple of days. She hasn't even given out about the breakfast-show presenter once. Mind you, out of loyalty to her, I've changed the station to RTE One.

As I enter, she's getting a little cross with whoever has called her. She's pacing about the kitchen in her slippers and miniskirt, the phone to her ear. Luke watches her as he sips one of his herbal concoctions, bits of branches sticking out of his mug. It looks vile.

'I left because I want to be taken seriously as a radio presenter,' Kate says sharply. Then, 'Well, yes, obviously I've grown tired of the whole sex thing. I mean, it does get boring after a while. I'd rather do something with women. I found that my listenership seemed to consist of seedy men.' A pause. 'Well, I'm not saying you're seedy because you listened . . .

236

can I get a word in here . . . oh, do you know what? Forget it.' And she snaps her phone shut.

'He'll probably write a nasty little piece on you now,' Luke observes, sounding amused.

'A nasty, seedy little piece.' I smile. I pour myself some of Kate's excellent coffee. Since she's spending her days under my feet, there is constant coffee on the go.

'I don't care.' Kate flings the phone onto the table and, as it starts ringing again, asks me to take it out of the room for her.

I look about at the chaos that used to be my lovely apartment. 'If I do, you might never see it again.'

'That would be a good thing.'

Instead of removing it, I take it and switch it off. 'It must be nice to know you're so famous.' I have to admit, I'm really surprised at the level of attention her departure has generated. The station is remaining tight-lipped on the whole thing, merely wishing Kate all the best in whatever she tries next. Of course, Kate says that they don't mean it.

'Mmm,' Kate says, squeezing in beside Luke. She cups her chin in her hand, looking up at me. 'It's OK.'

There is something in the way she says it, as if she's not really interested in talking about that but would like to discuss something else. 'Yes?' I quirk my eyebrows.

'Ooh, she's always been able to read me.' Kate flaps a hand at me, though she does sound relieved. She turns to Luke. 'She knows when we've got something to ask her.'

'When you've got something to ask her, you mean,' Luke clarifies. Then he adds, 'Can Kate ask you something, Andy?'

They're like two kids. I don't think they'll ever grow up. 'I'm sure she can.'

'We've got this idea, see,' Kate says.

'*You've* got this idea, see,' Luke clarifies yet again.

'Yeah, I do,' Kate thrills, all snuggled up beside Luke. From the body language, I reckon she's trying to charm Luke into going along with whatever it is too.

'Go on.'

'It was when Mabel appeared on my show, you see,' Kate explains, 'and she talked about how she felt lonely and how the yoga helped her. Well, we,' a pause, '*I* thought, wouldn't it be great to make a radio documentary on the subject of isolation and loneliness? It's not really talked about, is it? And Luke knows loads of old people who—'

'Ta very much,' he gawks, offended at her. 'I have lots of mates too, you know.'

'. . . and Mam and Dad are old—'

'They're not that old.'

'Well, Luke's mother is really old,' Kate says.

'Baby of the family,' Luke points to himself.

'And anyway, I thought, why not do this?'

'And?' I quirk my eyebrows. 'Where do I come in?'

A look is exchanged between Kate and Luke. 'It's more how your apartment comes in,' Kate says. When I don't reply, she adds, 'I'd like to record the documentary in it, you know, Luke doing his yoga, and then them all having tea and a chat and then I'll ask them questions.'

'Yeah, that should be fine.'

She smiles, nods. 'Great.'

It's not quite the ecstatic thank you I was hoping for.

'There's more,' Luke says, picking a branch out of his mug and poking her in the arm with it, 'isn't there, Kate?'

She squirms away from him.

238

Ahh, I think. The real favour.

'See, I think it would be better if I didn't tell you, but Luke says I have to.' Kate grabs the branch off him, sniffs it and glares at him.

'I said she has to,' Luke agrees, lying back in his chair and stretching out his legs, and generally acting as if he's not bothered by his girlfriend's obvious agitation.

'Which would you prefer?' Kate asks brightly.

Luke laughs. 'You're some tulip, do you know that?' Then he turns to me. 'Kate has, basically,' he pauses, 'what word would you use? Borrowed or stolen?'

'Borrowed.' Kate gives him another glare, this time more hardcore. 'I'm putting the equipment back in the studio every night. Well, my friend is.'

'Oh, right.' Luke nods. 'Well, Andy, Kate will be borrowing, without asking, some recording equipment from her old employers, and that's what she will be using in your house.'

'Oh Kate.' I'm a little bit shocked. 'What if someone finds out?'

'They won't.' That's Kate all over. She doesn't allow herself to think things through; she just goes for what she wants and deals with the consequences afterwards. A bit like what has happened with the radio show, in fact.

'How can you be sure?'

Kate squirms. 'OK, obviously I can't be sure, but this idea is a good one. I have to do it, you know. And, what's more, I'm going to do it, and if the only way I can is by borrowing a bit of equipment, then I will.' She looks defiantly at us. Luke is gazing at her half in admiration, half in exasperation.

I'm afraid for her. If she is caught stealing, that would put an end to her career. 'Well, once you know the risks, and you're prepared to accept the consequences without moaning if it blows up in your face, then I guess I'll say nothing more.'

'Put up with the consequences without moaning.' Luke stands up, and I notice that he is barefoot and that all he is wearing is a brown t-shirt and track bottoms. He must be freezing. Even though the heat is on in my apartment, I'm wrapped up in an oversized jumper and jeans. Luke mustn't feel the cold. He drains his disgusting concoction in one gulp. 'Well, that might be asking a bit too much.'

'I won't be moaning when the documentary wins awards,' Kate says smartly. She looks at the two of us. 'If you think too much about stuff, you get scared, so better just to do.'

And she waltzes by us out of the kitchen.

She has a point, I suppose. I spend hours thinking about going to Roy's shop, and planning out which aisles I'll walk up, and the shortest route within the shop so I can have my stuff in a basket without too many people seeing me. And sometimes the thinking does scare you as you see all the things that can go wrong. To be able to let go and just dive in the way Kate does is something I envy so much. Maybe, I think, maybe I should go to a place that I can't control as much the next time. Even contemplating this sends my heart stuttering and my stomach fluttering horribly. But what is the alternative? Living here and listening to second-hand accounts of my friends' lives? Listening to Alistair tell me about this girl he's besotted with, and never actually meet the two of them on a sunny street someday? Hearing Luke's funny stories about people coming into his health food shop and buying packets of organic biscuits, thinking that they won't put on weight? Even, damn it, walking past that photo shop and getting a dekko at the fella that joked about bringing me for

240

a drink? Or maybe accepting an award for Best Designer in front of a room full of strangers? I am curtailing my life, and it hurts. OK, there's Skype and webcams and Facebook and grocery online shopping, but meeting real flesh-and-blood strangers who might or might not become friends is what life is about.

'Andy, are you OK? You've gone pale.' Luke is peering anxiously into my face. I notice that his eyes are the strangest shade of green. 'I'm sure Kate will be OK.'

'Oh, I'm sure too,' I say. No time like the present, I think, taking a deep breath. 'I was, eh, wondering if you and Kate were going out for a drink sometime, if I could come with you?'

'Well, we're heading to a party tonight, but some day next week is good. We usually go out on a Wednesday if that suits?'

'Eh, yeah. Good.' Then I pause. 'Can we go to a quiet place? And maybe sort of dark, not too bright?'

'We don't normally drink in cemeteries.'

It's delivered so deadpan that despite my mortification, I laugh.

He pats my arm. 'I know what you mean. It'll be arranged just like that.'

'Thanks.'

Then he pulls his jacket straight out of the mess on the floor, which is amazing. A wink at me, 'Bye now.'

'See ya.'

36

*K*ATIE *FITZSIMONS THINKS Sex is Boring!* screams the headline from the paper the following week. OK, it's one of those shite papers that have naked women and celebrity gossip on every page, but hey, it's an attention-grabbing headline all the same.

Kate is furious as she reads it. 'Listen here,' she says as she stalks about the kitchen, just before we're due to go out to the pub. 'Katie Fitzsimons, sexy DJ for Dublin Live, who recently vacated her post on the show, admitted to this reporter that she is bored by sex. In fact, she is quoted as saying, "I'd like to do something with women."'

Luke splutters his water all over the table, and tries to stem the flow of it as it comes down his nose.

'Oh,' Kate flings the paper at him, 'you think it's funny, do you? How do you think it depicts you? As a boring sex partner, that's what!'

'Oh, my life is over!' Luke rolls his eyes dramatically. 'I'll just have to think of more interesting ways to do the business.'

Kate is about to pick up the paper and hit him with it when I say, 'Well, at least they called you sexy. That's nice.'

'Read the rest of it.' Kate thrusts the page into my face.

'It also says that I hated my listeners, calling them seedy. I mean, who will employ me now?'

'They were seedy.' I pick up the paper. A big picture of Kate, that seems to have been doctored, shows her spilling out of a tight white top as she grins lasciviously. Underneath is the caption, 'Katie admits lesbian feelings'.

I wish we hadn't found out about this article, but one of Kate's mates had rung to tell her and, of course, rather than ignore it, Luke was despatched down to the corner shop to buy the paper. Then it was pored over and dissected, and now it looks as if we won't be going out. I've spent the whole day petrified of this pub visit but determined to go through with it, and now I think Kate might chicken out, which would be a relief to me.

'So,' Luke stands up and slips his feet into a pair of trainers. Bending down to tie the laces, he says, 'We ready to go?'

Kate looks incredulously at him. 'Go?' she splutters. 'Go where? I can't go out. My God, it's humiliating.'

Luke, now finished tying his laces, gets to his feet and, as if he hasn't heard her, pulls on an orange Jesus jacket. 'Your sister,' he points at me, making me blush, 'has a scar on her face that she's really conscious of,' he turns to me, 'not that it's that bad,' he expands. 'And you,' he turns back to my sister, 'you are in a sleazy paper, looking great, I might add, and you are afraid to go out.' Pulling gently on her hair, he kisses her ear before saying, 'Get a life, gorgeous.'

'Everyone thinks I'm a lesbian.'

'Let me tell you something . . .' Luke pushes her hair back from her face. 'First off, it's no big deal if they do, second off, most guys would find that a turn-on.'

243

'Oh, God.' Kate covers her ears. 'Luke Mulcahy, you are mad.'

'Mad about you. Now,' he gives her a gentle push, 'coat.'

'OK,' she mutters. 'I'll go.'

Oh shit! I really thought she'd stay at home. 'It's cool if you don't want to,' I say.

'No,' Kate searches for her coat among the jumble of clothes on the kitchen floor, 'if you can, then so can I.'

And vice versa, I reckon.

Ten minutes later, I'm locking the door of my apartment, Kate and Luke waiting beside me, when Bert emerges from his apartment. He smiles at us, looking as usual like some kind of reject from *Saturday Night Fever*, before narrowing his eyes and peering hard at Kate.

'Hey, how you doing?' he says, straightening up and shoving his flowery, open-necked shirt into his tight jeans. 'I'd no idea I was living beside you. Nice picture in the paper today.'

Kate flushes. 'Well,' she says, 'none of the piece was true, it was all lies. I want you to know that.'

Bert runs his fat tongue over his thick fleshy lips and says incredulously, 'I don't *read* the paper, love. I just like to look at the pictures. Yours was the best. I have it on my wall.'

'Right.' Kate gives him a strained smile before hissing in an undertone, 'I think I just might die now.'

'I hope your girlfriend won't find out,' I say to Bert, 'it might make her mad.'

'She is gone,' he admits mournfully. 'I'm on the rebound. Half a pint and I'm anybody's.' He cackles a little before sauntering ahead of us, down the corridor.

'Do you think anyone else will recognise me?' Kate asks as

244

we let Bert increase the distance between us so we won't end up sharing a lift with him.

'So what if they do,' Luke says mildly. 'They'll be using you to wrap chips in tomorrow.'

'Thanks.' Kate is not impressed.

'They haven't wrapped chips in newspaper for a long time now.' I try my best, but even I know it's not a great consoling line.

'Let's just do this.' Kate strides on ahead of both of us.

'Yeah,' Luke grins at me. 'Let's just do this.'

Luke drops us off at the front door of the pub before driving away to look for parking. I stumble on my red high heels as I step out onto the pavement, and Kate has to catch me.

'Wow, I've got vertigo,' I joke, 'it's such a long time since I've been so high up.' But it's not my bloody heels that are the problem. Terror makes my legs shake. I really don't want to be noticed. But now Kate has been in the paper, so she might get noticed, and then me by default . . . It's awful being so vulnerable, I feel as if I'm in a cage surrounded by piranha fish. One false move and they'll start to bite. I dip my head, causing my hair to fall forward over my face, and follow Kate into the pub.

It had taken me ages to decide what to wear that night. Kate had looked at my initial jeans-and-sweatshirt effort and had told me sternly that there was no way I could wear that. Then she had marched me up to my room, flung open my wardrobe doors and said, 'Look, look at all your lovely clothes. You have got to choose something else.'

I looked at all my clothes, the majority of which I hadn't worn since before the accident. In fact, fingering

245

one particularly short skirt and glittery top combo, I found it hard to believe that I had once had the confidence to wear them. Most of my new stuff is shapeless and baggy, the way I like it now. In the end, I'd opted for a sedate pair of black trousers and a red and black top. I'd teamed it with a pair of black shoes, but Kate had insisted I wear her red stilettos, to give it a bit of bling factor. I hadn't wanted to, but in the end I'd agreed. It did look better with the red shoes, I had to admit.

The pub is gloriously dim inside. The kind of place so old-fashioned that it's only now coming back into fashion. Velvet seats in dark material, dark polished wooden counter, stained-glass windows. Small groups of people are scattered about in tiny alcoves, and only one or two look up as we enter. Kate finds a spot in the middle, facing the bar and, digging about in her purse, she hands me a twenty and tells me to go up and order.

'Me?' I swallow hard and shake my head, 'I can't, Kate.'

'Vodka, a water for poor Luke and whatever you want yourself. Go.' She makes whooshing motions with her hands.

I stare at the twenty in her hand while in my head, I run through various options. I could pull my hair over my face, lean on my hand while ordering, eh – I draw a blank. That is it.

'And show your scar,' Kate says. 'You can't hide for ever.'

'Will you come with me?'

'No.' She holds her hand up. 'And it's not because of the paper. It's because you have to do this.'

'I don't think I'm ready. I think I need a few whiskeys first.'

'Drink is not the answer,' she retaliates, sounding eerily like our mother.

246

'Oh yes it is,' I say back, making her laugh.

Kate scrutinises me. 'Look, Andy, you either want a life or you don't. Just go up there. Go on. I'll be here if anything happens.'

She really doesn't understand the fear. I thought she did, but she wouldn't ask me to do it if she did. Sitting here in the pub is a huge thing for me. My face is on show in all its gory detail. And I know I have to work at it, I know all the theory about it, I did months and months of counselling. But it didn't work, probably because I didn't see what I was missing. Now I know. I know when I see Kate and Luke together, when I hear about Alistair, shy-boy, moving on with his life. I want that too. I want it so badly that I've agreed to sit here. But I can't run, not just yet.

'Please,' I say to Kate.

There must be something in my eyes or the way I say it, because she nods without speaking and gets up. 'Watch the bags,' she instructs.

I look enviously after her as she walks to the bar. Such a simple thing. Leaning on it, she waves her money about and gets the attention of the barman. He smiles at her, rushes about to get the order ready and after a few minutes, she carries them back to the table.

'Now, your turn next. He's dead nice.'

I eye the whiskey she's got me. It looks suspiciously large.

'Double,' she grins. 'Maybe a bit of Dutch courage will work.'

'Hey.' Luke has arrived back, and to my horror, there are two lads with him. 'Look who I met outside.'

Kate obviously knows them because she stands up to receive a kiss on the cheek from each of them, calling them 'Davy' and 'Noel'. Then they turn to me as I cower pathetically in the corner.

'This is Andy,' Luke introduces us. 'Kate's sister.'

'Hiya.' Davy holds out his hand and takes mine in a strong grip. 'Nice to meet you.'

'You too.' I'm aware that my hair has fallen away from my scar. Davy doesn't seem to notice. Then, before I can rectify it, Noel grasps my hand and shakes it vigorously. Then they both sit down and take up Luke's offer of a drink.

My throat is suddenly dry; I can feel the beginnings of panic around the edges of my mind. Pushing it away, I lift the glass of whiskey to my lips, noticing that my hand is shaking slightly. I feel as if I've plunged back in time to the last occasion I went to a pub, everyone being so nice and me thinking that my scar didn't matter. And then finding out that it actually did . . . It made it so hard to trust what people told me after that.

I take a huge gulp of the neat whiskey and it burns its way down my throat and into my stomach, curling inside me like a cat. Another gulp. Another sip of golden-brown courage.

'How'd you get the scar?' Davy suddenly peers at me.

Holy shit. I gawk, horrified, at him. Whiskey sloshes out of my glass onto my top. I hastily put the glass back on the table.

Davy doesn't seem to have noticed. Instead, he pulls his shirtsleeve up, revealing a livid scar about eighteen inches long that goes from his wrist to just above the inside of his elbow. 'I got mine when I was scuba-diving off the Great Barrier Reef.' His scar is a lot more recent than mine, that's for sure. 'They said if I had cut a little further down towards my wrist, I'd be dead.'

248

'And what a loss that would have been,' Luke deadpans.

Davy lightly punches Luke on the arm for that comment. Then, rolling down his sleeve, he grins at me. 'Where did you get yours? It's a bummer it's on your face, but you're lucky you can get away with it.'

I blink. That was a compliment, I think. 'I was in an accident,' I stutter out. 'I, eh, hit my cheek off something.' Another gulp of whiskey.

'Oh right, so you don't remember?'

I shake my head. 'Not really.'

'Right.' He turns to Kate. 'And where did you get that nice t-shirt you were wearing in the paper? I knew there was a God when I saw it.'

Kate flings a beer mat at him.

'Have a bit of respect for my girlfriend,' Luke admonishes jokingly. 'She's very traumatised over the whole thing.'

'I can help you get over it,' Noel pipes up. 'Though the idea of you being a lesbian appeals to me.'

'I'd want to be desperate,' Kate jokes. 'In fact, I'd want to be the saddest person in the whole universe.'

Their banter eddies and sways around me. I don't know if it's the whiskey – which I've managed to gulp down in about five minutes flat – or the fact that the whole scar issue is now out of the way, but a lot of my tension has eased. These two guys didn't pretend that my scar wasn't there. By acknowledging it, they managed to banish it. Crazy, I know. But it's like trying to hide a secret and spending your time terrified of it being discovered, and when it is uncovered realising that in fact, most of the tension was in trying to bury the secret and not the secret itself.

249

And then Kate spoils my momentary calm by announcing, 'Now, the next round is on Andy. She's going up.'

'Oh no,' Noel waves that suggestion away, 'I'll get these.'

I'm tempted to let him, only now I'm afraid they'll all think I'm mean.

'No, it is my round,' I say, and my voice sounds a bit slurred. Am I drunk? I hope not. 'But you can help me carry them down if you like.' At least I'll have some support at the bar.

'I think he might have to carry you down,' Luke chortles.

'If I have to, I will.' Noel grins across the table at me.

It'd sound a lot more believable if he wasn't two inches shorter than me. Still, he's incredibly cute, with enormous brown eyes and a crooked grin. Or am I drunk?

A cheer goes up from the other three as, laughing good-naturedly, Noel stands aside to let me out and we make our way towards the bar.

'A water, a whiskey, a vodka and . . .' I look at Noel.

'Carlsberg and a cider.'

'No problem.' The barman nods and as he goes whizzing around the place, Noel angles his body towards mine.

'So, how come I've never seen you out with Luke and Kate before?' he asks.

Standing beside me, he's even shorter than I thought. He's got the kind of face that would get him the kid's fare on a bus. And his jeans look straight out of the boys' section in Dunnes. He's wearing a sweatshirt which declares to the world that he's mad, bad and dangerous. It'd look more convincing on a Labrador pup.

'Well?' he asks.

I shrug, trying for nonchalance. 'I don't go out that much.'

I make a big deal of scrutinising the change in my purse, and sifting my fingers through cents and five-cent pieces.

'Why not?'

'Just, you know,' big swallow, 'well, I work from home so I'm alone a lot, and, well, I guess this scar makes me a bit self-conscious.' I look directly at him as I say it. My face goes beetroot.

His gorgeous brown eyes widen slightly. 'Really? God, I'd love a scar on my face, it'd make me look tough.'

'Yeah, well, I've never had the desire to look tough. Just passably presentable.'

He laughs, rolling his eyes and snorting. 'Ah, come on! Everyone hates false modesty. You're more than passably presentable.'

His comment causes me to drop the money I've been fingering. It rolls all over the floor, and both of us dive down to get it and whack our foreheads together.

'*Ow!*' Noel howls, grabbing his head and laughing in pain.

I have to admit, I'm seeing stars, though I pretend it's nothing. 'Sorry.'

'Up!' Noel offers me his hand and drags me to my feet. The he crouches back down and retrieves the fallen cash.

The barman, who has our drinks lined up along the bar, is looking at us in amusement.

'Most guys would fall at your feet for cash,' he says, 'but this guy is making it a bit obvious, don't you think?'

I laugh. Noel hands me my money and as he does so, his fingers brush mine. I jolt. So does he. Our eyes flick away from each other. 'There,' he says, letting the coins drop into my hand. His face is red.

251

'Thanks,' I stammer out, wondering what on earth just happened.

Trying not to give it too much thought, I hand over a few notes to the barman, he gives me my change and together, Noel and I carry the drinks back down to the table.

The other three move up to let us in, so Noel and I end up beside each other.

'That was a nasty bang you had up there.' Kate peers at my forehead, which is throbbing.

'Any bang is better than no bang,' Noel chortles, causing Kate and me to go 'ugh' as the lads laugh.

'I can see why you have no girlfriend,' Kate sneers. 'Classy.'

Noel winks at me, and again I feel that jolt. Familiar, yet strange. It's . . . my befuddled mind tries to puzzle it out. It's . . . desire. Shit. I am drunk. But what a nice feeling. So I take another slug of whiskey, and another. I am seriously drunk. I cannot, in all objective honesty, think that this little guy is in any way sexually interesting. He's attractive in a cute kind of way, but I've never been a girl for cute men. I like tall men. Men like . . . Chas, I suppose. But Chas is not around, Chas doesn't know me any more and what he does know is a great big fat lie. But this guy, Noel, he knows that I hardly ever go out, which at the moment is the most important thing there is to know. I suppose there's nothing wrong with a little flirtation. It's been so long, I'm probably rusty, but I decide to give it a go.

'So tell me, Mr Mad, Bad and Dangerous, what is it you do?'

'If I told you that, I'd have to kill you,' Noel says, his brown eyes glittering mischievously, 'but in my pretend normal life, I'm a solicitor. I used to work with Luke.'

252

'Ohh.' I giggle a bit and slur out, 'D'you think you can get me off?'

Noel looks slightly taken aback at my clumsy flirting, and I wince. What have I just said? I flush and cough and stare into my drink. 'Eh, it was just a—'

'I'd have to look through your briefs first,' Noel smirks.

It makes me laugh.

My flirting goes very well, due to a combination of excess alcohol and the meagre attention I've had from men in the past while. Noel's total appreciation of me is an aphrodisiac that I've been starved of. Like someone who is tasting chocolate for the first time, I want it to continue, so when he suggests walking me home, I readily agree.

Luke, Kate and Davy are heading to a nightclub. There is no way, drunk as I am, that I could brave that.

'Are you OK, Andy?' Kate asks me as I make a mess of pulling on my coat. She helps me into my sleeves.

'Drunk but very much OK,' I slur lazily.

'Do you want me to go home with you?'

'No, Noel is bringing me, he's so cute.'

She looks doubtful.

'He's still a man,' she says.

'You sound like Mammy.'

That stops her from saying anything else, and to be honest, I don't want to hear any more. Yes, it's not like me to pick a guy up in a pub, but that's the great thing about drinking too much, it all makes sense when you're doing it.

Noel is waiting for me at the door, and I wish I hadn't worn high heels as he looks tiny beside me. Kate, Luke and Davy say goodbye and hop into a taxi. Then Noel and I walk through the almost deserted late-night streets of Dublin back to my flat. My feet begin to throb just as Noel slips his hand into mine. Then, as I'm considering abandoning the heels altogether, Noel snakes his arm about my waist. I soldier on, feet swelling, and just as we've hit the top of my road, he pulls me to him and I bend down to kiss his lips.

Oh God, it's all wrong, but I do it anyway.

His hand is now inside my coat. We walk, slightly unsteadily, down the road until we reach my block.

'Well, here I am.' I disentangle myself from his embrace. I wonder what to do next. I've never had a one-night stand before. I've always found that sort of thing slightly repulsive. But hey, Noel is Kate and Luke's friend, so I know him by default. And though I know people go on about self-respect and morality, I bet they're the sort of people who've never had a gap of more than twelve months between shags. Twelve whole months. Fifty-two weeks. And while part of those were spent in hospital, they still count. I would like to have sex, I decide, and this is the best opportunity to have presented itself in a long time.

'Any chance of a coffee?' he asks.

Oh, so he wants the same thing, I think. That's good.

'A hot and steamy coffee coming up,' I announce, trying to sound seductive. I turn and try unsuccessfully to jab the security number of the block into the pad at the doorway. It's hard because it's sort of spinning about. I try again. I concentrate hard on where I put my finger, and this time manage to hit the correct buttons. The door swings open.

'Come this way,' I beckon to Noel, and like an obedient puppy with big brown eyes, he trots along behind me. His tongue is even hanging out as if he can't believe his luck.

In the lift, as it too whirls around, just like my head, Noel attempts to grope me. Gently, I push him off. 'Wait,' I say, my fingers to my lips. He stops. He really would make a very good dog. 'You're not really mad, bad and dangerous, are you?' I run my finger down his cheek.

'Only when attacked,' he says.

'Oooh, maybe I'll attack you,' I say back, and his eyes widen.

God, I'm a slut.

But at least I can blame the drink in the morning.

In my hallway, it seems as if he can't contain himself any more. He takes hold of my wrist and pulls me to him, then jams his lips hard upon mine. It's gorgeous. I kick off my shoes, hitting him in the shin, but both of us ignore it. My feet ache with relief.

'Here.' Our lips still locked together, I pull him up the stairs towards my bedroom. It's not a very wise move because, going backwards on a stairs crowded with clothes and discarded pieces of electrical equipment is a dangerous business. I trip and fall down.

Noel falls on top of me, and we bang our heads together again.

'Jesus,' Noel winces. 'Christ.'

I don't want anything, not even concussion, to spoil things, so I haul him up and pull him towards the bedroom. It's not as messy as the rest of the place. Weak street light filters in from outside, a sort of yellow electric glow, and it's kind of romantic in a cityscape way.

Noel, his breathing ragged, drags off my coat. I drag off his jacket. He unbuttons my blouse. I pull his sweatshirt over his head. He unclips my bra. I pull off his t-shirt.

Groaning, Noel falls onto my bed, pulling me with him.

He lands on top of my cat.

Baz yowls and screeches and, extracting himself, pounces right on top of Noel's face and proceeds to hiss and spit and scratch.

'Oh, Jesus!' I yelp, and try ineffectually to whoosh Baz away.

Meanwhile Noel is struggling to get up, his hands around Baz's middle, and with a wrench he pulls the cat off him and throws him onto the bed.

'Fuck!' he says.

Unfortunately, any chance of that has disappeared, along with Noel's cute face. He's covered in scratches.

'Oh my God, I'm so sorry,' I say. 'It's my cat. I forgot he'd be here.'

Baz is still hissing.

'He attacked me.' Noel has hopped up, and is staring in terror at Baz.

'You fell on top of him. He was probably afraid you'd kill him.'

'I bloody well feel like it.' He sounds cross.

'He's not normally like that,' I lie. 'He's usually very gentle. Will I put some ointment on your scratches?'

'No.' Noel shakes his head. 'I think I'll go.'

'Oh—'

'I hate cats.' He scrabbles frantically around for his t-shirt and yanks it over his head. Then he looks for his sweatshirt. Glumly, I hand it to him.

'I could make you a coffee,' I offer, knowing I sound pathetic.

'No, no, let's just . . .' Noel shakes his head. 'No. Nice meeting you.'

'At least you've a bit of a scar on your face now,' I say, attempting lightness.

He doesn't reply, just shoots a filthy look at both me and my cat before stomping out of my apartment.

I sink down onto the bed, feeling really pissed off. 'You fecker,' I say to Baz.

His answer is to glare at me before settling down in his usual spot.

I decide to join him.

It mightn't have gone exactly to plan, but hey, I managed to pick up a guy. In fact – I grin a little – I probably could have picked him up, he was that small.

Baz begins to purr.

My thoughts exactly.

37

THE DAY IS calm and clear, yet the streets are busier than normal. Lexi stands at the top of the main road and watches the hustle and bustle of what had been a tranquil place up until now. She's slightly uneasy with it, but has to admit that it's great for her friends: they've told her that sales of angels and hats and music have increased. She waits apart from the crowd for Peter to show up. He's invited her to his house for a meeting and, as she doesn't know where exactly it is, he's offered to escort her. He's got someone he'd like her to meet, he has said and from the tone of his voice, she got the impression that it's going to be an important meeting, and so she's made an effort to look good. She's wearing a multicoloured skirt, borrowed from Cissy. It's a little long but the vibrant reds, yellows and blues of the material appeal to her. She wears it with a plain white vest top and a red summer hat, a present from Cissy in recognition for the extra traffic along the street. Her feet are clad in red sandals, bought especially for the occasion. She hopes it's worth it.

'Hi, how you going?' Peter catches her unawares from behind. 'How's my favourite offsider?'

Lexi turns. Peter is dressed in an expensive suit, one that

Lexi hasn't seen before, so she knows that buying the sandals was a good move. 'Your only offsider is fine.' She tries to stress the 'only', while copying his Aussie accent.

Peter laughs, obviously in a good mood. 'And can I say, as your boss, that you look very fetching today. Much better than the horrible green jeans you normally go for.'

'Sexual harassment,' Lexi quips. 'But I'll take it as a compliment.'

Another laugh. 'Right, come on.' Peter begins to stride ahead. 'We're going to meet the bloke I got to judge the competition.'

'Really?' Lexi trots alongside him. 'Who is it?'

There's a slight hesitation before Peter answers, 'His name is Dominic, he's up-and-coming.'

'Up-and-coming?' Lexi stops abruptly. 'Peter, we need an established artist. Up-and-coming? Who wants to be judged by an up-and-coming?'

Peter keeps walking, ignoring her.

'Peter!' Lexi has to run to catch up with him. 'Up-and-coming? This competition has had a lot of attention. You can't have an up-and-coming!'

'Trust me, we're cooking with gas.'

'Sorry?'

'It's all cool.'

He does sound cool, she thinks, but how can he be? 'You should have gone for established.'

'Eh, I'd appreciate it if you didn't express these reservations to my guest.'

'I'm your guest!'

'My other guest. I'm telling you, Lexi, it's cool, now just trust me.'

'I've got no choice, have I?' she mutters glumly.

'No, you don't.' His answer is firm.

Very soon they arrive outside a sprawling, many-windowed mansion. The door dwarfs both of them. It seems to have been hewn out of a redwood tree, or something equally large.

'Is this your place?' Lexi gawks around. The enormous gardens are a vibrant green. From somewhere she can hear the sound of water gushing.

'Nope, I just brought you here for the joke,' Peter says as the front door swings open.

'Aren't you the smart arse?' Lexi snorts, following him into a large hallway. Light pours in through the windows, bouncing off the floor, which is a beautiful shade of cream. Expertly hung artwork adorns the walls on either side of the wide expanse of shiny tile, fabulous abstracts depicting various woodland and seascapes.

'Wow.' Lexi stands in front of one of the pictures. 'These are great. Where did you get them?'

'Picked them up all over the place. This one here . . .' He points to the smallest picture. 'Do you recognise it?'

Lexi peers closely and then says, smiling, 'It's a copy of a Charles Ryan.'

'Yep. And an exy copy at that. You know your art.'

Lexi shrugs. She knows Chas's art like the back of her hand.

'Would you like to see the rest of the place while we're waiting?'

'I'd love to.'

His house is enormous. Way too big for one person, she thinks, though she doesn't say that. It might sound mean. In fact, as he leads her from kitchen to dining room to games room to bedroom after bedroom, she starts to feel a grudging admiration for Peter. He has great taste. Everything in the house is carefully chosen and well positioned. The furniture is unusual yet functional. Finally, just as he's finished showing her the cool gym with swimming pool and a voice-activated wave maker, the front door bell chimes.

'That would probably be the guest of honour.' He winks at her.

'I bloody know where I stand now, don't I?' Lexi says, following him back down the hall.

Peter opens the front door to reveal a tall, brown-haired man with a tanned face. Lexi grins. This guy has made no effort at all to dress up. Instead of a suit, he's wearing a standard-issue stripy t-shirt, white trainers and jeans.

'Hi, how you going?' Peter says, not at all taken aback at his guest's lack of etiquette. He waves a hand in Lexi's direction. 'This is Lexi, my offsider at the gallery.'

Dominic doesn't respond. He stands in the edge of the doorway, seemingly struck dumb.

'Hi,' Lexi says, nodding.

'Oh, eh, hi,' Dominic eventually blurts out.

'Come on in,' Peter urges, and Dominic, rather stiffly, steps across the threshold.

It's true, she thinks, most artists are bloody weird.

'We'll sit down, shall we?' Peter, fully in command, leads the way into his lounge and makes himself comfortable on one of the chairs. Lexi sits opposite him, the room is so enormous, and then Dominic lowers himself into a chair beside Peter.

'I was telling Lexi about you,' Peter says. 'About how you're, eh, up-and-coming?'

261

'Yes,' Dominic pauses. 'Up-and-coming.'

'So, how do you define up-and-coming?' Lexi asks. Damn it, she thinks, this won't be good. Who's going to respect a guy only a wet week out of art college?

'Well,' Dominic looks down at his hands, 'Saatchi is financing my work for the next five years.'

'Fuck off!'

Peter gasps at her use of language.

'Eh, I mean—'

''S'OK.' Dominic grins. 'That's what I said when he offered, too. In just the same surprised tone as that.'

'Wow.' She is seriously impressed. Saatchi, the millionaire who was largely responsible for the Brit Art revolution. 'So what do you do? You don't shove cows into formaldehyde, do you?'

'Nope. Just ex-girlfriends.'

She laughs, liking him, but still wary. 'Well, it's great, you must be talented, but I still don't get why Peter would—'

'Lexi!'

'No, Peter, this has to be said.' Lexi eyeballs him. She realises he could fire her for this, but damn it, who would like to be judged by someone they'd not heard of? Turning back to Dominic, she says, 'I still don't get why Peter asked you. I reckon people won't want to be judged by a complete unknown. Let's be honest, some of the people who have entered this competition are way better known than you.'

To her surprise, Peter doesn't jump all over her or tell her to shut up. 'Dominic?' he says instead.

'Well, Lexi,' Dominic says, 'by the time the competition ends, I'll be known. Trust me.'

'Trust you? I hardly know you.'

262

'We could change that.'

She's taken aback by his answer, so taken aback that she can't even speak.

'Good,' Peter says briskly. 'You've managed the impossible, to shut her up. Now Lexi, Dominic and I are going to discuss the judging. I have two favours to ask you. Number one is, don't tell anyone who's judging, it's a secret for now.'

'Yeah, only because you think it'll put people off entering. No offence to you,' she says to Dominic.

'None taken,' he says mildly. 'But you've no cause to worry. It'll be cool.'

'And the second favour is that you let yourself out.'

'I will.' Lexi stands up, knowing that Peter is going to walk them into a mess.

Thank God he doesn't really know her, she thinks. She can leave any time she wants.

'Oh, by the way,' she says to Dominie, 'can I see any of your work?'

'I have a crap website. I'm hoping to improve it soon, but yeah, you can google Dominic Grey and you should find me.'

'I'll do that.'

'Good, then maybe we can meet up and discuss what you think of it.'

Lexi ignores the comment as she makes her way to the door.

'I'll be around tomorrow, about seven or so.'

'She spends her time on the beach,' Peter offers.

'Er, hello? My life. My business.'

'See you tomorrow at seven,' Dominic calls after her.

She doesn't answer, knowing that there is no way she'll be around. Cocky little shit, though interesting, she has to admit.

263

Still, no point in being too available. She wants him to think she has a life, which is weird as she normally doesn't care what people here think of her.

Cissy is in her shop, expertly moulding some sort of material into a hat shape. The place has been transformed from a girly emporium into an edgy, slightly sinister spot. Doug's love of black is reflected in the shelving and on one of the walls. Lordi's angel towers against this wall, wearing a ridiculous cowboy hat. Lexi isn't quite sure what to make of it.

'Wow, don't you look nice,' Cissy teases gently as she walks in. 'Love the hat.'

'Do you? I'm not mad on it myself.'

Cissy squeals as Lexi laughs. 'So how did the meeting go? Has Peter got a good guy?'

'Don't even ask.' Lexi rolls her eyes. 'Plus, it's meant to be a big secret, but egg on face springs to mind.'

'I like egg,' Cissy smirks.

Lexi laughs a little before asking carefully, 'So, how's things with Doug? Is he a good guy?'

'What?'

'Have you got a better guy than Peter's got?'

Cissy stops her manipulation of the material and fixes her gaze on Lexi. 'You know Doug. You know what he's like.'

'I like Doug,' Lexi says cautiously, 'I do. But Cissy, he's having a rough time right now. Maybe it's not an ideal moment to plunge into a relationship.'

'It's not a relationship.'

'That's not what Lordi thinks.' She curses herself for dragging Lordi into it. 'Or me,' she amends.

'Look,' Cissy sighs, pushing her half-made hat aside, 'I don't mind admitting to you that I'm bloody lonely, Lexi. Every guy I've dated in my life has been a disaster. I've been used and abused like you wouldn't even believe. I am here to reinvent myself, I don't mind admitting it. And if I can have fun with a guy I like, then I'll do it.'

'Please take care,' Lexi says softly. 'Doug is on the rebound. His whole life seems to have gone belly up.'

'Mine is belly up all the time.'

'Oh Cissy, don't say that.'

'It's true. Now you know.'

'How is it belly up?'

Cissy buries her head in her work again. 'I'd rather not say. But trust me, being here has saved my sanity. You guys have saved my sanity.'

'Well, when you want to talk,' Lexi says as gently as she can, 'I'll always be here.'

'No one is always here,' Cissy answers. 'You'll go someday, Lexi, and you won't come back. You've got,' she pauses, considering, 'I don't know, but what you have I don't. I'll be here for ever.'

'You won't.'

Cissy doesn't reply, and Lexi isn't surprised. 'I'm lonely too,' Lexi admits. 'But you know, it's getting better. And it will for you too.'

Again Cissy says nothing. Lexi gets the feeling that there is nothing more to say, so she stands up and, touching her friend on the arm says, 'I'll be back tomorrow, and the day after and the day after that. OK?'

'I'll look forward to it.'

'And we'll all go out. You, me, Doug and Lordi.'

'Great.'

'So chin up. You do have mates.'

'Thanks.'

It should have reassured her, but as she leaves the shop, she feels anything but.

38

I NORMALLY LOVE VISITING Bob and Lucy. And it's not just their welcoming house I like; it's the idea of being out. Of being normal. Of escaping the confines of my cloistered existence for a few hours. But tonight, because of the row with Chas, I'm a puddle of nerves. What if Bob and Lucy know all the details of how we rowed? But how could they? Chas would hardly confide in them, he's not a kid. But Bob and Lucy are the sort of parents who notice stuff. They'd notice if Chas was in a foul humour. My mother wouldn't bat an eyelid if I went around with a razor blade in one hand and a noose in the other. Or she never used to, before the accident. But Lucy is the sort of mother who remembers to tell you to wrap up against the cold, the kind of mother who buys Lemsip at the first sneeze. It used to drive Lexi mad, but I thought it was cool. If Chas was grumpy, Lucy would definitely notice. But, I think, my mind going around in circles as I drive, even if Chas was in a foul humour, why would Bob and Lucy associate that with me? They wouldn't. And sure, maybe he isn't grumpy at all. Why should he be? He's probably fine. That would be good. But then that would mean that – Oh, God. I realise that I should have called and pleaded illness, but I reckoned that Chas would know and laugh at my cowardice.

The only way to deal to with this, I had decided as I'd left my flat, was to pretend that it never happened. Just smile at Chas, say hello and be mature. But I'd rather have trekked to Roy's shop than to this house. And the nearer I get to my destination, the bigger the knot of dread in my stomach. As I pull up outside, I realise that I feel sick. I can't bear to see the cold look in his eyes or – hang on a second – I peer out of my window into the darkness beyond the car. Chas's jeep is missing. I look out the passenger window – nothing. I crane my neck to look out the back window – zilch. He's not here. My heart gives a whump of relief, instantly making me feel even sicker. But in a good way. A tremendously relieved way.

Thank you God, I shout in my head before realising that I'll have to face him sometime and that I'm only delaying the inevitable. But still, it'll be at least another three weeks, which is *ages* . . .

Almost light-heartedly, I slam my car door closed and before I even make it to the door, Bob opens it.

'Hello, Andy,' he says, and his voice is sort of weird. He pulls the door open wider. 'Come on in. You must be cold; it's not a great night, eh?'

Bob never talks about anything as bland as the weather. I scrutinise his face for some sort of clue as to why he's doing that. His shoulders are slumped, he's finding it hard to meet my eyes and smile. As I step into the hallway, apprehension crawls up my spine. I try to think of something to say as I follow him to the dining room. Chas really couldn't have badmouthed me, could he? I mean, I didn't even mention it to Kate. I don't quite know why; maybe I was afraid of what she'd say.

'How are you, Bob?' I ask nervously as he lets me go before

268

him into the room. Lucy is sitting on the sofa, a big tissue in her hands. I stare at her and swallow. They know, I think numbly.

'Lucy,' I say softly. 'Hi.'

She looks up at me, and then looks back down at the tissue and something in me breaks.

They don't want to see me any more because I've hurt Chas. He's all they have left and they want him to be happy. I don't blame them. But I thought they liked me, I really did. And the row with him wasn't my fault. Not entirely.

'Sit down there, now,' Bob says, surprising me, as he indicates my favourite reclining chair.

I don't sit because I'm desperate to explain myself. I don't want to hurt these people. 'Bob, Lucy,' I begin, sounding a little desperate. 'About Chas—'

They both look a bit startled.

'He won't accept it,' Lucy says tearfully, knotting the tissue in her hands.

Won't accept it, I think. Jesus, he accepted it for over a year, when he was off making loads of money, and now that he's back he thinks he can just pick me up and ask me to be his friend? Won't accept it, my arse, I think a little indignantly. There is such a thing as protectiveness, but this is not fair. 'Well, that's just – just,' I search for the word, 'tough for him,' I mutter, a little tearful myself. 'He just has to.'

Lucy and Bob exchange shocked glances.

'He's a big boy now,' I add. 'He just has to deal with it.'

Bob frowns. 'Andy, pet,' he says, 'it's not like you to be so harsh. I know you feel he let you down, and maybe he did, but this is his sister we're talking about.'

'I—' I'm just about to launch into a speech about how I

know they love him but that they have to understand where I'm coming from, when Bob's words penetrate my stupid, self-absorbed brain. 'Sorry,' I jerk a tiny bit. 'What?' And then I realise, in a sort of slow-motion, almost comic night-mare way, that this is not about me. At all. 'Pardon?'

Lucy nods at Bob, who crosses to me and puts his hand on my arm. 'Now, now,' he says, leading me to the recliner like I'm an old woman in a nursing home, 'I don't know what you're talking about, Andy, but Lucy and I, we have some-thing to tell you.'

I sit down, almost as if I'm in a daze.

'We wanted to wait until you came to visit before telling you,' Bob goes on. 'Over the phone is too much of a shock.'

'Tell me what?' I gaze at the two of them, knowing that it has to be about Lexi. 'What's happened?'

'Well, it's good in a way.' Bob swallows hard, then sits down beside Lucy and puts his arm about her shoulder and hugs her into him. She still hasn't said a word. She wraps her arm about his waist, though. 'We got a call yesterday, to say . . .' Bob coughs and seems to find it hard to continue. 'We got a call to say that, well, they think they've located her body.'

At these words, Lucy hiccups back a sob, and Bob wraps his arm tighter about her.

I blink and open my mouth to say something, and then realise that I don't know what to say.

'Andy?' Bob gives me a probing look.

I swallow hard. 'They have?' I croak out.

Bob nods.

'Lexi's body?' The words themselves seem so fragile and tender. 'They found it?'

'They think so,' Bob says quietly.

'Where?' My voice is small.

'Apparently a man spotted it when he was hunting, or something.' He brushes his hand across his head as if it hurts him to think of the details. A pause. 'I don't know much else.'

'Oh.' It's too big to take in.

'We've to,' Bob swallows and his voice breaks as he says, 'you know, get dental records and and stuff, it could take a while. But they rang us to prepare us, just in case.'

Tears hit the back of my eyes and slowly start to leak out. I get a mental image of Lexi, lying in the undergrowth for a year, her beautiful face being destroyed. She didn't deserve to be left all alone on an isolated mountain-top, to be rained on and feasted on. My best friend, with her laugh and her high cheekbones and her annoying habits, which only endeared her to me more. 'Poor Lexi,' the words emerge in an anguished sob. 'Poor Lexi.'

Next thing, Lucy's arms are about me and we hold each other and cry and cry. I think we all know that it has to be her.

Bob leaves us alone, and reappears some time later with coffee and sandwiches.

Over uneaten food, the story unfolds of how the police called them on Saturday evening. When Chas arrived home, he'd found his parents in the kitchen and he'd instantly known something was up.

'When we told him,' Lucy said, 'he looked at us as if we were mad, or as if we were, I don't know,' she shakes her head to clear it, 'as if we were being disloyal for thinking that she could be dead. I mean, where does he think she is?'

'It's the shock.' Bob pats Lucy on the hand. 'He just got a shock.'

'No, it wasn't just that. He flat-out refused to believe it.' Lucy looks at me with distressed eyes. 'He really got cross that we'd accepted that she could be . . .' She doesn't finish. Instead she stands abruptly and walks to the fireplace, her back to us. 'I'm worried about him.'

'You're always worried about him,' Bob says gently. 'He—'

There is the sound of a key in the lock. The front door bangs open, then slams closed. 'Only me.' It's Chas.

The three of us look at each other. And I suddenly remember my earlier unease about meeting him. Pathetic, I know, but bad as it was, now it feels a million times worse. I feel desperately sad for him, and in no position to be able to comfort him. What do I say?

'We're in here,' Bob calls out. 'With Andy.'

'Yeah,' Chas pokes his head around the door, 'saw your car outside, Andy. How you doing?'

'Good,' I say automatically, then realise that my red eyes and tear-streaked face are far from good. 'Well,' I shrug, 'you know . . .' My voice trails off.

'We've just told her about the phone call yesterday,' Bob says. 'She's a little shocked.'

'Oh, um,' Chas nods, 'right.' He seems to swallow hard before saying, 'It's probably a mistake. I, eh,' he thumbs in the direction of the kitchen, 'I'll just get a cuppa, leave you all to it.'

When the door closes behind him, Lucy looks at me, her eyebrows raised. 'See?' is all she says.

'He might be right,' I find myself saying, 'you never know. It mightn't be her at all.'

It's met with silence. They stare at me.

'You never know,' I say again. I know I want to believe it.

'I think,' Lucy begins haltingly, 'that after all this time, I *want* it to be her. Right now, I just want to bring her home and know where she is and have some sort of peace. I can't live my life not knowing what's happened, or where she is.'

'I can't either,' Bob says.

And they embrace.

'She would have contacted us if she was alive,' Lucy says, her voice muffled by her husband's shoulder. 'Wouldn't she, Bob?'

His answer is lost as I gently close the door on them.

'You going?' Chas's voice from behind startles me. I'd been so busy making my exit that I hadn't noticed him in the hallway, sorting out his copious amounts of photographic equipment. He's on his hunkers and, as usual, to my heart-sore gaze, he looks beautiful. But how can he? His hair is all mussed up; he has about two days' stubble on his face and his eyes are ringed with huge dark circles. To more objective eyes, he looks wrecked.

We stare at each other before I gulp out an 'I'm sorry'.

He quirks his eyebrows.

'You know, for . . . for Lexi, and all.'

There is a pause. Then he stands slowly up, and I'm aware of how tall and solid he is. Softly, he says, 'You think it's her, do you?' He sounds hurt.

I flinch. 'I don't know. I guess I—'

'You know what Lex was like,' he interrupts in an urgent whisper as he crosses towards me. 'She was difficult. She was so bloody wilful. You know that.'

'So?' I wish he wasn't so close. I can smell his familiar scent, and it hurts.

'So? So, she's probably punishing them by not getting in

contact. They had a huge row with her the day she left, d'you remember?' He sounds as if he desperately wants to believe it.

'Chas, I think—'

He puts his finger to his lips and draws me away from the sitting room towards the front door.

'That's why she hasn't been in contact,' he whispers. 'Wouldn't you think so?'

He's looking at me so pleadingly, almost begging me to agree with him, but I can't. Yes, Lexi did row with the two of them because they found some dope in her haversack and yes, she had refused to ring them. Instead she'd called Chas, and kept him updated as to where she was. But it still doesn't make sense.

'She'd still contact you,' I say. 'She was mad about you.'

His eyes glimmer with sudden tears, and he turns his head away and looks upward, as if trying to keep them from falling.

'Or me,' I add. Then I wonder if she would. I'd rowed with her too. But it was only a minor thing. Still, it wasn't minor enough for me to tell Lexi's parents about. I keep thinking that if she's dead, she wouldn't be if she'd sat with me on the bus. And maybe they'd think that too. But Lexi would never be so cruel as to leave us all in limbo like this.

'Lexi would never do this to us,' I say. 'You couldn't think that of her.'

Chas's Adam's apple bobbles as he swallows hard and then his eyes, so brown and sad, meet mine. I suddenly have an acute urge to touch him. I reach out and my hand brushes his sleeve. He stares down at my hand, and then covers it with his free one.

We stay like that for a second. I don't know how he feels about it, but my heartbeat begins to escalate and the feel of

274

his hand over mine is like coming home. I have missed him. I have.

'I'm sorry if you think I left you,' he says softly. The change in subject catches me unawares.

I glance up at him. 'I'm sorry if you think I left you,' I say back, equally softly.

He smiles a little and inclines his head. 'I accept your apology.'

'Good.'

Another smile. The silence builds. Then he gently takes his hand away and I have no option but to release my hold on him.

'Friends so?' he says.

And though I want it, I'm afraid he'll start calling for me to go and have coffee with him, and then my carefully constructed lies will come tumbling down around my head. But how can I refuse? 'Friends,' I agree.

'Good.' He holds my gaze until I'm forced to turn away and open the door. As I leave, he calls out, 'Don't give up on her, not just yet.'

I think, and I know it's awful, that I would rather my best friend be dead than for her to be playing some elaborate hoax on us. I don't think any of us would survive that.

39

TWO DAYS LATER, Kate begins her project with the 'borrowed' radio equipment. Getting it into my apartment was a covert operation. Apparently Kate had to meet her friend in the middle of a field just outside Dublin, where the transfer from the friend's boot to Kate's boot took place. Kate has to have everything back to her friend by four o'clock. I've abandoned work for the day to help her set things up. Not that I could have worked, anyway. Ever since Sunday, when I found out about Lexi, I just can't seem to concentrate on work or on selling ads to people. I've had nightmares and don't want to be on my own, not even during the day, so helping Kate seems to be the obvious thing, even if I do seem to be getting in her way. To give her her due, though, she's biting her tongue and being very nice to me, and I bless my mother for persuading them to move in. If Kate and Luke weren't here, I reckon I'd spend the days lying on my bed, staring at the ceiling or sitting on the computer trying hard to escape my life. But the two of them keep me so firmly in the world. At the moment, I'm like a balloon that could go off in any direction, and they're the ones holding the string and keeping me from wandering too far away. I suppose they distract me.

This morning, Luke is going to give his yoga class in my front room, and then afterwards they're going to have tea in my kitchen while Kate records their conversation. They've to talk specifically about what the class means to them, and try to incorporate the feeling of camaraderie they all get from being together. My job is to monitor the sound levels. At least, I think that's what I'm doing.

I'm messing about with a button that Kate has told me not to touch, when my phone bleeps.

Do you think purple and black match?

Alistair. I grin slightly. I text back *Has she punched u? Do u have black eye?*

He texts, *What?*

But before I can reply the phone rings. It's him. 'I only got that joke now,' he says. 'But really, Andy, I'm serious. Does it match?'

'Has she agreed to go out with you again?'

'Just to thank me for the ad, she said. But that's good, isn't it? I mean, she didn't have to, did she?'

'So she's bringing you out?'

He pauses. 'Eh, I suppose so.'

Kate pushes past and glares at me. Obviously she knows I've touched the button. 'Andy!' she hisses as she twiddles about with the friendly-looking knob. 'Jesus!' she adds for good measure.

I move out of her way and into the hall. 'So where is she bringing you?'

Another pause. I can almost hear his mind tumble in panic. 'I dunno. Or maybe she wants me to bring her out. Oh shit! Do you think I should ring her?'

'No,' I answer firmly. 'Maybe you should just have a Plan

B. Book somewhere yourself, and if she's expecting you to bring her out, then at least you've somewhere to go.'

'But she said she was going out with me to thank me,' he says. 'So I reckon she's bringing me out. That way, you know, she won't feel too obliged to be nice to me.'

'Nice to you? You mean she won't feel obliged to shag your brains out?'

'Oh Andy!' He sounds genuinely hurt. 'I find that offensive. I would never expect—'

'Oh, keep your y-fronts on.'

'I don't wear y-fronts. I find that even more offensive.'

I laugh. 'Look, if you're going to worry about it, maybe you should ask her. Ring up and see if she'd like to go to a certain restaurant, and if she agrees, you know the bill is on you. OK?'

'OK. Ta.' He pauses. 'Do purple and black go together?'

'Black jeans, purple shirt?'

'Uh-huh.'

'Yeah, sounds grand. Only not too dark a purple.'

'OK. Sorry to be such a fecking eejit.'

'You are forgiven. And for God's sake, will you be yourself this time.'

'Unfortunately I have no other choice.'

I smile. 'Good. Let me know how you get on.'

He says goodbye and hangs up. I haven't told him about Lexi yet. I reckon he'll go all undertaker on me and be afraid to ask my advice, and so I've put it off. Not that he knew Lexi, but he knows what good friends we were. I shove my mobile into my pocket and go back into the kitchen. Kate is there, sipping on some coffee and looking nervous.

278

'You will be great,' I tell her. 'And Luke's yoga class can't wait for it. They'll be loads of fun.'

She smiles and pours me some coffee, and we sit in silence.

Luke's yoga class are struck dumb. When they troop into the kitchen after their session, they peer around at the micro-phones and the recording equipment as if they've just landed on a new and foreign planet. Very quietly, they sit down at the table, making faces of wonder at each other, and whisper their thanks as they accept cups of tea and biscuits from me.

Luke nods at Evelyn. She swallows hard and says, 'Well, that was a great class today, thanks Luke. It's so nice to get out and about.'

Good God, I think, she sounds like a robot.

'I like to get out and about,' says Fred. 'Especially since I had my heart attack. I know who my friends are.'

'Who are your friends?' A jerky response from Eileen.

'You are. I would be lonely if it wasn't for all of you. You visited me and—'

'Guys.' Kate claps her hands for silence. 'Eh, can we say this as if we haven't learned it off?'

There is a loaded silence. They all look at Luke.

'Jesus, yous haven't learned it off, have you?' Kate winces. 'Luke, you didn't tell them what to say, did you?'

He shrugs. 'They were all a bit nervous, they weren't sure what to expect. So, we practised in the yoga class.'

'I thought we did well,' Evelyn sniffs, taking another biscuit.

'It would be nicer if it was more natural,' Kate tries to say tactfully.

'I'll have you know, I was the star of a number of am-dram productions.' Evelyn is miffed.

279

'Maybe I'll ask the questions and you just respond,' Kate ignores her. 'We'll start maybe with you, Fred, if that's OK?'

'Fine,' he says, going pale and spraying biscuit all over the table. 'Just, eh, let me swallow this biscuit.'

We wait as he begins to chomp frantically before swallowing the result of his mastication down with a mouthful of tea. It all looks very painful, but eventually the biscuit is gone and he thumps his teacup onto the table. Then, taking a few deep breaths, like a fighter about to go into a ring, he nods to Kate.

'Now, it's no big deal,' Kate says.

'Oh, I know, I know.' He sounds utterly unconvinced.

'Right. As you know, this is going to be a documentary on loneliness and isolation. What I need from you lot is how getting out has helped you all. You spoke so well about it on my show, Mabel, and that's what prompted me to do this.'

'That, and the fact you got fired,' Evelyn points out matter-of-factly.

Kate bristles but again ignores her. 'So, Fred, give us a bit of background. Tell me all about yourself.' Kate nods at me to record.

'Well,' Fred says, 'I'm Fred.' He pauses. 'I'm in my late seventies and I live on my own. I have no family, but it was by choice.'

'Really?' Kate says.

Fred nods.

Kate makes motions for him to talk. He looks confused.

'You can't nod,' Kate says, 'you're on radio, Fred.'

'Oh yes, yes.' He finds this very funny, and so do the women.

Kate bites her lip. 'So, go on.'

'So, I live on my own, by choice. My own family, the one

280

I was born into, was all a bit chaotic. I'm not going to divulge that on the radio, that's all very private.'

Kate says nothing, but I can see her tense up. Fred continues, 'So when I grew up, I left my own family as quick as I could and I said to myself, "Self"' – an explosion of laughter from Mabel – 'I did say that.' Fred looks offended. 'I said, "Self, don't get caught in that trap again." And so I live on my own. I have no contact with my family and I tended to steer clear of people, not really trusting anyone. But I found that I was very lonely, and so I joined yoga.'

'What made you join up at the yoga?'

'Well, I originally wanted to do creative writing, but that was full, so I joined this. Sorry,' he says to Luke.

'No worries.' Luke grins.

'Anyway, I found the girls in the yoga class very nice. Not too nosy, just right.'

The 'girls' beam at one another, and I suppress a smile.

'Anyway, everything was fine, keeping people at a distance was fine, until I had a heart attack a few weeks ago.'

'And what happened?'

'Well, I was lucky in that I had it in my yoga class. There were people around. If I'd had it at home, I would have been alone and I could have died. And if I'd joined creative writing, well, it wasn't on that day, so I would have been at home. And I found that there is nothing so nice as people. I mean, the people in my yoga class visited me and looked after my home when I was in hospital. I realised that I need people. It's only when you need people that you realise you need people.'

'Oh, very profound,' Evelyn snorts.

Fred glares at her.

'What about you, Evelyn,' Kate says sharply, not the tone for an interviewer, I think. 'Have you ever felt lonely?'

'Of course.' She says it sharply, almost defensively.

'How? When?'

There is a pause. Evelyn's hard exterior vanishes for a second as she says, 'When I lost my beloved husband.'

'Now, now.' Eileen pats her hand.

'We were together for forty years,' Evelyn continues, 'and after he died I realised that everyone I knew was a couple. Not that it mattered at the time because I locked myself away and didn't want to go out, didn't want their sympathy or their cakes. I refused to socialise. Then one day, a long time later, I remember getting up and dressing and suddenly realising that I hadn't thought of my lovely Derek all that morning. Not that he was forgotten, but just that for the tiniest instant, I could contemplate living without him. Only there was nowhere to go, nothing to do. We had no children, he wasn't exactly a virile man, you know. Problems,' she dips her voice to a whisper, 'down there,' she points downwards. 'The only thing hard about it was the fact that it was hard to get up, that was his joke. His way of living with it.'

We all laugh. Evelyn smiles. 'Anyway, I had no one. I'd shut myself away for so long that no one called for me any more. So after a bit I decided that I had to get out again. I joined this yoga class and a painting class, only the painting is gone now because the hall got shut down. Thank God that I still have the yoga. I think I've made friends here.'

'You have,' Eileen, the big softie, declares.

'What does being lonely feel like?' Kate directs this question to Eileen.

Eileen looks a little baffled, then admits almost apologetically, 'I don't know. I've a great life. Thank God.'

'Mabel?'

There is the longest pause. Mabel swallows hard. 'It feels lonely,' she states. 'There is nothing worse than feeling that there is no one in the whole world that cares for you or about you. It is the lowest feeling to think that no one understands you. That you cannot have a connection with anyone. It's a state of mind, mostly. Because there is a person for everyone. A good friend, good partner, good group to be in. I joined the yoga out of desperation, I don't mind admitting it. I didn't care about being flexible or being fit, all I wanted was to belong somewhere, just for a few hours. Everyone needs that.' She stops abruptly and flushes.

'Wow!' Kate hops up. 'That's brilliant. Well done, Mabel. I'm going to use that in the beginning or at the end.'

'Oh,' Mabel seems overwhelmed by that. 'Fantastic.'

'Why were you so lonely?' Evelyn asks, stupefied.

Mabel shrugs. 'Well, when I was in my thirties, I got married. I'd known him for years. Eight months into our marriage, I find out he's having an affair. Apparently it had been going on well before the wedding. I suppose it shook my faith in people and in my own judgement.'

'Well it shouldn't have.' Eileen pats her hand. 'He was a shit. Not all men are shits. I have a lovely husband. We have three great children. Well, one of them is in jail and that broke our hearts, but we're still together and I am happy.'

'You're very lucky.' Fred nods.

'So is it luck?' Kate asks. 'Not being lonely?'

'I think sometimes being lonely is a result of bad luck,' Fred says. 'I mean, if you've been lucky and built up a lot

283

of friends and then something happens, well, you'll have your friends and you mightn't get left alone. But if you haven't . . .' He stops and shrugs. 'Like me.'

'It's the way you play it too,' I suddenly find myself saying, much to everyone's surprise, including my own. They all turn to look at me. 'That's it,' I mutter, mortified, and retreat back behind the sacred button that I cannot push. Jesus, I wonder what made me say that? For a second or so, I'd become so involved in what they were saying that I forgot I wasn't part of it.

'Do you think it's only old people that are lonely?' Kate asks, obviously gaining inspiration from my interruption.

'Well, I'm not old,' Fred says indignantly. 'I'm only in my seventies.'

'How about people in their twenties?' Kate says, shooting a not-so-subtle look at me.

I concentrate hard on the Button That Cannot Be Pressed and tune out the rest of the conversation.

For some reason, that evening, instead of going on my computer to congratulate my Facebook friend Julie on her pregnancy news or staying downstairs and chatting with Luke and Kate, I head up to my room and stare at the large blank canvas that rests on the easel at the end of my bed. For the first time since taking my art supplies down, I have the urge to paint. I stare at my brushes, all unwrapped and waiting to be used. They've survived their exile intact, and I mentally thank my dad for wrapping them up so well. I only ever had use for a couple of brushes, despite having about twenty. I mix up some water, get out my easel and gently, letting the ideas take me, mix up the colours I need.

I paint whiteness. Not a true white, just a sort of paleness. Then I colour shapes in the whiteness, blurs which might be anything, though they have the forms of people. And I sketch in the back of a head. Baz sits upright, watching me with his green slanted eyes. He gingerly moves in closer, finally coming to rest right beside me, lying curled up in a ball at my feet.

I keep going with an urgency that both delights and scares me.

I haven't felt so alive in a long, long time.

40

LEXI IS ON the beach, waiting for Dominic Grey, the so-called, would-be famous artist to show up. She's changed her mind about meeting him because there is something she has to say to him. Urgently. She had called into the gallery looking for him, guessing that that was where he'd be. But the only people in that day were potential customers, there to view the selection of artwork that was hanging on the walls. *The Global Shortlist* was emblazoned across one wall in black and white. The 'O' in global was done like a planet earth. Lexi was miffed. It had been her idea, and she hadn't even been told these were on display, much less that they had been chosen at all. OK, she hadn't worked in a few days, but still . . . Slowly she walked from one picture to the next, admiring the way the colours looked. A fairly brilliant shortlist, she had to concede, but then again, some of the pictures were so good a dog could have chosen them. Her heart leaped slightly to see Yellow T-Shirt's picture there; she hoped he'd be pleased, and wondered if he'd swing by to have a look. Probably not. Turning, she'd seen Peter and, deciding to talk to him instead, she called out his name.

'Busy, busy!' he called before disappearing. Or escaping. It sure looked like he didn't want to talk to her. Maybe he was embarrassed. He probably was. But she was baffled. How on earth could he have made such a huge mistake as to get an unknown to judge?

So she'd come to the beach and was now hanging around, just outside her little tent, waiting for Dominic to show. He'd told her that he'd meet her here, and she was sure he'd meant it. OK, so she was a few days late, but she guessed that this was her best hope. Maybe, she thinks hopefully, Peter has fired him, which would be good but which would also put them in a dilemma. The winner of the competition was due to be announced in three weeks' time, and finding a judge at such short notice would be a nightmare. But anyone was better than Dominic, in her mind at least.

And then she spots him. He's on top of the sand dune, scanning the beach. Is he looking for her? She waves over in a sort of friendly, glad-to-see you way, trying to put him off guard. To her relief, he waves back and begins to stride towards her. He is still wearing his stripy t-shirt. Or maybe it's a different one, though she doubts it. He seems anxious to meet her too, and she feels a little flattered, despite what she knows.

'Hello,' he says. 'You're a hard woman to track down.'

'I come and go.' Sitting, she pats the sand for him to join her.

For a second he stands there, hesitant, as if studying her, before gingerly inching himself in beside her. 'You must be a busy lady,' he turns to face her, 'only here now and again.'

'I do have a life beyond this beach.'

'Good.' He stares out to sea, suddenly silent. 'What sort of a life?'

Lexi laughs. 'None of your business. Jesus, you're bloody

nosy. What sort of a life do you have,' she pauses, 'Faker Boy?'

'Faker Boy?'

'Uh-huh.'

'Why do you say that?' He sounds taken aback.

'I say it because you're not a big-shot wannabe at all, are you?'

'No, I'm a gonna-be.'

'Ha, ha. I saw your website. If you could call it that.'

'Yeah, I told you it would be crap. The colours didn't come up right on the page. I've to get a better camera.'

'All your pictures were plastered in "sold" signs so that I couldn't even see them properly. It was like you didn't want me to.'

'Oh yeah,' Dominic has a sneer in his voice, 'I deliberately designed my site so that you couldn't see the pictures.'

'Not me, anyone. And there was no mention of Saatchi on your site, either.'

'It needs updating.'

'Or on the web anywhere. The only reference to Dominic Grey was on your site.'

'I'm not that well known yet.'

'You must be on a site somewhere!' This was not going how she'd thought. She had been under the impression that he'd fold. As far as she was concerned, the evidence that he was a chancer was overwhelming.

'May I suggest, Lexi, that you mightn't know how to use a computer properly? Googling is an art form, you know.'

'More of an art form than the pictures on your site,' Lexi snaps.

'That's a horrible thing to say.' He doesn't sound offended.

288

But she has to admit, it is horrible. And if he's being honest, then her comments are pretty unacceptable. Though she still can't help feeling that something is amiss. 'Sorry,' she says. Then adds, 'Look, I just don't want you taking Peter for a ride. He's irritating, but he's OK. And I think he's a very lonely man, and you better not spoil this chance he has of making his gallery work. This competition has been a brilliant idea, far more successful than we ever imagined.'

'I promise I won't take him for a ride,' Dominic says with impressive sincerity. 'And yes, I agree, Peter is a good guy.'

'I still can't understand . . .'

'So, tell me where you're from.'

The sudden change of subject catches her off guard. The fact that he's not offended at her criticism of his pictures is strange. Maybe he really believes that he's great, in which case what she thinks of him wouldn't matter. And yet . . . 'I hope you mean what you say.'

'I do.'

And even though she distrusts him, there is something very likeable about him. His voice especially. All warm and inviting. But con men are likeable, that's their big weapon. 'Cross your heart?'

He smiles. Does a vague crossing motion.

'And hope to die?'

There is a pause. 'Er, nope. I don't hope that at all.'

'OK, I'll let you off that one. But I'm warning you.'

'So, where are you from, Lexi?'

Obviously her warning isn't too worrying for him. 'Ireland,' she says with a bad grace.

'Oh. Me too.'

'Yeah, I read your website, remember?'

289

'And where are you from in Ireland?'

'You going to track me down one day?'

'You never know.'

'Well, in that case, I'm not saying. I don't encourage strange men in that way.'

'I'm not strange.'

She says nothing.

'I bet you're from Dublin.'

'Obviously you're better at gambling than art.'

'You wound me.'

'I will if you don't shut up asking me questions.'

He laughs.

They spend the next hour walking the beach. Lexi tells him about her friends in Salue. It wasn't meant to have gone that way at all.

41

THE INTERCOM BUZZES for about the hundredth time that morning. Kate's phone calls have paid off. She has spent the last few days ringing various charity groups and hospitals looking for participants for her documentary. So far, the response has been amazing. I suppose people don't mind talking on the radio because they can retain their anonymity. Contrary to what I expected, not all the contributors are old. Not that I've seen too many of them. I decide that if these people want to remain anonymous, well, then I should respect that and not go tromping through my kitchen making copious amounts of coffee, which is what I usually do when I'm working. So instead, I've made a large flask full and brought it into my office. Downstairs I hear Luke, who is helping Kate with the recordings, answer the door.

'Andy,' he calls, 'it's for you!'

I feel a rush of momentary panic, the fear that always grips me when I've an unexpected caller. Luke gives no clue as to who it might be, so I'm forced to walk to the stairs and look down.

Chas. Oh shit! I groan inwardly. He seems to specialise in calling over when I look my very worst. Sensing me, he looks up and smiles. I cower away, trying to cover up the fact that

I'm in my comfy grey track bottoms and oversized sweatshirt, my hair tied up in a messy ponytail. 'Hiya,' he says, 'have you got a second?'

'Eh—'

Baz pushes past me and at Chas's invitation, runs lightly down the stairs, already purring loudly. Chas rubs him.

'Wow,' Luke is gobsmacked. 'You've got a magic touch.'

Chas looks confused. 'Magic touch?'

For some reason, I don't want Chas knowing how grumpy the cat usually is, so following Baz downstairs, I make hasty introductions. 'Chas, this is Luke, Kate's boyfriend. Luke, this is Chas.' I pause. 'An old friend of mine.'

'Lexi's brother.' Luke makes the connection immediately and, as he shakes Chas's hand, his expression changes slightly. 'Any news on your sister yet? Have they identified her?'

'Nope,' Chas answers, his face impassive, 'it'll take a few weeks. That's if it is her.'

'Of course.' Luke nods, looking embarrassed. He thumbs in the direction of the kitchen. 'Nice to meet you. I'd better get back or she'll kill me. We've someone else coming in a minute.'

'They're making a documentary in there,' I explain as Luke disappears.

'Oh.' If Chas is confused, he hides it well.

And then the person Kate is expecting buzzes up from the front door. 'I've been told to come here for a documentary?' The line crackles, but the voice is female.

'OK, flat 22b.' I bleep her in.

'Have I called at a bad time?' Chas asks. 'You seem to be really busy.'

'It's Kate's gig,' I tell him. 'I'm working upstairs. Come on up.'

Before he can follow me, the doorbell rings. I nod for him to open the door. He does, to a hugely overweight girl in her mid-twenties. She's made an effort to look good, and wears a black trouser suit with a white blouse. Her hair is a wispy mousy brown and hangs poker-straight to her shoulders. Her make-up is too brown and too heavy. Her blue eyes are mascaraed an unnatural inky black and, blushing deeply, her chin almost sinking into her shoulders in embarrassment, she says, 'Documentary?'

I frown. Something about her is familiar. I shake my head. I can't quite place it.

As her gaze rests on me, I turn away, the habit of hiding my scar too deeply ingrained to avoid.

'In there,' Chas answers for me, pointing to the kitchen.

'OK. Thanks,' the girl says breathlessly, already highly agitated. 'Thanks.' Chas joins me on the stairs, making way for her to pass him.

Then the two of us head up to my study. I don't know why I was embarrassed to be seen in my tracksuit, as Chas has made no effort to look good either. He's in navy Adidas bottoms and trainers and is wearing a heavy blue jumper, yes, a *jumper* over his tracksuit. The look is slightly horrendous, but he's so handsome he just about manages to pull it off. He's a long way from the poseur guy I used to know. It's unbearably sad, for some reason.

My study looks satisfyingly scattered and important. In fact, it makes me appear to be a busy lady with a *life*.

'Wow,' Chas has spotted a rough I've done of this month's magazine cover on my computer screen. 'Great stuff, Andy,' he sounds impressed. 'I like the way you've merged the flowers into the headstone montage.'

293

I smile, delighted. 'Thanks. It's not too obvious, is it?'

'Nah, I like it.' He turns to me. 'So you really do like working for this magazine, do you?'

'Yeah, do you find that hard to believe?' But I'm joking, and he smiles.

'And do you still paint? You used to be quite good.'

'A bit,' I mutter, remembering the burst of energy I'd had a couple of nights previously. 'I gave it up for a while but I'm slowly making my way back to it.'

Now he looks as if he's sad for me. 'Well, if you ever want me to have a dekko at anything . . .' He lets the sentence hang.

'Thanks.' I'm grateful for the offer. Chas is a brilliant critic; he helped me a lot once. 'Maybe, you know, when I feel . . .' I don't finish either.

'Sure.' He nods.

'So . . . ?' I quirk my eyebrows.

'Oh yeah,' Chas says, sounding suddenly serious, 'you're probably wondering why I'm here.' He gives an awkward laugh. 'I'm, eh, looking for pictures of Lexi so I can—' He stops abruptly, his gaze riveted on the picture I have of his sister beside my computer. The one taken in Dublin airport the day we left Ireland. 'Hey.' He crosses over, his voice lifting in delight, and picks up the snapshot. 'Perfect. Wow.' He stares at it, his expression alternating between wonder and regret. 'Wow,' he says more quietly. Then, as if remembering me, he lifts his eye from the picture and asks, 'Can I take it? I'll have it back to you in a week or so.'

This picture is my only happy link to that time, the one photo I can look at without my heart twisting up. 'Why do you need it?' I resist the temptation to grab it from him.

'It's perfect for a project I'm doing.'

'On?'

He refocuses on the picture. His finger traces the outline of his sister's face. 'It's for Mam and Dad.' He shrugs and says vaguely, 'Just a Lexi scrapbook photo thing.'

Maybe on some level he does realise she might be gone, I think, wanting to hug his pain away. But what could I give him? I'm not much better myself. I nod, hating the way I almost didn't want him to have my photo. 'Sure,' my voice is soft, 'take it so. Just – just bring it back. Please.'

He must sense my reluctance. 'You can scan it and email it to me if you prefer.'

I wave that away. 'No, it's fine. Go on.'

'You sure?'

'Totally.'

'Thanks.'

There is silence for a second. We regard each other across what seems to me to be a chasm of unarticulated emotion.

'I—'

'Can—'

We stop. Smile. I wave my hand. 'You first.'

'Can you tell me about it?' He nods to the picture.

'Oh, yeah . . . sure.' That's not what I'd hoped for. It's not what I'd been about to say. But to my relief he doesn't ask what I'd been about to blurt out. 'Sit down,' I indicate my office chair, 'and I'll get a spare seat from my room.'

'Nah, let's go somewhere more comfortable. How about I buy you a coffee down the road?'

Oh shit. Balls. Damn. My expression freezes. My stomach heaves. Sweat breaks out under my armpits and on my forehead. Shit!

Chas half grins. His gorgeous smile breaks my heart. How could I ever have thought Noel was cute? What I wouldn't give to walk down the road with this man.

'It's only a coffee.' Chas smiles roguishly. 'And you did say you were my friend.'

I know my refusal will hurt him, but I can't accept. Not for the first time I curse myself and the state I've let myself get into. I indicate my office with a sweep of an arm. 'Look around. I've piles of work to do. I'm really sorry, but I don't have the time to go out.'

'You must have a lunch, surely?'

'Not today.' I aim for regret, but instead my voice notches up an octave and leaves him in no doubt that I'm lying.

'OK.' He's gone a little cold on me, and I can't blame him. 'Get that chair so.'

I detest myself, despise my weakness. If only he'd chosen Roy's shop, I'd have been OK. We could have chatted among the aisles of breakfast cereal or fruit. I vow to venture down to the coffee shop on the corner very soon. But I know that two rebuffs are two too many for Chas. I don't think he'll ask me again. But hell, maybe I'll ask him. When I get better. And I will get better . . .

So, sitting opposite him, I take the picture from his hands and stare at it. It was a Wednesday, I tell him. Though he knows that much, as he'd driven us to the airport where I'd made a fool of myself by bawling loudly as he'd waved us goodbye. I had wanted to turn back. If only I had. I don't tell him this, though. I say that it had been a rare sunny Wednesday morning. Lexi had been standing in the duty-free area in Dublin airport, a baker-boy hat holding back her glorious dark hair. She was giving an oratory on what she wouldn't miss about Ireland. I can even hear her voice, that sing-song inflection she had that was crossed with an unmistakable Dublin lilt. She wouldn't miss the weather, the traffic, the food, the ugly men or her super-controlling parents. I laugh, and tell her that if my folks had found dope in my haversack, my mother would have tried to ban me from going altogether. 'You're twenty-seven,' she said, laughing loudly, 'they can't stop you from doing anything.' And snap. I'd caught her. Her expression is pure obstinate, defiant, entertaining Lexi.

Then she'd taken one of me. I'd had red, swollen eyes and looked awful. Only I don't say this to Chas either, as he sits there, drinking up every word, his eyes hungry for information. And then, I say, we'd had some guy with an equally enormous haversack take a picture of both of us. I don't know where those pictures are now. I try never to look at pictures of myself any more. And I don't tell Chas this last part either. And then, I'm finished. I pull back out of that day and hand the photograph back to him.

'Thanks.' He flicks his gaze over it one more time before pushing it into a jacket pocket. Then he stands up and thanks me again. I walk him down the stairs and, at the end, just before he goes, he turns to me. 'Bye now.'

'Bye.' Just then, the kitchen door opens and Kate walks out accompanied by the girl who'd come in just after Chas. 'Thank you very much,' she says sincerely to the girl.

The girl, looking a lot happier now, thanks Kate.

Then Kate sees Chas and, shrieking loudly, arms open wide, she lunges forward and hugs him. 'Hey Chas, long time no see. Luke said you'd called in.'

297

'Kate.' Chas laughs, sounding genuinely pleased to see her. 'You're looking great. Sorry to hear about the show.'

'Excuse me,' the girl says, and again I have the eerie feeling that I know her. 'Can I get out by you both?'

'Of course you can, Cathy,' Kate says, 'I'm sorry.'

Cathy scuttles out as quickly as she can, her head down. I don't know anyone called Cathy, so I must be mistaken.

'Poor thing,' Kate says as she closes the door on her. 'She's had an awful time. I'm definitely using her story in the documentary.' Kate links her arm through Chas's, and I envy the ease with which she does this. 'So, how you been? Have you time for a coffee?'

'I've been good.' He smiles down on her. 'Working hard here, getting some pictures together, portraits mainly.'

'Your pictures sell for a fortune, you jammy bastard,' she says, making him laugh. 'Feck's sake, all you do is press a button and earn thousands. Life is not fair.'

'Oh, I dunno. You got to talk sex to the nation for a fair fee yourself.'

'Do you not read the papers? I'm a lesbian now.'

'Only sends your stock even higher,' he says, grinning.

I watch this exchange with a little sadness. We used to banter like that.

'So, coffee? The kitchen is free for an hour or so. Or Luke can make you something disgusting, your choice.'

'The "something disgusting" sounds tempting, but I got to go. I've to meet someone in town.'

'Oh, someone nice?' Kate teases.

'Well, not as nice as you, obviously.' Chas grins down at her. 'But yeah, someone nice.' He turns to me. 'See ya.'

'Bye.' I wonder who he's meeting.

When he leaves, Kate makes a big 'oooh' with her mouth. 'Is there something I should know?'

'Nope, he only called for a picture of Lexi. He's doing a scrapbook up of her for his parents.'

'Yeah,' Kate scoffs, rolling her eyes. 'Oy! Luke!' She yells.

He comes running. 'Yes, o loud-voiced harridan?'

'What do you think? Chas calls, looking for a picture of his sister. He has tons in his own house, yet he takes one,' she holds up a finger and repeats, *'one* from Andy. Would you call that an excuse just to see her?'

Luke frowns. 'Hmm, I dunno. Seems a bit off, using his sister like that.'

'He wants to see you.' Kate ignores Luke's analysis, as if she'd never even asked for it. 'I betcha he wanted you back.'

'No he didn't,' I brush her off. 'Sure he was going out anyway. And he did ask me to go for an innocent coffee, but I couldn't.'

'Well, I suppose he knows you don't go out. Sure his parents probably told him that.'

There must be something in my expression, or my lack of response following her words, because Kate has not been an interviewer on the tackiest show without gaining some experience on reading people's reactions. 'You've not told them, have you?' she gasps.

'Nope.'

'But—'

'How could I?' I flare up, my shame at being found out making me harsher than I should be. 'Their daughter died, what would they think of me? I'm alive, and I'm so self-indulgent that I can't go outside the door without having a panic attack? Come on!'

'I wouldn't call you self-indulgent,' Luke speaks softly. His hand is on Kate's shoulder, silencing her. 'There's nothing self-indulgent about being scared. I'm sure they'd understand.'

His sympathetic analysis makes my eyes water.

'Yeah, you've done so well, Andy,' Kate says. 'You nearly died, for God's sake. It wouldn't be normal if you were,' she pauses floundering, 'eh, normal.'

'So I'm not normal?' My lips twitch. 'Is that what you're saying?'

'No!' But she sees me smile and smiles a little back. 'You should tell them. I mean, what do they think you do? Do they think you go out?'

'Uh-huh.' I sigh. 'I can't tell them now. It's too late. It's gone on too long. Anyway, the way I see it, in another couple of months I will be going out. So it'd be pointless.'

'True.' Luke squeezes Kate's shoulder a little harder, stopping her from jumping in. 'So, let's see. The best thing to do is to bring you to a coffee shop next, just in case he asks you again. Or do you want to go with him for a coffee?'

I shrug, feigning indifference.

'Of course she does!' Kate snorts. 'She's so into him, she's almost wearing his jocks.'

'Ugh!' Luke and I both go together.

'Sorry,' Kate apologises. 'Throwback to my sex-show days.'

300

42

LUKE'S MOTHER IS a surprise. I think I'd expected an ageing hippy or someone in flowing robes waving incense, but instead, she's dressed conservatively in a two-piece navy suit with a white frilly-collared blouse. Shiny patent mid-height shoes and a patent bag complete her outfit. Her hair is the blonde preferred by older women, styled in a short, neat cut. Her face, with eyes the same green as her son's, is subtly made up, and the whole impression is of an elegant creature with a whiff of sadness. Or maybe I imagine the sadness because she is taking part in Kate's documentary, and so far, most of the contributors have had some sadness or other, though there has been a lot of humour too. I'm helping Kate today, as Luke is working. I think he's deliberately allocated his mother a slot on a day when he won't be around. According to Kate, Luke told her about his upbringing once and since then he has never referred to it again.

'Hi Marsha,' Kate greets her cheerily. 'Sit down here.' She motions her to a seat. 'This is my sister, Andy.'

'Hello Andy.' Marsha's voice is as clear and as tinkling as a Christmas sleigh bell. 'I hope my sloppy son isn't being too much trouble.'

'Not at all.' I relax under her friendly gaze, my self-consciousness dissolving bit by bit.

'The mess in the hallway is all mine,' Kate chuckles. 'Luke is so good. He tries to fold everything away.'

'Are you sure it's the same Luke?' Marsha jokes.

We laugh, though we all know it doesn't actually merit the big belly laugh from Kate.

'OK,' Kate says, pretending to recover from her fit of laugher, 'all you have to do, Marsha, is describe your experience of loneliness. What words would you use? I'm not looking for specifics. Just a few words to say how you felt when you were at your lowest.'

Marsha nods. She takes off her navy jacket and hangs it carefully on the back of the chair. Then, rummaging about in her bag, she pulls out a piece of paper, unfolds it and smooths it out. 'Is it OK if I read this? I'm afraid I might get all tangled up.'

'Absolutely.' Kate points at the microphone, adding, 'Talk towards that in as natural a way as you can. It'll pick up whatever you say.'

'OK.' Marsha licks her lips. 'Will I go now?'

Kate nods. I press the 'record' button as Marsha begins to speak.

'Loneliness is not just being alone,' she reads. 'It's also being surrounded by people who don't know that you're living a lie. It's being surrounded by people who think that you've got a happy marriage, that you've got everything you need, when in fact, behind closed doors, things couldn't be further from the truth. Loneliness is not being able to break out of the prison of a sham marriage. Of a sham life.' She pauses, nods slightly. 'That's it, really. That's what I think.'

302

Kate nods to me, and I click off the recorder, surprised at the brevity of the interview. And yet moved by its truthfulness.

'Great,' Kate says. 'Nice and succinct. Would you—'

Buzzzzzz.

Buzzzzzz.

'Hello?' I press my intercom.

'Only us!' It's my mother. 'Thought we'd call in. Your father just received his driving certificate.'

Kate and I look at each other.

'It's a computer driving licence,' Dad corrects patiently.

'They know that,' Mam says impatiently. 'Don't be so pedantic.'

Kate leans across the table to Marsha. 'Brace yourself, you're about to meet my parents.'

Marsha looks a little bewildered at Kate's warning tone. 'Oh, that'd be nice,' she says, and she sounds as if she means it.

'Come on up.' I buzz them in.

Half a minute later, I've ushered them into the kitchen. Kate has just served Marsha a cup of tea and is placing a full pot on the table for our parents. They've stopped dead at the sight of this stranger in my kitchen, and also at all the wires and stuff all over the floor.

'Mam, Dad, this is Marsha, Luke's mother,' Kate makes the introductions.

My mother looks as if Kate has just announced that it's the President sitting having tea at the table. Her surprise is palpable. Like me, I suppose, she'd been expecting someone a little more like Luke. Instead, she is forced to acknowledge that Luke's mother is a neat, normal-looking woman with classy dress sense.

303

'Well,' my mother says gushingly, 'how nice to meet you. I'm Lil, and this is my husband Donald.'

'Nice to meet you too,' Marsha says. 'Kate has told me so much about you.'

'And Luke has told us about you,' my mother lies gaily. 'Hasn't he, Donald?'

My dad looks blank. 'Maybe when I was out,' he says eventually. 'I really can't remember.'

'He's like that,' my mother says brightly, 'he can't remember his own name sometimes.'

'Oh dear!' Marsha looks horrified.

'Just an expression,' my mother explains hastily. She looks around. 'Where is Luke, and why is all this stuff in your kitchen, Andy? Is it for the magazine?'

'Luke's out working . . .' Kate pours them both a cup of tea and they sit down as she continues, 'and all this stuff is mine. Remember the documentary thing I was telling you about? On loneliness? Well, that's what this is for. It's recording equipment. We're almost finished up now.'

'Oh.' Mam nods, lifting the cup to her mouth and sipping delicately. 'I see. Well, that's wonderful, Kate. Wonderful.'

'I was just helping Kate with it,' Marsha explains, 'so that's why I'm here.'

'Oh.' My mother looks taken aback. 'How are you helping? We weren't asked to help. Were you asked to help, Donald?'

'No.'

There is an awkward silence.

Kate fills it. 'It's a documentary on loneliness, Mam. Have you ever had crippling loneliness?'

'Well, no, of course I haven't. I—' The penny drops, and Mam realises exactly what Marsha is doing there. The effect on her expression is comical. She now looks as if she's mourning the loss of a puppy. Her voice dips about ten octaves and drips with sympathy. 'Have you been lonely?' she asks Marsha. She gently touches the other woman's arm. 'Isn't that terrible? And what did Luke do? Did he help you?'

'Mam—'

'He was only a child at the time.' Marsha shrugs. 'There was nothing he could do. Oh, he'd cuddle me and tell me he was going to box his dad about when he got bigger and stronger, but it's not right for a child to say such things, is it?'

'No!' Agonisingly for Kate and me, my mother misses the point. 'All children should love their parents. What would make him say a thing like that?'

'Lil,' Dad tries to intervene.

'Well, his dad was a very angry man.' Pause. 'Violent,' Marsha expands, just in case my mother should misinterpret things again. 'So naturally Luke wanted him gone.'

My mother's mouth opens and closes like a fish. As does mine. OK, I'd suspected as much when I'd heard her speak, but for her to say it in such a blunt way shocks me. Especially when my own dad is a complete pushover.

'Oh.' My mother is flustered now. Her hand goes to her face in agitation and embarrassment. 'Oh dear, I am sorry. I didn't mean to pry. Oh my God, poor Luke.' She swallows. 'And – and – him such a nice boy.'

I suppress a smile. 'Nice' is not a word she's ever associated with Luke. 'Weird' and 'strange' are the more typical ones.

'Isn't he?' Kate makes the most of the opportunity. 'My mother adores Luke,' she tells Marsha, who beams with pleasure.

'Well, he is a great boy,' Marsha agrees. 'After his dad died, he got a job and gave me every penny he had. Every penny. Even though he hated his job he stuck with it. Then one day I told him to go out there and do what he wanted. Life is too short to live a lie, I said.' She smiles a little. 'Of course, I had no idea he was going to do yoga and sell health food. And grow his hair into those awful scraggy things.'

'They suit him,' my mother declares staunchly, causing my dad to splurt his coffee everywhere. 'Oh, Donald,' she shakes her head, 'I can't bring you anywhere.'

'Well, I suppose they do in a way.' Marsha nods. 'It's who he is, isn't it?'

'It certainly is,' my mother agrees. 'He's a lovely boy with scraggy hair.'

An hour later, Marsha has left but my parents are still in situ. At first, the topic of conversation had been all about poor Luke and poor Marsha, and of how my mother had never known, and of how she was going to be so nice to Luke from now on. 'If you had told me he was from a dysfunctional background, I would have been extra nice to him,' she informs Kate in an accusing tone.

'You would not,' my dad says. 'You would have warned her off him and said something along the lines of "like father, like son".'

'I resent that, Donald!'

'Do you,' he says mildly. Taking a rolled-up scroll from his pocket, he flattens it out and hands it to me. 'I was presented with this this morning. I can now go on a computer and find my way about.'

'Well done, Dad!' I jump up and hug him.

306

'I said,' my mother repeats, not going for the change of subject at all, 'that I resent that.'

'That is great, Dad.' Kate hugs him too. 'This calls for some vino.'

'It's way too early in the afternoon for that,' says my mother, waving the suggestion away.

'I'll just have a glass,' my dad says.

'You won't.'

'I will.'

'I don't think so, Donald.'

'I don't care what you think.'

'Obviously.'

'A glass, Kate,' he says firmly.

Buzzz.

Buzzz.

'Hello?' Oh God, please don't make it be someone who doesn't know my parents, I pray. They're brewing for another row.

'Is Kate Fitzsimons living here?'

'Who is this?' I ask my caller.

'Police.'

Kate looks askance at me.

'Kate, the police are at the door.' I say.

My mother is looking at my father. 'What are the police doing here?' my mother asks.

Kate gawps at me, then, with a slight edge of panic in her voice, she says, 'Andy, take the tape we did today out. Take all our recordings and hide them. They can have the equipment. Let them in.'

'Girls?' My dad has caught my mother's hand and is squeezing it. 'Why are the police here?'

307

We both ignore them. I buzz the cops up and hastily do what Kate has ordered me to do with the tapes, stuffing them into a press. Meanwhile, Kate stands by the door awaiting their arrival.

'What is going on?' My mother has gone pale.

'What is going on?' Dad asks too.

'I'm going to be arrested, I think,' Kate sighs.

My mother gives a shriek as the police arrive in. Dad holds her close and I half envy Kate as she is led away, because it'll be me that'll have to explain the whole thing to my mother and father.

Story of my life.

43

KATE HAS BEEN released on bail, though her solicitor has berated her for refusing to name her accomplice, the one who supplied her with the recording gear. But I'm proud of her for that. I tell her as much when she arrives back to the apartment with Luke.

'How are Mam and Dad taking it?' she asks as she sinks into a seat, looking very despondent indeed.

'Badly,' I answer.

'Damn.' She bangs her head lightly against the tabletop. 'And we were so nearly finished.'

'Yeah, well, at least all the stuff is here.' I show her where I've stored the digital tapes. 'And I've spent the afternoon uploading most of it to your computer. We can finish the rest later.'

'Oh, Andy, thanks.' She manages a smile.

'Luke?' I glance encouragingly at him.

'And,' he says, sitting opposite her and taking her hands in his and giving them a gentle squeeze, 'seeing as your birthday is coming up, me and Andy clubbed together and bought some online editing software for you.'

'No!' Her face is a picture of incredulity.

'Yep.' He winks across the table at her. 'It's the best we could get, and it wasn't even that expensive, was it, Andy?'

'Nope.'

'So,' Luke grins, 'get working, jailbird.'

Kate's shriek of pleasure makes us both laugh. 'I hope they have radios in jail,' she half jokes, 'so I can listen to it when it goes out.'

Of course, we have to make the inevitable visit to the folks. There is no point in putting it off, I tell my sister as we bundle up in warm jackets to brave the driving rain in the dash to Kate's car later that evening. Luke has wisely opted out, even though we've informed him that my mother's impression of him has undergone a dramatic U-turn.

Hopping into the car, shaking the droplets from my hair, I shiver and it's not just from the cold. My parents are a formidable force when they're rattled. We're better off getting it over with, I've told Kate. If we go to them, we control things. Even though we are on their turf, we can walk out and leave when we want. Kate agrees with that.

She is understandably quiet on the journey over, her finger dancing over the radio controls to find any kind of music to take her mind off the lecture and recriminations that will definitely be dished out. While Kate has always done pretty much what she wants without bothering about what Mam and Dad think, she knows right now that breaking the law is not something she can justify to them. They have her cornered for perhaps the first time ever.

Twenty minutes later, we pull up outside. It's almost as if they've been expecting us. My mother comes to the door and hastily ushers us inside. I can imagine she's delighted that this has happened in the winter, when it's dark early and none of the neighbours can see her law-breaking daughters enter.

'I hope you're proud of yourself,' is her first comment to Kate, as we take our jackets off and hang them at the end of the stairs.

'Well, yes, the documentary is brilliant,' Kate answers flippantly.

I wince.

'Oh.' My mother throws her eyes heavenward. 'You can give all the smart answers you want, lady, but you've broken the law, you've received and used stolen property.'

'I know.' Kate nods, her head low as she stares at her furry boots. 'But Mam, you have to understand—'

'Understand?'

'I was desperate, I had no job, I—'

'And whose fault is that?' Mam sweeps by us into the sitting room, which as usual is pristine. 'Donald, your daughters.' She sits down beside him on the arm of the chair and he takes her hand in his.

Kate and I follow her in and sit together on the sofa, like two children waiting outside a headmaster's office. They glare at us.

'I'll probably only get a fine,' Kate chirps up.

'Oh, fantastic.' My mother shakes her head. 'That's all right, so.'

'There's no need to be like that, Mam,' I speak quietly, annoyed at her for some reason, what I can't quite fathom. In fact, I'm annoyed at both of them.

'No need to be like what? Angry? Disappointed? Upset?'

'Sarcastic,' I say, falling into my usual role of defending Kate.

'Well, this is our house,' my dad speaks for the first time, 'and if we want to be sarcastic, we will be. I can't believe you did what you did, Kate.'

311

'Well said, Donald.' My mother nods.

'So . . .' Dad leans forward in his chair. 'What on earth were you thinking of?'

'I was thinking of making a documentary,' Kate says back, her spikiness reasserting itself.

'But you stole equipment.'

'Borrowed,' Kate clarifies. 'My friend was putting it back every night for me.'

'Borrowing without permission,' Dad says, 'equals stealing.'

'My friend had permission. She lent it to me.'

I can almost hear her scraping the bottom of the barrel.

'Yes, Kate stole it,' I jump in, 'but it was minor. They'd treated her badly at that station, in case you didn't know. And she was upset, and she had a great idea for a documentary and it was the only way she could make it. If this was a film, she'd be a hero.'

Scraaaaaape!

'A hero?' Dad lifts his eyebrows. Then, without waiting for me to answer, he shakes his head and sighs. 'I am disappointed. Especially in you, Andy. You're her elder sister, you should have warned her.'

'I am not her babysitter!' The fury of my response stuns even me. And then it hits me what's annoying about this whole scenario. The two of them, all cosied up to one another in their disappointment of us. Normally they'd be bickering and sniping and getting one over on each other while Kate and I cringe. But now they're together against the world. All the times I've tried to smooth things over have never been as successful as this. 'I am not her babysitter, nor yours, for that matter.'

Their looks of puzzlement are sort of satisfying.

312

'I don't think you're in any position to be throwing tantrums,' my mother says, sounding shocked. 'You've always been the good one, Andy, that's why we can't understand—'

'I have always been the good one to keep the two of you happy, to stop the two of you from murdering Kate because she's always done exactly what she wants.'

There is a silence.

'I haven't always done what I wanted,' Kate says meekly.

Now I feel cross with her. 'Yes, you have. You've spent four years talking dirty on the radio and shocking the knickers off our mother.'

'That's a very crude expression,' my dad says tightly.

'I only did it initially because,' Kate stops and shrugs, 'well, you're right, Andy, it's the only thing that unites them, isn't it? Their raging horror and shock at me.'

More gobsmacked silence.

My mother is the first to recover. 'So,' she says, sounding all indignant and hurt, 'you're blaming us, are you? What are you saying, that we haven't been good parents? That you stole radio equipment to save our marriage, or something?'

'No.' Kate eyeballs my mother. 'But you have to admit, you and Dad are as happy as two gorillas with a bunch of bananas right now.'

'I am not a gorilla,' my mother snaps, a little tearfully. 'I find that very hurtful.'

'It's just an expression, love.' Dad pats her on the back. His eyes dart from me to Kate and back again. 'Your mother and I are not happy at all at what you've done, Kate. And for your information, we did our best with the two of you.' He speaks with his customary quiet dignity. 'In general, you

313

made us proud, we never stopped you both doing what you wanted, not when Andy went on that trip with Lexi, not when our daughter became the most famous shock jock in the country. Yes, we voiced our opinions, but we're your parents, that's our job. And we both agree what we want for both of you. Do not try to blame us for what you have done, Kate. Don't even try.'

'She wasn't,' I say back. My voice is not as dignified as his, unfortunately. In fact, I sound like a kid again. Maybe you always do when confronting your parents. 'But you and Mam, you never stop bickering.'

'Kate and Luke never stop either, from what I can see,' Mam says.

'We're not like you.' Kate's voice sounds a little strangled.

'Yes you are,' Mam says dismissively. 'You're always bossing him.'

And she is, I realise, only it doesn't seem the same. But then again, Kate and Luke are not my parents, so it's not as threatening to me. Or as embarrassing. And I also realise, with the shock of a sudden fall, that Chas and I never had an argument. Well, except for that one time when he'd come to the apartment. But I'd been a nervous wreck afterwards. Before that, however, in our halcyon days, I'd never fought with him or, my mind says, the thought sneaking up on me like a mugger on a street, fought *for* him. I'd been so determined never to be like my parents, I'd gone the opposite way, fighting for nothing. Keeping everything calm and steady, not rocking the boat. I hadn't even fought for my life until recently.

'Luke doesn't mind being bossed.' Kate's voice seems to come from a great distance.

'Neither do I.' Dad shrugs. 'Your mother and I enjoy our little tiffs.'

'We do.' My mother nods vigorously.

'Well we don't.' I swallow hard, zoning back in. 'I have spent years trying to foresee arguments developing between the two of you and head them off at the pass. I've—'

'We never asked you to,' Dad says. 'It's none of your business.'

'Well then,' Kate stands up, sensing an opportunity, 'what I do is none of yours.'

'Actually, madam, it is,' Mam says sharply. 'Sit down.'

Kate does.

I'm vaguely aware of Dad lecturing us, of being told that what Kate has done is terrible and inexcusable and of Kate meekly acknowledging this and apologising for calling Mam a gorilla. I'm aware that she explains to them about the documentary, and of how she was compelled to do it and the fact that Dad is glad that she's not a shock jock any more and that they will help her out any way they can. I am aware from my daze that Kate has jumped up and hugged him and he her. And that Mam has joined in. But I stand apart, as if I've just stepped off a waltzer in an amusement park and am trying to stop the world from tipping sideways. It was none of my business. My obsession with playing peacemaker was a waste of my time. My letting Chas go should never have happened. I should have fought for him, with him. Told him I'd wait and that I'd kill him if he went off with anyone. Instead I'd stepped aside, never told him of my shame, never forced him to confront his friends about what they'd said. Hidden in the shadows while that girl had talked about me on her phone. Anything rather than confront her. Fights scared me. And in being like that, I'd lost so much. And the only time I had fought with my best friend, she had been killed in a bus accident.

'Andy?' They are all looking at me. 'Are you OK?'

'No.' I shake my head. There's a pressure mounting behind my eyes. A huge lump building in the back of my throat. I feel sick.

'Hey.' Dad comes over to me. He rubs the length of my arms with his hands, as if trying to warm me up. 'What's the matter? We'll sort it out, we will.'

'I fought with Lexi the day she died.' The words tear out of some deep part of me. 'I never fought with anyone before, and then she died.' Tears spill over onto my cheeks.

A puzzled silence follows my words. Then Dad has me in an embrace. 'Hey.' he sounds bewildered. This is not what he was expecting. 'Come here.' He hugs me hard.

'I didn't deserve to have a life afterwards. I fought with her and she sat away from me and she died. It's my fault.'

'Hush now, hush now.' He rocks me gently. 'Where is all this coming from, hey?' He pulls his face level with mine. 'Hey?'

'She needs a drink,' my mother says. She's stroking my hair. 'Get her a drink, Kate.'

'I thought this was my moment,' Kate tries to joke.

'It'll be your moment for a kick up the arse if you're not careful,' Dad grumbles.

I hiccup out a laugh.

'That's my girl,' both my parents say together.

By the time we leave, Kate is quite upbeat, while I'm swollen-eyed and sniffly. Still, I feel as if part of a weight has lifted

316

from me. Of course, they assured me that it wasn't my fault Lexi died but hey, they are my parents. But if I'd sat beside her or her me, who knows how things might have been. Still, just to tell my story about that awful evening is a relief. Just to tell them and not read condemnation in their eyes is so brilliant.

The test, though, will be in telling Lexi's parents, which I know I have to do. My whole relationship with them since the accident has been one long lie. They think I go out, they think Lexi and me were great friends to the end. I have to start afresh, let them know who I really am, who their daughter was. Face the music. Stand up and be told off.

Rock the boat and hope we all survive.

At least I'll be me.

44

'HEY.' LEXI POKES her head around the door of Lordi's shop. 'Have you seen Cissy anywhere?'

Lordi looks up. His shop is even more cluttered than Lexi remembers. Now he seems to have stocked up on posters emblazoned with encouraging slogans.

An angel is a friend. Friends are everywhere.
Angels come in all shapes and sizes. Just like your favourite jeans.
Praying is a telephone call to God.

She suppresses a grin as her gaze rakes over the white posters with the colourful lettering. Each letter is composed of a series of tiny feathers.

'You may think they're funny,' Lordi sweeps over to her, his white cloak billowing behind him, 'and that's good. Anything that makes a person smile is a good thing.'

'Do you ever get sick of all that wise talk?' Lexi asks cheekily as she lounges in his doorway.

'Wise? Thank you very much.' Lordi bows elaborately. 'Now, what were you asking? Have I seen Cissy?'

'Yeah. I talked to her about three days ago. I can't find her anywhere today. You know Cissy, she's always here.'

Lordi nods. 'I saw her maybe two days ago, but I haven't seen her since. Have you talked to Doug?'

'He doesn't know either.' Lexi checks that Doug isn't around. 'But I don't believe him. He wouldn't talk to me for very long, made some excuse to go. And you know him, he never goes anywhere, really.'

'You're better off staying out of it,' Lordi says.

'I told Cissy I'd be around for her, but the past couple of days I haven't.'

'If she wants you she'll find you. You'd be better off worrying about yourself.'

'What?'

Lordi pauses before saying carefully, so as not to alarm her, 'A certain man has been making a lot of enquiries about you. I think it's a little odd.'

'Who?'

'A Dominic Grey. That's when I was last talking to Cissy. He'd been asking her about you too.'

She feels a shiver of nervousness. 'Dominic Grey? The guy judging the art competition?'

Lordi nods. 'Is he? Oh, maybe that's why, then.'

She realises suddenly that she probably shouldn't have told Lordi that information. 'That's top secret. Peter doesn't want anyone to know just yet. Apparently Dominic is an unknown quantity, and Peter thinks it might put people off.' She pauses. 'What sort of stuff was he asking about me?'

'Like to walk?' Lordi indicates the road towards the beach. 'I'm in the mood for a walk.'

Lexi joins him on the path outside his shop and slowly, side by side, they begin strolling along. The sun is high, the sky as clear as the smooth sea. 'So?' Lexi asks.

319

'Well, at first,' Lordi says, 'I didn't think much of it. This Dominic fellow was wandering about the shop, he bought an angel from me, commented on the place and talked in general about the people here. Then he asked if I knew you, and of course I said that I did.'

They've reached the sand dunes. Lordi begins to walk up and Lexi follows.

'Then he asked how long you'd been here, and I said a few months. And he asked where you were from.'

'He did? But I already told him.'

'Did you? Well, I told him you were Irish, and then he said that you seemed like a nice girl and he asked if I knew any more about you.'

'And?' Her heart has skipped a beat. Please no, she thinks.

'I said no.'

'Good.' She's relieved, for some reason. She doesn't need people knowing about her accident. Thinking back, Dominic's questions upon meeting her at the beach had been pretty up front. 'Is there anything else?'

Lordi nods. 'I did ask him why he was so interested in you. I wondered if he was a friend of yours that you'd told to meet you here, or something.'

'And what did he say?' An idea is forming in her mind, an idea so awful in its implications that she can't believe it to be true, and yet . . .

'He said that he'd met you through Peter, and that he liked you and that he wanted to find out more about you. So I told him to ask you himself. He left then.'

'He only met me twice. He can't like me that much.'

'I took the liberty of asking Cissy if she'd been talking to him, and she said that he'd called in to her too.'

320

'What?'

'He bought a hat from her, some music too, so she liked him, but again, just like in my shop, he led the conversation around to you. She thought it was curious, but she said there was nothing much she could tell him.'

'Good.' She feels suddenly sick. She wonders if she should go in search of Dominic, or if she should steer clear of him. But steering clear means that she mightn't get to see Cissy, and she's promised Cissy that she'd be around for her. And for some reason she thinks that it's important to be around in case Cissy needs her. Doug is not going to make her happy, he's too deeply unhappy himself. 'Maybe I'll go and see if I can locate Dominic and ask him what the hell he's at.' Then an idea strikes her. 'Or maybe I'll corner Peter.'

'Peter? What would he know?'

'I have a feeling he knows a lot more than he's letting on.' They've reached the top of the dune, and down below them the beach with its series of tents, stretching long and wide.

'Ah, if only life were like this,' Lordi says, 'a panoramic view. You could see all before you.'

'Yeah, but you can't see behind you.' Lexi smiles.

'You should never look behind,' Lordi retaliates. 'Always look forward.'

Neither Peter nor Dominic is around, much to Lexi's frustration. She thinks of leaving a message for them but changes her mind, preferring to wait in the gallery in case they show up. She spends the next hour looking at the shortlisted pictures once more. It's quiet, only the sound of her boots on the floor breaking the silence. The pictures Dominic has chosen are colourful pieces, some realistic, some not, all with a massive

321

vibrancy to them, a life force emanating from them. She appreciates his taste, enjoys what the pictures represent and wonders what the hell is going on. Maybe it's time to move on. Literally. She came to talk to people, and she succeeded. Before this, she'd been ambling about in the wastelands of the world, her contact with others ebbing and flowing like debris on a river. She feels more grounded now. More in control. Maybe it is time to let go of this place. But there is Cissy to consider. And she remembers Cissy's words the last time she saw her. She'd predicted that Lexi would leave, and she doesn't want to prove her right. She can't leave Cissy. Not until she is sure Cissy will be OK. But if she waits around and her suspicions about Dominic are even half correct, things might just start tumbling all around her.

Hobson's choice.

45

A LISTAIR HORRIFIES ME when he comes over to my place on the Saturday that we've put the magazine to bed. I'm obviously not shocked because he is calling, but because he has somehow managed to persuade his new girlfriend to come with him.

When he announces through the intercom that they've both called to say hello, I flirt with the idea of telling him that I am sick, that I've got some contagious disease, but he won't buy it because he already asked me if it would be OK to come over and I said that of course it was. To be honest, I thought he was going to have a moan about his love life again, and I reckoned I could tell him all about Noel and Chas and we could have a moan together.

Instead, he's a loved-up man. I feel a little jealous, actually. Not of him, though. Just for Mandy, that she has him.

I open the door on both of them, trying to convey with a surreptitious glare at him as to how I feel about being ambushed on my own territory. Alistair smiles easily at me. 'This is Mandy, Andy.' Then he sort of snorts nervously, which belies his earlier smile. 'God, how does that sound, eh?'

Mandy actually looks quite normal. I don't know what I'd envisioned, well I do know, a sort of drippy, skinny, brown-cardigan-wearing 'Mavis'. Instead, Mandy is a miniskirt and piles of make-up kind of girl. She also has massive teeth, like tombstones, which is apt, I suppose. She displays them to me in a wide smile.

'Andy, hello, we meet at last. Al has told me so much about you.' She enfolds my ragged, nail-bitten hand in hers, which is white and soft with shiny, manicured nails. It doesn't seem to me to be the hand of someone who wrestles with thorny roses all day.

'These are for you.' She nods to Alistair, and on cue he produces a massive bunch of lilies. He knows I hate lilies, but obviously he hadn't the heart to tell Mandy. And neither do I.

'Oh, thanks.' I take them from him, wanting to kick him for bringing her here. Has he no sensitivity? He knows I get terrified around strangers. He could have warned me. Though then I would have told him not to come. Mandy has the sort of face I envy, clear and unblemished. Her clothes, though casual, make mine look like cheap bargain-basement. Well, they are, I guess, but still . . .

Sweat breaks out under my arms and I find it a little hard to breathe, suddenly. It dawns on me that I've never had a guest in this flat, not since the accident. All the people that have passed through here have been comfortable ones for me, or ones associated with Luke and Kate. No one has ever gone out of their way to visit me. This visit, as perceived by ordinary mortals, would be seen as a welcome diversion, a pleasant surprise. For me, it's a horror to be endured. Baz senses my unease as he starts to miaow plaintively at my feet. He always does this; I used to think it was because he cared about me, but now I believe it's that he's afraid I'll become so wrapped

324

up in my own problems that I'll forget about him. I'm *heee-re*, he's miaowing.

'Oh, a kitty cat,' Mandy says, sounding ridiculously like a five-year-old. 'Isn't he cute?'

'I wouldn't,' Alistair says, touching her gently on the arm. 'He's not very friendly.'

Kind of like his owner, I want to add, but don't. Then I wonder if our behaviour affects our animals. Maybe that is why Baz is so antisocial. Maybe it's my fault. 'Yeah, best leave him alone,' I say, holding the flowers up to my face to cover my scar. 'Go in and sit down. I'll put these in water.'

Alistair and Mandy climb over all the bits and pieces to get to the sitting room. In fact, Mandy seems to find it difficult, and Alistair solicitously holds her hand. In the kitchen, I take a few deep breaths and mentally tell myself to calm down. Inside, I hear Alistair telling Mandy that he's just going out to see if he can help me in with some glasses. I steel myself and, opening up a press, pull a vase from it.

'You all right?' Alistair asks a tad nervously from the doorway.

I don't answer. Instead, I turn on the tap and fill the vase with water. Then I take a scissors and start to cut the stems on the flowers.

'I, eh, think Mandy might have done that already,' Alistair says, coming to stand beside me, his hands sunk deep into his jeans. I notice that he looks quite nice. New jeans that actually make him appear fatter than he is, and a red and white striped rugby shirt. He's had his hair cut too, all sort of spiky and cool. He doesn't look half bad. OK, he looks quite handsome, actually.

I still don't answer him, chop, chop, chop.

'I, eh, bought some wine,' he says. 'Will I grab three glasses from the press?'

'How could you?' I hiss in an undertone. 'How *could* you?'

He looks a little defiant. Then a little ashamed. 'I thought it would be a surprise.'

'Yeah, it is.' I nod. 'Kinda like the way the bus crash that gave me this bloody scar was a surprise.'

He flinches.

'You know how I am about meeting new people,' I go on as I pull a leaf viciously off the stem of a white lily, causing yellow powder to scatter all over my sleeve. 'You know.'

'Yes,' Alistair nods, 'I know. You're ridiculous about it. I decided to be proactive.'

'It's not your business to be proactive. This is my life, and you can't just bring people here without me knowing about it. I could have a – a panic attack, and I'd be mortified.'

'You're not going to have a panic attack.' He sounds a little pissed off. 'Kate told me you went to a pub a few weeks ago.'

'Yeah. But I had to screw my nerve up.'

'What do you think Mandy is going to do?'

I dump the flowers into the sink and turn to face him, my hands on my hips. Baz is regarding the two of us from his big, lantern-like eyes. 'You had no business. You know what I'm like. You're being insensitive.'

'Nope, I'm trying to help you. You deserve—'

'Am I to take it that I'm an experiment, here?' Mandy speaks from the doorway, and she doesn't look a bit pleased. At our looks of horror, she says, her eyebrows arching up into her perfectly straight fringe, 'I'm sorry, I couldn't help overhearing. What is going on, Alistair?' Now her hands are on her hips, which are gorgeously in proportion to her waist. How did Alistair manage to get her, I wonder idly?

Alistair flushes beetroot-red and stares down at his trainers. New ones, I notice, branded and expensive. 'I, eh, well . . .' he stammers.

'Yes?' Mandy is waiting.

'It's, eh, her.' His eyes flick to me.

'Her?' I say, adopting Mandy's tone, 'her is the cat's mother.' I don't even know what this means, it's just something my mother says.

Alistair glares balefully at me. 'The cat's mother,' he says grumpily, 'doesn't go out much.'

I am beginning to feel sorry for him now. He likes this girl a lot, and I don't want to ruin it for him. Yes, I could kill him for making me uncomfortable and for not thinking of me at all, but at the same time he *was* thinking of me. 'I, eh . . .' I lift up my hair. 'I have this scar,' I mumble, flushing bright red at the embarrassment of showing it off.

'And?' There is no sympathy in Mandy's voice. In fact, she doesn't even cluck out some platitude.

'Well, it's made me embarrassed to go out,' I stammer. 'And I get nervous meeting new people. And—'

'Am I to take it that you didn't tell Andy I was coming tonight?' Mandy barks out.

Alistair jumps a little. 'I thought I'd surprise her,' he says.

'So you used me to help your friend.'

'No, it wasn't like that—'

'It was exactly like that,' Mandy's voice is a whip. Now she doesn't look all cool and collected. Her gaze flicks from me to her boyfriend. 'How dare you, Alistair. How dare you. I am your girlfriend. In fact, I was pissed off at coming to visit your friend tonight. I thought we might do something really interesting—'

'Andy is interesting,' Alistair flounders weakly.

Aaah! I almost forgive him at that comment.

'And instead, I get dragged over to your best friend's house. Well, don't,' and here she points a finger at him, 'don't call me ever again, you – you fecker.'

'Oh hang on,' I rush in, 'please, I'm sure Alistair didn't mean it like that. He was trying to be nice to me, and also to introduce you into his circle of friends.'

'Circle?' Mandy looks at me. '*You* are his circle of friends?'

'I have more than one,' Alistair says, but his voice has dipped, as if he's given up the fight.

'Well, you'll have one less from now on,' Mandy says.

'Ah, Mandy—'

'Don't "Ah, Mandy" me, you little shit. You were using me. How do you think that makes me feel?'

'He does that to everyone.' I try to make light of it.

'Shut up,' both of them say together.

Then Mandy turns on her heel and we hear her in my front room as she obviously grabs her coat from a chair, and then we watch her as she staggers over all the junk in the hallway until finally the door slams behind her.

The silence is profound in her wake.

Even Baz is cowed, and he slinks under the table.

'Do you think another full-page freebie would work?' Al jokes feebly.

'Nope.' I sit down at the kitchen table.

He sits opposite me.

'I'm sorry, Alistair.'

He shakes his head. 'No. I am. I never should have done

that, to either of you.' Then he rubs his hand over his face and groans. 'Jesus.'

'Can I throw out those lilies now?' I ask.

'I was afraid to tell her you didn't like them.'

'They remind me of funerals.'

He cracks a grin.

We sit there for another little while in silence. The clock ticks away the time.

'The only thing that ever worked out for me in my life was the magazine,' Alistair says eventually.

'I am not sitting here listening to your moany "poor me" stories.'

'This is not a moany "poor me" story,' Al says indignantly. 'Thank you very much.'

'I don't think you and Mandy were right for each other anyway,' I say, changing the subject. 'You seemed a bit scared of her.'

'Eh, yeah,' Alistair says, as if it's obvious. 'I was trying hard to hang onto her. I mean, she was gorgeous.'

'If you like women with big horsey teeth.'

'That's my ex you're talking about.'

More silence. Eventually I reach across the table and grab his hand. 'I'm sorry. I really am. And I know you were trying to help me and all, so I feel responsible.'

He clutches my hand in his. 'I promise never to try to help you again.'

'Well, you'll have to help me drink that bottle of wine you bought, unless you want to go after your ex.'

'We came in her car; she didn't like mine, so I think I'll stay here and get drunk with you, if that's OK.'

'That's great.'

He smiles at me, and I'm glad he came over.

How dare she not like his car, I think.

We both get seriously sloshed. I'm sitting on the sofa, my legs tucked up under me, a huge glass of wine in my hand, telling him about Noel. Alistair is cracking up, his head thrown back, his laugh loud and infectious. In my very drunken state, he actually looks quite sexy. He has nice teeth, not at all horsey, and his hair is mussed up and his eyes are sparkling and the kindest shade of dark brown. I give myself a mental shake and tell myself to get a grip. It's the cloistered life that's doing this to me, I think.

Eventually Alistair stops laughing and, kicking off his trainers, he plants his big feet up on my coffee table.

Big feet. Mmmm. I'd never noticed that before.

'Ah, Andy,' he swirls his wine about in his glass, 'you can always make me laugh.' His eyes meet mine. A flash of white teeth. The smell of his aftershave. He wiggles his toes. 'Jaysus, those trainers are a ton weight.'

'They're nice, though. And you look really good.'

'Hmmm.' This time he gives me a glum smile. 'Wasted on you though, eh?'

'I wouldn't say that.' I cock my head to one side. 'If I didn't know you, I'd fancy you, I think.'

'Is that a compliment?' He looks bewildered. Then he shakes his head. 'Nope, it's an insult.' He takes a massive gulp of wine.

And then I lean over and run my fingertips up and down his arm. What am I doing? What the hell am I *doing*?

Alistair watches me. 'What are you doing?'

'Eh,' my hand stops, freezes, 'I don't know, actually.' I give an embarrassed laugh and pull my hand away.

'I liked it.'

'Yeah, well,' I shrug, feigning indifference, my fingertips zinging from the contact, 'you're meant to be broken-hearted, aren't you? Your girlfriend just dumped you. You're looking for comfort.'

'I guess.' He smiles. 'You better watch out, a man on the rebound is a dangerous thing.'

'Dangerous men are exciting.' Am I flirting? With Alistair? Ugh.

He snorts in derision at my comment, and pours himself some more wine. We're on bottle number two at this stage. 'Andy?' He holds the bottle over my glass.

'Go on.'

He pours some for me.

And it's that profile, his hair flopping over his forehead, his nose, his quirky grin, his Adam's apple, his fine fingers, his big feet, that suddenly all come together and I find myself, inhibitions gone, sliding across the sofa and taking the bottle from his hands and putting my hand to his cheek and turning him to face me and pressing my lips on his. Oh God, it feels gorgeous. He smells divine.

For a second, he's startled and doesn't respond, then his hand slowly slides its way up my face where it knots itself in my hair, and he presses his mouth to mine. I gasp. Alistair's kiss grows more insistent. I press myself into him. He pulls me to his hard chest and I moan. The man can sure kiss.

Mmmmm.

Then he freezes, and almost throws me away from him across the sofa. 'Shit.'

I am stunned, gawking up at him.

'Too much to drink,' Alistair says standing up, presumably

to get as much distance between us as he can. 'Not a good idea. Let's call this a night, Andy. Talk whenever.'

I can't reply. I am mortified. Mortified sober. I can only stare at him as he fumbles about looking for his jacket. A gorgeous brown leather one which I hadn't noticed. He doesn't even put it on; instead, he throws it across his arm.

'Sorry,' I stammer out.

'Eh, yeah, me too.'

I'm a bit insulted at that. Sorry I kissed him? Thanks a lot, pal.

'See ya.' He manages a strained smile as he exits.

I listen to the front door slamming closed and sigh. What on earth was I thinking? Wearily, I top up my wine and spend the night finishing off the bottle.

46

THE PAPERS HAVE somehow got wind of the fact that Kate is in trouble with her former employer. There's a small piece on page three on one of the tabloids – *DJ Kate in Hot Water* – accompanied by a picture of Kate in a bath of bubbles. The picture had been lifted from a shoot she'd done years ago for a 'conserve water' campaign.

'I wouldn't mind, but I did have my clothes on in the bath,' Kate fumes as she scans the article. 'This makes me look like one of those awful reality TV contestants.'

'Chill,' Luke stands behind her and massages the back of her neck, 'let it go. When you get the documentary done, you'll have the last laugh.'

Kate moans under the pressure of his hands. 'Yeah, I'm thinking of seeing if I can cut a deal with Dublin Live. I'll give them the documentary to air on condition they don't press charges.'

'They don't do documentaries,' I say, joining in the conversation, from my position at Baz's feeding bowl.

'It's a brilliant piece of work, though,' Kate says, never one for underestimating her talent. 'They'd be fools not to use it.'

'They don't have a documentary slot,' Luke says.

'I'm going to offer it to them all the same,' Kate murmurs.

'You're wasting your time, I'm telling you. They might see it as bribery. You should talk to your solicitor.'

I can see Kate stiffen at the words. As she tenses up, ready to let fly at him, I jump in and blurt out, 'I tried to kiss Alistair on Saturday night.'

It has the desired effect. The impending argument dissolves under my confession. And then I mentally curse myself. Hadn't I sworn not to do that any more? Hadn't I promised myself that I'd never get between two people who were about to have an argument? So at their looks of incredulity, I say, 'Sorry, forget I said that. You go on fighting.' I scoop the rest of the cat food into Baz's bowl and try not to look at the two of them as I dump the empty can in the bin.

'Forget it?' Kate is gawking at me, her gaze following my progress across the kitchen. She pushes her hair behind her ears, which is a sure sign she means business. 'Forget *that*? Forget that you tried to kiss your boss?'

'It was nothing.' I take my cup of coffee from the table and, with a fake nonchalance, attempt to exit.

'It's sexual harassment,' Kate says.

I turn to face her. 'He is not going to say I sexually harassed him.' The idea of it makes me laugh. 'Anyway, he kissed me back, for a bit.'

'He kissed you back!' Kate shrieks. 'Oh my God. Alistair?'

'I thought he had a girlfriend,' Luke chimes in. There's a note of disapproval in his voice.

'I'm not that bad that I have to steal someone's man,' I splutter. 'It was all over with her.'

'He's on the rebound, then.' Kate is horrified. 'I mean, how long has his relationship been off?'

That question I am not prepared to answer. I don't think the words 'about an hour' would go down too well. 'I said, forget it.' I glare at the two of them. 'I only told you both to stop you arguing and it's worked, so talk later.'

Mercifully I manage to make it to the foot of the stairs before Luke calls out cheerily, 'First Noel, now Alistair. Where will it all end?'

In bed with someone, I hope, I snigger to myself.

It's around three o'clock, and the apartment is empty. Kate has gone to meet Luke for lunch, having spent most of the morning editing her documentary. She asked a couple of times for advice on where to cut certain stories, but what did I know? I told her my opinion, and was flattered when she went along with it. Baz is watching me from his position in his basket. He knows the routine at this stage, and is fully expecting to be fed in a couple of minutes.

For about the thousandth time that day, I check my email. There is nothing from Alistair. Not that he emails me a lot, but I thought he might even drop me a line to tell me how many units of the magazine had been sold on. Though he rarely does that either, at least not on the first day. But sometimes he just mails a 'hi' or a 'how you doing'. I do hope that our brief kiss hasn't ruined things. I love our friendship, and would hate to think that we'd be forever awkward with one another. Besides, I'd miss him in my life, I realise. I'd miss his dry humour and his bewildered outlook on things. I couldn't take it if things changed. So I take the plunge.

Hi I type, *I hope you're currently not filing a report on my sexual harassment of you.* I put a little smiley after that. Then take it out. Then put it back again. *You did ply me with powerful wine.*

335

Then I delete that. Then I sit for a bit, thinking hard on what to say. Baz miaows.

'Shut up,' I say to him.

He gives me a glare and miaows again.

I ignore him, and stare at what I've written. Shit, might as well just be honest. So*rry about what happened, and I hope it won't spoil our friendship.*

I press send.

Then I wait, counting down the minutes. After three minutes I check my mail. Nothing. I wait another two. Still nothing. OK, if he hasn't replied in fifteen minutes, I'll go and get some lunch. So I sit and wait, but before the deadline has ended, my mobile rings. Without even looking at the number, I pick up. 'Alistair?' I say breathlessly.

There is a pause. 'Eh, nope. It's Chas.'

My heart plummets, then rises, then gets all confused and bangs out a tattoo. 'Chas,' I repeat dumbly.

'Yeah, sorry, were you expecting a call?'

'No. Yes. Oh,' I flap my hand, 'don't mind me. What do you want?' I croak the last bit out.

'Well, I got your number from the ma. Hope you don't mind.'

'Not at all.' I'm flattered that he has called, and then wonder with some apprehension what he wants. This is becoming ridiculous. If he asks me out again, I'm going to have to refuse, so I head him off as quickly as I can. 'There's no rush returning the picture, you know. You can post it on if you like.'

'Well, I was hoping to call over to you this evening. I've something I'd like to ask your opinion on.'

'Me?'

'Uh-huh. Would that be OK?'

I hesitate, my mind whirling. I hope it's not my opinion on the coffee in the coffee shop he wants. I'm fully planning to confess all my phobias to his parents on Sunday. But maybe if I tell him first . . . maybe . . .

'You're the only one I can think of to talk to before I talk to the folks.' He breaks into my thoughts, obviously sensing my reluctance. 'It's, eh, sort of connected with the picture you gave me the other day, of Lexi.'

'The photo album you're working on?'

He hums an affirmation.

'OK,' I agree. 'I finish work here around six, so you can call over any time after that.' I pause. 'And there's something I'd like to say to you too, if that's OK.' Oh God, now I feel sick.

'Yeah, sure.' He doesn't sound sure, though. Then he asks, 'Will we be alone?'

What does that mean?

'Well, Luke and Kate might be here, but you can come upstairs to my office if you like.'

'Sounds like a plan.' I think he's smiling a little. 'I'll be there around sevenish. I'm in Dublin today snapping, so I'll get back early.'

I smile too. 'See you so.'

He clicks off.

Oh God, I can't eat lunch now. I feel sick and weirdly emotional. Tonight he'll know what a liar I am. Still, the part of my brain that tends to look on the bright side says, At least you know he's coming over. You can at least look good.

I forget about Alistair and hop down the stairs, Baz almost tripping me up in his eagerness to be fed.

337

47

A T SEVEN O'CLOCK exactly, Chas pulls up in his jeep. It's dark outside but peering through my blinds, I know it's him. The way he hops from the vehicle and jiggles from foot to foot, spending a bit of time rummaging around in the back for whatever he has planned to bring inside, is instantly recognisable. I am familiar with his confident stride; I know it's him because he is the only guy I am acquainted with who has a camera permanently slung about his neck. I watch as he saunters up to the door, loving the look of him. A second later, the buzzer goes.

'We'll let him in,' Kate calls cheerily. She has high hopes for me tonight. She reckons Chas still fancies me and is just making excuses to call over. I don't know if I want her to be right, which is strange. All I know is that I miss the way we used to be.

'Bye now.' Luke pokes his head into the room and winks. 'A word of advice, don't jump him the minute he gets in.'

'Feck off.' I give him the finger.

'Do so jump him,' Kate shouts over Luke's laughter. 'I would.'

'Yeah, and crush him beneath your massive bulk,' Luke teases, unaffected by envy.

'I can understand why your dad hit you,' Kate jokingly belts him.

I gape, horrified by her comment, but Luke merely chortles and then they are gone.

I love their relationship, I think, as the sound of their happy voices fade away down the corridor outside. I can hear my neighbour, who seems to keeps an eye out for Kate passing by, calling out to her that he loved the photo of her in the bath. She tells him to 'drown himself'.

'Can I do it in your bath?'

I smile. Life goes on, even when your own has stopped. It's good.

Buzzz.

I shake my head, not used to such profound ideas, and, taking a deep breath, I open the door on Chas.

My first thought is that I have made an effort and he hasn't. Not a sign of a man planning to seduce me. I am wearing my best pair of jeans, bought off the internet, a very lucky buy. They flare slightly and make my hips look thin. On top, I have a gorgeous long blue wool jumper with a cowl neck. I've a large belt slung around it. The blue of the jumper makes my eyes appear even bluer. Chas, on the other hand, is in his trusty tattered sneakers, a pair of green combat trousers and a red sweatshirt with frayed cuffs. His hair, which has grown, has an unkempt look about it, as has his unshaven face. He looks like a guy that is all work and no play, and a million miles away from the Chas I used to know.

'Wow.' Chas smiles. 'You look good. Are you going out somewhere?'

I'm tempted to lie, only I'd been planning on telling him

about my reclusiveness, so I can't. I wonder how he will take it? 'Nope. I'm just dressing for comfort.'

He gazes at my stiletto boots in surprise.

'Coffee?' I ask brightly, my face going red.

'Sure.'

He follows me into the kitchen. 'We're on our own,' I tell him.

'Yeah, I saw Kate and Luke heading off. That's good.'

I notice with a little unease that as well as his camera, he's also carrying a laptop bag. But perhaps he just took it out of his car so that it wouldn't be robbed. That seems likely.

I flick on the kettle, which I have filled earlier. Two mugs are standing by.

'You're probably wondering what I'm here for,' Chas says, sliding into a seat, his laptop bag on the table in front of him.

'Tea? Coffee?' The fecking laptop is making me nervous.

'A strong coffee,' he says as he begins to unzip his laptop bag.

My hand shakes, and a pile of coffee ends up in his cup. I spoon some of it into mine.

His laptop now lies on my table, and he switches it on. Oh Christ. Oh shit. This can't be happening.

Baz distracts Chas momentarily as he trots in and begins to purr at his feet. Chas reaches down and pets him. I say nothing, just watch the two of them in a sort of surreal daze. The next few minutes, if I'm right about this, will be hell. The kettle clicks off and I make us both a drink. My hands are now visibly trembling as I slide Chas's across the table to him. He barely notices it. He has stopped petting

340

Baz and turned back to his computer. I think he's keying in his password because a second later, his computer makes a bleeping sound.

I slide into a seat opposite him, afraid to talk.

Chas looks at me from over the top of his computer. 'Come here, Andy, I want to show you something.'

'You do?' I can barely get the words out.

'Come here.' He beckons me over.

It's like a nightmare. Like when, in your dreams, you can see the man running at you and your legs are like glue. When you can see all your life unravelling out like a piece of material to be blown away by the wind. Please God, I pray, as I join him in front of his laptop, let me be wrong about this, let me be wrong.

'Now, you have to bear with me,' Chas says. He sounds cautious. 'I want you to read something.'

Read? That doesn't sound bad. Maybe God *is* listening. I gently let go of my breath and breathe out, trying to slow my heart. Chas goes into his email programme and rapidly scans his inbox, coming to rest on an email entitled 'Art Competition'.

I'm going to be sick.

It's all becoming too clear.

'Read that.' Chas, oblivious to my turmoil, points to the screen.

I gaze blankly at him.

'Go on,' he urges. 'Please.'

Is there any way I can get out of this? Anyway at all? None that I can think of, right now. I read the email slowly, trying to buy time to think.

341

Dear Charles Ryan,
My name is John Robinson, and among other things I run
my own very successful web-design business in Australia.
My latest business venture involves running an online gallery
in an internet virtual-reality programme called 'Second Life'.
An employee there suggested that in order to make the
gallery more successful, I should run an art competition.
This competition will be unique, in that it will be advertised
online in virtual reality and online in actual reality. In this
way, I hope to reach as many people as possible. I would
very much like if you could judge it. Obviously, I can pay
you for your time at a fee to be mutually agreed.
Yours sincerely
John

The world is beginning to spin.

'Well, I refused,' Chas says, his voice seeming to come from
far away. 'And then he sent me this.'

Another email opens and I'm forced to read it, though I
think I know what it says.

Dear Charles,
I am sorry to hear that you are not interested in judging
our competition. My employee, whose avatar is called
Lexi, said that she knew you, and I thought it would be
worth a shot. No hard feelings.
Yours sincerely
John

Chas waits until I read this and says, his eyes shining,
'Lexi? I mean Andy, how much of a coincidence is that?

342

So I emailed this John fella and told him that I might reconsider, on condition that I could meet this Lexi person, and also on condition that she didn't know who I was. And John sent me the details of how to set myself up in Second Life.'

Chas's voice blurs. I watch, holding onto the back of his chair as he presses the 'Second Life' icon on his computer to connect with the virtual online world.

'The first time you try to join Second Life, you have to download the Second Life programme,' Chas explains unnecessarily. 'Then, when this downloads, you can create a person to represent you in this Second Life world. Your person is called an avatar. You can be anyone you like, and you can design your own face and everything. I created a guy called Dominic Grey. Then I entered the 'Second Life' world. It's exactly like here, it's totally bizarre. I dunno why anyone would bother with it, though. It's like living your life online while sitting at home. Anyway, then John met up with me online, only he calls himself Peter there, and we went to his house and I met—' Chas presses more buttons, logging himself into the programme. His avatar, Dominic Grey, materialises on the sand dune. 'This is me. And then I met up with this other avatar called Lexi.' Chas turns to me. 'This is what she looks like.'

He types the name Lexi Ryan into his 'search' box and the avatar Lexi pops up. She's wearing the green denims and the green hat. The same clothes as in the picture I lent to Chas.

Chas's eyes are searching my face. 'She's offline at the moment, Andy, but don't you see? It has to be her. It's too much of a coincidence.'

343

I can't utter a word. I open my mouth to say something, then close it again.

'Oh shit,' Chas hops up from the chair, 'I've given you a shock, haven't I? Andy, sit down. I know how you feel, I felt like that too. It's a lot to take in. Basically, I'm saying that this Lexi is our Lexi. It has to be. She looks the same. Here, sit down.'

I sit on the chair. I think I might be sick.

'So, it can't be her body they've found, don't you see?' He crouches down in front of me. His eyes are so full of hope that it breaks my heart a little. 'I've talked to her online, but she won't give anything away about herself except to say that she's Irish.'

Can he not see, I wonder? If Lexi was alive, why would she do that? Why would she sit at a computer and do that? 'It's me,' I whisper, forcing the words out before he can go on, 'me.'

A pause.

Chas blinks. 'What?'

A tear slides down my face. I jerk as each word falls from my lips. 'Lexi is me. I made her. I copied her from – from the photo.'

More silence. Chas blinks again. 'What?' he says, swallowing hard, the light gone from his face as his mind filters what I've said.

No one was ever meant to find out. Lexi was my escape from the prison of my house. She was my way of seeing my friend. Of keeping her alive.

'I discovered Second Life last year,' I say, as more tears slide down my cheeks. I am crying for the hope I gave him. 'And . . . and I thought I'd give Lexi a second life. I made her

344

as best I could, it took me ages, and then I let her have adventures and meet friends. I missed her.'

Chas stands up, looking at me like a man suffering from shell shock. 'You?'

I can only nod.

'So, she's not out there?' It sounds like the plea of a little kid.

'I don't know if she is or not, but that online Lexi is me. I'm so sorry, Chas.'

'I thought—'

'I know.'

I try to touch him, but he pulls away.

'I think maybe I should go now.' He rubs his hand over his face and blinks rapidly. Then he stands there, unsure of what to do. I move away and let him switch off his laptop.

'Chas,' I speak to his back, 'you were never meant to know. It was just, well, it helped me. I—'

'Right,' he says without looking at me, 'impersonating my dead sister helps you, that's fine so.'

'No!' I'm crying and snuffling. 'It's not like that. It's—'

'Don't!' The abrupt tone stops me. He lowers his voice and shakes his head. 'Don't, Andy, just . . . don't.'

I watch as he picks up his laptop and shoves it into his bag. Then, without looking at me, he leaves.

The next hour is spent in a daze. I am unable to do anything. I just sit in the kitchen, two cups of untouched coffee on the table, Baz pacing in an agitated manner up and down the room. I stare straight ahead, like those comatose people in movies. I think I'm crying but I can't be sure. All I know is that I've lost both Chas and Lexi. It hurts more to lose Lexi,

345

I think. I created her to keep her alive in a computer programme that would last for ever. I created her and gave her a life and a second chance, and I looked after her and felt her emotions and I made her funny and popular, just like she was in real life. The graphic designer in me had laboured to make her face photo-perfect, and no one was ever meant to find out. I suppose I should have been more suspicious of Dominic Grey, but I didn't want to be. I'd known there was something familiar about his voice, but I'd dismissed it. I wanted it to go on. And now look what's happened, my head yells, you've hurt people that—

The front door bell buzzes.

I freeze.

Then it rings again.

I stay sitting at the kitchen table, not moving.

Then my mobile jangles its happy tune. The screen says *Alistair*.

There's no harm in answering that, and I am relieved that at least my boss is ringing me after the fiasco on Saturday. I can't afford to lose any other friends. And Alistair can't see me. 'Hello?' I make my voice cheery.

'I'm outside your door, can you let me in?'

Oh shit. 'Eh, I'm busy. I can't.'

'You're not busy,' Alistair scoffs. 'You don't go anywhere. I mailed you and told you'd I'd be over, and I told you not to mail me back unless you had something else on.'

I'd forgotten about checking my mail once Chas had rung. 'Well, I forgot to mail you back.'

There is silence. 'So I take it that our, well, I'd hardly call it a snog, has affected our friendship, eh?'

'No, no it hasn't. I still want to be your friend.'

'Are you OK? You sound all choked up.'

'I'm fine.'

'You don't sound fine.'

'No, no I am.' And then, to my mortification, I dissolve into tears. It's the concern in his voice. The fact that he cares.

'Open up now, you idiot. I'm not leaving. Are you on your own?'

'I have Baz.'

'Oh well then, you're fine.' A pause. 'Feck's sake, open up.'

And I do.

I think he races up because seconds later, he's at my door. I open it, turning away slightly so he can't see how puffy my eyes actually are. But he takes a step closer to me, tips up my chin with his finger before enfolding me in his arms and saying, 'Jesus, what the hell happened with you, eh?'

'I did something stupid,' I wail. 'You'll think I'm mad.'

'I think you are stupid and mad, but far too gorgeous to be so upset.' Alistair brings his face level with mine. 'Come on, spill.'

His arm about my shoulder, he leads me back into my kitchen. He makes me sit down before nodding at me. 'Go on, tell me. It won't go any further unless you want it to.'

I begin haltingly, mortified to be admitting what I've done. But once I start, it's like munching my way through a packet of biscuits, I'm unable to stop until it's all finished. Only when I eat biscuits, I don't cry and hiccup and sniffle.

Alistair listens, leaning against my cooker, his arms folded, his long legs apart. He doesn't comment all the way through but when, finally, I've stuttered to a halt, he says calmly, 'What you did was no big deal. I understand.'

The words wrap themselves around me. No big deal. It's comforting that he thinks that, but maybe he's only saying it. 'It was a big deal.' I sob a little. 'You can't understand.'

'Andy,' he says, and he sounds firmer than I've ever heard him sound before. 'You bloody well haven't gone outside your door in a fucking year. You had no friends, no social life. Your computer was your gateway to the world. This virtual reality game was the closest to the world that you could get. You did it to survive, anyone would have.'

His insight momentarily stuns me. 'No, I did it for Lexi.'

'Maybe, but I think it was for you too. Jesus, Andy, we all could see it. You were as lonely as hell. I worried a lot about you. You *needed* it.'

Yes, I admit, I had been lonely. I was one of those girls that loved the social scene. Despite my shyness, I enjoyed meeting people, having a laugh. But it had been taken away. And I'd been scared by that. Not only had my life been taken away, but so had my identity. I hadn't a clue where I was going. Who I was, without my pretty face to rely on. And I needed company. Alistair's right, I think, stunned. By bringing Lexi to life, I'd brought a little bit of myself back, too.

'That's why you're an ace ad seller,' Alistair goes on, smiling a little. 'You feel confident when you're talking to people you can't see.'

'Can you explain that to Chas,' I sniff. 'I think he hates me.'

'Ah, no,' Alistair shakes his head, 'he doesn't hate you. He's probably just devastated that his hopes of finding his sister are gone. That must be pretty hard for the poor guy.'

'I'd rather he hated me.'

'Ah Jesus, come here.' Alistair crouches down in front of me, and I wrap my arms about his neck, sobbing again. 'You'll be OK,' he says softly. 'You will.'

'Yes, but will your shirt, with all my tears?' I hiccup out.

He laughs gently, and holds me even more tightly.

When Kate and Luke arrive back, they are stunned to find Alistair making me a toasted sambo as I clutch a mug of cocoa in my hands. He has laced it with sugar for shock.

'I thought you said it was Chas that was calling.' Kate flings her black patent bag across a chair.

'It was.'

My downcast voice catches her attention, and she peers more intently at me. 'Have you been crying?'

'She's OK now.' Alistair slides a tuna and sweetcorn in front of me. 'Anyone else?'

Luke asks for a cheese toastie, while Kate waves his offer away. As Alistair slices the cheese and butters bread, I once again tell my embarrassing tale to my sister and Luke.

However, rather than being shocked or confused, Kate claps her hands together. 'Wow, that is *exactly* what one of our interviewees did on the documentary.' At our questioning looks, she says, 'Her name was Cathy, apparently she logged onto that game too and she said she got hooked on it. She had to go for counselling to get off it, it was an addiction, she said.'

'Oh, yeah.' Luke nods. 'I remember her. Ta,' he says, as Alistair gives him his toasted cheese.

'Well, I'm not addicted,' I pipe up.

'Do you remember when we came here, Luke, and Andy would spend all her time on the computer?' At Luke's nod,

349

she turns to Alistair. 'She'd go to bed really late at night, we thought she was working. We thought you made her work too hard. You weren't working, though, Andy, were you?'

'Kate, stop, would you? You're embarrassing me.'

'So you weren't!' It's as if she's just solved a mystery. 'No wonder Luke and I could hear you talking sometimes. It was into the computer, wasn't it?'

'Kate, stop!' Luke says firmly.

'I just—'

'Ah-ah, stop!' He holds up his hand.

'Sorry,' Kate says to me. Then, 'Can you show us?'

'Show you what?'

'This virtual reality thingy.'

'You really aren't being very sympathetic at all, are you?' Luke snaps, though his eyes are twinkling. He loves Kate's unshockability and I have to confess, at this moment, so do I. Between the three of them, they're almost making me feel normal.

'You really want to see?' I ask.

They all nod.

'OK, but just for a second, I'm not going on for long. Come on upstairs.'

The four of us tromp up to my room. With them all standing around me, I boot up my computer, key in my password and wait for the homepage.

'This is the icon here,' I say, clicking on the Second Life icon. 'I downloaded the programme from the internet. It's free.'

In seconds, the homepage of Second Life is displayed.

'That's my name.' I show them where *Lexi Ryan* is

displayed in the left-hand bottom corner. 'Now I just key in my password.'

The password is accepted and there I am, as Lexi, standing where I last logged off, on the beach.

'Wow,' Kate says. 'It's cool.'

'That's my tent,' I say, pointing to my tent.

We all look at the screen. The silence of the beach seems to mesmerise us. It's daylight, the sun is up. The sea is flat and the sound of the waves can be faintly heard. Someone somewhere has added a lone gull to the mix, and it cries plaintively.

'Is she wearing—'

I cut Kate off. 'Yeah, she's wearing the same clothes as in the picture I lent to Chas. I designed them. It's what she wore the day we left Ireland.'

'And can she wear anything else?'

'Uh-huh.' I click on the 'inventory' tab on the right-hand side of my screen and then when it displays its list, I click on the 'clothing' tab. A list of my avatar's clothing pops up. 'You just click on whatever you want her to wear and on it goes.'

'Cool.' Kate is impressed.

'And she can earn money for working,' I explain. 'The money is transferred into her account online. Linden dollars is the currency they use. If you earn enough Linden dollars, you can change it to real money. Some people have become millionaires in this game.'

'Have you?' Kate sounds enchanted.

I splutter out a laugh. 'No.'

'Oh look.' Kate jabs a manicured nail at my screen. 'Someone is coming.'

It's Lordi, striding across the strand towards Lexi.

'Lordi,' Kate reads in the sign over his head. 'What a nutter. Look at what he's wearing.'

'He's nice,' I say. 'I'll just say "hi", then log off.'

They all watch as Lordi comes nearer. I turn Lexi to face him.

'Hello, Lexi,' Lordi bows.

Kate shrieks. 'Wow, it talks.'

'Yeah, some people talk and some type in what they want to say. I do both.' I press the relevant button on my computer and say, 'Hi Lordi. I can't stay, I'll see you again.'

'OK. Talk later. I'll be here until around ten.'

And I log off.

'Awesome!' Kate pronounces. 'And is he a real guy, out there somewhere in the world?'

'Yeah. He told me he sells angels in real life somewhere in London.'

'No way! You should go meet him.'

'Eh, no thanks.'

'I never knew you could do that stuff on computers.'

'Me neither,' Luke says. 'Cool.'

I smile weakly, glad they don't all take me for some sad freak. 'I'm glad you think so. But Chas . . .'

There is a silence. 'Mmm,' Kate eventually breaks it, 'poor Chas.'

'I think maybe I should go over later tonight and explain,' I mutter.

'Maybe you should,' Kate says. The other two murmur that that might be a good idea.

Part of me hadn't expected them all to agree. In fact, I'd hoped they would tell me to steer clear until Chas calms

352

down, but I know he'll be upset, and while there isn't anything I can do to make it easier for him, the least I can do is explain properly.

If I can . . .

If I can.

48

K ATE DRIVES ME to Bob and Lucy's. I had wanted to go over myself, but she insisted. I think she's half afraid they'll run me out of the house, and I'll be too upset to drive home properly and might have another crash, or something. When we arrive, I ask her to wait in the car. This is something I have to do on my own.

'Good luck.' She smiles gamely at me as I hop out.

'Thanks.'

I will be so glad when this awful day is over. But as Luke said, the day has already been ruined, so I should just keep going. At least tomorrow I can lick my wounds and start to recover. He has a point.

Bob and Lucy both answer the door, and I follow them to their front room. I'm touched that they both smile encouragingly at me. I've rung ahead and told them that I've a bit of a confession to make, and that it might be a difficult conversation. Bob has said that I'm not to worry, and to just come over. But it's easy to say when he doesn't know what the problem is.

As Bob and Lucy sit down, I hesitantly ask where Chas is.

'He's upstairs,' Lucy says. 'Do you want him here, too? I have to warn you, he's not in the best of form.'

'Ask him if he would come down,' I say. 'If he doesn't want to, tell him I'll understand.'

Bob gives me a curious look before heading upstairs to his son's room and a few minutes later, Chas slinks in behind his dad, his eyes flat and blank as he surveys me. His fists are jammed into the pockets of his combats.

'There is no need for this,' he says, his voice cold.

His tone hurts, though I suppose I can't expect anything else from him. 'You don't know the whole story,' I say softly, trying to keep my voice from trembling. 'I'd like you to hear it.'

Lucy and Bob shoot a curious look at each other.

Chas glares at me but sits down, his arms folded.

'This is hard for me,' I begin.

Chas rolls his eyes, and the brief motion makes me want to cry.

'Don't get upset, pet,' Bob says, patting my hand before joining Lucy on the sofa. 'It can't be that bad.'

But it is, I think. I wish now that Kate was here. I take a deep, shaky breath. I'm still standing, I just can't sit. My gaze rakes the three of them. 'I have been coming here since, well, since Chas went away.' My hands knot themselves around and around.

'And we've been so happy to have you,' Lucy says supportively, nodding at me. 'We've really appreciated it. We've loved having you.'

I try to ignore the words in case I break down. Instead, I focus my gaze over their heads at a picture on the wall. One of Chas's earlier works. Like him, loud and bright. I think he'd paint differently now. As I have been doing. 'Well,' I continue, 'what I, eh, didn't tell you was that your house and

355

my parents' house were the only places I visited.' I have to sit down. The words are like a punch from inside my gut. I'm releasing part of me that I've kept hidden away for so long. I plonk down on a chair away from the three of them and stare hard at my hands. 'I was . . . have been . . . effectively housebound, agoraphobic. I still am.' I risk a glance upwards.

Bob leans forward on the seat, looking puzzled. 'But you told us—'

'I know,' I interrupt, biting my lip, not wanting to hear all the lies I'd told them. 'I lied to you both. I don't go out.'

'But why?' Bob is baffled. 'Why lie about it?'

'Because,' I gulp, trying to keep the sob out of my voice, 'I didn't want you both to think that I was pathetic because, well, your girl was maybe dead but at least I had my life.'

'We would never think that.' Lucy is horrified. She puts a hand to her throat. 'Oh Andy, never.'

They both look shocked.

'You do go out,' Chas snaps, sounding angry. 'You were out on the street the day I called in to talk to you.'

I flinch at his tone, but nod. 'Yeah. It was the first time I'd ventured out alone to the shops in almost a year. I'm trying, but it's hard. My scar, see—' I stop abruptly.

'The scar didn't bother you when I knew you. We went out.'

'Chas, if you can't speak to Andy in a nicer tone, leave.' Bob's voice is a whip crack.

Chas glowers.

'It did bother me,' I say, 'but you were around, and you kept telling me that I looked OK.'

'You did.' He holds my gaze. I can't make out the expression in his eyes.

356

'Yeah, well,' I falter, before gathering myself together and continuing, 'the first night we went out, after the accident, one of the girls in your group told her friend that my scar was awful. I overheard her.' The memory brings so much pain with it. After all this time, it's hard to believe how much it hurts.

'Oh, Andy.' Lucy impulsively crosses over and sits on the arm of my chair. Wrapping an arm about my shoulder, she cuddles me to her. 'You poor thing.'

'Remember that night I didn't come back into the pub?' I ask Chas. 'It was the first and last night I ever went out with you.'

Chas blinks, remembering, I think. 'Yeah,' he says softly. 'I do.'

'Well—'

'Why didn't you say something?'

'I was too hurt, too embarrassed. I didn't want a scene. But it ruined my confidence. And so I just stayed in.'

'Is that the reason you didn't come with me to India?'

'Part of it.'

'Oh Andy, how awful,' Lucy repeats. She rubs her hand up and down my back, the way my mother did whenever I was sick as a child.

I really don't want her to feel too sorry for me until she's heard the rest of the story. But her being beside me is comforting.

'And so,' I say, 'I became really isolated and,' I swallow hard, 'I went online and invented an avatar.'

I explain what an avatar is to them. I tell them how I'd identified so much with the character on my screen. Even though she was a version of Lexi as I remembered her, she

357

was also what I'd left behind of me. Chas remains motionless in his chair. Finally, I say, 'It started out as Lexi 'cause I wanted her to live for ever. You see, I, well, I felt responsible for her death. We had a row that morning, and she didn't sit with me on the bus, and as a result . . .' I can't finish. I get all choked up, the emotion of the day overwhelming me. The whys and what ifs and the guilt. I stare hopelessly at Lexi's family, totally tongue-tied, with no words to explain it all from there. There are no words left in me. They know what I mean, anyway.

I wait for the denouncement. I brace myself for their reactions.

'I bet the row was Lexi's fault,' Bob says gently, after it becomes apparent that I can't talk any more. He comes to sit on the other arm of my chair. 'I bet she annoyed the hell out of you.'

'She was,' I sniff, 'late for the bus. It was so trivial. I completely overreacted.'

'That was Lexi.' Lucy peers down into my face as she strokes my hair. 'Always late for everything. And I bet she refused to accept the blame.'

I say nothing, not wanting to give out about my friend.

'Sure, don't you know Andy,' Lucy smiles a tiny bit, 'that we had a row with her before she left? And to punish us, she never rang us once. We spent the two months cursing her, but it didn't mean we didn't love her.'

'But we were glad she had you.' Bob wraps an arm about my shoulder. 'You were sensible.'

'It was the only reason we were happy about her going,' Lucy agrees.

'Really?' I look up at these two lovely people. I don't deserve their kindness.

'Uh-huh,' Bob says.

'And wanting to make her live for ever on the computer, well,' Lucy blinks hard, a tear drops from her eyes, but she smiles, 'that's a lovely thought. Lovely. And if it helped you, well, that's even better.'

At this point, Chas exits the room.

Our eyes follow him.

'Chas,' I call, but Lucy's hand on my arm stills me. 'Leave him. He'll be fine in a day or so. Chas needs time, that's just the way he is. Can I just say one thing to you?'

I nod.

'What upsets me the most is the way you lied to me and Bob. Andy, we would never have judged you, you were a great friend to Lexi, and that meant so much to us.' She squeezes my hand in her tiny one. 'OK?'

'Thank you,' I whisper.

For the first time in two years, my whole life is a clean canvas. A clean canvas, waiting for me to use it.

And I know now what I have to do.

49

I T'S TIME TO leave. To say goodbye to my other life, because it has been a life, no matter how odd it seems.

Logging on later that night, I join Lexi on the beach, savouring the last contact with this world. It's dark and still. Night only lasts a few hours here. Soon it will be daylight again. It's three in the morning in reality.

'OK,' I whisper, 'you know what you have to do.' I press the controls.

Lexi turns and begins the walk towards town. Down the now familiar stretch of sand where Yellow T-Shirt used to stare out to sea, over the sand dunes and along the road beside the exotic flowers. She knows that, if she wanted to, she could fly but always wanting to keep it real, Lexi has walked everywhere. Walking is good anyway, more to see, more to wonder at. After five minutes' tramping along, the three shops come into view. One now closed, the other two still in business. Lexi peers through the window into Cissy's. Doug is there, prowling around, gazing up at the shelves.

'Hi,' Lexi says, entering.

'Hi.' Doug nods.

He used to be terrible at typing, she thinks. All his words

would come out wrong. Now he uses the built-in microphone on his laptop. 'Is Cissy around?'

'Haven't seen her for days,' Doug mutters. He feigns being busy, moving things from one area of the store to the other. She notices that he is putting Cissy's hats in the worst display places.

'Can you give her a message from me?' she asks.

There is a pause. Doug finally sits down on a jazzy-looking red velvet seat. 'I doubt we'll see her again,' he says.

'Why?'

'We met up, the two of us, offline. Turns out we both live in the same place, give or take fifty miles. Anyhow, I don't think we liked the look of each other. Cissy looked nothing like I thought she would.'

She feels cross, no, more than cross, furious. 'You honestly expected her to look like Cissy?'

'I don't know what I expected,' he sounds defensive. 'But it wasn't what I got. And after we met up, she plagued me. I told her I didn't mind being her friend but that we couldn't have a relationship.' He pauses, then mutters, 'Anyhow, I'm back with my girlfriend.'

'You selfish shit.'

'I am not. I did nothing wrong. I promised her nothing.'

'She let you share her shop. She said she was your friend. She was lonely.'

'I pay rent when I can. I said I'd be her friend. It's not my fault if she's lonely.'

There is no point in continuing on with this argument. Doug had appeared to be nice enough, but really, how well could she ever know him? How well could he know her? She liked to think that she was what she appeared to be online.

361

She knew that the best part of herself emerged when she wasn't so self-conscious. That she was wittier, friendlier when she couldn't be seen. She imagined that Doug was probably as selfish in real life as he had proven himself to be in the virtual world.

'Do you have a mail address for her?'

'Nope.'

She wasn't going to say goodbye to him. He probably wouldn't care anyway. Instead, she turned on her heel and marched out of the shop.

Lordi isn't around, so she continues on past his shop to the gallery. She reckons if she waits long enough, she'll catch Peter. The little fecker has been avoiding her for days, and now she knows why. Big, fat guilty conscience. She is so going to enjoy this encounter.

The gallery is deserted, which doesn't surprise her. She sits in a chair behind the desk in the foyer, determined to wait as long as it takes. Half an hour later, a woman wanders in, she nods a 'hi' and goes into the gallery to look at the pictures. Maybe it's one of the artists, she thinks. Might as well talk to her, it beats sitting around. 'Did you do one of the short-listed paintings?' she asks, following the woman. Whoever this woman is, she has christened her avatar 'Avatar'. So much for imagination.

Avatar turns awkwardly, obviously a newbie. 'I did,' she types. 'The picture in the far left-hand corner is mine.'

Lexi looks. It's a big picture, full of bright circles and odd shapes. It's probably a massive canvas in reality. 'I just came to wish it luck,' the woman says. 'Decision day is on Wednesday, isn't it?'

'That's right.'

'Who is judging it, do you know?'

She smiles to herself. 'It's a well-known artist. I can't say, though. He likes bright pictures, as you can see.' Her hand sweeps in an arc, encompassing all the pictures.

The woman laughs. 'High standard, though. Wow, isn't this Second Life a fun programme? I never knew about it until I entered the competition, and when I made the short-list I decided to come here.'

'It's fun,' Lexi acknowledges, 'just don't get too addicted to it.'

'My God,' the woman said, 'I wouldn't have the time. Two kids to ferry about the place and an art career to manage.'

'The best way to be,' Lexi answers.

Just then, she sees Peter, who has arrived at the entrance to the room. 'Excuse me,' she says to the woman. Then, turning to Peter, she yells, 'Don't move!'

She must sound threatening enough, as Peter freezes and the woman vanishes.

'Don't even think about it!' Lexi shouts again.

'Think about what?' Peter attempts nonchalance.

'Think about trying to avoid me,' she pauses. 'John,' she adds.

'John?' he splutters. 'I'm – I'm Peter.'

'John Robinson, web designer and owner of the biggest web-design company in Australia. You started off in—'

'Stop!'

'It is you, isn't it?'

'How did you find out?' Then he stops. 'Chas Ryan,' he says crossly. 'He had no right to reveal my identity.'

'You had no right to entice him here by using my name.

363

Well, my avatar's name. And you had no right to try and fool me with this ridiculous Dominic Grey.'

'It was his idea.'

'Yeah, but you helped. You designed his website, didn't you?'

'I might have.' He's defensive.

'Well, it was pathetic.'

'It was done in a hurry.' A pause. 'So, why did he want to keep his identity a secret from you?'

'That is none of your business, John.'

'Will you stop calling me John! For Christ's sake!'

'I know your email address now, I saw the one you sent Chas. I am going to send you an email with my address on it. If you see Cissy again, you are to forward her details to me. Immediately.'

'What?'

'You owe me one, Peter. It's the least you can do.'

'OK.' He nods, then adds, 'But won't you see her soon?'

'I've decided to go. This is goodbye.'

'You're gonna shoot through? Why?' He seems genuinely upset.

'I want to.'

'But where am I going to find another offsider like you?' There is desperation in his tone. 'You thought of the competition. It was a ripper idea. It's being judged on Wednesday in London, most of the art came from there. I was going to invite you. I'd a liked you around. I'd like to meet you.'

'What you want and what you can get, Peter, are two different things. You can take the credit for the idea yourself, I don't care.'

Peter comes towards her. 'You're spewin', aren't you?'

'If that means cross, then yes, I am.'

He hangs his head in shame. 'I'm sorry. This Chas bloke, he said it was really important.'

'Yeah, well, I suppose it sort of was.'

'So? I did the right thing then.'

'No you bloody didn't, Peter. You fooled me.'

'Are you just shooting through here, or shooting through the whole thing?'

'The whole thing.'

He says nothing for a bit. Finally, he mutters, 'I had planned a surprise for you on Wednesday.'

'Yeah, well, bet it's not as big a surprise as finding out that you lied to me.'

'Ah, Lexi, I said I'm sorry.'

She feels a bit mean. He's not the worst, and he paid well, and if she was to stay she'd earn enough to buy a house and everything. Plus he did give her loads of days off. 'I know you did.' She pauses before admitting, 'In fact, you probably did me a favour.'

'So stick around.'

'No. I have to go.' She holds out her hand. 'It's been a blast.'

'You any good at designing websites? I could give you a ripper job.'

'I have a ripper job, thanks. Bye, Peter.'

'Call me John.'

'John.'

'Have a great life,' Peter says, as he touches her hand.

'I do have a great life.'

And as she walks away, she knows that she means it.

Now there is only one person left to take her leave of. This will be the worst, she thinks. In the last while, she has grown very fond of Lordi and his little philosophies. He'd been so nice to her, listened to her as she told him about the accident and about the row she'd had with her friend. He'd helped her, she realises suddenly, helped her get perspective and given her the courage to tell her parents. It's bright daylight when she walks out of the gallery and back up the street. This time, Lordi is in situ, just exactly as she'd found him months before. He's dressed in white and sitting languidly in his angel chair.

She feels a deep pang of regret as she looks in at him.

He spots her and waves her inside. 'Hello.' He smiles. 'How are you?'

'I'm leaving,' she says, not knowing any other way to broach the subject.

'Leaving this town, or . . .' He lets the words hang.

'Leaving this whole virtual thing, Lordi.'

Lordi stands up, adjusts his cape and crosses towards her. 'You are?'

Lexi nods. 'I came to say goodbye.'

'I'm with Bob Dylan on this one,' Lordi answers. 'Don't say "Goodbye", say "Fare thee well".'

She was glad she couldn't be seen because tears were forming at the corners of her eyes.

'Fare thee well,' she says, her voice trembling.

Lordi turns his back on her and begins rummaging among some shelves. Finally, he pulls out a small white angel in a blue dress, holding a trumpet. 'For you.' He bows as he presents her with the angel. 'Healing.'

She is touched. 'I was actually going to buy it from you today,' she says. 'In fact, I was going to spend all my money in this shop.' Well, half of it. The other half she wanted to give to Cissy and Doug, but there was no way she was doing that now.

'Today is not the day for buying things.' Lordi holds the angel towards her until she takes it. 'Today is the day for receiving gifts.'

'Thank you.' She places the angel in her accessories file.

'And even if you never come online again,' Lordi says, 'it'll be for ever in your kit bag.'

'I know.' A pause, before she says, 'I have about 1,150 Linden dollars saved. I want to give it to you—'

'Absolutely not.' He holds up his hand.

'—so that the next time,' she interrupts, 'that you see someone who needs an angel here, you can give it to them for free.'

'Absolutely.' He nods.

They both laugh. Then she right-clicks on Lordi, and when the circle with the various options pops up, she clicks on 'pay' and transfers all her money to him. Now she is as she was when she came, penniless. 'And Lordi, if Cissy drops by, tell her that if she asks Peter, he'll pass on a message to me. I know Peter's offline identity, so I've sent him my email address.'

'I will do that.'

'You're a good man, Lordi.'

'Yes, I know.'

'And a modest one.'

'Always.'

They smile at each other. Then Lordi bows, vanishing before she can say goodbye.

I log off, crying silently, missing already those people who I'd shared my days and nights with in virtual reality. But I know I've chosen wisely.

50

WEDNESDAY MORNING, AS the news headlines blare out on the kitchen radio, Kate receives a summons to appear in court. She scurries into the kitchen, hyperventilating and waving a piece of paper about. I've just turned the volume up on the radio as one of the news items is to be about the art competition.

'I thought I was getting a present or something in the registered post,' she wails, standing in the doorway in her tight pink jeans and leopard-print top, 'but it's a court summons from those bastards at the radio station.'

Luke and I look at each other, then at her.

Luke moves towards her saying, 'It won't be a good idea to think of calling them bastards in court.'

'Wankers, then.' Kate allows him to lead her to a chair, and she sinks down jadedly before pointing wearily at the coffee pot.

I pour her a cuppa, and with all the energy of an eighty-year-old, she lifts it to her lips and takes a shaky gulp. My concern for Kate and my interest in the news vie for precedence.

'Wankers is not a good word either,' Luke half jokes.

'Shut up.' Kate squeezes her eyes closed as if she might cry.

I have no choice; I turn the radio down. Luke pulls a chair towards him and sits, facing Kate, peering into her face. 'Look,' he explains patiently, and from his body language and tone, I think he must have been a good solicitor, 'you did wrong, Kate, whatever way you look at it. On the positive side, you're going to be tried in the district court, which is good. There's only a judge there, and the sentencing is lower. In fact, you'll probably get away with a fine.'

'I'd rather prison,' Kate says dramatically, 'I can't afford a fine.'

'You said you wouldn't complain if you got caught, d'you remember?' I remind her.

'Yeah,' Kate says as if I'm thick, 'but I didn't think I'd get caught, did I?'

'Well, there was always the possibility,' Luke says.

'Oh, don't be so smug,' Kate grouches. 'Polish your halo, why don't you?'

Luke glares at her as he rises abruptly from his seat. 'I give up.' He shrugs. 'You go to jail if you want to. You annoy the judge if you want to. When you decide you want my advice, you can get me on the mobile.'

'Oh, Luke—'

But he's gone, tripping over a pair of my shoes as he exits.

In the silence that follows, Kate asks meekly, 'He was smug, wasn't he?'

'No,' I answer sternly. 'He's only trying to help you, and be honest, it's all your own fault. And Luke does know what he's talking about.'

She narrows her eyes before sipping on some more coffee. I turn my back on her and flick up the volume control on the radio. I really can't believe her attitude. She'd been fine up until now, very accepting of her fate. *'And now, more on the online art—'*

'I suppose I just got a shock, seeing my trial date written down,' Kate mumbles a little tearfully. 'Me? In court? And everyone knows, it was in the paper again yesterday. It's humiliating.'

'Ah, Kate.' Once more I abandon the radio and rush to console her. I wrap my arms around her and she hugs me.

'I am sorry for what I did,' Kate sniffs, 'and I will be contrite, but I just want to give out about those feckers too, d'you know what I mean?'

'Totally.' I hug her harder. 'But Luke is worried about you.'

'*I'm* worried about me.'

'You got yourself into this mess.'

'Yeah, I know.' She pulls away from my embrace and reaches for her mobile phone, which is on the table. 'Do you think I should call him?'

'Do you think you should?'

Kate snorts crossly, 'Who are you? My counsellor?' Though she smiles a little. 'Right,' she says, flicking her phone open, 'I guess I'll call him.' She pauses. 'And apologise.' She selects his number from her contacts and presses 'call'.

Her phone has just connected and she's blurted out the word 'Luke?' when he marches triumphantly back in the door.

I laugh. He obviously knows her well. Meanwhile, the piece on the art competition ends and I haven't heard a word.

'You ready to listen to sense now, you grump?' Luke asks, grinning.

'I am ready for anything,' Kate answers, mock suggestively.

Or maybe there's no mock about it, as Luke bends over her and brushes his lips with hers.

371

I'm glad I'm dressed appropriately, in a green jumper, because I feel like a big gooseberry.

Later that day, as I put the finishing touches to an ad, my landline rings. There is only one person who uses that number, and it's my mother. I hate being distracted by phone calls when I'm designing, but if I don't answer she'll freak and think that something is wrong. So I tromp downstairs and pick up the receiver. 'Mam, hi.'

'How do you know it's me?' she sounds suspicious. 'Were you warned that I would ring?'

'No, why would someone warn me?'

'Because I'm very cross with you, that's why!'

'Cross with me?' There's a turn-up for the books. Her ire is usually directed at Kate. 'Why?'

'You obviously didn't enter my picture for that competition.' She stresses the word 'obviously'.

It takes a second for my mind to click into what she's talking about. 'The fruit-basket monochrome?'

'Monochrome? The black and white fruit-basket,' she clarifies. Then, sounding hurt, she adds, 'Why didn't you enter it?'

'I did.'

'Well,' she says as if playing her trump card, 'you couldn't have because I didn't win.'

She hadn't even made the shortlist, but obviously she didn't know that. I bite my lip so I won't giggle. 'Mam, your fruit basket was great but—'

'I *know* it was great. It was way better than the awful yoke that won. I've just seen it on the telly. And I couldn't make head nor tail of it. It was like a car crash, if you ask me.'

'What? They've announced the winner? Who is it?'

'I don't know, I didn't catch the name. But the picture . . .' There is a shudder in her voice. 'Good God, the only colour the artist seemed to know was red.'

So Yellow T-Shirt didn't win, I think. I try to remember what picture was mostly red, but I can't. There were quite a few of them.

'And I wouldn't mind,' my mother ploughs on, 'but Chas Ryan judged it. Well, I never thought he was much good as a painter, way overrated, but he'll never make it as a judge, that's my opinion.'

I suppress a smile. 'Well, Mam, I can assure you that I did enter your picture. Chas likes bright colours, though, so maybe your black and white just didn't appeal to him.'

'Well I'll know that the next time I enter a competition. I just have to slap a load of bright paint all over the place and call it something meaningful, and I might have a good chance.'

'There you go.'

'Don't patronise me, Andy.' She pauses and changes tack. 'So how are things with you?' Without waiting for an answer, she dips her voice and continues, 'Did you sort that business out, you know, the way you were pretending to be your dead friend? I was telling Julia Kelly about it down the road and—'

'What?' My stomach heaves.

'She said you should maybe get some counselling. An inability to let go. I told her you were always like that. Even as a child you dragged around a smelly teddy for years before we took it off you.'

'Mam,' I am reeling, 'please don't discuss me with your

373

neighbours. This is my business. I don't tell everyone about you and Dad.'

'Me and your father? I'm not surprised you don't. What's to tell? He's as boring since he got his driving licence. He's pressing all sorts of buttons and looking up things on the internet and surfing and whatever. Last night he looked up the origin of the word "pineapple".'

This conversation is growing bizarre.

'We had a bit of an argument at dessert. I gave him pineapple. He said the fruit didn't look like an apple or a pine cone. I said it did. Do you know what he found?'

'How could I know?' I ask drily.

'Well apparently it is something to do with a pine cone, though I can't remember now. But I was right. Anyway, your father will tell you all about it if you ask him.'

The likelihood of that is minuscule.

I try to finish up the conversation. 'So, Mam, I can assure you that I did enter your picture for the competition, and—'

'You never told me you were running it, though, did you?'

'That would have been unethical, and anyway, as I said, that was my business.'

'Hmm.' She pauses. 'Right, I believe you entered my picture, though the evidence points to the contrary.' She pauses as she waits for me to refute this, but I remain silent. She then asks, 'Have you gone out lately?'

I squirm. Not something I want to discuss. 'Just to the shop.'

'Get Kate to bring you out again.'

'I will. I promise.' And I mean it.

'I'll forgive you everything if you get better.' Her voice is softer.

'Gee, thanks. That'll spur me on.'

She laughs before putting down the phone.

That evening, as good as my word, I ask Kate and Luke if they've room for an interloper.

"Course we do.' Kate is snuggled up in Luke's arms on the sofa. She keeps telling him that it might be their last time together, and he jokingly tells her that he's going to make the most of it so. 'We'll ask some of our friends, too. Get you socialising.'

'Not Noel,' I say hastily.

They snort a little at this, and then Kate asks slyly, 'How about Alistair?'

'Sure. That'd be great.' And then I realise what she means by it. 'As a friend,' I clarify.

'Oh yeah, yeah, sure.' Kate nods. 'Of course.'

I ignore their juvenile laughter.

The nine o'clock news comes on the TV then, and with it, right at the end, is a feature on the art competition.

'Shussh,' I say, as Luke and Kate start up a mini-argument on which of them is the funnier.

'And now,' the newsreader says, 'the art competition with a twist. We go to our reporter Celia Hurley for details.'

Celia Hurley, complete with oversized microphone, informs us that some months ago an online art competition was initiated, in which artists could jpeg their pictures into a site and their pictures would then be displayed in an online gallery, just as in real life. The pictures were whittled down to twenty, which were then displayed for a month in the online gallery. She gave the online address and details of the Second Life programme. 'And today,' she said, 'in London, the surprise judge was announced, and it was wonderful to see that it was an Irish judge. Chas Ryan, hello.'

Chas's face appears on the screen, and Kate and Luke whoop and clap. I haven't heard from him since going to his house that awful night. God, he looks gorgeous. He has made no effort to dress up, but he certainly makes an impression on Celia, who is actually blushing. 'So Chas, how and why did you get involved, especially as we all know that you've abandoned the canvas in favour of photography?'

Chas lies easily, 'Well, Celia, I've a photographic exhibition coming up in a few months' time, and then next year it transfers to London and I thought, well, the publicity won't do me any harm. Plus, it's nice to see good-quality art again.'

'What made you choose the winning picture?'

'The vibrancy, the life it represents.' He pauses. 'Initially, I had picked another one but when I saw the last twenty canvases in reality, this was the one that made the most impression on me. It's stunning.'

Then there is a shot of Chas to the left of a tall man. On the other side of the tall man is a relatively young man in a wheelchair. The man in the centre holds a fabulous picture towards the camera. I remember the picture now, though I don't know if I would have chosen it above some of the others.

'Who are the other guys?' Kate asks.

'And there we have it,' Celia wraps up her report, 'Toby Gates, the artist, flanked by Chas Ryan on the left and John Robinson on the right. John is the Australian businessman who financed the award.'

The piece ends. I am unable to tear my eyes from the screen, not even when the weather forecast comes on. John

Robinson. He was the man in the wheelchair. A strange sort of sadness overtakes me. I hadn't known. But why should I have?

Still, it makes sense. It all makes sense.

Things are becoming clearer all the time.

51

SATURDAY NIGHT. ONCE again, I'm assailed by the demons of socialising. I haven't slept in the last two nights, worrying about everything from the conversations I'll have with people to the looks I'm bound to get from them. I assume, however, that Kate and Luke have told all their friends about me, which is a little horrifying, but at the same time makes things easier. To compensate for my scar, I've really tried to make the rest of me look good. Kate has straightened my hair, and it now shines like something from a shampoo commercial. I've more make-up on my face than I've used in a decade and Kate has kindly lent me some of her clothes. She's thinner than I am, but nothing I own quite hacks the 'trendy pub' scene any more, and so I'm forced into sporting an almost-too-tight-to-be-comfortable pair of black jeans, a white long-sleeved blouse and high-heeled black boots. The only thing that's mine is the wide belt slung over the blouse. Kate has also lent me some black and white bangles and a black beaded necklace. Viewed from the left-hand side, I look fantastic, if a little uncomfortable.

Luke wolf-whistles as I enter the kitchen. He's dressed up, too, in that he's ditched his long coat in favour of a leather jacket and his jeans for black trousers. His t-shirt, though, tells whoever reads it to 'Save the planet, damn it!'

Kate looks stunning. Short and tight is her motto for the night. Her petite frame makes her appear sexy rather than tarty. But as I stare at her, it occurs to me that it's November and it's cold out.

'Are you sure you'll be warm enough?' Her legs are bare. Her skirt is teensy.

'Oh,' Kate pinches my cheek, chortling loudly as she says, 'listen to Mammy!'

'Well, madam,' I do a passable impression of our mother, 'you'll be laughing the other side of your face in a few hours, when your legs go purple with the cold.'

'I'll be off my face in a few hours,' Kate retaliates.

We laugh. 'So,' I try to sound casual, 'who's coming tonight, again?'

'Would you give it a rest.' Kate rolls her eyes. Pulling on her little fake-fur jacket, she adds, 'You'll be fine.'

'Alistair,' Luke answers quietly, 'and two girls from Kate's old job, Maya and Eithne.'

'They're sound,' Kate interrupts.

'Also about three guys I know,' Luke continues.

The word 'about' reeks of uncertainty. Maybe it'll be more than three, maybe they'll invite others and a whole hoard of people will descend on the table. I try to quell a slight flutter of panic. 'So, about six people?'

'Uh-huh.'

The pub will probably be crowded with others, though. Crowded with people all looking at me. But why would they all look at me? It'll be a bit dark, surely. Anyway, I know I have to do this. I have to get back out there, and thus far,

I've been doing OK. Plus, I look good. I do. *But only on the left side*, the uncertain voice inside my head whispers. *Only on the left.* It's like someone has pressed the switch on a tumble dryer inside my brain; one thought leads to another and another and they jump about, tumbling over and over. I close my eyes and try to turn them off by reminding myself that I do look good. Nice clothes, nice hair, nice figure. *Scarred face.* These thoughts have a direct effect on my heart. Its beat intensifies, then picks up speed. *Stop*, I think. Stop. But it's no use, I can't seem to remember how to breathe, my rhythm has gone all funny. In. Out. In. Out.

'Andy?' Luke's voice comes from far away. 'You OK?'

In. Out. In. Out.

One of them leads me to a chair. I drop my head to my knees and tell myself that it's only a panic attack, nothing is going to happen to me. I am not having a heart attack. Part of me wishes I was, though. At least a bad heart can be worked on by someone else, instead of it all being in my control. But it is in my control. I can do this. I can. In. Out. In. Out.

The kitchen grows further away, voices whoosh and fade as I work hard to hold myself afloat. Then, after what seems an age but is probably only a few minutes, things slowly stabilise. Equilibrium is glimpsed and the panic trickles away like melting ice. A few seconds tick by, and I find the courage to glance up. Kate is clutching Luke's arm, her fingers white. The expression of absolute terror on both their faces makes me giggle a little, more out of embarrassment than anything. Kate looks as if she's just witnessed the birth of the anti-Christ. 'Sorry,' I get out before beginning to titter again.

380

'It's not funny,' Kate says in an anguished tone. 'Oh my God. Oh, I have to sit down. Oh God.'

'D'you want a drink of water?' Luke solicitously grabs a glass from the press.

'Yes,' I answer, then realise that he's talking to Kate.

'I need a drink. Alcohol. Pronto,' she says.

Luke fusses over her, and I marvel at her ability to turn it into her drama. But maybe she's done it deliberately. In fact, I think she has.

'I'm fine now, ta,' I say from my position on my chair. They both glance over at me.

'Great,' Luke says before turning back to Kate.

It's a chance to compose myself. I wipe the sheen of sweat from my forehead and hope that it hasn't ruined my make-up. 'I'll just go upstairs and retouch my make-up.' I thumb in the direction of the stairs just as the doorbell rings.

It's probably Alistair. He's driving the three of us over. Moral support for me and all that. I am so glad he'll be there.

But when I get back down, after slapping on some more bronzer, instead of Alistair in the kitchen I find Chas. He's looks rough, unshaven and pale-faced. A large parcel, wrapped in brown paper, sits against the wall. I'm about to ask what it is when Kate says, 'We'll, eh, wait outside for Alistair. See you, Chas.'

'Uh-huh, bye now, have a good time.'

The two of them leave in suspicious haste and I'm left alone with him. It's strange how they didn't ask him to join us. But Chas isn't dressed for going out, so maybe that was why. But then, as Chas raises his eyes to mine, something clicks. This isn't a social call. Chas looks beaten. Defeated.

My eyes search his, and he gives a slight shrug without saying anything, and involuntarily my hand flies to cover my half-opened mouth. However bad I'd felt a few minutes before, it's nothing to how I feel now.

'Lexi!' I stumble over the name; I don't even know if that's what comes out of my mouth.

Chas understands though, and nods dumbly.

'Oh Chas, I'm sorry,' I hiccup out, through sudden shocked tears.

He holds out his arms and I fall into them. He pulls me tight and lets me cry. I've cried before over my friend, cried when they couldn't find her after the crash, cried when the search was called off, cried when they found a body, but now I was crying for the loss of hope, for the finality, for the brutal ending. Tiny slivers of optimism float away on my tide of sorrow. She was not out there playing some silly Lexi prank on us all. She was not in cyberspace, where I might have found her. She was gone. Gone somewhere that I couldn't follow, not now. Gone for ever.

I become aware that Chas is rocking me slightly, making comforting noises and kissing the top of my head, the way a mother might a child. Oh, how I'd longed for his touch, ever since that night in his parents' house when he'd lounged across the sofa, a big toe poking through a red sock. But I didn't want it to be like this, not in these circumstances.

He pulls away slightly, brings his face level with mine, his hands on my shoulders. 'You OK?'

His own eyes are red-rimmed and puffy. I hadn't noticed.

I nod and scrub my eyes, which surely are a mess now, and they sting as mascara, supposedly waterproof, gets into them. 'Oh, Chas . . .'

382

'I know.' He hugs me again, his chin resting on the top of my head. Finally we sit at my table, me still scrubbing my eyes and gulping hard and wishing I had a hankie.

'When did you—'

'Today. The folks are devastated, though I think they're glad she's been finally found.' He swallows, composing himself. 'So, to give them some space, I said I'd come here and let you know. You might have heard it on the news anyway.'

'I am so sorry.' I reach out and grasp his hand and hold it hard. 'So sorry.'

He squeezes my hand in return. 'I know,' he answers softly.

We sit in silence for a bit before he breaks it by saying, 'I just – I just wanted her to be out there, you know,' his voice breaks, 'raising hell, like she was good at.'

'Me too.' A tear slides down my face. I wipe it away and blink hard. 'Even though it's been such a long time, I can't believe it.'

'Me neither.'

I wish I could curl up in bed now, into a ball, and be on my own so that I can get my head around it. She is gone. Like Yellow T-Shirt and Cissy, she's lost to me in time and space. Like my old carefree life, vanished. Like the old me. Like the old Chas. And in that moment, as I glance up at his beautiful but grief-stricken face, I know that there is no chance of the two of us ever getting back together. I was in love with the old him. The old, carefree, poseurish him. And he loved the old me. Life has changed us. Maybe for the better, but certainly not for each other.

'When will,' I wince; there is no delicate way to ask the question, and yet I feel I have to ask, 'well, the funeral and—'

He gulps. 'I dunno. Ma and Da want to fly over to bring her,' he stumbles a little, 'home. So—'

He lets the sentence remain unfinished. His gaze drops to the tabletop.

'You'll let me know?'

''Course.'

We fall back into silence, unable to find words to comfort each other. Baz pads into the kitchen, but obviously sensing the atmosphere, decides it'd be too much trouble to bother attracting our attention and so, his tail in the air, he exits haughtily. Finally, as the silence stretches on without either of us knowing what to say to make it better, Chas stands up. 'I'll go now.'

I rise with him, relieved to be left on my own. 'You sure? D'you want a cuppa? Are you OK to drive?'

'Yeah,' he pauses and continues. 'Audrey drove me here, she lives nearby. I'll call into her place for a lift back.'

'Audrey?'

'My agent,' he pauses again before smiling a little uncomfortably and admitting shyly, 'well, more a girlfriend now, I guess.'

'I'm glad,' I say, and to my surprise, I mean it. He deserves to be happy.

'I'm sorry if I ever hurt you,' he blurts out suddenly. 'And for being such an asshole about the internet thing.'

I shake my head. 'You weren't an asshole. I don't blame you for a second. I wish – I wish you had been right.'

Tears fill his eyes, as they do mine.

Impulsively, I cross to him and hug him hard, and he smells just like I remember and I feel his loss so keenly. I breathe him in as he hugs me too, before we both pull away. He

384

ushes a strand of hair behind my ear, looks at me for a bit
n silence and then turns to go. Just as he reaches the kitchen
door, he stops abruptly. 'Oh, I almost forgot.' Indicating the
object wrapped in brown paper, he says, 'That's for you.
There's a note with it.'

'What?' It's so unexpected, I don't think I've heard right.

'The note explains it. The news about my sister will have
ruined it, I expect, but you'll love it.'

Then he's gone, without explaining any more.

I approach the parcel with caution. It's large and rectan-
gular. Sellotaped to the outside is a white envelope. It feels
all wrong to be getting a present in the midst of such terrible
news, but I pull the envelope open anyway. A small, folded-
up piece of white paper is inside. Pulling it out, I unfold it
and read:

Dear Lexi (or whoever you are),

 I want you to have this as an expression of my sincere thanks.
You made me smile, you made me cross and you made me RICH!!!
If you do not like it, I can change it for any of the others, but I
think I know what you like.
Take care – Peter / John.

There's a lump in my throat as I peel off the brown wrapping paper. How incredibly thoughtful. He'd said he had a
surprise for me, but I hadn't envisioned . . . The final piece
of paper falls away, and Peter is right – he does know what
I like. It's Yellow T-Shirt's canvas, the one depicting the sky
and the sea in Salue. The boundary between reality and
fantasy and how blurred it can get. He must have bought it
from the artist for me. It must have cost him a fortune. I sit

in front of my brand new work of art and in that moment even though my best friend is never coming back, I fee grateful for all the people in my life and for everyone who has passed through it.

It seems so apt to get this painting just now.

52

I T'S THE DAY of Kate's court case. Luke has advised her to
wear a sedate black skirt and a grey blouse, and I hardly
recognise my sister as she slouches into the kitchen. Over the
blouse she has donned a small leather jacket. Her hair is
scooped up in a bun and she looks like a stereotypical librarian.

'Good,' Luke says approvingly.

'Very nice,' my mother agrees. She and my father have
been in my apartment for the last two hours, as they want
to travel with Kate and Luke and offer their support en route.
'God knows,' my mother had whispered, 'she needs all the
support she can get. The press will be crawling all over it.'

I try not to smile at my mother's melodramatic statement.
She's been watching too many political shows, I think.

'Why can't you dress like that more often,' my mother says
then, pouring herself some more tea. 'You look very
respectable, Kate. Most of the stuff you normally wear is a
little on the small side.'

'Eh, so you want me to go to court more often, do you?'
Kate slumps down in a chair beside my mother.

'You know what I mean, don't be ridiculous.' Mam pushes
a piece of toast towards her. 'Eat up now.'

'I can't, I feel sick.'

'It might be the last piece of toast you get for a while,' my mother says ominously. 'Jail food isn't that nice, I'd imagine.'

Kate is about to snap at her when Luke interrupts with, 'Ah, she won't be going to jail, Mrs Fitzsimons. She'll probably just get the probation act.'

'Really?' Mam blinks hard, looking thrilled. I don't think she knows what the probation act is, but anything is better than jail, in her opinion. 'Oh, that's marvellous. I didn't know that. Me and Donald were looking up the net last night all about visiting her in jail and how we'd cope with the strip-searching on the way in, weren't we, Donald?'

'We were.' Dad nods. 'I'd imagine it'd be an unpleasant experience. I've never been strip-searched.'

'They don't strip-search you,' Luke says.

'Do they not?' Dad sounds almost disappointed. 'Well, that explains how they manage to smuggle all those drugs and mobile phones into prisons, doesn't it?'

'Yeah, people shove them up you know where,' Kate says with relish, 'then they take them out and smuggle them across.'

'No!' Mam looks disgusted. 'That's disgusting.'

'One prisoner even had a twenty-inch TV in his cell,' Luke grins.

Dad splutters out his tea. 'Jesus, how on earth did they get that in?'

'I don't think it bears thinking about,' Mam says faintly.

'I'm really not hungry now.' Kate wanly pushes the toast away.

'Will I make you a strong coffee?' I ask, hovering. There is nowhere for me to sit.

'No, ta. How are you today?' Kate asks.

Their heads swivel in unison to peer at me.

388

'OK.' For the past two days, I've been all over the place emotionally. One second I'm glad they've found Lexi, and the next, I'm crying with the loss of her all over again. It's a different sorrow to the pain I had at the beginning, though. It's knowing that I never will get to say sorry. It's the futility of the fight we had. It's the pain of finally acknowledging that I'll never, ever see her again.

'I was talking to Lucy on the phone last night,' my mother says in a lowered voice. She always does this when referring to someone who has been bereaved. Her head dips and her voice takes on a reverential air. 'She and Bob are flying out on Sunday to claim the body. She sounded quite stoic about it, and she said she's glad she can bring her daughter home.' My mother's eyes fill with tears. 'The poor woman.'

'Indeed,' my father agrees. 'I have to say, though, Lexi was a wild young wan. I was always worried about you being her friend, Andy. She led you astray terribly. Mitching school, smoking, hanging around with older lads.'

'That's called having fun, Dad,' Kate leers.

Dad frowns at Kate before continuing, 'Then she made Andy give up her great job to go travelling.'

'She didn't make me, Dad. I wanted to.'

'I don't know why you wanted to, though; you had a great job, and you were mad about that young fella, Lexi's brother. You seemed happy.'

I was happy. 'Lexi just made life fun,' I state simply.

And, I realise, it's something I'd never quite managed to do for myself since she'd gone.

At half nine, the four of them start fussing around, grabbing coats and jackets, and Luke is on the phone to Kate's solic-

itor telling him that we're leaving now. I accompany them to
the door.

'Good luck, Kate,' I say.

'Aren't you coming?' my mother asks. 'I thought you were
coming.'

Before I can answer, Bert appears at his apartment door
in a vest and boxers. 'Hey, Katie girl, good luck today. Blow
the judge a kiss he'll be putty in your hands.' Then he pauses,
cocks his head to one side and adds, 'Not long before he'll
go all stiff and hard, though.'

'Who is that man!' my mother demands, disgusted, as Bert
slams the door, laughing loudly.

'Oh, just the local pervert,' Kate yells through his door,
though she is grinning a little.

'Pervert is right.' My mother wrinkles her nose in disgust.
'Donald, how could you let that man speak to your daughter
like that?'

'Do you want me to deck him?' Dad asks, quirking an
eyebrow and rolling up his shirtsleeve.

'Oh, don't be facetious,' Mam snaps. Turning back to me,
she asks again, 'Are you not coming to support your sister,
Andy?'

'Well, I, eh—' Oh God, I think maybe I should. After all,
Kate has been there for me for the past few months, but it
just hadn't dawned on me to go, and Kate hadn't asked, and
I just don't know if I could . . .

'It's fine,' Kate says, touching me gently on the arm, 'don't
worry, we'll text you.'

Now I feel really mean. There she is, thinking of me, and
all I can think of is myself. 'Well—'

Just then, the buzzer on my door goes and, pressing it, I

hear Alistair say, 'Hey, Andy, thought you might like a lift to the courthouse.'

'Well now, isn't that nice,' my mother is impressed. 'And there, he has come over all this way, so you have to go now, Andy.'

'She doesn't have to go,' Kate says, 'not if she doesn't want to.'

But with Alistair there, I suddenly feel it'll be fine. He reassures me, I realise. I feel safe with him. I believe what he tells me because it would never occur to him to lie. He has no guile, he just says what he means, and while this is a problem for his love life, it is exactly what I need.

'No.' I smile at her. Admittedly, it's not as confident a smile as I would like to give. 'I'll go. You lot go on, Alistair and I will catch up.'

Kate gives me a brief hug and thanks me, and I know suddenly that if I hadn't gone, she'd have missed me.

Alistair is waiting for me outside in his car. The noise of its exhaust reverberates up and down the street. He pops the door open for me and I sit into the low bucket seat. The first thing that strikes me, very uncharitably, is that he is wearing grey jeans and a green top. The green is probably the only shade available in the whole world that does not go with the soft grey of his jeans. Of all the colours in all the world, Alistair would choose this one. It makes me smile a little.

'Hey.' He smiles back. 'How you doing?'

'Thanks for coming.'

He revs up his car and takes off in a screech of rubber, not even bothering to reply.

*　　*　　*

The courthouse is very busy, with solicitors and barristers running up the steps, files under their arms, coat tails flapping. A group of women stand huddled against the wind, having a quick smoke before their cases are called. Photographers from local and national papers mooch about, looking for news. I have alighted from Alistair's car and he has walked with me to the entrance of the courthouse, his arm slung casually about my shoulder, drawing the bad side of my face into the soft leather of his jacket. As I spy all the commotion at the entrance to the courthouse, I freeze. Alistair looks questioningly at me.

'It's quite crowded.' My voice shakes slightly.

'No one is going to be looking at you,' he says firmly. 'They all want to see Kate.'

Yes, he has a point.

'Will you keep your arm around me?'

'Pleasure.' He grins down at me, brushes my hair away from the right side of my face and something in me melts at his expression. I don't have time to ponder it, though, as Alistair begins to walk forward with me, and he is right – a few casual glances are flicked in our direction but no one stares. As we ascend the steps, we see my mother doing her best to elbow the press out of her way, telling them loudly that she and her family would like some privacy. That Kate will talk to them when her 'ordeal' is over.

'Is your ma loving that, or what?' Alistair says, amused.

As we cross towards my family, a small, stocky man in a suit hurries towards them from the other direction. My stomach does a nose dive. Oh God. Oh, no.

'Problem?' Alistair reacts to my involuntary groan.

'Cat man,' I hiss.

Alistair's eyes flick briefly towards Noel as he greets Kate with a firm shake of the hand and turns to introduce himself to my parents.

'What is he doing here?' I can't believe it.

'Looks like he's your sister's solicitor,' Alistair remarks. 'Jesus, Andy, what were you thinking?'

'Shut up.' I elbow him, suddenly overcome with a fit of giggles. 'I was feeling a little desperate, OK?'

'You could have had me, then,' he says, sounding wounded.

'Desperate, not completely desperate,' I smirk.

He sticks his tongue out at me and asks, 'You OK to go over?'

'I don't have a choice,' I hiss, as Kate suddenly notices us and waves us over.

We come abreast of them. Noel, who, I'm convinced, has been aware of my approach, turns and openly studies Alistair. Then, with a sort of catty smile on his face – no pun intended – he says, 'How are you, Andy?'

'I'm good.'

'How's your cat?'

Mam and Dad can't understand how Luke and Kate start to splutter with laughter.

'My cat is fine,' I answer back, proud of my detached voice. 'How's your ego?'

Alistair guffaws loudly and tries to turn it into a cough.

Noel chooses not to dignify my petty response with one of his own. Instead he nods and says to Kate, 'Come on with me and we'll run through a few things again, OK?'

Kate gives us a little wave as she leaves.

'Oh, are we late? Are we late?'

It's Eileen, with the rest of yoga class trotting behind her.

They're all dressed up, I see in amusement. It's as if they're going to a race meeting instead of a dingy courthouse. Fred looks very dapper in a yellow shirt and a cream linen suit.

'Oh Luke, how are you?' Eileen asks Luke as she hugs him.

'Grand,' Luke says.

'I hope you've said your goodbyes,' Evelyn says ominously. 'My cousin was in court last year. She stole a pair of knickers from a store. Now admittedly they were expensive knickers, but she got' – a dramatic pause – 'ten years in jail.'

'Oh, don't be ridiculous,' Fred scoffs. 'They don't give you ten years for stealing a pair of knickers!'

'They do if you tell the staff member who caught you that you're going to shoot him,' Evelyn responds.

'That's different, then,' Fred says. 'Stealing the knickers was not the major offence.'

'And is this the same cousin who stole a TV before?' Mabel pipes up.

'Yes,' Evelyn concedes with a bad grace. 'But—'

'Eh, guys, these people here are Kate's parents,' Luke interrupts before she can say any more to upset my folks. 'They don't need this.'

Evelyn reddens like a bold child. Then one by one the four of them introduce themselves to my mother and father. Just as they're explaining how they know Luke, the court usher shouts out: 'Dublin Live versus Kate Fitzsimons!'

'That's us,' my father says, and he gives me a tremulous smile. The poor man is terrified, I realise. With a sudden burst of courage, I leave Alistair's side and link my arm through my dad's. He, copying Alistair, pulls me into him, disguising my scar as my mother links him on the other side. The three of us take a deep breath and march into the courtroom, which is little bigger than a classroom. Finding some free seats, my dad sits down beside a young man in a grey suit, and to my relief, he makes sure that I can sit on the edge, and we watch as Kate and Noel take their places on the other side of the courtroom. I recognise the director of Dublin Live from his picture in the papers as he, too, takes his seat. The whole room smells of old wood and polish.

Members of the general public are there, old women with their knitting and their takeaway coffees. In fact, for a Monday morning, the place is packed. There is a definite buzz as Kate is recognised. And no one looks at me. Not one person peers in my direction, not one person whispers behind their hand as their eyes scour my face. No one cares about me at all. A tiny bit of tension leaks out of my body, though I still remain on high alert.

The court clerk calls out the name of the case. Noel stands up, takes a deep breath and begins to talk. He's confident and assured, without sounding arrogant. 'Judge, Kate Fitzsimons is deeply sorry for the offence she has committed. She states that she had asked the station for the equipment to record the documentary, and when they refused, she was unable to let the idea go, such was its hold on her. I would like it recorded that the accused is from a good family and has never been in trouble with the law before. She has pleaded guilty, and is prepared to take whatever sentence is handed down. She has also agreed to turn the tape over to Dublin Live, or to donate all proceeds from the sale of the documentary to a charity nominated by the station. My client's aim in making the documentary was not profit, but a desire to highlight loneliness in our society.'

Then Noel sits down.

There is silence. It seems to go on for ever. Finally, the judge, who only looks about forty, begins to speak. 'There isn't a man in this country who doesn't know Kate Fitzsimons,' he begins, to a smattering of laughter. 'So I would be foolish to pretend otherwise. Kate was wrong in what she did, but as she has never before been in trouble with the law, and as she has pleaded guilty and is unlikely to reoffend, in this instance I feel the Probation Act will suffice on condition that she will pay a five-thousand-euro fine to Dublin Live for the rental of the equipment, and as for the documentary, that is a matter entirely for her to discuss with the station. Case closed. Next!'

The man in the suit beside my father stands up. 'Excuse me,' he said. 'That's my case now.'

'Oh,' Dad who is beaming with relief, smiles up at the man. 'What happened to you?'

'Beat a fella up outside a night club.'

'Oh.' Dad's face is almost comical as he jumps up like a rabbit to let the man out. Once the man has passed, he mouths to me, 'You just can't tell, can you?'

All I know is that we can all breathe again.

The fact that Kate hasn't been sent to jail is a cause for celebration, despite her having to find five thousand euro from somewhere. As we file out of the room to let others in for the next case, Noel is in deep conversation with the director of Dublin Live.

'We're going to find a nice place for lunch,' my dad announces jubilantly. 'Who's coming?'

The four from the yoga class demur, saying they'd just come to support Kate and Luke, and are now going to head on home.

396

'But yous are all dressed up,' my dad says. 'You can't let it go to waste. Come on.'

The three women titter delightedly at the compliment and agree that all right, they'll go. Fred nods too.

'I'll head off home,' I say, from the safety, yet again, of Alistair's shoulder. 'My boss is a slave driver, I have to work.'

'And I'll drop her,' Alistair says, 'make sure she goes straight in and to work.'

'You have to let her celebrate,' Evelyn snaps at Alistair. 'Her sister has just been let off a serious criminal charge.'

'He was joking.' I smile.

'It's her scar,' Eileen mouths, making big slashing motions down her cheek, 'she's afraid to go out. She has picnic attacks.'

Evelyn blushes. 'Oh yes, yes, I forgot.'

My mother kisses me briefly and hisses, 'Does Luke only know weird people? Lunch with these women will be a nightmare. I wish you'd come.'

Laughing lightly, I pull away. 'I'll talk to you later.'

Noel joins us then, with the news that Dublin Live are happy to nominate a charity and that Kate has permission to sell her documentary to any station she likes. Kate cheers and kisses him, and Noel, beaming, agrees that Dad may indeed buy him lunch.

I am really glad I'm not going!

'Fancy lunch in my place?' Alistair asks as we pull off from the kerb. 'Promise no one will see you, and it'll be a change of scenery.'

'OK,' I agree, surprising myself and him, but if Alistair says no one will see me, then no one will. 'I didn't know you could cook.'

He looks slightly startled. 'Eh, I was thinking of a sandwich.'

'Sounds fabulous.'

'Sarcastic bitch!'

Twenty minutes later, I'm sitting at Alistair's small, shiny kitchen table. For obvious reasons I've never been in his apartment before, and despite its newness – he has had it about eight months – it's filled with mismatched pieces of furniture. His table is glass-topped and is surrounded by four funky-looking steel chairs. His kettle is yellow, and he has a retro-looking toaster sitting on a worktop. Various ornaments are scattered around, trying to give the place a homely feel but the effect jars, especially when one sees a small modern sculpture alongside a picture of a hen sitting on an egg.

'It's horrible, isn't it?' Alistair asks dolefully as he catches me staring. 'I just can't seem to get it to gel. But hey, it's somewhere to sleep.' He turns to a blue bread bin. 'Now, what sort of a sambo would you like? I've cheese, ham, tomato.'

'Sounds good. Any coleslaw?'

'Yeuch.'

'I take it that's a no.'

'Yep.' He pulls out the bread and begins buttering it. Then he lopes to the fridge and pulls out the cheese, tomato and ham. 'I had a call from Mandy yesterday,' he says, his back to me.

'Oh yeah? She rang you?'

'She did. She thanked me for the free ad, said it got her a good few orders for wreaths, which was great, and secondly to tell me that there's no way she's going to the Magazine Ireland Awards with me.' He slices up the cheese and sniggers a little. 'Like I actually thought she would, after what happened.'

I laugh too.

'Shove on the kettle, will you?'

I fill the kettle and make us some tea as he lays my sandwich on a plate. When we're both sitting down, he says, 'So, I'm going to look like a big loser at this thing in December.'

'You won't. You'll be fine.' He makes a damn fine sandwich.

There is a moment's silence, then, through a mouthful of bread, he says, 'Come with me, will you?'

I almost choke on my tea. 'What?'

He chews and chews and swallows before saying, 'Ah, come on, Andy. We'll have a blast. And no one will look at you, they all know you anyway.'

'They don't all know me. No, Alistair, I can't, I'm sorry. I'm just not ready for something that big yet.'

'Well, I'm not ready for escorting my mother to it, and that's what'll happen if you don't come. Please, Andy?'

I laugh at his anguished expression. Then, pushing my sandwich away, I shake my head. 'I'm sorry, Alistair, I'd love to go with you—'

'So come. I swear, I'll look after you. If anyone says anything, I'll deck them.' He's almost leaning across the table now, his eyes pleading with me.

'It's not just that. I get panicky in places like that. I'd make a show of myself.' Even thinking of it makes my stomach flutter. 'I really am not ready, Alistair. I—'

'You went to court today.'

'I know, but that was different. What if I win this thing, and have to get up in front of a room full of people? I – I couldn't. Really.'

'Think about it, eh? You've got nearly a month to change your mind.'

'I don't think a month will make a difference.'

'You've done quite a lot in the last few months. Just,' he pauses, 'think about it.'

It seems easier to just nod.

53

L EXI'S FUNERAL TAKES place two weeks later in her local church. Kate and I slip in just as it gets started, as I want to hover around at the back and not be noticed. My mother flipped when I told her.

'Lucy wanted you to sit with them,' she says. 'What will she think?'

But I knew I couldn't, and when I'd told Lucy, she had understood. 'You sit wherever you are comfortable,' she said. 'I know you care, that's all that matters.'

So, Kate and I stand in the back of what is a packed church. Glancing quickly about, I spot some girls that we'd gone to school with. I see people from Lexi's old job. I even spot an old boyfriend. Everyone from each phase of her life is gathered in one place. It's a strange sensation. Up the front, stunning pictures of Lexi dominate the altar. Chas's work, I'm sure. I am unaware that I'm crying yet again for my friend, but when finally Bob stands up to talk at the end, I have to wipe my eyes to stop them blurring. I'm sort of amazed to note that while I was terrified of coming to this packed church, my sadness for Lexi, rather than my self-consciousness, dominates my thoughts. I haven't even registered if anyone has looked at me.

'Thank you all for coming,' Bob begins, coughing slightly. 'It means a lot to Lucy and Chas and me.' He pauses and grips the lectern tightly before taking a deep, shaky breath and continuing in a slightly stronger voice. 'There is something I'd like to say to you all today and it's this. On the surface, Lucy and I have it all. Good marriage, nice home, plenty of money. The things we all aspire to. But what Lucy and I don't have is the one thing we would gladly give everything away for, and that is one more moment of time with our little girl. We would trade everything one hundred times over to take her in our arms for a fraction of a second. We'd take that moment and we would remember it, the warmth of her, the feel of her hair, the smell of her skin. I would sell all I have for one more perfect second of her life.'

There is the sound of sniffles and people blowing their noses.

'So, my message to you is, if you have children, cuddle them always, tell them you love them no matter what, make them feel special. The hardest thing about today is that Lucy and I have to accept that our time for that has passed. But our comfort is that we know that Lexi truly lived. She blasted her way into our lives, fought with us, argued with us and then got what she wanted. Every single time. And I'm so glad she did, because her time was over so quickly.'

He bows his head and his shoulders heave. Lucy and Chas join him on the altar. Lucy wraps her arms about him and Chas takes the microphone. 'What my family would like,' he says, 'is for you all to stand and applaud a life well lived.'

And it seems so right to do just that. The whole building erupts into applause as Lexi's coffin is carried down the church by her brother and her dad and her uncles. She's on a new ourney now, and I know that if Lexi can see us, she would ove this moment, being, as she always was, the centre of attention.

Has Chas got a girlfriend?' Kate asks on the way home from he graveyard. I'm still sniffling into my hankie, scrubbing my huge puffy red eyes, and all Kate cares about is if Chas has a girlfriend.

'I think so,' I sniff.

'I think so, too.' Kate indicates to turn onto the main road. 'That girl who was with him, did you see her? She was tall and had red hair. Quite nice-looking. She had her arm around him.'

'I really didn't notice, Kate.' I sound all snuffly, so I blow my nose. 'Wasn't the church lovely, all those photos of her?'

'Of who? His girlfriend?'

'Lexi.'

'Oh yeah, Chas can take a mean picture. I hope everyone claps me when I die. That'd be nice. Would it upset you if he had a girlfriend?'

'No, we had our chance and we blew it. I think I loved his image more than I loved him.'

Kate smiles. 'Yeah, the two of you were like a pair of poseurs. Do you remember the night he brought you to his gallery opening and you wore matching outfits?'

'Stop!' I groan, half laughing through my tears with the embarrassment of it. We'd worn red tops and black trousers. We must have looked like two gobshites. 'Oh, God! Stop!'

'I like you better now,' Kate says simply.

And, despite everything, I think I like myself better now, too.

* * *

403

That evening, Luke abandons Kate and me to go out with a few mates. I'm sitting on my bedroom floor, sipping a glass of wine and idly flicking through some old pictures of Lexi that I'd unearthed earlier in the evening. For some reason, it feels good to look at them now, therapeutic, as if by seeing them I can finally say goodbye. I smile a little shakily as I come across one of us taken at our debs' ball. Lexi's dress was her own design, and at the time I'd thought it was cool. Black and goth-like, it came to just above her ankles. She'd teamed it with black lace gloves and copious feathers. Her hair had been spiked with some sort of hardcore gel, and I'd joked that it was a dangerous weapon. The guy she'd brought along for the evening towered over her in a black tux and shirt. They'd looked like something from the Munsters. I'd been demure in a pink sheath dress with sparkly shoes and jewellery. The guy I'd brought along looked as boring as he'd been in reality. The four of us looked young, hopeful and excited. I'd no idea what happened to the two guys in the photo. Another picture shows us out in Lexi's back garden one summer's day. I think her mother had taken the shot. I'd just dumped a bucket of water over Lexi's head, and she was standing in a puddle, dripping wet as I fell about the place laughing. She'd promised to get me back for that, and she'd put a spider in my coat pocket as I left her house and when it had crawled up my sleeve during the car drive home, my scream had almost caused my mother to crash the car.

'Andy?' Kate pokes her head in the door, sees what I'm doing and flushes. 'Oh, am I disturbing you?'

'Nah, it's fine.' I manage a smile for her. 'What's up?'

'Will you have a listen to my documentary?' she asks,

404

sounding suddenly shy. 'I've finished it and RTE have expressed a cautious interest, so I'd like it to be just right.'

'Yeah, sure.' I drop the photos, haul myself up from the floor and follow her to the computer. I think I've remembered enough about Lexi for tonight. 'Though you know me, Kate, I don't have a clue.'

'Most people listening in won't have a clue,' Kate says as she presses 'play'. 'I just want you to tell me what you think of it.'

The music she has chosen starts up, and as it fades out, Luke's mother's sweet tones open the piece as she describes what being lonely meant to her. This is followed by the yoga women, who provide me with a few laughs, thus breaking and yet highlighting the seriousness of the issue, and then one by one Kate's other contributors chime in with their own comments and experiences. Like the building of a wall, brick by brick, voice by voice, it dawns slowly on me that it could be me talking, that every single one of the participants could be me. Then Cathy talks about her computer addiction, and I wonder suddenly if it could be Cissy. Yes, it could, I think, but it could be me, too. Her story is mine. By the time the documentary draws to its close, I'm so choked up with emotion that I can't speak. Then, as the final music plays, Kate's voice, piping clear, says, 'This is for Andy.' And the disc clicks off.

The silence afterwards is supplanted by the silence in the room. Kate looks anxiously at me. 'Well?' she presses gently.

'You dedicated it to me?' I blurt out at last, meeting her eyes.

'I *made* it for you,' Kate says with passion. 'To show you that you're not on your own.' A pause. 'I had to do it, even if I had to steal every bit of equipment to do so.'

405

I bite my lip and sniff a bit, and blink hard.

'Well?' she asks again.

'Thank you,' is all I can manage. 'It's great.'

She smiles at me and says nothing, just takes the disc out of the computer and kisses it. 'For luck.' She grins as she puts it into an envelope.

But luck isn't everything, I think. Sometimes we make our own luck by doing what we know is the right thing. So I hug her, hard, making her laugh.

54

So?

It's Alistair. He's been texting me every day, asking me to reconsider the Magazine Awards. Every day I text back to tell him nothing has changed. The sneaky git even got Kate on my back, and now she's pressuring me too.

Love to but can't. I text. And I mean that; I would love to go out with Alistair. I reckon we'd have a great laugh. I kick myself for my weakness but on the upside, it's made me determined that, in time, I will conquer my fear. I can already, with Kate's help, go to the local coffee shop, and indeed both of us met Chas there yesterday. He bought me a celebratory cappuccino. He still looked beat but then, an hour later, the redhead, who Kate had seen with him at the funeral and who I reckon must be Audrey, had met him outside the coffee shop, and the smile he had for her had lit up his face.

'Told you he had a girlfriend,' Kate hissed as we bade him goodbye.

I'd watched as he'd walked off with her, his arm loosely about her shoulder, and found that I was smiling.

I press send on my mobile. I'm not quite ready for big parties just yet.

I jump as Kate bursts into the room, shrieking. She wraps

her arms around me and attempts to lift me off my chair as she jumps up and down.

'I take it you've got some good news then?' I deadpan.

She laughs. 'I sold the documentary.' A big grin before she shouts, 'To RTE! Can you believe it?'

Now it's my turn to shriek. RTE, the premier Irish radio station. What a coup for her. 'Yeah, I can.' I hug her back. 'Of course I can. It was a brilliant piece of work. Well done!'

'And Dublin Live are giving the fee to a charity for loneliness in the elderly.' Kate grins. 'Oh God, it's all worked out so well. Want a drink to celebrate?'

'It's eleven o'clock in the day!'

'Yeah, so we've loads of time to devote to it.' Kate gives a wicked laugh.

'I've to sell a few more ads first,' I tell her, 'then maybe I will.'

'Hey, hang on, isn't tonight the night of the awards do?'

'Yes, and I'm not going. I've just texted Alistair that.'

Kate bites her lip. 'I don't think he's going to give up. He told me it was you that said to him to go for what he wanted.'

'What?' I gawk at her. 'When did he tell you this?'

'The other day when I told him I really didn't think you'd change your mind. Well, he said that you'd told him to be persistent. And that he was going to keep asking you until you said yes, or until the dinner was over, whichever came first.'

'That's ridiculous. I meant, be persistent when he wanted that Mandy one to go out with him. He's going to end up missing the bloody dinner himself if he's not careful.'

'His mother must be a real minger,' Kate observes wryly, and we both giggle a little.

My phone bleeps. *How about now? Have you changed your mind?*

I wonder if I should ignore it. Then I text back, *Going to ignore all ur txts. Not going.*

He texts back, *We'll c.*

'I think he likes you,' Kate observes. Then, poking me in the arm, she teases, 'That kiss you gave him must have been something special.'

I smile. Even thinking of that kiss sets my heart racing. But for God's sake, it was only Alistair. And that, for some stupid reason, sets my heart racing faster.

At seven thirty that evening my front doorbell buzzes. Kate answers it. We are sitting in our tracksuits watching *Fair City*. Kate is ebullient. That afternoon, she'd been approached by someone looking for her to do another radio documentary as the quality of her work had impressed the bigwigs so much. This time she'll have access to equipment and facilities. It basically means she'll have a job again, temporarily at least. The only thing I'm sad about is that it won't be long before she and Luke decide to move back out into their own place. I'll just have to make the most of them while I still can. I pluck some more popcorn from the bowl in front of me, while in the hall I hear Kate opening the front door.

She shrieks, then starts to laugh in a semi-hysterical way.

'What is it?' I jump up, the bowl of popcorn tumbling from my knees and scattering all over the floor.

'Hello!' It's Alistair's voice. 'I've come to bring you to the ball.'

I stomp out to meet him, wondering if he's thick or just stupid. 'I said I'm not – OH JESUS!' I recoil in fright.

Alistair grins and quirks an eyebrow. 'Thought if I got this

409

done, no one would look at you tonight. So, what do you say? You coming, or what?'

He's got a very ugly scar running from his ear, down the side of his cheek, under his chin and down his neck. It's red and raw and sore-looking. I gulp, hardly able to get the words out. I'm transfixed by his face. 'Wh – what? How? Did—'

'I went to a make-up artist this afternoon. I told her I wanted something to make people stare. I've discovered that I quite like being looked at.' He winks at me.

I don't know what to say.

'Isn't that romantic?' Kate says, beaming.

'Romantic?' I gawk at her. 'How could you call getting that on his face romantic?'

There is a silence.

'Have I offended you?' Alistair looks contrite. 'I didn't mean to.'

I'm not quite sure how to feel. He looks utterly ridiculous. It's the sort of scar you'd see in a comedy about someone with a scar. And yet, it is a sort of charming thing to do, in a perverted kind of way.

'I just wanted you to come with me tonight, Andy,' Alistair says, looking up at me from downcast eyes. 'You're the one who told me to go for what I want, and to be honest, all I've ever wanted was you. Well, that's not technically true. I suppose I wanted Mandy as well, but I just didn't realise how much I liked you, and then when—'

'I'd quit while you're ahead,' Kate states drily.

'Then when what?' I ask, wanting to kick Kate for interrupting him.

'What?' His brow creases.

410

'Then when what?' I repeat. 'You said, "Then when", and I said "what?"'

'Oh, well, then when you kissed me that night, I realised that all along I'd been waiting for it to happen.' His scar isn't that well put on. It doesn't seem to move when he talks. 'Well, not *waiting*,' he clarifies, 'as I hadn't expected anything to happen, like you're way out of my league, you are gorgeous and I'm just, well, just me. But when it did happen, I knew there was no one else for me, only I thought you were drunk and—' He stops and says, sounding annoyed with himself, 'You *know*?'

'Are you trying to say you fancy her?' Kate asks bluntly.

'Yeah,' Alistair replies. He looks at me, opens his hands wide. 'This is very nerve-wracking for me, Andy. I meant to tell you before now, but it just never seemed the right time, what with you being a computer avatar and your sister in court and your friend dying and—' He pauses. 'Anyway, I thought if you turned me down it would wreck our friendship, but I decided that won't happen. I set up the magazine with no regrets, and I figured you were worth a shot too. No point in living with regrets.'

He's dressed in a black suit and a navy bow tie. I reckon he thinks the tie is black. He's going to regret that suit and tie combination if he ends up in a photograph. I find myself smiling.

'Well?' he asks, biting his lower lip, his brown eyes fixed on my face and making my heart tumble about in a most peculiar way. 'What d'ya say?'

He's just him, he'd said. And how lovely that sounded. He's just Alistair. Funny, wry, witty Alistair. He'd eased his way into my life with his fancy bottles of wine, his vintage

411

car and his disastrous love life. He'd called into me each time we finished a magazine and kept me in touch with the world. That kiss had said everything I'd probably been unable to say to him. The knowledge that I actually fancy this man is a bit like when I design a page for a magazine. I come up with a concept, I fill in the detail, but it's only when I pull right back and look at the whole page that I actually realise I've achieved perfection. I'm seeing Alistair as a whole for the first time. He is perfect for me. He has always been, only I was too blind and too absorbed in my own misery to notice. Plus he has gone and got a massive scar on his face that he's prepared to wear for me. I find my eyes tearing up. I brush a hand across them.

'Shit.' Alistair glares at Kate. 'I've just ruined everything.' The bit of scar on his neck lifts up and he presses it back down.

'Alistair,' I say a little tearfully, 'you're fecking weird, but you're the best thing to *ever* happen to me.'

'I think I'll go now.' Kate makes a not-so-discreet exit.

A slow grin spreads across Alistair's face. His eyes crinkle up and he looks questioningly at me. 'I don't think I'm that weird.'

We stare some more at each other, not quite sure how to proceed. Then he slowly takes a step towards me and my heart starts racing. I cross towards him. He circles my waist with his arms. It feels so good to have him touch me. In almost erotic slow motion, he bends his face to mine and caresses my lips with his. My whole body zings at the contact. I press myself closer to him and feel hardness through his black trousers. His kisses turn hungry, his breath ragged. His scar sort of squelches under my lips.

'Can you remove that revolting thing?' I giggle, pulling away.

'My suit isn't that revolting,' he jokes back as I laugh.

We don't go to the awards in the end. Even with Alistair there, I wouldn't be ready to face such a large crowd, and I honestly doubt that they'd have let Alistair in. Plus, I have nothing to wear. Apparently he never considered this. Instead, we spend about twenty minutes trying to coax a very irritable Baz out of my bedroom, and once he's removed, we begin getting to know each other properly.

Though I reckon I know all the important stuff already.

This moment I know I'll remember for ever.

Epilogue

One year later . . .

L ONDON. THE CITY is hopping. Alistair and I stand with
a tourist map in the middle of St James's Park. It's my
first time abroad since I had the accident. The past year has
seen a slow improvement in my condition. Finally, I can see
light at the end of the tunnel. According to Alistair, I've
mastered the important things – coffee shops and pubs. Offices
and shops can wait, as Alistair reckons they're overrated.

This trip to London was something I'd aimed for, a sort
of landmark in my recovery. Finally, after almost a year, I've
made it. It's a November weekend; a glorious winter sun is
bathing everything in brilliant white light. We've just come
out of Chas's photographic exhibition, which has received
rave reviews in all the papers both here and in Ireland, and
deservedly so. His reputation as one of the best photographic
artists has been well and truly cemented. I take out my phone
to text him a congratulations while Alistair studies our map.
'I think this is the street we want.' Alistair points to a little
road off Piccadilly Circus. 'I hope your boots are up to walking
that far,' he grins.

'Of course they are.' I'm lying, I'll be crippled, but I can't

414

admit that to him as he'd warned me not to wear them. I send my text, and linking my arm through Alistair's, instruct him to 'lead on'.

A few minutes later, my phone bleeps with a message from Chas. *Tanx. BTW Baz is fine. Also Audrey showed your pic to a friend of hers and he happy to include you in exhibition in January. So happy painting.*

I blink and reread. Then blink again. Then with a shake in my voice, I relate this to Alistair. He startles everyone by whooping in delight and lifting me up and swinging me around.

I'd finally screwed up the courage to show Chas some of my pictures about six months ago. He'd called in with an album of Lexi he'd made up for me. It was a beautiful thing, done like a child's storybook with chunky cardboard pages. *Once upon a time, there was a beautiful girl*, was printed on the opening page, and there followed a collage of pictures of his sister and me and him and everyone else in Lexi's life. The last page had, *And they all lived happily ever after*. Which of course had made me burst into tears. Anyway, while I was busy drying my eyes, Chas had seen a painting I was finishing up sitting on an easel, and he seemed to really like it. He asked what else I'd done, and I shyly showed him some finished pieces. He'd borrowed one, saying that if I was interested he might be able to fix something up for me. Of course I was delighted, but as the months went on, I'd forgotten about it.

'My wonderfully talented woman.' Alistair is grinning at me. Then he taps my nose. 'But don't let it go to your head. I mean, you weren't even good enough to win a prize at the Magazine Awards last year.'

415

I laugh. 'Well, at least I was pipped at the post, which was more than you, you talentless git.'

'That's not what you said last night.' He wraps an arm about my shoulder and pulls me in close. 'I think I might just love you, especially if you become really famous and make us rich.'

'If I become really famous and make us rich, I could dump you.'

'You could, but you wouldn't.' He kisses me on the cheek.

'Nah, how could I? Oh, and in case you're interested, Baz is fine.'

'Damn.'

I laugh. Baz and Alistair barely tolerate each other. Alistair does his best, but Baz isn't stupid. He knows when someone is trying to buy him over. The only person I could leave the cat with when I went away was Chas, who visits each day and feeds him for me. Apparently Baz hates Chas's girlfriend too, and hisses at her if she so much as sets a foot inside my door.

'I think he just has a longing for his parents to get back together,' Chas joked one day when we were doing a trial run.

'Well, at least we're civil for his sake.' I smiled back.

Chas laughed. 'Yeah.' Then he'd added sincerely, 'And it's great.'

It is too. I suppose the fact that I visit Bob and Lucy regularly helps. Chas has moved out, but whenever he's in the country he calls to them on a Sunday, so I bump into him quite a lot. It was he who'd offered to mind Baz for me, when he heard that it was proving impossible to get volunteers to take care of him when I was going away. Being on

416

good terms with Chas makes me feel even more connected to Lexi.

'OK,' Alistair breaks into my reverie as he points towards a sign saying Piccadilly Circus, 'this way, I reckon.'

Twenty minutes later, just as my feet are beginning to cramp up, we arrive at the top of a street that barely makes the London map. It's small and narrow and seems only to have a few shops along it. The shops are squashed in between tall grimy office blocks. Hesitantly, the two of us start to walk, our footsteps echoing off the walls. We're halfway down when I spot what I'm looking for. A white shop with a sign done in swirly letters, proclaiming that this is the Angel Shop.

My heart stutters on a beat before speeding right up.

'You OK?' Alistair asks.

I can only nod. As we draw alongside the shop, I see that it isn't half as nice as the one on the internet, but that's the internet, a dreamer's paradise. This shop is the three-dimensional reality. Grimy, but with windows gleaming. Inside, angels of every shape and size peer eerily from the shelves.

'Holy shit!' Alistair exclaims, his face pressed to the window.

I laugh. 'Holy being the right word, OK.'

He guffaws, then asks seriously, 'D'you want me to come in with you?'

I shake my head. This is one thing I have to do on my own. Alistair nods and sits on the low windowsill. Pulling a magazine from his pocket, he smiles up at me. 'Well, you know where I am, eh?'

'Yeah. Thanks.' Taking a deep breath, my heart pumping fit to burst, I push the door open. It announces my arrival with a small 'ping'. My eyes are immediately assaulted by the dazzling whiteness that bounces off every surface. The whole

417

place is painted white. The shelving heaves under the weight of countless angel memorabilia. The place is seriously bizarre. One or two people are browsing. My eyes search for an assistant, and then I spot an old man, sitting behind a white till, with white fluffy hair and a very lined face. He looks to be about eighty. I stand and stare at him for a minute, wondering if it could be . . . Then, without giving it any more thought, I walk towards him. He is impeccably dressed in a grey suit and tie with a white shirt.

'Yes?' He smiles up at me, brilliant blue eyes glittering like sunlight on water. I wonder again if this is him. I feel somehow that it could be. It's hard to tell, as voices get distorted online.

'I'm looking for an angel,' I stammer out.

He smiles. 'Well, you've come to the right place, petal.'

Petal. It *is* him. It has to be. 'I'd like,' I pause, trying to stop the slight tremor in my voice, 'a Healing angel, please.'

He blinks. 'A Healing angel,' he repeats.

'Yes.' I swallow. 'I was told a while ago that I should get one.'

He studies me for a second without saying anything. Then he gets slowly up from his chair and shuffles towards a shelf laden with goods. I think he must have arthritis. Finally, he turns to me, holding an exact replica of the one I'd received online. 'Is this what you're looking for?' he asks.

'That's it exactly,' I say softly as I pull my purse from my bag.

He holds up his hand. 'It's on the house.'

We meet each other's eyes. A slow smile makes its way across his ancient face. 'On the house,' he repeats, holding it towards me.

'Thank you.' I take the angel from him and offer him a

418

fifty-pound note. 'Maybe you can use this to treat someone to an angel of their own someday.'

'You're a very kind girl.' He takes my money and nods. 'Very kind.'

'You're a very kind man.'

In the background, the deafening sound of a choir starts up. We both wince.

'Sorry,' one of the browsing customers calls out apologetically, 'I just pressed a button. I didn't know that was going to happen.'

'Life is like that, petal,' the old man calls back, winking at me. 'You do things without ever knowing what's going to happen.' Then he adds, 'Press the button again.'

Immediately the sound ceases.

'Panic over,' the old man says, smiling at me.

I smile back. 'Well, thank you for this.' I hold up the angel.

'Thank you for calling,' the old man says. 'Fare thee well.'

'Yeah.' I nod. 'Fare thee well.' I reach out to touch his sleeve, but he has turned away and is making his slow passage back to his seat behind the white till. I leave without seeing him turn around.

A week later, I visit Lexi's grave. On my own, in the daytime. I stand in front of it and marvel at the peace to be found in a place where the dead are buried. Leaves have fallen from the trees above her grave and are scattered all across the ground in brilliant patterns of red and gold. Somewhere in the bushes that line the graveyard, animals are preparing for their long winter sleep. Dusk will come early, and long nights will creep up on us until the days begin to lengthen again. Life goes on. The sleep ends. I hope it will for Lexi, too. I

419

place the angel carefully on her grave among the hardy winter shrubs her mother has planted there.

'Sleep well,' I whisper, knowing that the angel, like the one she has online, will be with her forever.

Acknowledgements

To all who helped in the writing of this book:

Thanks to my editor, Caroline Hogg, who did a great job with this book, and to all the Little, Brown staff.

Grace Aungier from Magazines Ireland who told me all about the Magazine Awards and answered my questions. Any mistakes are mine.

Alice Marchand and her Australian friend, Ali, who put me right when my Aussie slang went a little over board.

To Tony Joyce, my brother-in-law, who proof read the court case scene and stopped me from looking stupid!

For all the computer techies who helped me with any computer queries. To the site that's mentioned in this book – thank you for the free access.

To Joe Duffy and all at Liveline – for having me on last year and giving me and my books some lovely mentions. It's appreciated. Loved meeting you all. And if you ever want an Abba impersonator on your show again – you know who not to ask!

And a big thanks to Kevin Egan of Efree Media for designing me such a wonderful website and for being so nice to a rookie like me!

In memory of Pebbles and Caesar who died last year (I know, but I loved those two cats). They were not a bit like Baz but Baz is in the book because of them!